GIFT

D1407986

THE
SCARLET
RIDER

Lucy Sussex

TOR®

A TOM DOHERTY ASSOCIATES BOOK
NEW YORK

THE SCARLET RIDER

A Tor Book
Published by Tom Doherty Associates, Inc.
175 Fifth Avenue
New York, NY 10010

Tor Books on the World Wide Web:
http://www.tor.com

Tor® is a registered trademark of Tom Doherty Associates, Inc.

ISBN: 0-812-54923-6
Library of Congress Catalog Card Number: 96-18115

First edition: October 1996
First mass market edition: April 1999

Printed in the United States of America

0 9 8 7 6 5 4 3 2 1

This book is dedicated to the memory of four doughty Victorian women, my great-grandmothers:

Marion Sperring Wilson
Jane Bailiff Fyfe
Emma Melvina Harrison Hearn
Nancy Wardman Sussex

Acknowledgments

Thanks are primarily due to my editor, Harriet McDougal, for her hard work on this manuscript. Many others helped in the production of this novel, commenting, answering questions, and reading extracts, particularly Les Harrop, Dr. Craig Hilton, Daisy Rose, and Sue Martin. Meg Tasker and ASAL '92 gave me the opportunity to do a reading from *The Scarlet Rider* in the historic ballroom of Craig's Hotel, Ballarat. William Gibson permitted me to quote from *Count Zero*. A number of biographers let me pick their brains about their experiences, among them Deidre Bair, Brenda Niall, Russell McDougall, and Penne Hackforth-Jones. Thanks are also due to Yvonne Rousseau and Greg Egan.

Thanks are due, too, to the various nineteenth-century writers whose work informed the novel within a novel: "William Burrows," Susan Meade, Ellen Davitt, James Skipp Borlase, and various diarists, journalists, and letter writers, too many to mention. Special apologies are due to Marcus Clarke, who may well be rolling in his grave at having parts of his "Human Repetends" transmogrified into Jesperson's confession. However, the major influence upon this novel was the life and work of Mary Fortune, pioneering woman detective writer. In 1987 I was researching Fortune and found myself becoming a little too involved with the biographical search. That much is true, but the rest of this novel is LIES.

THE
SCARLET
RIDER

Prologue

At first, all you can see are silver-nitrate ghosts, framed by ornate metal, also silver, a heavy jutting border incised with gum leaves and wattle blossoms. It distracts the eye from the old photograph, and the glass above is dingy, too. You turn the frame on its face and find only a backing of brown paper. Suddenly a vandal in your desire to see the ghosts better, you stab the cardboard with the ivory-handled paper knife, and tear it away. Underneath is a square of dirty, yellowed cardboard, and below that is the photograph.

You pull it out and hold it up to the sunlight. There are three in the picture, not counting the photographer, who surely influenced the composition of the horse and the two young humans. He must have been sweating under his hood: his equipment has captured a hot day in the 1880s. The grass in the foreground of the photograph looks seared, and while the gums at the back seem in rude health, somewhere nearby an imported apple tree has wilted, its fruit scattering underneath the horse's hooves.

Certainly it seems too warm to be horse riding, but the girl looks determined on it. Her chin juts out. She is fifteen? sixteen?—but dressed with no concession to her youth in a heavy dark gown, up to the neck, down to the wrists and ankles. From her shoulders to her hips the habit fits like a glove, without wrinkles, tightly molded to her corseted form. Only her hair is unconstrained, coiling wildly around her face and neck. Her mouth shows a tinge of wry amusement, perhaps at being recorded so windblown. She stands in front of the horse, holding the reins firmly in one hand, the other clutching her riding crop. The old photographs are monochromatic, sepia or silver, but this horse has tones suggesting a light brown, maybe a chestnut. It has one eye cocked at the photographer, as if in half a mind to bolt.

The third in the picture is a small child, boy or girl is hard to say, as all tots in those days wore their hair long and their frocks short. He—somehow you sense it is a he—perches on the hard leather saddle, his chubby legs almost at right angles to the broad back of the horse. They are encased in stiff, starched frilly trews, above them a broderie anglaise petticoat, above that the skirt of his tartan dress. He looks uneasy: his wide mouth is set tight.

You step over the thin barrier of white at the bottom of the photograph. Dry grass, the drought fodder of over a century ago, crunches under your shoes. A hot wind blows, carrying the smells of eucalyptus and horse sweat. You go closer, taking care not to kick over the photographer. The horse shifts its footing, and the little boy's starched clothing creaks as he twists around nervously in response.

"Don't be fearful," the girl says to her brother. "She may be a big horse, but you're her master. Take hold of the reins."

The girl flips the reins over the horse's head and down the

mane, and presses them into the boy's plump, unresisting fingers.

"She obeys her rider. Pull on her mouth and she'll go anywhere you want, do anything you want."

She smiles, revealing irregular teeth. "Let me show you!"

With one quick movement she puts her foot into the stirrup and vaults up, seating herself comfortably behind the boy. One buttoned boot kicks the drum of the horse's belly; her hands clasp the reins within the child's small mitts, and shakes them.

"Gee up!"

The horse strolls away. The photographer has already packed up his kit and gone, to take anthropological shots of Queen Martha, the last of her Aboriginal tribe, and the only black face for miles. Now there is only semi-cleared land in front of you, with eucalypts and a single, sickly apple (previously hidden behind the horse), whose tiny green fruit bruise under your feet, yielding a sickly-sweet scent. You step back, and you are leaning against a window ledge, staring at an old photograph. The girl stands holding the reins, the mare shows the white of her visible eye, the child looks scared.

We have photos, letters in crabbed handwriting, journals, scraps of petticoat lace, cuttings from newspapers, paper-thin pressings of flowers and ferns, detailed listings of births and deaths on the flyleaves of family Bibles. Yet, with all this memorabilia, how can we know how they spoke, how they felt, all these our influential ghosts? How can we know what they were really like?

A Monkey on Her Back

*But away with reflections and proceed with
relation.*

—Janet Ronald, shipboard diary

Mel stares at the white paper in front of her and
feels blank terror, writer's block. She picks up a
pen, holding it as if ready to stab. What words can
she write that will send her story down the slipway of the page
as effortlessly and inexorably as the actual events she recalls?
How can she begin her narrative? Where to start it?

She inches her fingers down the pen until she is holding it
normally and writes, "Once upon a time I had a monkey on my
back, then I lost it." Each letter she shapes carefully and tidily
as if keeping accounts in the old blank ledger, her writing book.
Then she looks at the sentence, sighs, and scores out her words
savagely. I could do with some help, even from a monkey, she
thinks, and glances over her shoulder, warily. But failing that,
I'll just have to make do with what I learned from the association. Monkey see, monkey do . . .

"I" she writes, the first word of the new beginning, then

stops abruptly. I, I, I . . . But the "I" of Mel now is not the same as the "I" of Mel then. Too much has changed. When I look back, it's like staring at another me, another person, she thinks. She pauses, nib against paper, and it moves in her fingers, delineating the word "She."

Is the cat's mother, she thinks, then speaks the words aloud. The chubby ginger kitten on the bed half wakes, stretching luxuriously across the largest item in this day's mail, photocopied records from an orphanage on the other side of the continent, business for the future Mel, once she has finished with her past self. It yawns, then, pillowing its small round head on the other piece of mail, a love letter, slumbers again.

Mel turns back to the white paper, closing her eyes momentarily. She thinks: I, in this room, bent over a desk, watch, in my mind's eye, she, Mel past. Third person, then, she decides, and opens her eyes to the sight, through the open window, of birds playing stunt pilots in the summer breeze. She watches them, distracted, before her thoughts involuntarily, dutifully, return to her task. Sammy's funeral, she thinks. Maybe it all started there, when Nola didn't show up, and felt so guilty afterward that she had to make amends. "Nola," she writes, then suddenly tears out the page and crumples it, leaving an expanse of pristine white in front of her again.

It did start with Nola, she determines, not at the funeral, but later, the day she met me in the street. Sure there's a whole story behind that moment, my whole life, my parents' lives, grandparents' even, the story of the colonization of Australia, the history of the world, the first atoms clumping together in the void . . . but I put my pen down on that moment, *then*, and skewer it. Stop squirming and start my yarn for me.

Slowly, very painstakingly, her story travels from the synapses of her mind, through the nerves of arms and fingers, coming to rest as scrawls of black ink on a white page.

* * *

Someone was watching her. She, Mel, felt that, stronger than
the late-autumn wind that shrieked between the high-rise buildings and peppered her cheeks with grit. One of those smart
beautiful women, she decided, as her eyes watered in the blast,
making the passersby a yuppie blur. She could have wept from
the shame of it all. I must look so out of place here, a misfit, she
thought, gawky tall tatterdemalion of a girl, shuffling along. . . .

A blur of bright red topped with green spoke to her:

"Stone the bleedin' crows!"

Mel wiped her eyes, to see a woman as gaily attired as a parrot in knitwear, hat, and gorgeous full-length coat.

"Mel!"

The face was tanned, creased in the corners, but despite the
familiarity in her speech it seemed that of a complete stranger.
Mel peripherally checked the woman's clothes again. Something about that combination of vivid colors was reminiscent of
. . . of whom?

"Mel, you ain't changed a bit. Still with your lovely head of
bronzy curls. First time I met you, I said to Sammy, Can I put
in an order now for a little baby curlyhead, just like Mel?"

One of Dad's girlfriends, Mel thought, but damn it, which
one?

"What, doncha recognize your almost-stepmother?"

And next moment they were hugging in the middle of the
street.

"Nola!" How she'd changed. Mel had last seen Nola in
Sammy's motel room, the tears washing mascara down her
cheeks until she looked like a Pierrot. She had been wearing the
red negligee she had slept in, with the green tracksuit pants she
had hastily donned when the doctor arrived—and this was hours
after Sammy had gone out, horizontally, through the motel
doorway. Mel had placed a box of tissues handy but Nola

wouldn't touch it, instead had sobbed like a magdalen into her hood of hennaed perm.

The perm was gone, now, as was the henna—the hair beneath the knitted cap was as straight and brown as coffee poured from the pot. And Nola was beaming!

"Mel, lemme buy you a coffee. I owe you, don't I?"

Yes, thought Mel, you're in my debt, Nola, for running away and leaving me to organize my dad's funeral, all by myself.

"C'mon!" Nola still had her arm around Mel, and the wool of her sleeve warmed both sight and touch, like a smoldering red log. "Let's catch up on the last three years, eh?"

She led Mel around a corner into a lane paved with uneven chunks of bluestone. It was like a river valley, carved between two crags of hard rock high-rise, the hotel and the bank headquarters, and at its end was a building—amazingly—of just two stories, its lower floor a coffee shop. As they entered, an ambience of soft babble and enticing food smells surrounded them like an embrace. They sat themselves at the long counter, watching the staff move like clockwork in the narrow workspace.

"Cappuccino," Nola said. "You, too, Mel?"

Mel went googly-eyed at the display of sinfully rich cakes, and Nola grinned.

"Which one do you want? I'll shout you coffee *and* cake—how 'bout that? You look like you need a special treat."

"Thanks," Mel said, touched. "In that case I'll have the chocolate."

"And I will too."

"Two cappuccinos, two sacher tortes," repeated the waitress.

Mel sat back, the confession unmade that she was budgeting herself carefully until her next unemployment payment. Nola stripped off her thin leather gloves, and Mel noticed that her fingers were naked, unadorned with any ring. What has she been doing these last three years? Mel wondered, recalling the wild talk in the motel room about Sammy being her last hope, her last chance. . . .

"You look well," she said, as the cake and coffee were set in front of them.

Nola grinned again. "I'm doin' well too. See, I got outta the travel agency—"

That was how the pair had met, Mel recalled: she'd organized Sammy's Gold Coast holiday and had ended up accompanying him.

"—though it had its uses . . ."

Mel suddenly stopped spooning off the top of her cappuccino, recalling something as bitter as the froth of milk and chocolate was sweet. Nola read her expression and sighed.

"Yeah, I know. Buggered off to Bali, didn't I, and left you holding the baby."

Coffin, thought Mel.

"I'm sorry about that, but it was, well, necessary. And I was right: Bali saved my life. See, I fell in love again. . . ."

Mel shrugged, still aggrieved but unable to resist the warmth of that smile. Nola took a swig of coffee, and continued: "And after that, things just got better and better. Now I've got this great job, office manager for a publishing company, going up in the world, eh? Ever hear of us? Roxana Press."

Mel tried to look noncommittal.

"After the private detective, Roxana Reul. Don't tell me you've never seen the books. Kaye Tollet writes Roxana's adventures, and they finance us, partly. All those lovely Yankee royalties and movie rights go into a dinkum little Aussie publishing company. The revenge of the colonies, Kaye says."

She stopped and picked up her chunk of cake. Mel had just swallowed her first mouthful, acutely aware that she had skipped lunch to save money. Now she just wanted to devour the food as quickly as possible. However, a gap in the conversation should be filled, whether with mortar, fluff, or sweetened cream. Social intercourse abhors a vacuum.

"So you publish detective fiction?"

"Not always," Nola said indistinctly, then swallowed. "Hey Mel, why don't you talk for a bit, while I eat 'n' listen. What's happened to you?"

Mel was mildly flabbergasted by the change in subject. Nola must have mistaken the expression, for she said, frowning:

"And don't start by saying old Sammy had a good send-off. I knew you'd do him proud."

Mel considered telling her about the whole bizarre farce of the funeral, but decided that Nola didn't want to know now. Maybe I could tell her later, she thought . . . if there was a later.

"Always knew you were one of the capable types," Nola added, taking a second bite.

"Me? Capable?" And Mel started to laugh. It died out after a few splutters, leaving Nola looking concerned.

"Said the wrong thing, did I?"

"I'm on the dole!"

"Thought you were at uni."

"I finished my degree a year ago."

"You liked study. I remember Sammy 'n' me meeting up with you outside the old library and you talkin' all through our lunch about the funny facts you'd dug up."

"I loved it, especially the research. But when I finished at university I found that all the time spent in libraries, writing essays, and arguing in seminars just gave me a piece of paper with 'Unemployable' written on it. I've spent the year since wondering what to do with the rest of my life."

She stopped, embarrassed at speaking so freely, and addressed herself to the cake, filling her mouth so as not to say more.

"Mel, that's awful," Nola said. One of her bare hands crept

across the counter, as though to comfort with a touch, but Mel kept eating furiously. The hand withdrew, and coiled around Nola's cup.

"Seem to remember it was Aussie history you were studying—convicts and gold rushes."

"Yeah, well, my major was in history, but . . ."

Nola didn't let Mel finish. "I reckon I owe you, a lot more than coffee and cakes'll fix. You're down on your luck? I might be able to do somethin' about that. See, Roxana needs someone who likes fossickin' in libraries, and it would be useful if they knew their Aussie history."

Mel gulped, literally. "Nola, I'm not a Ph.D. or anything. I only got second-class honors, that's good, but not enough to get me a scholarship for further study. And . . ."

"Mel, love, anyone who's been to uni looks good to me. And I know you're brainy—Sammy was real proud of that. I think you'll do us just fine. Ever done detective work? Well, what we want is a private eye, to find out things about this lady crime writer, who was around at the time of the gold rushes. Wrote about them, she did, bloody well. And that's why we want to know all about her."

She fished out a mesh purse from somewhere in her coat, opened it, and extracted a business card. It had ROXANA PRESS on it, the O a huge magnifying glass through which a determined-looking woman peered. Nola stabbed a finger at the address.

"Turn up tomorrow, say eleven o'clock. And we'll do a job interview, informal-like."

"But aren't you advertising?" Mel swallowed the last of her coffee with difficulty. It seemed as if her throat muscles had suddenly turned to jelly.

"We don't have time. And—" Here she pulled up one coatsleeve and glanced at a nifty green-and-red Swatch. "—neither have I! See you tomorrow morning, Mel."

She handed payment to the waitress, then stood, shaking out the folds in her coat. Then all of a sudden she swooped down, her nose nearly pecking Mel's ear.

"Another thing, Mel," she said softly. "Don't mention how we know each other, and 'specially not me 'n' Sammy! With the boss it'd be all right, but she's in Yankee-land, and the number-two boss, Sorrel, she can be a bit starchy sometimes. Not to worry, though."

"But . . ."

She was too late, for Nola had left, the door jangling shut behind her. Mel watched her progress down the bluestone, bright as a minor nation's flag. I should run after her, she thought. Well, it's too late now. She eyed Roxana Press's business card. The doughty girl gazed through her magnifying glass, and after a while Mel looked away. The cartoon figure had stared her down, the way everybody else did. At that unwanted thought, she got up and ventured into the marble-and-glass canyons again. On the corner a gust of wind laden with dust and dead leaves caught her full in the face. She knuckled her eyes, but they still streamed. Then, between fist, salt water, and grit she saw a telephone booth, open only on the leeside of the wind. She sheltered in it, and gradually her eyes returned to normal.

What to do? she thought. I don't know where Nola is, so I can't ring and say: "Sorry, the interview's off. I'm a fraud!" I could ring Roxana, but what if I got this fearsome Sorrel? "Er, your office manager asked me to come in tomorrow re the research project, but she had her wires crossed. I haven't done Australian history since first-year university, but I didn't get a chance to tell her that."

Mel heard a cough, and glancing over her shoulder spied a sleek young businessman. She hastily began riffling through the topmost phone book, as if looking for a number, but stopped suddenly at the sight of her own surname. Kirksley, E. Her aunt Edith, Edie for short.

Mel had last seen Edie three years ago, about a week after Nola had hopped on her life-changing plane to Bali. Edie had come to Sammy's funeral, with her older sister, Alice. Among the confusion of the wake, all tears, tea, fruitcake, and Sammy's ex-girlfriends, all of whom wanted to tell Mel how much they'd meant to him, aunt and niece somehow had a brief conversation. Edie had told Mel that now she was retired from nursing she was writing the family history. She had even started to talk about her findings—Kirksley gold miners had been mentioned, as Mel recollected.

However informal tomorrow's interview might be, Mel would fail it miserably unless she could show some knowledge of Australiana. I need a refresher course in the subject, she thought, and how to research it, and in a hurry too! The only person who might be able to help was old Edie. She felt the coins in her coat pocket. A phone call wouldn't break the budget, and it might even clinch the job with Roxana.

And as the coins clattered down through the machine Mel knew that she wanted this work. Passionately.

TWO

The World of Publishing

Mel lifts her pen from the page, thinking: What now? I could give an account of the phone conversation, and how I walked home afterward, to save the tram fare, but what I most remember is being in a fever of anticipation the whole time. I didn't want the sun to rise and for there to be a new morning, with a job interview slap in the middle of it, but at the same time I couldn't wait. Just as now—the sentences that form in my mind describe the trip to Roxana, not the time I spent mentally and physically preparing myself for it.

By Mel's local tram stop was a clump of shops: a newsagent, a particularly unwholesome pizza parlor, and a barber's, with its door framed by a full-length panel of mirror. She inspected herself in it.

"Vanity, thy name is woman," Sammy used to say if he didn't like a new dress. If he did like it, he'd ask for the next dance. From woman to woman this formula never varied; he said it to Edie and Alice, his sisters, he said it to his ladyloves, and he said it to his daughter.

Well, Mel would never know what he thought of her interview outfit, but nonetheless she felt under an invisible parental scrutiny. She had decided on looking scholarly, but neat: a silk blouse that Sammy had brought back from the Philippines; a plain black skirt, from a secondhand shop; her last unladdered pair of tights; flat shoes; and her boyfriend Marc's sports jacket, a present from his wealthy parents, with the cuffs hurriedly tacked up. Most things fitted both Mel and Marc, but he had the longer reach.

It was a sunny day, but chill; Mel was the only person at the tram stop not warmly wrapped. She had no choice—her one coat, a tatty old duffel, was definitely not interview wear. By the time the tram arrived, she was goose-pimpled and very glad of its central heating. Far too soon, it seemed, she disembarked into cold again and to keep warm speed-walked through the crowds of commuters. The pace stopped her from shivering, but did nothing to appease the major lepidopteran war in her stomach.

She turned a corner into another bluestone lane and saw Roxana's emblem, the girl with magnifying glass, on the antique brick wall of a converted warehouse. The accusing gaze, when painted large, was even more intimidating, and she longed to be as careless as the old drunk sleeping in the opposite doorway. Without stopping, she smoothed down her mop of reddish hair with the mental injunction: Look tidy, you, for the first few minutes at least! Then, teeth clenched in case they chattered, Mel strode into the warehouse and up the single flight of stairs to the Roxana offices.

The first thing she saw disconcerted her almost as much as the giant logo: a receptionist with a hairstyle of short, brightly dyed dreadlocks, which stuck straight out from her head like fluorescent nails.

"Um, I've got an appointment. Mel Kirksley, that's the name. I'm here to see Nola . . ."

She paused, her mind an utter blank at Nola's surname, and the butterflies began a major offensive. The receptionist glanced down at her appointments diary and, turning, bellowed:

"NOLES!"

Mel cringed, astonished, but then Nola appeared, in red-and-green angora. "Hi, Mel! The intercom crashed, but we're in luck 'cos Rube studies opera."

A Rasta diva for a receptionist, Mel thought, following Nola out of the foyer—it's like something out of a novel. They walked around partitions, like a maze of cards, and came to a meeting-and-tearoom space, with easy chairs grouped around a low table, on which sat several dirty cups.

"Get yourself some coffee," Nola said. "I'll find Sorrel."

She left, but not before gently squeezing Mel's shoulder. Alone again, however briefly, Mel sat with her cup, glancing up at the open-plan, eye-height walls, which were decorated with posters, all of book jackets. Roxana Reul glared at evil-looking men; warily peered around alley corners; delivered what looked like a terrific judo kick to an androgynous punk with a purple mohawk; and drove a sportscar at speed into the exit lane of a motorway. Among all the covers two things were constant: Roxana's neat little platinum gun, and her trap of a jaw. Mel fervently hoped that Sorrel wasn't the model for these images.

Nola returned, looking wary. Accompanying her was a diminutive woman, dressed entirely thirties-style: bob, round tortoiseshell glasses, tweed suit, and patent lace-up shoes, shiny as cockroaches. Something about face and dress was familiar, but Mel immediately rejected this woman as a flame of Sammy's: the gaze behind those glasses was cold and hard as battle-ax steel.

"Intros," Nola said, as the pair seated themselves. "Mel Kirksley, meet Sorrel!"

If there was a surname, it wasn't forthcoming, and, unable to think of any response, Mel was silent. The pause lengthened. The soft sounds of work from behind the partitions, the ruffling of papers, the tap of computer keys, became excruciatingly audible. Finally Sorrel spoke.

"Nola tells me you have research qualifications." Her voice sounded like something from a sitcom of the British bourgeoisie.

"Yes. Bachelor in history."

"Honors?"

"Two-A."

Sorrel blinked, very slowly and deliberately.

"It was nearly a first," Mel said apologetically.

How that rankled, even after a year.

"Which university?"

Mel named it, and Sorrel nodded as if in recognition.

"I will require proof . . ."

Mel put her coffee cup down on the floor and produced her university degree, still in its protective cardboard roll, the paper inside stiff, thick, and creamy, an imitation parchment. Sorrel inspected it, her face expressionless.

"Roxana's main interest is whether Ms. Mel Kirksley can research. That we will find out quickly, I daresay. The other quality we require is discretion, which is harder to ascertain."

Nola interrupted. "Mel's not a gabbler, if that's what you're getting at!"

"We're obliged to take your word for it, are we?" Sorrel said.

"Find out for yourself, then!" Nola retorted. For a moment

they eyed each other; then Sorrel turned her neat head slowly toward Mel again.

"I want you to undertake not to reveal to anyone what I am about to say to you."

Swear, should I, Mel thought, in sepulchral tones, like Hamlet to his father's ghost? Instead she merely said, "I promise."

"Good." Sorrel leaned back, relaxing a moment, then sat forward again, her spine stiff as a post. "*Jackanory* time! I have a detective story to tell you."

"About Roxana Reul?" Mel asked incautiously.

"In a sense," Sorrel said tartly. "Roxana the publisher exists owing to Roxana the fictional character. Kaye Tollet founded this company with capital from the Roxana books. And the Tolletown winery."

"I know it." Dinners chez Marc's parents, with the bottle of wine, like a mast in the middle of the table, a clean linen napkin tied around its neck, came to Mel's mind.

"Kaye is a fifth-generation Tollet. She and her cousin Lillian inherited the winery from their grandfather."

Nola chuckled. "It only goes to show there's some justice in the universe. You see, Mel, the Tollet winery was a boys' club, handed down father to son. But the lads in Kaye and Lil's generation were so hopeless—vinegar-makers, the lot of them—that finally Grandpa had to admit the granddaughters were his best bet. He even talked Lil out of a high-powered marketing job and into winery school before he went to the great vineyard in the sky."

Sorrel gave her a dark look at the interjection, but continued: "Lillian and Kaye very quickly came to an agreement. Lillian bought out Kaye, and Kaye founded Roxana Press."

Nola grinned luxuriantly. "Now we come to old Rosie . . ."

"Kaye and Lillian's great-great-aunt, and the best bookkeeper the Tollets ever had," Sorrel said rapidly, cutting off

Nola. "Lived to be a hundred, all by herself in the original stone . . ."

She paused, looking nonplussed. "I can't think of the word! If I were in England I'd say manor house."

"Homestead. Tiny little shack in the middle of the vines, with climbing roses and a kitchen garden. Rosie's Place. It was special, for Kaye and Lil—they were the only family Rosie let visit. She'd had a gutful of the Tollet boys, what with ten hulking big brothers. Lil showed me this old sepia print of the family, and I thought, What big bruisers, what an unhappy little kid. But then Lil brought out a Polaroid of a white-haired old lady sitting all alone in her parlor and grinning from ear to ear."

"Thank you, Nola," Sorrel said icily. "Perhaps I would save my breath if you continued the narration."

"OK. Well, Rosie went to sleep during the Minister of Agriculture's speech opening the new wine-tasting building, and never woke up. Completely stole the show, she did. Tollets respect family wishes, even of the dead, and so the old house was left alone, a time capsule of Rosie's century, for Lil to sort out. But she never quite got around to it, and then Kaye paid a visit. Cunning Lil asked if she'd like to go through Rosie's Place, find herself a keepsake. Oh gawd, what a job! Rosie never threw anything out, so the house was full of preserving jars, bottles of old buttons, tight little balls of knitting wool . . ."

"Don't forget the newspapers," Sorrel said pointedly.

"Oh yeah, neat piles of the *Women's Weekly*, and the *Australian Journal*, even a few late issues of Louisa Lawson's *Dawn*. But the real find was in a tin trunk. Kaye thinks Rosie kept her mother's things: top was a dress from the 1880s, tobacco-brown frills it was, yucky, and underneath was an ivory box with eleven locks of baby hair in it, tied with ten blue ribbons and one pink . . ."

"And at the bottom was what we are interested in. Eighteen-sixties issues of the *Tolletown Chronicle*, the local newspaper."

"Mother and daughter must both have been readers," Mel said, feeling some comment was needed.

"Discriminating readers," Sorrel said. "For in the twenty-nine issues of the *Tolletown Chronicle* was preserved a complete serialized detective novel, never published in book form, absent from the canons of your Australian literature. And, though it was written when Conan Doyle was still in his cradle, the plotting, Kaye says, anticipates him eerily."

"It's bloody brilliant!" Nola said. Sorrel smiled, all the interrupting, the hostility between the two, lost in this common enthusiasm.

"And this is what you want me to research?" Mel said.

"Yes. Kaye would do it, but she's in America, on the promotion trail. And we can't wait until she comes back."

Mel was mentally reviewing her conversation with Edie, and now felt that the moment had come to prove her veneer of expertise. "Well, if you give me the name of the writer—Nola said it was a she—I can search the Birth, Death, and Marriage indexes on microfiche. Birth records may give us her children, if she had any, marriage gives parents' names, date of birth, place . . ."

"Hold on," Nola said. "We don't know her name."

"What?"

Sorrel stood up, and called, "Rube, pass over the old newspaper, please. It's sitting on my desk!"

"OK!"

There was a long pause; then over the top of the partition appeared a folio-sized cardboard folder. Sorrel took hold of it, and drew it down into the tearoom.

"Here!" Nola hastily cleared the table of cups and wiped the surface down. Sorrel set the folder upon it as if she carried raw eggs. She opened the wide wing of cover, smoothing it out with one white hand. On the top was a sheet of clear plastic, through which was visible the first page of an old newspaper, with the heading *Tolletown Chronicle*, and a Latin motto, in smaller letters, underneath. The words of the title were supported by two burly, bearded men, one carrying a pickax and the other a flat bowl that slopped water.

"Gold miners," Mel said.

"Tolletown began as an alluvial goldfield, although the first Tollets found it more profitable to grow vines. The rush was over in a few years, so the illustration isn't accurate, not by 1865. But it is where our story begins."

Sorrel lifted the sheet of plastic and turned the page over. Mel came and sat beside her, to see rightside up, and as she did, glimpsed advertisements, for patent medicines, farm implements, quartz-mining equipment. On page 2 were columns of print: unbroken text, some of it indented, with quotation marks. Her gaze traveled to the top of the page. In the far left column was a title, *The Scarlet Rider: or, a Mystery of the Gold-Diggings*. There was no name underneath it, just the heading "Chapter One" and underneath some lines of verse.

"It was not uncommon," Sorrel said, "for novels to be published anonymously in the colonial newspapers."

"And this is all you've got?" The butterflies had returned with a vengeance.

"We have only a text."

Mel stared again at the title, and the space underneath it, where the author's name should be.

"If there's no name, how can you know it's by a woman?"

"Strong female representation," Sorrel said.

"The narrator?"

"No, the 'I' of the story is a policeman. So are most of the characters. There are only four women in the book, actually. A washerwoman, a little girl, a simpering young miss with blue eyes, golden curls, and all the intrinsic interest of a jar of saccharine—and the novel's real heroine, who subverts the ethos of the conventional Victorian female, the Angel in the House, utterly."

Mel was recalling Sammy's haphazard choice of bedtime reading for her small self, which had included Wilkie Collins's *The Woman in White*. "A strong female character doesn't necessarily mean the author's a woman. Wilkie . . ."

"There's other things," Sorrel continued. "When George Eliot's first novel was published, one reader thought that it must be by a middle-aged man, with a wife from whom he got the beautiful feminine touches—"

"The box under the bed," Nola said, "with the sketchbook, cards of thread, tortoiseshell hair combs, and all the other bits and bobs. It didn't half remind me of Rosie's trunk."

"THE DESCRIPTION OF HOW TO MANAGE YOUR SKIRTS SIDESADDLE!" contributed Rube from behind the partition.

"Biddy's description of how to wash lace!" added another invisible Roxana.

"Plus the genuine insights," finished Sorrel, "into the psychology of a real Victorian woman, not a Charles Dickens dolly like Dora. If you read the novel, you know it's not the work of a man. It's as simple as that."

"But you want me to prove it."

Sorrel half-lidded her eyes. "And quickly."

Why? Mel wondered, but something about Sorrel's demeanor said, Don't ask.

Nola cut in, "Well, does Mel get the job?"

"I suppose so!" Sorrel said ungraciously. She leaned back again, looking so stern that Mel could barely concentrate on the details of pay and working conditions that Nola was outlining. Finally, in a very small voice, Mel said:

"When do I start?"

Sorrel looked as if she would have liked to say "Now!" but

Nola came to the rescue: "Tomorrow morning, nine o'clock. I'll fix up the paperwork in the meantime."

Sorrel had her hand on the folder, seemed about to close it, but Mel said, "Just a minute, please!"

"I beg your pardon?"

"That piece of verse at the beginning. Can I copy it down? I'd like to know where it came from, for a start. There's dictionaries of quotations I could use."

"It's probably Tennyson, or wordy old Wordsworth," Sorrel said. "But you may as well transcribe it."

At this point Mel realized that though she had a pen in her bag, there was no paper—she had used up her notebook during yesterday's phone call to Edie. So she copied the little poem onto the back of the degree. When Mel lifted her head, Sorrel was gone.

"Phone call," Nola said. "C'mon, close the folder now and I'll pass it over the wall again."

Mel did as she said, although she itched to just sit and read the novel.

"I'll see you out," Nola said. As Mel rose, she noticed on the floor her mug of untasted coffee, forgotten all this while. But she had no time to taste it, for Nola strode ahead, leading Mel not only out of Roxana but down the stairs and into the lane. The sleeping tramp apart, this space was private in comparison with the open-plan office, and Nola's first act was hearty congratulations, a pat/slap on Mel's back.

"Good on ya!"

"I was terrified most of the time," Mel confessed.

"Oh, that's just Sorrel. See, she doesn't know a thing about the unis here, nor about the wild colonial days, 'cept what Kaye told her, but she'd never admit it. That's why she was putting on her act."

There's more that you haven't explained, Mel thought. Like the emphasis on speed, and why the pair of you fenced with words and glances during the interview. But it's not my place to ask, not just yet.

Nola moved her hand so that it rested on Mel's shoulder, gripping hard. "Remember that Sorrel said you weren't to talk about this project? She meant it. And so do I. See, I can't recall if you were the discreet type or not—Sammy's a long time ago now. But I said you were, crossing fingers. And I don't want you to let me down, comprenday?"

"Yes," Mel said quietly. The door closed behind Nola's red and green, and, quaking a little, she started down the lane. It was not only physical cold that she felt. To do this job properly, she needed more than notes hastily scribbled down in a phone booth. She had to speak to Edie again, and thus she would begin the work by breaking the promise of silence. Oathbreaker! Mel admonished herself, and then found herself dancing on the spot. She was employed!

THREE

Edie

With a hop, skip, and jump, Mel burst into the street, landing right in the path of a woman in a double-breasted suit and stiletto heels, who tottered, waving her briefcase and umbrella wildly in an effort to retain her balance. Mel put one hand on her shoulder, steadying her, then fled, up two steps and into the warm maw of a tram stopped at the traffic lights. At the city center Mel disembarked, soberly, normally, just like an office worker, which indeed she was now, and took the tram that trundled down the cold iron rails to the suburb where Edie lived.

The vehicle was a movable travel brochure, painted with beaches and palm trees, and within it the heat was almost tropical to match. Yet though Mel warmed up quickly, she couldn't seem to shake her shivering. Despite the warnings from Sorrel and Nola, here she was, not even on their job, and off to gabble already. And while yesterday Edie had given the preliminary information Mel needed, over the phone, she hadn't seemed pleased to hear from her only niece.

"Who?" the cracked, old-lady voice had said at the other end of the line. For a moment Mel wondered if she had dialed the wrong number; then she repeated her name again.

"Oh," Edie said. "Jammy Mr. Sammy's little girl. Big tall girl, the last time I saw her. Grown any more, these last three years?"

The question was casual, but the tone was unfriendly, even reproachful. It translated as: Where have you been all this time? Before Mel could reply, Edie added:

"I've shrunk slightly. Old people do. I suppose you've quite forgotten your aunt Alice?"

Another barb. Sammy's oldest sister had not been the sort of person you could forget, especially not at the funeral, where she had plucked flowers from the wreaths and stuck them into the buttonholes of her black coat and in her hatband. At the wake she had even come up to Mel and stuck one of these flowers behind her niece's left ear.

"Is Alice dead?" Mel blurted, suddenly realizing that the entry in the phone book had read Kirksley, E., not A. and E.

Edie's voice softened a little. "No. And yes. She's in a home now. Senile dementia."

That was no surprise, given her graveyard behavior.

"When did that happen?" Mel asked.

"Two years back. The old nurse network got Alice into a decent place, with people who'll take care of her unto the grave. It doesn't matter much to her, but it puts *my* mind at rest. I've stopped raging at the dirty tricks nature can play on people."

"I'm sorry," Mel said. "I should have been in touch before. It's just that with study . . ."

That was one reason, but another, that Mel couldn't voice, was that living with Marc, and her girlfriend Mayzee, she had sufficient, self-chosen family.

"Hmn," Edie said, beginning to prickle again. Mel quickly added, "But it's your study I want to talk about—the family history. Can I pick your brains about research in that area?"

After that Edie had been fine, rattling off the names of the useful source books, the helpful people at the archives, the libraries that had good collections, so rapidly that she was almost untranscribable. But still Mel approached Edie's front gate with trepidation.

Last time she had met her aunts, Edie had just retired from nursing and come to live with Alice, the two sisters sharing the old terrace house that had belonged to Gran Kirksley, who had died before Mel was born. Mel had leaned on this gate many times, staring at the iron lace, with its motif of blossoms; the fanlight above the front door, the glass etched with the name APPLEBY; and the tiny front yard, where everything Alice had tried to grow had withered. Apart from the garden, which had been given a good dig, plus an infusion of the original local flora in the shape of a dozen hardy little native shrubs, it looked much the same. Dire thoughts of teas with Alice, in the days when she had been sane, but appallingly austere, came back to Mel. She shrugged them off, walked up the crazy paving, and rapped with the bronze knocker on the front door.

There was silence. Hell, she thought, Edie's gone out. I should have phoned first. Nonetheless she rapped again and crouched against the door listening intently . . . until she heard, echoing down the passage, arthritic footsteps.

When Edie finally opened the door, they stood looking at each other for a moment, without words. Yes, Mel thought, she has shrunk in height, if not around the waist. Edie was distinctly puffy now, even the joints on her hands swollen. How old is she? wondered Mel, mid-sixties? Yet she was clearly aging with grace, her silver-gray hair cut very short, framing her face, with its pointed chin and rather too large nose, on which were perched small round spectacles. They put Mel in mind of a skier at the top of a precipitous slope.

Below the neck, though, this decorous old lady became something of a bag, with her toes showing through ancient karate shoes, which she had teamed with faded batik pants, under a long moth-eaten cardigan. Her hands were filthy black, and with a vague pang Mel remembered Mayzee, at the funeral, referring to her aunts as Alice in Fairyland and Seedy Edie, although at the time it seemed that Edie's sobriquet was purely rhyming slang. Now both names suited her, for she looked grotty and dotty, her outfit finished by a threadbare apron with the remains of a cross-stitched bunny on the bib.

"You've come in the middle of a cleanup," Edie said, breathing hard. "I'm not dressed for visitors. Neither's the house. But come in and stop your shivering."

With that she stood aside for Mel to enter into the hallway, its framed watercolors and flowered wallpaper familiar, but not so the brooms, dustpans, and other cleaning implements lining the walls and even marching up the stairs. Edie closed the front door and ushered her into the front room—in family argot, the "library," due to its glass-fronted cabinets of books, which had held everything from leather-bound editions of the classics to the copies of the Book of Mormon Alice had been too shy to refuse. She had at least six, hidden somewhere behind the Dresden figurines, the cowrie shells collected on beach holidays, scraps of carved scrimshaw and other knickknacks, occupying the narrow space between books and glass for lack of anywhere else to display them. It was a small room, and the windowsills and the carved marble mantel above the iron grate, where pinecones burned, were already chockablock with Kirksley memorabilia.

Edie gestured at the old fireside rocking chair, where Mel sat to find, draped over the facing sofa, a wrap crocheted in multicolored squares and several embroidered and fringed silk shawls. An old-fashioned suitcase gaped open by the hearth, with around it about ten pairs of antiquated shoes.

Mel said, "This isn't so much a cleanup as a major archaeological investigation."

"Well, somebody had to do it," Edie said. "And there really was only one person: me."

"This reminds me of a certain old lady's house, on the Tollet vineyard estate."

"Well, I am an old lady," Edie said.

"She kept everything, just like the Kirksleys. And in a trunk under her bed, her great-niece—"

Or had it been Nola? Mel's almost-stepmother had definitely been there at the time. Yet Sorrel hadn't, Mel realized, and that was a sore point.

"—found a novel. That's why I got in contact with you. I'm supposed to research it for my job. The thing is, I'm not allowed to tell anybody, but I have already: you."

Edie inclined her silvery head.

"Mel, I haven't been a nurse all these years without being discreet."

"Sorry, I didn't mean that. Edie, I need help with this project, or my bosses will sack me."

"You want me for my Australiana. One may as well be wanted for something." She stood, untying her apron. "That's enough cleaning for the day. I'll make myself tidy and we can talk over tea."

"Thanks."

Edie darted out the door, leaving Mel to bask in the heat of the cone fire like a cat. When Edie returned, her hands were freshly scrubbed and her ragged cloth shoes replaced by patent-leather boots. The mothy cardigan remained, though.

"I'm off to get some milk from the deli. While I'm gone, you can make yourself useful. Advise me. Take a look at those old clothes and tell me what should be thrown out."

Mel had finished by the time Edie reappeared with milk and a small plastic container of cakes.

"Baklava," Edie explained, from the doorway. "I do like multiculturalism—such a change from the dull old provender your father, Alice, and I grew up on. Scones like stones, interminable fruitcakes, dishwater coffee . . ."

Despite her words, she served her bought cakes in traditional style, on a tray decked with an appliquéd napkin and bone china. The tea table, though, was unconventional, for she simply closed the suitcase and set down the tray on its lid.

Mel said, "Before we get our hands sticky with pastry and honey, I want to show you something."

Edie took the certificate and stroked the fake parchment. "Well, nice, you graduated. Sammy would have been proud."

"The other side."

Edie read, very slowly and deliberately:

My eyes behold a beauteous world,
My ear hears nought but merry glee,
My very lips sing songs of praise,
Beloved, these senses V are full of thee!
This frosty heart is ice no more,
True words of love do nourish me:
"Precious," "My dear," and "My sweet Amie"!

My lips would speak her darling name,
But Ah! such freedom's not for me.
My lovely rose is hedged by walls around,
Strong gates, tall yews, owned by mine enemy.
Ours is a secret yearning, undeclared,
We have no friends to urge our amity.
And so, in bliss, in pain, in secrecy,
I must conceal my love, my sweet lady,
I must conceal my love, my sweet lady.

"Who wrote that?" Mel asked.

"I haven't the foggiest." Edie turned, eyeing the bookshelf. "Though I'll wager it's out of the old school readers. We had to learn such deathless verse by heart, you know. I once recited all of 'The Charge of the Light Brigade,' without a prompt, at the school concert, and then couldn't get it out of my head for weeks." She sighed. "I had a good memory when I was young. Not anymore. The human brain is a finite box: there's only so many memories can be fitted into that small space. Just as well, I suppose. I don't want to remember the Great Depression, nor the war."

She fell silent, belying her words, remembering sorrow all too well. For a while they just licked honey off their fingers, until, Edie's gaze returning to the shoes and shawls, she asked:

"Well, what should stay or go?"

"Umn, nearly all the shoes were moldy."

"Hardly surprising, as they were out in the back shed."

"But I liked those little boots with the jet buttons."

Edie reached over and grabbed the pair, holding them by their uppers, of very soft leather, scalloped at the top.

"Your great-grandmother's," she said. "And the shawls?" She leapt up, took a step over the suitcase/tea table, and, lifting up one length of cloth, then another, draped all three around her. They clashed hideously.

"Well?"

"I suppose if you want a bed rug or something, you could keep the crochet. But otherwise I'd say just the silks."

Edie nodded, satisfied, and divested herself of the yards of cloth. "You chose well. But not what I was expecting you to, not at all. For all I knew, you could have been deeply into art deco, or the 1970s, like the young people I see on the street. The buttoned boots, the embroidered silk shawls your great-great-grandfather brought back from India—they're of an era. You went unerringly for the Victoriana."

"Did I? I wasn't even thinking about it."

* * *

Another door was in front of Mel now, not set in a frame of iron-laced verandah, but stark in a dirty brick wall on the topmost floor of the block of flats. The contrast was striking to Mel, but she merely took out her key and entered the flat, her home sweet home.

"Mel-pet!" said a voice from the big swivel chair with the ripped upholstery. As she closed the door it revolved, to reveal Mel's flatmate Mayzee, her skinny body folded around her habitual accessory, a secondhand paperback. They kissed, and Mel smelt old wood pulp in the fluffy hair, which was almost the same shade as May's skin, both being a sallow jaundiced color suggestive of decaying paper. Mayzee was an invalid, but Mel was still half inclined to ascribe her coloring to the paperbacks she loved. A pile of them sat on the floor, in dangerous proximity to her dangling feet.

"Mayzee had a dullsville old time at dialysis, but read three spy novels. What you bin doing with yourself, pet?"

Edit, Mel thought. Mayzee liked to interrogate her on the day's events, but if Mel confessed to a family tea there would be sarky comments. Friend and aunt had met only once, at Sammy's funeral, but Mayzee had taken one of her instant dislikes.

"Guess," she said.

Mayzee eyed Mel's interview rig, her pale eyebrows raised. "Auditioning for the rat race?"

"Right first time. I *was* auditioning for a job. At a publisher's—Roxana Reul."

"Prunefaces," Mayzee said. "Read one of the books once—everything bad is men's fault. They'd never give you a job."

Mel just stood there, grinning like a cheese. "They did. Publication assistant. Part-time casual!"

Mayzee threw her book up in the air and caught it. "Wow! Partykins time!" she said.

"With Marc?"

"He's gone bye-byes."

Mel sighed: Marc being an intern on shift hours, his sleep was sacred. Mayzee dug deep into the recesses of the chair, her skinny hand finally emerging with a purse, which she tossed at Mel. "Pub champers. This is Mayzee's shout."

"Thanks," Mel said, catching it. Mayzee settled back in the chair luxuriantly.

"I'll just be a moment," Mel said. "Get my coat first."

The room Marc and Mel shared was off the living room, and Mel gently opened the door, squeezing into the male-smelling darkness. She knew the space by heart, and could move around without barking her shins on the few items of furniture. Cautiously she felt in the wardrobe, replaced Marc's sports coat on its hanger, and found her duffel by its worn nap. Donning it, she tiptoed to the bed, listening to the soft, slow breathing. She felt the edge of the pillow, and following its indent, touched coils of hair, faintly warm. Mel stroked that hair softly, for Marc was a light sleeper.

"Dream of me, Marc," Mel whispered. "Dream of me tomorrow, in my brand-new job."

FOUR

A Room of Her Own

Mel looks up suddenly, wrinkling her brow. Drat, she thinks, ruffling back through the pages filled with writing, already a fat slice of the book, I've gone and left out something. She rereads a passage or two, half impressed at the bulk of her work, half despairing at the mess of it, the sprawling skein of memory tangled by scratchings and the occasional doodle. Yes, she thinks, I forgot to mention the visit to the library.

She opens a drawer and takes out a sheet of foolscap. This she inserts in the ledger, between the visit to Edie and the return home to May. She closes her eyes, thinks hard for a minute, then picks up the thread again. The yarn unravels down the page. . . .

The old library looked like an antique wedding cake, its grimy white pillars and towers dwarfed by skyscrapers, the wedding party about to cut into the marble, slice it, and devour it. Mel neared, small as a mouse at the feast. She entered the great door, with its pediment of Shakespeare amid scantily clad musettes, crossed the chessboard marble of the entrance hall, and veered into the reference center, bypassing the card catalogs and computer terminals until she came at last to an imposing walnut desk.

Mel had never quite established to which sex this librarian, an Eton-cropped, tweed-suited, middle-aged, middle-sized person belonged. It was immaterial—what was important was a mind that, if given a query, whether it be betel-nut statistics, quasar formation, or arcane lexicography, would speed, with very little fuss and noise, down the corridors of knowledge, to return invariably with its quarry.

"Now, what have you here for me?" said that voice, neither high nor low in tone, but in between.

"I want to know who wrote this." Mel unrolled the poem. There was a long pause, as the Eton crop drooped over the writing.

"Hmn. Victoriana—nobody else was so florid."

The unadorned fingers took the certificate from her hand, gazed briefly at the official, university side, then reversed it again.

"From where did you transcribe this poem?"

"An 1865 bush newspaper, the *Tolletown Chronicle.*"

"Good winery," the librarian said. "But not, I imagine, in the 1860s."

"No, Tolletown was more of a mining settlement then, but big enough to support a thrice-weekly newspaper."

"And all you have is the text? Oh, lovely! Do you know how much poetry was published in the nineteenth century? It was practically a disorder of the age. Verse overstuffed, overornate . . . if anyone had invented a patent cure for poetasters, they'd have made a mint. This'll take hours!"

But he/she looked overjoyed. How rare, Mel thought, as she strolled out into the cold again, how wonderful, to enjoy your work so much. It was something that she kept recalling acutely the next day . . .

Here Mel runs out of foolscap paper, and turns the pages of the ledger, returning to where the narrative broke off earlier.

. . . at her new work, the offices of Roxana Press, Ltd. To begin with, Mel arrived with a hangover from the champagne celebration with Mayzee, to find Sorrel waiting, again immaculate, thirties-style, and again displeased to see Mel. It was drizzling and Mel wasn't game to risk pneumonia from another coatless day, so the only alternative was the duffel coat. It looked very seedy in contrast to Sorrel's suit.

"Where's Nola?" Mel asked.

"Not here."

Mel's mood sank even lower.

"She'll be in this afternoon. In the meantime, you can hang that *thing*"—with a disdainful glance at the duffel—"in the coat cupboard. Then come and see me."

She turned on her heel, leaving Mel alone with Rube. Mel untoggled the duffel dutifully, suddenly aware she had no idea where the coat cupboard was.

"TEAROOM," Rube said, in what must have been intended to be sotto voce, but still projected like a foghorn.

"We haven't been introduced," Mel said lamely, holding out her hand. "Though I know you're Rube."

"AND YOU'RE MEL." They shook hands formally, and cheered by this human contact, Mel threaded her way through the partitions to the tearoom. Yet, as she hung her duffel, she had a curious sense of being observed. She glanced warily at the eyes on the posters, but Roxana et al. stared blankly. Next she inspected the tops of the partitions without finding any spying eyes. She left until last the corner directly behind her, where the sensation was strongest, twirling all in one movement, to see, for the third time—nothing. Tapping her head, she set out through the maze of partitions to Sorrel's lair, encountering sundry Roxanas in little cubicles, and two women in white overalls with pots of paint and a ladder, before coming to face her personal ogre in a room dominated by a window showing cityscape silvered by wet.

"Nice view," Mel said, although all she could see were roofs, with distant workmen like ant on the framework of a new, hard, thrusting building.

Sorrel gave a snort. "I trust you won't spend your whole time here staring at it! You're here to read the *Tolletown Chronicle*, remember?"

The open folder almost covered the desk.

"I'll be in conference all this morning, so this office is—temporarily—yours."

Mel heaved a mental sigh of relief as Sorrel stalked out, then, very nervously, perched on the ergonomic chair behind the desk. Facing her on the wall were several photos, the largest of a narrow-faced woman who bore a vague resemblance to Sorrel herself. Grandmother, Mel thought, noting the clothes in the photo, which also were thirties-style. Something about the image was reminiscent of something, but Mel turned away from it, to the first chapter of *The Scarlet Rider*. Try as she might, though, it was impossible to concentrate. The sense of being observed persisted, and now she had the feeling of being an intruder in Sorrel's den. She couldn't even progress beyond the verse at the beginning—her gaze traveled down the lines, came to doggerel's end, then started again. Snapping the folder shut, she eyed the office phone, an elegant flat model clinging like a moth to the wall.

Mel lifted the receiver, tried dialing out, but got Rube instead.

"HI MEL. WHATYA WANT?"

As she spoke, Mel moved the earpiece sideways, but could still hear the voice clearly from two inches away. "The old library, reference section. I'll give you the number."

There was a long wait, then at the end of the line, Mel heard a polite, androgynous voice.

"Ah, the poetry girl," the librarian said. "Well, you pitched me a curly one. I went through all the relevant dictionaries of quotations, checked the literary histories, collections of nineteenth-century verse, with no luck, no luck at all. It has been fun, but fruitless. Would you have any more information, perchance?"

"Not much. The poem appears at the beginning of a serialized novel."

"A common Victorian habit. Tell me, who wrote the serial?"

"I don't know. It's anonymous."

"Like the poem. Had you considered the possibility that the two anonyms might be one and the same? Many a Victorian novelist also wrote verse."

"No, I hadn't," Mel began, but just then Sorrel entered. She glared.

"Not gossiping on Roxana's time, I trust."

"No," Mel said. "Just checking the source of that poem. You can talk to my proxy, if you like."

"No," she said, irritably. Mel thanked the librarian, then hung up. Sorrel was flicking through the contents of the filing cabinet, her back straight as a poker.

"Sorrel?"

"Yes?"

"What happens this afternoon, when you're back from your meeting? I don't think this office is big enough for both of us."

Sorrel frowned, and Mel knew then she had struck upon a knotty point.

"We don't have much room at the moment. I had thought of moving you here or there, where space permitted."

Mel took a deep breath. "If I had a copy of the serial, then I wouldn't need to be on-site. I could work at home, or in the old library—where I'll have to spend a lot of time anyway. With a copy at hand, I could research intensively. Otherwise, every time I saw something that looked relevant, I'd have to dash back here to check the text."

Sorrel hesitated, just enough to make her "No" seem qualified.

"It really isn't very efficient this way," Mel wheedled.

Sorrel glanced out the window and back again.

"How can I know you're trustworthy? If we make you a copy, what's to stop you—"

She cut that sentence short, with a slight shake of her head. Stop me what? Mel wondered.

"I'll have to consult with Kaye," Sorrel continued, "and she's almost impossible to pin down at the moment, what with her going from signing to interview to literary dinner to airport, to signing . . . and so on. In the meantime, you stay here and keep reading. After lunch I'll put you in Nola's bolthole—no, she'll be back by then. And the painters are starting work in Kaye's office!"

Her mouth opened, and her small square teeth met for a moment. She's going to grind them, Mel thought, fascinated. But the instant passed, and Sorrel composed herself.

"The tearoom?" Mel inquired innocently. "But that wouldn't be any good, would it, because the novel might get coffee spilt on it."

Sorrel glanced at Mel suspiciously, as she continued, keeping her voice neutral, "Well, then, perhaps I should take myself off to the old library, to see what I can find out about

Tolletown circa 1865. I suppose there's been some sort of local history written."

"No, there hasn't!"

How odd. The dig re the tearoom hadn't caused Sorrel to lose her icy cool again, yet mention of local history had. Perhaps now, Mel thought, if I press, I'll get some proper answers. But Sorrel was saved by the bell, for just then the phone rang. Mel was closest to the receiver, and lifted it, almost dropping it at the peal of Rube's voice in her unprotected eardrum.

"She says it's Kaye," Mel informed Sorrel. "In Baltimore. I'll get out of here, so you can have a private conversation. Can I go to the library this afternoon?"

Sorrel had put one, long, delicately manicured finger on the receiver, and seemed about to wrest it from Mel's hand.

"Oh, all right, all right! But if you see a man there, tall, bald as a coot, with a waxed mustache, you are not, repeat not, to speak to him. If you do you're sacked!"

This place is a madhouse, Mel decided.

By midday, the sky had cleared, and Mel went out the door of Roxana into faint sunlight. With enormous relief at escaping Sorrel, she dodged the empty cans the wind was blowing down the lane, nearly dancing again. Out in the street a tram had stopped, its destination shown as Edie's suburb. On impulse, she leapt on, showing the conductor her all-day ticket (Mayzee, on the strength of the new job, had loaned Mel money until her first paycheck). Why not a lunch-hour trip to consult with Edie, on the way—a very roundabout way, certainly—to the library?

In the tram, she sat by the door, experiencing, every time it opened, the outside world, with its wind, smog, and noise. When, by the post office, the tram passed a shaggy pony drawing a buggy full of Japanese tourists, Mel got a sudden, vivid taste of the sounds and smells of a former age: the clip-clop of hooves on road, and the sharp reek of equine sweat. This continued for several blocks, with the horse-powered cart catching up at the traffic lights, only to be passed on the way to the next set of lights, and so on. Several times Mel could almost have reached out and stroked the long, coarse mane.

It put her in mind of the beginning of *The Scarlet Rider:* a man, riding through the bush and singing the verse at the beginning of the serialization. Mel thought, Why didn't I realize poem and novel were by the same person? It seems blindingly obvious now. And there's something about that song, too, that I can't quite put my finger on. Uncanny, that's the word. Might it be the key to *The Scarlet Rider?*

When Mel got off the tram, at Edie's stop, she almost ran down the street to the house, so eager was she to talk. It wasn't until she was staring at the ironwork flowers again that the possibility crossed her mind that Edie might not be in. But the bronze knocker brought her aunt to the door, breathless and aproned again.

"Two visits from Mel in two days! I suppose I should be honored?"

"I'm picking your brains again."

"That's what I thought. I'll just finish washing up my lunch things, then I'll be with you."

Mel wandered into the library, nearly upsetting a small stepladder, set plumb under the brass chandelier, its shelves laden with rags, cleaning fluid, and a number of small, frosted glass shades. The chandelier looked naked without them. Mel fingered one, and felt a layer of gray dust, as thick and soft as pussy willow. Some of it, dislodged by her touch, fell—onto the layer of yellowed newspaper, which covered most of the floor, protecting the elderly Persian carpet. Paper crackled under her feet, then tore, as Mel suddenly darted toward the glass cabinets. Somewhere within her head, an invisible librarian had pounced upon an errant memoir, blown off the dust, and opened it to the gaze of her mind's eye.

Ever since Mel had seen the buggy, she had been vaguely musing, not on horses for courses, but on horses and verses, which juxtaposition had now unexpectedly recalled one dire summer afternoon, spent in this very room. It was as clear as if Mel had suddenly gone back in time, a disembodied entity, and was observing her ten-year-old self, with Alice. Sammy had taken his latest flame for a seaside holiday, and dumped Mel at Appleby, flummoxing her aunt completely. For lack of anything else to do, Alice had brought out the old school readers, a bad idea, for the first story Mel read had been a moral tale of the *Black Beauty* riding school, featuring a truly saintly pit pony, whose deathbed, surrounded by sorrowing miners, had made Mel weep inconsolably.

"Oh dear, oh dear!" Alice had said. "Shall I bake some fairy cakes?"—but they had been more like goblin cakes, scorched and lumpy, the hundreds and thousands on top leaching multicolors into the thin white icing. Then she had opened a box of special Christmas chocolates, only to find they were from several years back, dry, hard, and tasteless. When these attempts at placation had reduced Mel to near hysterics, Alice had frantically rung Sammy at his beach hotel.

It had been late evening by the time he walked into the house, leaning heavily on his walking stick. His jacket had smelt of the night damp, his tobacco, and, very faintly, sea salt. Mel buried her face in it.

"Eh? What's the matter, lass? You've got Allie all upset."

"Don't care. Get me out of here."

"Now, suppose you tell me why."

"It's boring, and the food's horrible and there's no kids around, and aunty can barely talk to me. . . ."

"She's shy," he said. Mel released him and backed away, her bottom lip protruding. He looked at her, his head on one side.

"We'll have to do something about this," he said, and knelt, careful of his game leg, by the bookcase.

—in the same position Mel was now—

examining the volumes visible behind the double curtain of glass and ornaments. "Here's something you two can do together," he said, finally, opening the cabinet door and extracting a small book from behind a china shepherdess.

Now Mel had the cabinet open, her hand moving along the edge of the shelf. There was a sudden gap in the bric-a-brac, and through it she could see four shabby books, the old readers, and beside them a spine lettered in gold with the words: *Britannia Compendium of Parlour Games*.

"Do you remember?" Mel said, when Edie reappeared. "How one of the few things that could break through Alice's shyness was word games?"

Edie nodded her cropped silver head, and Mel held out the book, open to the title page, with its steel engraving of a happy paterfamilias and his plump, crinolined spouse, surrounded by a score of children in Eton collars and corkscrew curls. Sammy had re-created a Victorian family evening with Alice and Mel, here in this very room, playing handkerchief tricks, charades, and puzzles. And it had worked—after he had left, whenever things got awkward, the two had sat down and played the games in the book. Alice, as if briefly freed from some spell, had smiled, even thrown back her head and laughed, as they teased their wits with what soon was a mutual passion, complex anagrams and rhymed acrostics.

"She was good at those things," Edie said. "Could toss off those fiendishly hard poems, the ones with secret messages hidden in them."

The two copies of the poem, in the *Tolletown Chronicle* and on the back of Mel's degree, were absent, but repeated readings had caused the lines to stick, like "The Charge of the Light Brigade," in her memory. She recited it aloud as she flipped through the *Compendium* to the section reserved for verse games.

"That's the poem you showed me yesterday, isn't it? I looked through a couple of the old readers, but couldn't find a source."

"I don't think it was a quote. I think it was at the beginning of the serial for some other reason."

Edie had put her head on one side. "Recite it again."

Mel did, and Edie commented, "The words used are . . . odd. In several instances I could very easily replace them with synonyms which not only would suit, but would scan better. The poet's clearly not got a tin ear, but there's places where the verse seems tortured, twisted, and not for aesthetic reasons either."

"Yeah!" Mel said impatiently. "And why spell 'five,' as in 'senses five,' as 'V'? It doesn't make sense. I think there's something hidden there. Have you got a pad, or something, handy? I want to work on this."

"You mean, in here?" Edie was gazing at the ladder. "Oh, Mel, I'd rather you didn't. That half-cleaned chandelier is looking all reproachfully at me, and I just know I won't be able to rest until I've finished it. Why don't you work in more civilized surroundings? The spare bedroom is positively tidy, in comparison. Go on up, you know where it is."

Mel strolled upstairs to the small spare room, where her child-self had slept during visits to Alice. It was unchanged, except that the narrow brass bed was piled high with what looked like the entire contents of the linen cupboard. The desk by the window, though, was free of clutter, an ideal workspace.

"There's writing paper in the top drawer!" Edie called from downstairs.

"Thanks!" Mel replied. She made several circuits of the room, like a dog moving around and around its basket, before drawing the upright wooden chair up to the desk. The room fitted her; a space all to herself, not like the flat, with the living room Mayzee's space and the bedroom Marc's, whether sleeping or studying, nor like Sorrel's borrowed office. A room of her own . . . and Mel suddenly realized the woman in Sorrel's photo, whom she had taken to be a grandmother, was actually Virginia

Woolf. She knew a few things, did old Virginnie, she thought.

The paper filled with calculations and word combinations, to the distant accompaniment of housework downstairs. Once Edie brought coffee, which Mel sipped absently, engrossed in the puzzle. Edie glanced over her shoulder for a moment, then remarked, "Alice absolutely bamboozled me one rainy afternoon, when we were girls, with an acrostic, her name hidden in a poem, spelt down one side and up the other."

"I thought of that already. It doesn't work out."

She left, and Mel bent over the poem again. Time passed, with a ray of feeble sunset lightening the desk, then sliding away. She scribbled and scratched out, aware, but not aware, that it was getting late, that the room was dimming; she was too intent to move away even for the seconds it would take to switch on the electric light. Then, suddenly, a string of letters detached from the text of the poem.

My	eyes	behold	a	beauteous	world,	
My	**E**ar	hears	nought	but	merry	glee,
My	very	**L**ips	sing	songs	of	joy,
Beloved,	these	senses	**V**	are	full	of thee!
This	frosty	heart	is	**I**ce	no	more,
True	words	of	love	do	**N**ourish	me:
"Precious,"	**"M**y	dear,"	and	**"M**y	sweet	*Amie*"!

My	lips	would	speak	her	darling	name,
But	**A**h!	such	freedom's	not	for	me.
Her	lovely	**R**ose	is	hedged	by	walls	around,
Tall	gates,	great	**Y**ews,	owned	by	mine	enemy.
Ours	is	a	secret	**Y**earning,	undeclared,
We	have	no	friends	to	**U**rge	our	amity.
And	so,	in	bliss,	in	pain,	**I**n	secrecy,
I	must	conceal	my	love,	my	sweet	**L**ady,
I	must	conceal	my	love,	my	sweet	**L**ady.

Yuill? Odd surname, Mel thought. Then it struck her.

"Melvina Marie? That's what I'm called," she whispered.

FIVE

The Happy Orphans Club

All her life Mel had borne this outlandish name, that she knew came from a poem popular in the last century—but she had never once encountered a namesake. Puzzled and disbelieving, she swept the worksheets into the wastepaper basket, put the final copy into her pocket, and crept downstairs. All she wanted was to ponder the coincidence at her solitary leisure, but good-byes must be said. Light came from the kitchen, and she went toward it, to find Edie seated at the table, cleaning the dismantled brass spider arms of the chandelier.

"You off home, then?"

Mel nodded.

"Well, come back anytime, if you want a quiet space to work. I never use that room."

Edie suddenly stood, reaching up to the shelf above the old-fashioned iron range. Amid the usual Kirksley clutter was a tin shaped like an English cottage. She lifted the thatch/lid, and extracted a long length of string, with knotted on one end a key.

"If I'm not in, use this. Alice doesn't need it anymore."

"Thanks," Mel said—offhandedly, she knew, but her mind was fully occupied by Melvina Yuill. She started down the hall, then, with the front door open, called back:

"Who gave me the names Melvina Marie?"

Edie sounded surprised.

"Myrie, of course. Why do you ask?"

"No reason," Mel lied, and shut the door. The night air bit, but she pulled up the hood of the duffel and set off, hugging the information, the secret name revealed.

Myrie had been the one woman, among Sammy's many loves, who had led him to the altar, or in this case, the desk of a West Australian registry office, Myrie being rather too round-bellied for a church wedding. The marriage had lasted six months, largely spent, Mel had heard, in a slow, cross-continent tour, Sammy selling insurance in the backblocks, with Myrie in the passenger seat of his car, squinting over her bulge at the map spread across her lap. Mel wished she had a copy of that map, to trace in red their route across the country. It had ended in this city, with nineteen-year-old Myrie dead of an aneurysm. Mel had been less than two months old.

Myrie had left no keepsakes, no memories, nothing except genetic matter. To gaze into the one photograph Mel had of her, a bridal snapshot showing head and shoulders only, was almost like staring into a mirror. Mother and daughter had the same thick, curling, reddish-bronze hair; same skin, which tanned dark apricot in summer; same full mouth and snub nose. Myrie had been tall, too, standing nearly a head above Sammy, just like Mel.

When she got back to the flat that evening, the first thing

she did was take the photo from her bedside chest of drawers. She sprawled across the coverlet, studying the framed image. The woman in the photograph gazed back, in repose, but with the corners of the mouth turned upward, as if about to smile. She had a reason, Mel thought, for giving me the Christian names of a dead novelist.

Behind her, soft footsteps sounded on the hall carpet. The next moment the bed heaved violently as a mass, a human body, leapt onto her back.

"Marc!"

"Yep," he said, sitting down firmly, his bare knees gripping her by the waist. Unable to rise, Mel craned her neck around, gazing over her shoulder. The lopsided view she got of Marc showed him in his bathrobe, hair still damp from the shower, and grinning broadly.

"You scared me," Mel said. "I thought nobody was in."

"Hey, what's wrong with being friendly? Specially when I ain't seen Mel-baby for days." He bent, pulled back the hood of the duffel, and blew a raspberry on the back of her neck. "What're you doing?" he said. "Putting on makeup? Hey, that's your picture of Mommie Dearest."

"Don't call her that," Mel said, to the reflection. "She might have made a good parent."

" 'They fuck you up, your mum and dad,' " he said, the one line of poetry he knew, and rather than argue Mel replaced the photo. As she did, the angled glass showed first Marc's face, then her own, superimposed on Myrie's.

Marc sat heavy as a sack of onions. "Can I turn over?" Mel said, and in response he rose slightly. Mel rolled, the duffel and skirt rucking around her waist.

"Congrats on your job," he said, and bent down in a kiss, his mouth leaving the overwhelming taste of junk food. "Shall we celebrate? I'm not due back at the hospital for a few hours yet."

Mel mentally groaned, not minded to have another Cheezels kiss, nor indeed to do anything except ponder the mysterious Melvina Yuill. But Marc was slipping the loops off the toggles, one by one, in a progression down her body. He hunkered back.

"Are you aware," he said, "that you have a hole in the crotch of your panty hose?" He demonstrated with a pinch. "And your knicker elastic has gone slack in one leg."

"I'll take the tights off before you make them any worse, as I haven't got a fresh pair. Oh, you want to do it, do you? Hey, hold your horses! You'll ladder them right down to the ankle!"

Mr. Willing, Ready, and Able, Mel thought, using one of Sammy's expressions. And I'm not, just at this moment. Could I possibly ask him to clean his teeth first? Too late now . . .

The only sound in the flat was Marc's slow, steady breathing, but then Mel heard the key turn in the front lock. Mayzee's brisk steps sounded down the hallway. Over Marc's shoulder Mel saw her briefly silhouetted in the doorframe, before May reached out and pulled the door shut, quietly but still with enough noise to momentarily distract Marc.

"No damn privacy here," he muttered.

"Hush. She's gone." Mel's arms encircled his back. Almost despite herself she was beginning to get interested, but before it amounted to much Marc winced, let out his breath sharply and collapsed on top of her.

"Marc, I can't breathe. Marc, I mean it, I'm suffocating! Get off!" Mel elbowed him hard in the side. Slowly, still lost in his private pleasure dome, he rolled over and away from her. Mel sat up abruptly.

"Marc! You pig! You've dribbled on my coat."

"Not for the first time," he muttered, and Mel flounced off to the bathroom. In the living room, Mayzee was coiled up in her chair, a paperback open in her lap.

"No damn privacy here," Mel repeated to herself, slamming the bathroom door behind her. She rubbed the duffel with tissues, then stripped off her remaining clothes. When she turned on the shower, the water emerged brownish and lukewarm, but sufficient to douse her head to foot. Hidden by a cloak of water she stood, momentarily alone.

It had been in a shower room that Mel had first met Mayzee, five years back, and at that time she hadn't wanted to be by herself, she had been desperate for company. Mel had moved into university college some weeks before her first year started, with the idea of making friends. Instead, she had found herself living on what seemed the set of a postholocaust film. Walking down the corridors, Mel would hear distant voices, footsteps on the fire stairs, but when she turned the corner, there would be only vistas of beige carpet, and shut, anonymous doors. In the canteen, mealtimes would summon a few people to huddle at tables, their only company the textbooks propped in front of them. Mel should have been used to institutional living, after years of boarding school, but she shrank away, too shy to make contact with these solitary diners.

Thus it was that, when alone in her college room, Mel heard the rattling of the shower in the women's bathroom two doors down, she leapt up, wound her wrap tightly around her, and went haring down the corridor. Clouds of heavily scented steam emerged as she opened the door of the bathroom; that, and a light female voice, softly singing. Mel took the cubicle next but one, hung up her wrap and took her second shower in thirty minutes.

She had planned to intercept her fellow bather when she finally emerged, but the other washed for what felt like hours, while Mel waited under the water, her fingers wrinkling like a crone's. When the shower finally ceased, Mel counted to sixty before turning off her own, then realized that she had left her towel back in her room. She wiped herself down with the wrap, for lack of anything else, then found that the damp cloth clung lewdly. Oh, well. Outside the cubicle, she could hear the hand dryer, and decided it was time to introduce herself.

To—someone bent double under the stainless-steel nozzle of the dryer, her short wet hair spiking in the gale of warm air. As if that wasn't odd enough, she was naked as a skinned rabbit. The stranger grinned, relishing Mel's polite, frozen astonishment.

"Hi," Mel said, for lack of anything else to say.

"Beg parding?" shouted the other above the cyclone of the dryer. It stopped, and Mel repeated, "Hi."

"Hi also. Can you be a pet and pass my pay-nwah!"

"Your what?"

The answer was an imperative point, at a robe hanging on the back of the cubicle door, red satin embroidered with golden dragons. The girl cast it over her nakedness, then padded over to two little purple velvet slippers, with gold bead fringe. She stepped into them, and gave Mel a wink.

"Somebody's gotta liven up College Dullsville."

"I suppose so," Mel said, politely.

"I'm this corridor's tutor, May Zeehan, it says on the door, but to my special people I'm Mayzee."

"I'm Mel." To anyone, she thought, whether they like me or not.

Mayzee was eyeing Mel disconcertingly. "Pleastameetyou. Come and have supperkins."

"In the canteen?"

Mayzee wrinkled her nose. "God no. Chez me, the room at the end of the corridor, behind the magic door with the Day-Glo name tag. Hour's time, okay? Bring that brother of yours along."

She wafted her red satin and embroidery out of the bathroom.

Oh thank you, oh thank you very much, Mel thought. Then, puzzled: Brother, what brother?

Back in her room she dressed, and to pass the hour went for a wander around the college yet again. In the front lobby, she found people mostly too old to be students, all wearing name tags. A conference, she realized as she entered the crowd, which was eerily silent. A large banner explained all: this was the third annual Sign Language Symposium, a signal success, to judge from the animated faces, the delegates all talking at the tops of their fingers. Near the outside door Mel could hear the anomaly of a voice, coming from the public phone booth. "Ma, I haven't left home to come back every weekend for meals. No!" it said. The receiver slammed down, and next moment the door of the booth opened and she was suddenly face to face with—herself.

Tall and slender. Thick, curling red-bronze hair. Skin tanned to apricot. A full mouth and snub nose. Only the cropping of the hair, and the Adam's apple jerking beneath the chin as his jaw dropped, convinced Mel that she wasn't gazing into a mirror.

"So the comments about a twin . . ."

"The brother . . ."

They were speaking almost in unison. Embarrassed, they stopped, started again:

"I'm Mel Kirksley."

"And I'm Marc St. Cyr."

"I start arts this year."

"I'm second-year med."

"At least we're not the same age." They both said that, and Mel turned her face away, sure she was blushing and not wanting to see if he was, too. Two delegates were watching, exchanging comments on their fingers.

"We're a raree show," Mel said.

Marc glanced around. "Too right. Let's get out of here."

A little later they were walking down the main road beside the college, trucks and buses thundering past.

"I never knew of any relatives called St. Cyr."

"Nor Kirksley. I could ask Ma, though. She's into the family history. Or maybe I should just mention the milkman factor to her. . . ."

"What's that?"

He grinned. "Every large study of inherited differences has failed, because a certain percentage of the children have different biological characteristics—like a different blood group—to their putative dads. In other words, they were fathered by someone else. The joke is that the milkman's responsible."

Sammy, Mel thought, you didn't . . . She almost laughed at the thought, sobering when she looked at Marc, and saw him like her and Myrie—not at all resembling Sammy.

"Do we have the same blood group?" Marc was asking.

"I think . . . O. Yes, I'm sure of that."

He replied lightly, though his face twisted: "Damn, and I thought I had proof of illegitimacy, or of being adopted."

"You're . . . ?"

"I'm AB positive. Same as my parents."

They walked in silence for a little while after that, shooting sideways glances at each other.

"I got invited to supper by this tutor called Mayzee, and she said I was to bring my brother along."

"Well, then," he said. "Let's go and play happy families."

So it continued as they circumnavigated the huge block of the university, to reach the college just in time for Mayzee's supperkins.

Mayzee opened the door, took one look, and said, "Ah! The glimmery gingery twins. Unrelated, as I just found out from Rictus the Rector. Mel I've met, and you are . . ."

"Marc St. Cyr."

"I'm Mayzee, the resident eccentric."

As if it wasn't obvious, thought Mel. Entering, she glanced around the tutor's big room, decorated in the dullest shades of beige, and sympathized with Mayzee's desire for color. She still wore her red peignoir and purple slippers, but had tied a turquoise scarf, twenties-style, around her narrow head.

Marc was goggling a little at her getup, but said, "I like you calling the Rector Rictus. 'S a good name for the old spy."

"Spy?" Mel said.

"Dr. Ricketson's a friend of my parents. I don't doubt he's reporting on me."

"Then you must misbehave, extraspecially, to give him something to report," Mayzee said. She sank to her knees before a coffee table, on which were arrayed glasses, nibblies in an open packet, and cheap white wine. She poured out drinks all round, and stilted conversation started, thawing as the wine took effect.

"Now tell me, you not-twins, what are you doing in College Dullsville, so early in the academic year?"

Mel said quietly, "I've nowhere really else to go." Not with Sammy off with his latest love, Edie overseas, and Alice so strange lately it was impossible to live with her.

"I've run away from a home classified by the National Trust," Marc said. "Full of antique furniture, pictures of ancestors by famous artists, and mementos of the St. Cyr history of squattocracy."

It sounded not unlike Mel's family, with better financial management, but she said nothing, thinking Marc had probably had enough coincidences for the day. Mayzee opened her mouth, sang a line:

"Ma-uh little runaways. Just like May. Except I've dee-vorced my family, for being terminally dull."

"Wish I could," Marc muttered.

"Kindred minds, we are," May finished.

Mel opened her mouth to disagree, then closed it. The wine was going to her head, and she wasn't sure she could express herself coherently. Better to just listen and maybe explain later.

"A club," Marc was saying. "Ooh yes! What'll we call ourselves? The Runaways? The Waifs and Strays? How about the Happy Orphans' Club?"

Marc and she clinked glasses. Mel didn't like the sound of that, of being without Sammy, the only parent she had left, but nonetheless held out her glass to these new friends.

It was after midnight when Marc and Mel strolled back to their college rooms.

"She's nice," Mel said at her doorway. "I thought tutors would be stuffy."

"That's what old Rictus'd like. I wonder how long she'll last. He won't like her being pregnant."

"What?"

"When she put her feet on the table. You might have only noticed her glitzy slippers, but the trained medical eye, ahem, the half-trained medical eye, saw that her ankles were swollen. Dead giveaway."

"But she can't be," Mel said, thinking back on that white body in the bathroom. May's belly, from what she could recall, had been flat. But she didn't want to tell Marc that she had seen Mayzee naked, so the conversation ended there. He left, and Mel lay in her bed, wrapped in the warm memory of that evening. She felt something rare, contentment, apart from the slight niggle of Marc's diagnosis.

Three weeks later, Mel was in still much the same state, and first term had started. Mayzee held a party for the students of the corridor, in her room, which she decorated with balloons and about thirty bright silk Indian scarves, stuck to the ceiling with tape to form a billowing, patchwork canopy. She eschewed her gown and slippers for this occasion, choosing a fifties dress of ochre crepe, which she teamed with a velvet beret the color of claret, and bare feet with cerulean toenails. It was all a bit too much for the first-years, the football jocks, the conventional little girls from the country, the suburban kids from good immigrant homes, and mostly they sat around the walls looking sullen, while Mayzee talked to Marc and Mel. Even Marc thought she was being over the top, and more disturbingly, her feet looked puffy to *Mel's* untrained eye; but still she seemed enormously likable.

Then things started to fall apart, just as things fell neatly into place for Marc and Mel, on the night he christened her then new duffel coat for the first time. Mayzee came rapping at the door:

"Mel-petal, Mel!"

Mel wriggled out of Marc's arms, and almost immediately got tangled in the rag-bag of discarded garments they had strewn over the bed. Her thoughts were similarly confused— maybe Marc could hide in the little clothes closet, or under the bed itself. Finally Mel extricated herself, tied on her wrap, and went to the door. Marc heaped the clothes over his nakedness, and lay back, grinning goofily.

Mayzee pushed past. "I just got a bum at my window!"

"Er, what?"

"I heard a tap-tap-tap, so drew aside the curtain, and saw this huge pair of hairy cheeks! With pimples! I rushed outside, but only found heavy footprints . . . and hearty laughter, far off. I bet it's that Henry cretin. I bawled him out for playing his heavy metal too loud. Oh . . . hi, Marc."

Despite her jaunty tone, she looked deeply upset.

"Complain to Rictus," Marc said.

"Someone already has, about May-the-bad-influence! Rictus won't say who, but I can guess. Little Holier-Than-Thou down the hall, with the plaits. She was singing hymns in the shower, so I responded with 'Eskimo Nell.' "

"Umn, Mayzee, was that wise?" Mel said.

May looked aggrieved. "Anyone would think you're as prissy

as the rest of the students here, the Non-Happy-Orphans."

Marc cleared his throat. "Mel's not, and you know it."

Mayzee bit her lip.

Marc continued: "'Scuse me for asking, but it's a cold night, and your toes must be freezing. Are you being a hippie, or have you forgotten about shoes?"

Mayzee looked down at her feet and up at Marc again. "May's shoes just don't seem to fit, anymore."

"Then," Marc said, very gently, "I suggest you see a doctor."

Mel returned to the bed and took Marc's hand.

May pouted. "You want to go back to your fucking, pets. Well, don't mind May, who was just letting off steam. Shan't disturb you any longer. I'll sit in my room and plot revenge on thicko Henry and that sick little girl. Night!"

After May left, Mel said, "Look, I don't think she's pregnant."

Marc said nothing, just drew her back into bed again.

They were a happy couple, but Mayzee looked increasingly strained and miserable over the next weeks. She had had, by her own account, hugely enjoyable confrontations with Henry and Holier-Than-Thou. Both had denied everything, but the bum at the window had recurred, and poison-pen letters, written in precise rounded capitals, had come under her door in the wee hours.

The atmosphere in the corridor was like a crypt, cold and creepy, hardly romantic, but it never seemed to put Marc off during his nightly visits. Late one evening, Mel rolled away from Marc, suddenly stirred into wakefulness by a noise in the corridor.

"Wozzat?" he said muzzily.

"I think they're persecuting Mayzee again. I'd better go and stop it."

Mel pulled on her wrap and opened the door. Nothing was visible except the usual closed doors, but she heard, near her feet, a whimper, coming from something that looked like a huge red ladybird. Mayzee was hunched on the carpet, her red satin arms clutching the crown of her head.

"What is it?"

No response, except for a sniffle. Mel bent down and lifted Mayzee to her feet. Inside the room, Marc was pulling on his jeans; even before Mel walked Mayzee inside and sat her down in the one chair, she could guess, from his face, the mask of woe that finally turned toward her.

"Mayzee! What's happened?"

Her mouth worked, tears streamed down her face. At last one word emerged, incomprehensible to Mel, although it sounded vaguely medical. Marc suddenly sat down hard on the bed, his fly still undone.

"What did she say?"

"It's . . . a kidney disease. A nasty."

Mayzee was moaning, a sound that finally translated into words: "Didn't want to interrupt your fucking. But, but . . ."

"But what?" Mel knelt down behind the chair, put her arms around it and Mayzee.

"Get me out of here, pets," she finally said.

And that was that. They were out of the college in two weeks flat, the parting gesture being Mayzee's. On the night before she was due to hand in her master key, she entered Henry's room at 3 A.M. with a bucket of soapy water and poured it straight down his snoring throat. Holier-Than-Thou might have suffered likewise, but, as Mel heard later, that night she was on the other side of the college with Billy Carboni, a sleazy law student who specialized in virgins.

Where is she now, Mel wondered, as the water dribbled down her from scalp to toes. Unmarried mother? Good dull wife? What did she make of herself, in the years while we lived in this flat, three happy orphans? Memories swirled in her mind, like the dirty water in the shower drain, first funny—Mayzee coaching Marc for his exams, a mortarboard made from an ice-cream carton on her head—then sad. After Sammy's funeral Mel had sat in the living room weeping, with Marc and Mayzee cuddling her, all night long, in shifts. She would always be grateful to them, and indebted too, for that.

The thought of Holier-Than-Thou lingered. What would she think of me? Mel suddenly had the sensation of seeing herself as others might view her, as if she had stepped outside her body for a good, dispassionate, and critical look at herself. It lasted only a moment; then she was back, standing on moldy tiles, with a new feeling: disaffection for the way she had come to live.

Putting One over Sorrel

Mel previewed the next day in her mind, lying alone in bed that night, imagining the smile on Sorrel's face at the sight of the solved acrostic, Melvina Mary Yuill revealed in all her trickster glory. It was a wish-fulfillment fantasy, somewhere between sleep, waking, and dream, and after a moment Mel realized there was something strange about it; instead of viewing the scene through her eyes, she seemed separate from it.

Mayzee had recently brought back a book from the Paperback Exchange on the subject of what she called "oobys": Out of Body Experiences. Loony stuff, she had said, really only worth reading for giggles. Yeah, Mel agreed, rolling over and burying herself in the pillow. She tried to imagine herself floating up near the ceiling, gazing down at her body, and failed. Yet there had been a strange sense, in her fancied meeting with Sorrel, and while she had showered that evening, of *witnessing* herself.

In the event, her fantasy was quite wrong. When she entered Sorrel's space, she found an additional figure in the scene, Nola, forming a tableau with Sorrel, *Women with Paperwork*. Nola smiled in welcome, but Sorrel merely asked, irritably, "Do you have anything to report?"

From the tone, it translated as: "If not, skedaddle!"

Mel took a deep breath and began to explain her word games. The tableau watched intently, unsmilingly, and her voice began to falter. When Mel had at last come to a slow, grinding halt, Sorrel said, her voice even more English than usual, "Are you serious?"

Mel nodded slowly.

"Nola, what do you make of this?"

"Well, Mel means it, I can tell that. . . ."

"Mel," Sorrel said. "*Mel*vina Mary. Coincidence? Mel, what is your Christian name in full?"

"Melvina Marie." It was the one piece of information Mel hadn't wanted to impart—and now she had.

"Never knew that," Nola drawled. "I thought you were a Melissa, or a Melanie."

Sorrel narrowed her eyes. "Nola, I thought you knew this person!"

Nola said nothing, and Sorrel, after a moment, returned her attention to Mel. "I suggest you're projecting."

Mel was stung. "Then how do you explain that the verse forms a name?"

"Merely coincidence. Like those songs played backward, that somehow produce dark satanic messages." Sorrel made a shelf of her hands and rested her triangular chin on them. "This is, quite frankly, not good enough. In fact it's verging on the loopy. You'll have to do a lot better. In fact, if over the next few days you don't come up with some goods, Roxana'll drop *Mel*vina Marie Kirksley from the payroll."

The phrasing of the name was an implied jeer and it stirred memories in Mel, hidden deep because unpleasant. Before the child Melvina had abbreviated her name to the somewhat more normal "Mel" she had suffered agonies at school, and now she felt as if she were in the playground again, about to sob in front of this adult bully. But then, from a great distance, Mel heard herself say, "Sorrel, you spoke to Kaye Tollet on the phone yesterday. Did you ask her?" Now she sounded almost as accusing as Sorrel.

"About what?" Nola said.

Sorrel unclasped her hands. "The novel. Mel wants a copy of it."

The tone implied that Mel had been asking for the moon and stars. In response, Mel opened her mouth and her voice issued forth, unexpectedly forceful: "I was only suggesting it would be more convenient to have the research text handy when I do library or archival work. And I wouldn't be cluttering up Roxana."

"Makes sense," Nola said. "Well, Sorrel, did you put that to Kaye?"

There was a pause. Sorrel pursed and unpursed her mouth. "Yes," she said.

Mel could have kissed her hard, cold cheek.

"But Kaye said, only as a last resort. Kaye said, 'She's not to show it to anyone, nor discuss it.' "

"Mel wouldn't," Nola said staunchly.

Oh yeah? Mel thought of Edie, with guilt but no repentance. She met Sorrel's gaze and held it, until Nola broke the eye contact by lunging between them and grabbing the *Tolletown Chronicle* from the desk.

"Last resort!" Sorrel repeated.

"Sorrel, since you're looking like a bad fairy, maybe you can change Mel into a mouse, and that way we could find her workspace! Because otherwise we ain't got the room!" The newspaper clutched firmly under her arm, Nola headed for the door. "Mel, c'mon! We're going photocopying!"

As they slaved over the warm copier, Nola murmured, "You put one over Sorrel. That's rare."

"You helped."

"Yeah, but you did most of it yourself. Pleasure to watch. Wouldn't have thought you had it in you."

Mel wouldn't have either.

"And just for that, I'll let you in on a little secret."

Why Roxana are so paranoid about the novel? Great!

"You musn't let on, though."

"Oh, I won't!"

"Around the office, when Sorrel gets into one of her moods, we call her Spinach."

Mel shut the lid of the photocopier on her hand. Then she laughed, half vexed, half amused at the anticlimax.

A half hour later, Mel stood under the Roxana sign clutching an expanding folder stuffed full of *The Scarlet Rider*. The photocopying had reduced the format slightly, but the novel was still an armful. She started toward the library, only to find herself, after a block or so, increasingly lopsided under the weight.

To her left were shining panes of windows, framed inside by heavy velvet drapes, giving a view of small mahogany tables, set with crystal vases of hothouse flowers, and, seated at them, sophisticated old ladies and trendoid business couples. The Victoria and Albert Hotel tearoom—a place Mel had never dared enter before. Yet, here she was, perhaps emboldened by the encounter with Spinach, setting one foot after another, up the marble steps, the man in the stiff suit outside the door actually opening it for her, despite the disgusting duffel with its Marc stains. Mel strutted into the tearoom, and was ushered to a vacant table at the back, under a huge engraving of the Victoria and Albert Hotel when its namesakes had still been conjoined.

A starched and frilled waitress appeared at Mel's elbow, and she ordered cappuccino and a brioche, already preoccupied with the *Tolletown Chronicle*. The novel sat on the table before her; its pages drew her gaze inexorably.

A Victorian Detective Officer

My eyes behold a beauteous world,
My ear hears nought but merry glee,
My very lips sing songs of praise,
Beloved, these senses V are full of thee!
This frosty heart is ice no more,
True words of love do nourish me:
"Precious," "My dear," and "My sweet Amie"!

My lips would speak her darling name,
But Ah! such freedom's not for me.
My lovely rose is hedged by walls around,
Strong gates, tall yews, owned by mine enemy.
Ours is a secret yearning, undeclared,
We have no friends to urge our amity.
And so, in bliss, in pain, in secrecy,
I must conceal my love, my sweet lady,
I must conceal my love, my sweet lady.

Such was my song, as I rode through a parklike expanse of bush in the colony of Victoria, and felt myself as near to Heaven as any man living can hope to be. The road before me was but a rough bush track, winding amongst the eucalyptus trees, and here and there I could see the little lizards, blinking their eyes in the sunlight, the bare patches in the scrub that signified a parliament of ants, and even the monster of the bush that is the Australian iguana, lolling his four foot of scales along a white-barked branch. As I raised my voice in song, my easy-going nag pricked up her ears, the bell-birds made their "tinkle-tinkle," the natty magpies sounded their clarinets, and it seemed that I had quite the appreciative audience—until the shriek of a parrot declared itself the critic. I could but laugh; on such a pleasant sunny day, amidst such agreeable surroundings, there was little that could destroy my equanimity.

It was rare for me to experience such blissful serenity; for I will tell you now that in the normal course of my duties there was little time to contemplate the beauties of nature, although one would sometimes think wistfully of them, given that my fate was to mix daily with the worst humanity had to offer. I was, in short, an officer of the mounted police, something that back in dear England, at my Oxford College, I would not have thought of becoming; but after six months scrabbling around in colonial dirt for the ever elusive alluvial gold, near-starving in the process, I was right glad of the chance to wear the smart blue and silver uniform and eat three meals a day.

My route was taking me from our district headquarters, a large provincial town, still prosperous despite its aureate fields being well nigh exhausted, to a smaller settlement, where the gold fever still reigned. Here, in contrast to the alluvial diggings where I had broken my young heart in pursuit of Moloch, was a nuggety goldfield. Those of minuscule means could not hope to survive there, as they might not see the "colour," not only for days, but for weeks and months. Yet the lure of a glorious

find, such as had happened to two young Cornishmen the previous spring, with a nugget the length of a man's forearm, and
shaped, so they fancifully claimed, in the form of their native
county, kept many there.

My simple bush track soon met with another, wider, with
the signs of the surveyor's work on it, and so, with regret, I left
the sights and sounds of the natural world, and neared what
passed, in this remote region, for civilisation. This road led up
and over the summit of a hill, and at the top I pulled up my
horse, to gaze down upon the river valley at my leisure.

To the untutored eye, Cornish Flat was like many another
goldfield, and if you have not seen anything of that sort, I must
needs describe the scene. There were no trees, no bush creatures, only as far as the eye could see dirt, flat or in heaps of
"stuff" beside the claims. Had the lucky nugget been shaped like
nothing in particular, I do believe the goldfield would have
been named after its most distinguishing characteristic, viz.,
the colour of the earth. Before me was an expanse of chalky
white, not even relieved by the clustering tents of the diggers,
for they also were that same drear colour.

Cornish Flat was a maze; for such had been the haste to get
to the precious metal that absolutely no attempt had been made
at a street plan. Indeed, had I arrived at night, I would have
found it positively dangerous to proceed, for the holes of aban-
doned claims were all over the place, twisting and diverting the
rough tracks from any semblance of order, so that my mount
was often obliged to squeeze between a yawning gap on the one
hand, and the canvas flap of a tent on the other.

Despite having to keep my attention on my path, I gazed
keenly about me, for it is the business of us police to know
everything about a place and everyone living there. Yet at this
hour of the day there was little to see, bar a few sleepy dogs, tied
at the entrances of the tents; for the diggers were hard at work,
down their claims with pick and shovel. Even the places of busi-

ness, with their flags and bunting blazing forth the proprietors' names, were closed until the return of the customers at sundown.

As I rode, the fancy came to me, no doubt prompted by the continual monotony of white all around, that I had perhaps died, back in the bush, and my spirit rode through the realm of the dead. It was an idle phantasy, not long entertained, for I soon saw in front of me, not a ghost, for no ghost ever washed her baby in a bucket beside a goldfields tent, but a genuine Irish "colleen," broad, tousle-haired, red of face; in short such a specimen as can be found on any diggings. From this young woman I gained directions to the police camp, where I quickly wended my way, as much as the nature of the terrain would allow.

The little wood-framed station was erected on a rise, surprisingly still covered in green grass, close to the centre of Cornish Flat. Although the wealth of distant gullies had already begun to lure the population away from its neighborhood, the camp was a close-to-ideal location for overlooking the diggings, or for idly lolling outside with a pipe of tobacco, watching the busy world of a gold rush go by. Indeed, on most days, Metcalf, the constable in charge, was to be seen in this position; but today he was not there.

"Good heavens!" I said to myself. "Ned Metcalf, the laziest man in the mounted force, not indulging in his usual *dolce fa niente*, as the Italians have it? Something is up, for certain!"

At that moment, drawn by the noise of my horse's hooves, Ned himself came to the door of the camp, but oh, poor fellow, so shipshape, with his cap-cover white as snow and his high boots shining with polish, that I knew instantly that Cornish Flat had been favoured with a visit from the district Inspector, James Renfrew Justperson. I was on reasonable terms with this august presence, as his family had been acquainted with mine, back home; indeed it had been his recommendation that had gained me a place in the mounted force. I knew well, though, that he was quite the martinet, given to arriving at the stations under his jurisdiction without notice, and fining the constables heavily if the slightest hair in the forelock of a police horse was out of place. Thus, I was always on my best behaviour anywhere that Justperson and I might meet.

"Say nothing, Ned," I murmured as he came and took the bridle of my horse whilst I dismounted. "I have guessed. What was it? A lost button? You should tell that Irishwoman who launders for you to take more care with your uniform."

"Five shillings he fined me!" responded Ned, equally *sotto voce*, "but we can't talk about it now. He's in there now waiting for those despatches in your saddlebag, and if you don't get them to him immediately there'll be even more fining!"

Thus warned, I straightened my uniform, and leaving Ned to look after my horse, marched up the rise to the police camp. As I have mentioned before, it was a wooden building, simple in construction, built for two constables, with an iron roof, which on days of bright sun made the place a veritable oven. When I entered and stood at attention, drops of sweat sprouted on my brow; but the man seated at the rough table appeared as cool as the proverbial cucumber. Pen, ink and paper, the blue sheets on which we police made our reports, were in front of Justperson, and he continued tracing his calligraphy down the page, before signing it with a flourish. Then, with an inclination of his head, just so, he indicated that I should approach him with my despatches.

He read them, whilst I glanced around the room, and saw it was in as apple-pie order as a police camp could be, with the straw pallets on which Metcalf and his assistant, Constable Dacre, slept, looking so respectable one might almost have believed they did not harbour fleas. Despatches read, Justperson folded them, and after calling for Ned to make tea, keenly regarded me for a moment. He had a pair of eyes like pale green glass marbles, in which a man might fancy his misdemeanours, real or otherwise, were reflected, coldly and with censure. Yet being tidier by nature than poor Ned, and aware that my peccadilloes, such as they were, could hardly have come to Justperson's attention, my base camp being far away, I met his gaze with composure.

"I have already discovered," he said, leaning forward, "that Constable Metcalf is, in the matter of tea-making, exceedingly slow. Shall we, whilst he takes his time, perambulate briefly?"

I nodded, although deep within me, my heart missed a beat. Might he know something, after all? Or perhaps he had bad news from home, which he wished to communicate to me privately, away from Ned's inquisitive ears. I forced myself to grin and look agreeable as I followed Justperson out of the door of the police camp, with its skillet of a roof, and indeed, outside it was far more pleasant than inside, with a faint breeze just arisen, carrying to us the distant noises of the miners. Justperson strode down the rise at a great rate, stopping at a point just out of earshot of the police camp, but where we could still gaze across the expanse of white tents and earth.

"Miles, I have known you long," he finally said, his gaze fixed on the horizon, as if he espied evil-doing there.

"Indeed you have, sir, since I was in short petticoats."

A different man might have smiled at the incongruity of myself, a strapping young fellow of six feet and more, recalling my days in frills and lace, but Justperson remained impassive.

"It has come to my attention," he began, then stopped, so that my poor brain frantically searched for whatever minor misdemeanour of mine might have been reported to him. "It has come to my attention, Miles, that you have applied to join the Detective Force."

"That is correct, sir." For though I loved the outdoor life of being a mounted man, days of settling disputes between miners, and dealing with the consequences of the spiritous liquors, alas, so freely used on the diggings, had begun to pall on me, and I craved something involving a little more brainpower, and I will be honest here—money.

"Humph! I was not aware you had any facility for detection."

I said nothing.

"You are of course aware that your admission into the Detective Force will depend on the recommendation of your senior officers."

I was well aware of that, and indeed had been seeking the good opinion of my Sergeant and the Inspector himself, although without being too obvious about it, lest I be chaffed by my fellow constables. Justperson turned from his perusal of the landscape, and said, with a sidelong glance at me: "Miles, if you wish to be a detective, I shall require you to prove your eligibility for the position!"

"How, sir?" I asked cautiously.

"You are acquainted with Constable Dacre?"

That I was; a handsome fellow, younger even than myself, for he still had down on his face rather than hair, who spent his days doing, with apparent good spirit, all that lazy Ned had left undone.

"Young Aynsley Dacre also entered the force on my recommendation, his family, back home, being distantly related to mine. He has, by all reports, proved a competent and efficient officer of the law. Yet now I fear he may be about to do something to dishonour both his uniform and his name."

He glanced around again, as if seeking the miscreant.

"Aynsley is not here at the moment. I sent him to Constable Surtees at Peg-leg Gully, with despatches. Would I could send him there permanently—but I fear the evil would merely follow him."

I did not know what or even who this evil might be; but in the next instant he lifted one hand, his finger stabbing the air.

"Do you see that tent below, flying the golden flag?"

I did; a large round canvas erection, some thirty feet wide, supplemented at the back by several smaller tents, which clung to it as oysters cling to a rock.

"What is it? A dancehall? A shanty?"

"It calls itself a restaurant," he growled, "though I have no doubt that spirits are sold on its premises. Sometimes it seems that every tent on the diggings is dealing in unlicensed liquor! I could order Metcalf to 'stick up' the place tomorrow; but that would alert Dacre to my design. I do not doubt that he would warn the proprietress to cease her illicit custom temporarily, if Metcalf did not tell the woman himself. Sometimes it seems that I can trust neither of my constables at Cornish Flat."

"Who is this proprietress?"

"The miners call her Red Meg," he said, staring down at the tent as if it was a poisonous toadstool that he would at any moment stamp upon with his booted feet, and grind into the dirt. "A well-spoken woman, though not quite of the gentry. I cannot call her a lady, given her trade. She may seem respectable enough, but Miles, I know in my mind that she is a whited sepulchre! I would not care, for there are many of her sort on the diggings, but I am informed that she is Dacre's inamorata. Do you recall young Jarvis, from Spring Hill?"

"I do sir; did he not resign from the force and join his beloved in her shanty?"

"He did, for I reminded him of the regulation, which it is my duty to enforce, that the wife of a police officer must be of good repute. Jarvis was the son of a fishmonger; but for Dacre it would be ten times worse, for his father is a gentleman! I owe it to old Dacre, and to the rest of the family, that Aynsley should make no hasty and ill-judged connection."

"Is that so, sir, that Dacre wishes to marry this restaurant owner?"

"He denies it, but I cannot believe him," he said, still staring down at the tent. "For he will hear no ill of the woman, though I have remonstrated with him. I have no evidence, Miles, none but an instinctive certainty, a knowledge within my brain, that she would come within my jurisdiction, if all her secrets were known. Thus, when Dacre asked me to state why he should quit the witch's company, I was silent, I had no reasons to give him. There is no case, Miles—but I require of you that you should find such evidence as will make a *case* against this marriage. Need I remind you that much depends on it, for you?"

"No, sir."

"Then prove yourself a detective! Find who Red Meg really is, where she comes from, in what diggings she has plied her trade, what is rumoured of her. Prevent this misalliance, I beg you. Nay, I order you!"

EIGHT

The Chase

O time, thou hast played strange tricks with us!
and we bless the stars that made us a novelist, and
permit us now to retaliate.

—Bulwer-Lytton, *Paul Clifford*

Peel the layers off the onion. Innermost, perhaps, is the nineteenth-century novelist, Melvina Mary Yuill herself, writing the layer around her, the two policemen standing in the midst of a busy gold rush. Then there is Mel, Melvina Marie Kirksley, in the Victoria and Albert tearoom, reading of Miles and Justperson, but visualizing the scene differently, for her perceptions of the goldfields are formed by television costume dramas, rather than from experiencing the originals in all their grit and glory. And around her, Mel again, the autobiographer, describing her former self, from a few months back.

Perhaps they parallel each other, the Melvinas, just as the outermost layer of onion has the same shape, the same curve, as the innermost. Thus, after writing "I order you!" in precise copperplate script, Melvina Yuill lays down her quill pen temporarily and sits back in her chair, her mind still full of the scene she has described. Nearly one hundred and fifty years later, Mel Kirksley uncrooks her back, and puts aside the first chapter of *The Scarlet Rider*, to reach for a cup of coffee, hot no longer. At her desk Mel the memoir-writer pauses, momentarily at a loss for the words to describe her reactions to a sunny afternoon at Cornish Flat with Miles and Justperson. Then she picks up her pen and starts a fresh page.

The coffee, even when cold, was so strong that the physical sensation alone brought Mel back into the modern world. She had been little more than a pair of eyes over the past hour, one slowly ticked away by the tearoom's magisterial granddad clock. When that clock was built, she thought, was Melvina Mary alive? Might she have walked past a shopwindow, in her crinoline—here she glanced up at the print of the Victoria and Albert in 1860, to see what else women were wearing then—her crinoline, poke bonnet, and paisley shawl, and paused for a moment to admire the brand-new clock?

If so, Mel thought as she put down the cup, how do I trace her kid-leather steps? She noticed for the first time a folded paper on a little china dish, placed discreetly by the flower vase, and unfolding it, read incredulously. No wonder she had never been in the Victoria and Albert tearoom before! But it had been worthwhile, she decided, the perfect atmosphere for reading *The Scarlet Rider*. She paid, then wandered out into the street again, carrying the novel like a baby in her arms.

It was only a block or so to the library, and Mel was so eager to get there, she could have run the distance, baby and all. In the end though, mindful of her burden, she settled for a brisk walk. I'm gonna get you, Melvina Yuill, she thought. Somewhere in the library, behind that marble façade, is information, all about you, who you were, where you came from, why you wrote *The Scarlet Rider*. I'll have it all, I'll pin you down—and wipe the sneer from Spinach's face!

Yet as Mel passed beneath the sculpture of Shakespeare and his fan club, she was struck by sudden doubt. Shakespeare might be among the immortals, but very little was known about him. A second-best bed, Anne from Shottery, a coat of arms . . . not a word about what he thought of anything, let alone why he wrote thirty plays. What chance did she have, with one novel by an author of whom she knew only the name? Then Mel cheered slightly. Shakespeare might be some five hundred years away from his scholars, but Melvina Yuill was, at best, only a century's remove from her.

She gave the novel and her coat to the cloakroom attendant, and went to the walnut desk, seeking her tame librarian. To her annoyance, he was off-duty, in his place a hipster librarian in denim and black leather, though looking plainly terrified at his current customers, two genuine bikers, huge, hairy, and grizzled, not his tidy imitation of rebellion. Mel savored the scene a moment, then circumnavigated the reference center, in hopes of finding the Eton crop bent over a dictionary, or a catalog drawer. But in the end Mel was back staring at the walnut desk, with the real and fake bikers, feeling acute frustration. The Hound of Information had gone to earth.

The library's phone was in the corridor leading to the ge- nealogy section, and she made a Mel-line to it.

"Edie? It's Mel again."

They must have had a bad connection, for Edie's voice was faint and distant. It seemed she was far away mentally, as well, for she said, "Mel? Who? Oh, Melvina Marie Kirksley." There was a pause; then she added, more brightly, "Do you want to pick my brains about your namesake Yuill?"

"How *did* you know that?"

"Well, after you left, I went upstairs to get your coffee mug, puzzled why you'd suddenly mentioned your naming . . ."

Her voice trailed off. "Excuse me while I sit down," she said. Then, "Mel, are you still there?"

"Yes. You all right?"

"Just had a spot of the dizzies. Well, when I was upstairs I saw you'd filled the wastepaper basket. I'm a Kirksley, a squirrel, so I went through the paper, looking for sheets that still had white, useful space on them. At the bottom of the bin was your first transcript of the poem, with all the letters in squares."

Mel had been trying to establish whether Alice's acrostic, her spelling "Alice Una Kirksley" down the side of the left margin and up the right, would work on *The Scarlet Rider* poem.

"Well, I smoothed it out, and the name just leapt out at me. Melvina Mary Yuill. Clever lady, I thought. That's how you know the really good acrostics, Alice used to say, once you see the key, it seems so obvious. No wonder Mel came downstairs in a brown study, I thought. Well, congratulations! You've found your mysterious author!"

"I need more. Just the name won't satisfy Roxana."

"Proof," Edie said. "*Cherchez la femme.* Where was the newspaper published?"

"Tolletown."

"Go to the genealogy section and check the post-office directories for the period. They at least listed who was living in the area. If a Yuill's in Tolletown, then it's game, set, and match!"

"Thanks," Mel said, and hung up.

In the genealogy section she found a Senior Citizens' Club, where she was the odd youth out, the only person under sixty. All around, grey, or white, or mauve rinsed heads were bent over microfilm or microfiche readers. The center of the action was a carousel, gilled like a fish, each narrow plastic slit stuffed with color-coded fiche. Mel checked the guide hanging on the wall beside it, written in very large lettering, for aged eyes she supposed, and selected a fiche from the segment marked DIRECTORIES. *T* for Tolletown, she thought. Well, here goes.

There were few free machines, and Mel squeezed in between a sweet-faced elderly man with a pepper-and-salt beard, and a plump woman in shocking pink. The fiche at first skewed this way and that, as she struggled with the controls; then she slowly got the hang of it, and scanned the squares, miniaturized pages from some elderly, dog-eared, much repaired book. Tatyoon, Tintaldra, Tolletown! Under that heading was an alphabetical string of names. Mel scanned to the end, and found *Y*s: Yarrow, Fergus, miner, followed by Young, Adalbert, publican. There was nothing in between.

"She's not there!"

Mel's neighbors exchanged glances. "Heard that before, haven't we?" the bearded man said. "Some days the ancestors play hide-and-seek with us!"

"What's the name, dear?" the pink lady asked.

"Yuill. Spelt Y-U-I-L-L."

"Hmn," the man said. "Me, I'm a retired schoolteacher, and the first thing I found when I came in here was that the ancestors couldn't even spell their own names. Try Ewell, E-W-E-L-L."

Mel turned back a page in the microfiche. "There's Ewbanks, Arthur—he's another miner. He's followed by Ezekiel, Moses, ironmonger. Hey! Where are all the women?"

Mel scanned up and down the list again. Adams, Matilda, hotelier. Binton, Thecla, hospital matron. Fingle, Edith, dressmaker. O'Brennan, Margaret, laundress. Turk, Augusta, schoolteacher. Zieger, Elizabeth, fruiterer. The A–Z of Tolletown, the year *The Scarlet Rider* was published, contained only six women for the two hundred men.

"Us girls didn't have professions much, in those days," the

pink lady said. "Except being wives and mothers. And the family being the private sphere, rather than the public, there was no need to list Mrs. Ewbanks or Mrs. Ezekiel. Unless a woman was independent, had income, she was invisible in the directories."

"Melvina Yuill might have had money," Mel admitted, staring at the list again. "See, I don't know very much about her. I don't even know if she was married. I suppose she can't have had a husband, if there's no Mr. Yuill in the directory."

"Not necessarily," the man said. "You're looking at what year, 1865? That was still gold-rush time. There was a big floating population of transients, never stayed in one place long enough for their names to be written down before they were off to the next rush."

"Maybe I should try the electoral roll," Mel ventured. The woman gave a little sigh, and the pink silk of her neck scarf fluttered.

"Women didn't vote then, dear. They weren't allowed to."

Mel must have looked downcast, for the woman patted her on the wrist.

"Oh, cheer up! We're about to break for afternoon tea. Come along and we'll give you some tips."

She lumbered to her feet, the man lending a helping hand. What an odd couple! Mel thought. I wonder how they got married in the first place.

"Didn't have a clue when *I* started," the man said as they headed out of the genealogy section. "But I'd see Dot across the room, looking just as perplexed, and I knew I wasn't alone. It was when we reached for the same microfiche that the penny dropped."

"Never saw Nev before in my life," Dot said. "But we had a great-great-grandfather in common. We're distant cousins!"

Mel looked from one beaming face to the other, seeing not the faintest family resemblance.

"For all you know, dear," Dot said, "there could be cousins of yours here today, slaving over a hot fiche reader."

"We weren't the only family reunion over the microfilm," added Nev. "It's uncanny. You could almost believe the ancestors were leaning down from their clouds and saying, 'Come on, junior, it's off to the library with you!' "

"Oh, I felt it stronger than that," Dot said. "Almost like someone stood behind me, nudging me along."

Much later, Mel sat by herself in another tearoom, this time the library's, which featured formica tables, plastic chairs, and tablecloths, all tinted by the art-deco stained-glass windows. They colored the pages of *The Scarlet Rider* rose, leaf green, and sky blue.

It was a moment of calm after a word storm. The cousins had talked incessantly, all the while drinking tea and devouring huge hunks of fruitcake. The "tips" had rapidly become a dialog on their old ancestors, fascinating to them, but incomprehensible to Mel. When they had left for yet more research, Mel had thanked them politely and gladly returned to *her* fascination, Melvina Yuill.

She had started by flipping through the pages of photocopy, looking for more verse, in the hopes of another acrostic. As she did, she read a word here, a paragraph there. Halfway through, she found a mistake in the photocopying—Chapter Nine had not been copied in full, for one page had accidentally been folded under, revealing a large triangle of the following page, a window into another world, the *Tolletown Chronicle*'s personals column.

Followed the Advertiser, a Bull and Terrier Dog. The owner can have him by giving description and paying expenses. Apply A. Young, Spell-Oh!

Wonder if that's Adalbert Young the publican, she thought,

and continued reading down the line of advertisements.

If this should meet the eye of John Brown, who sailed from Liverpool on the CALLIOPE, October 1852, and was last heard of in the Tolletown vicinity, he will find his brother at Adams' Hotel.

That must have been where Matilda Adams was hotelier, Mel decided.

Arthur Ewbanks wishes to state that Mary Ewbanks, his wife, having left her home on the 6th inst., in company with another man, he will no longer be held responsible for her debts.

Wow! Mel thought. Adalbert Young, Matilda Adams, and Arthur Ewbanks had only been names in the post-office directory, but now she had learned much about them. The personals were clearly a rich vein of social history. What else might she mine from the whole of the seam in the *Tolletown Chronicle?*

This time Mel did run the distance from the library to the Victoria and Albert tearoom, and beyond, to the offices of Roxana. It was dusk, but lights still burned in the upstairs windows. She pelted up the stairs, and for lack of a free hand, for she was still clutching the photocopy baby-fashion, kicked at the door with her foot, once, twice, three times. Please don't let Spinach be the only one working late, Mel prayed, and—answer to prayers!—when the door opened she saw Nola's familiar green and red.

"Mel! I was just closin' up."

"Let me in," Mel panted, and Nola held the door wide open. She led Mel to her office, which was little more than an alcove, and Mel flopped into the nearest chair, still clutching the novel.

"Now suppose you tell your almost-stepmother what's up?"

"I've got a hunch. But to prove it I need the original of the *Tolletown Chronicle.*"

"And after you went to all that trouble to get a copy! Sorrel was spittin' for hours afterward!"

"Where is the paper? In the safe?" Mel asked feebly, and Nola laughed.

"Nah. Doesn't fit. You wait here, and I'll get it from Lady Spinach's office."

She did, and Mel spread the newspaper across Nola's desk, reading rapaciously. She devoured the advertisements, the extraordinarily verbose editorials, and the mining news, reserving particular attention for the personals.

"Hey Mel, whatcha doin'?"

Mel looked up, blinking. Somehow she had quite forgotten Nola, though she was less than two feet away.

"Chasing Melvina Yuill," she said. "You might have photocopied the novel for me, but the rest of the paper is an absolute gold mine! Did you know what our ancestors got up to? Looky here—Margaret O'Brennan the laundress announces that since she hasn't heard from her husband Michael for six years, and assumes he is dead, she intends to remarry! It's all in the classifieds!"

"Since the serial was run over twenty-nine issues, you're gunna be round awhile. I'll keep you company."

Mel read on furiously, so intent on the paper she barely noticed that Nola now sat on the floor thumbing through a heap of glossy brochures. Time passed. Nola yawned, looked at her Swatch, found other work to do. Then Mel, as she bent over her text like the miner of the newspaper heading, with his cradle full of water and river sand, spotted the faint glint of gold. A cry of "Eureka!" might have been appropriate, but all that happened was that she suddenly let out her breath like a pricked balloon. Next moment Nola was leaning over her shoulder.

"In luck?"

"Yes. Now Spinach can't accuse me of projecting myself into the text of *The Scarlet Rider*. See there."

Nola read, not moving, so that each exhaled breath goosed the skin of Mel's neck.

"It's a lost horse," Mel said. "A mare, chestnut, sixteen and a half hands tall, with a white blaze down her face. Five pounds reward. Apply Mrs. Yuil."

NINE

Dreaming of You

A fine day; sighted land at 10 o'clock P.M. It would astonish you to have seen the joy it gave us all when we first saw land; it appeared like coming out of Sodom into Paradise.

—Sarah Ann Raws, shipboard diary

"Pet! *Where* the dickykins have you been?"

Mel closed the door, shutting out the late-night cold, and shutting herself into the warm rising damp/old socks/wood pulp miasma of the flat.

"Working," she said abruptly.

"Well, I hope the prunefaces pay generous overtime, so you can soon repay the moolah you owe me."

"I'm well aware of the debt!" Mel retorted.

"Don't you be narky to May!"

"I'm sorry," Mel said. Anything to quiet Mayzee, so that she could keep her mind on the mystery of Melvina Yuill.

"So you should be, in spadefuls. It was your turn to cook tonight."

"Was it?" With the confusion of Marc's entries and exits, Mel had never really kept track of the flat's roster system. If Mayzee said it was Mel's turn, she cooked. If it was Mayzee's turn, they ate sardines, or pickles, or Spam, with crackers. It was curious, but Mel couldn't remember the last occasion May had actually cooked anything.

"Marc came home ready to eat a gee-gee, and so I opened a tin of baked beans, which we shared before he went sleepykins. There's none left."

Thanks, Mel thought sarcastically. She was hungry enough to have eaten horseflesh, had any been available. She wandered into the kitchen, and opened the fridge, a loan from Marc's parents, and thus reasonably new and in good order, though filthy, because nobody ever quite got around to cleaning it. From semi-stale bread, withered lettuce, and cheese that was, thankfully, fresh, she made a rough sandwich and returned to Mayzee in the living room.

May was bent over her book, with light from the standard lamp gilding her face, making her fluffy hair into a halo. She's like a picture, Mel thought, despite being ill. And she's my friend. I shouldn't snap at her. It occurred to Mel that she could make May a present, a show of trust, by telling her about Melvina Yuill. Mayzee read detective mysteries, along with everything else in the Paperback Exchange. Vaguely Mel wondered why she'd been so closemouthed before. Must have been terrified of Spinach, she decided. It seemed odd, but she hadn't said a word about the nature of the Roxana work to Mayzee or Marc, not that they had inquired about it. Silly me, she thought, and opened her mouth . . .

Then the next moment closed it like a nutcracker, so abruptly that her teeth clicked together. It was as if she were three again, with a mouthful of cauliflower, courtesy of Sammy's latest ladyfriend, who seemed to think the way to a man's heart was stodgy home cooking. Mel had made such a face on tasting the cauliflower that Beryl? Meryl? Laurel? had taken Mel's chin in one red-clawed hand to prevent her spitting out the food.

Sammy had burst out laughing at the sight. "Like daughter,

like dad!" he had said, and winked at Mel. Beryl had released
Mel angrily. Since Sammy was, if only temporarily, on her side,
Mel had skipped outside. While the adults argued she had bent
over Beryl's prized cactus plant and spat the white mush all over
the tall, prickly stem. Sammy had found that funny, too, even
though it had been the end of the relationship. "Good rid-
dance!" he had said to Mel. "Fish and chips, lass?"

Now her mouth was open again, but Mel had no desire to
speak. Instead she bit into the sandwich, watching Mayzee read
on, quite oblivious.

"Mel! What d'you think you're doing?"

Light cut across the darkness of the bedroom, illuminating
Marc, sleep-eyed and scowling. Mel shook her head, muzzy
from the shock of sudden waking. Somehow she was sitting bolt
upright in the bed, with her arms wrapped around her.

"What happened?" Mel said. "Why'd you wake me?"

From her dream, her beautiful complex dream, that with
every second was receding away.

"What happened? Jesus, Mel! You woke me! I've gotta get
up at five for my shift, in case you don't remember. I don't need
you shouting stuff about Leggo."

"It was Land-ho," Mel said.

"I don't give a damn what it was. Just don't do it again,
okay?" He flopped down on the bed again, and pulled the coverlet over his head. Only a wire of his bronze hair showed. Mel
reached out and stroked it, but Marc's only response was "Hurry
up and turn off the light!"

Mel reached across and did as he ordered, then snuggled
down in the bed again. Her skin was already goose-pimpled;
they always switched the flat's heating off before going to bed,
to save the power costs, and it was cold in the room. Mel hugged
herself, to warm up, noticing after a moment that unconsciously

she had returned to her waking position, as if clutching an imaginary cloak.

What had she dreamt about? First there had been Sammy, driving Mel to the railway station in his old car. That was mundane enough, for the dream world, but the train she caught was like Stephenson's rocket, a clanking monster, breathing clouds of white steam. The destination was the seaside, and if Mel missed the high tide she'd never get her university enrollment form in—though why, she couldn't guess. Dreams have no logic, not one penetrable in the waking world. Somehow Mel had found herself playing paper boats with the forms, launching them into the surf. . . .

Then there had been an abrupt discontinuity. Mel was standing on the deck of a ship, not paper, but full-sized, in mid-ocean, with a stiff breeze whipping the tops of the waves into cream. The moving, bucking deck was deserted, except for a cloaked form leaning against the rail of the ship, apparently intent on the seascape. To judge by the long coils of hair, dark with spray-damp, that escaped from the hood, it was a woman, but face, age, other details were obscured by the cloak. The figure stood so still she seemed to Mel a model, a doll, but then she suddenly gestured at the horizon, the line where blue-black sea met sky. At the same time a voice had cried:

"Land-ho!"

It had come from above, from the mast. A man's voice, Mel thought, which I apparently echoed, waking Marc.

Beside her Marc breathed, in the rhythms of deep sleep. Moving as quietly as she could, she put on her dressing gown, and felt her way out to the living room, nearly tripping over a lump that proved to be her shoulder bag, still on the floor where she had dropped it earlier that night. She unzipped it and felt inside, her hand finally emerging with her new notebook, personally issued by Nola from the Roxana stationery cupboard. In the kitchen, Mel turned on the light, set the kettle to boil, then quickly noted down what remained of the dream. She sat for a while sipping coffee, and running a mental magnifying glass over her memory of the dream.

What was the ship like? she thought. I know the carriage was horse-powered, and the train a steam-powered antique, but thanks to Marc I have no clear image of the vessel. I don't remember any sails, or smokestacks. All I have is the woman. As she wore a cloak, unless she was at a fancy-dress party—in that weather?—she would have to be traveling on a sailing ship. How like a museum of transport that dream was!

Her thoughts skittered off on a sidetrack. What a trip, she thought. Months shut up on those little ships. Dot and Nev had talked for ten minutes alone on the subject, giving what Mel would have sworn was an eyewitness account of their common ancestor's shipwreck, barely a day after he had departed the shores of old England. He had escaped with only the clothes he was wearing, and even before they had dried, it seemed, had hopped on another boat to Australia.

Records of ship passengers, Mel suddenly thought, and dived down to her shoulder bag again, almost braining herself on the table leg. The original notebook that she had filled with Edie's genealogical advice had, over the passage of days, worked itself down to the very hull of the bag. Mel repacked everything that had been above it, then riffled through the pages, recalling Edie's words:

"Oh, and another thing, Mel. Remember the white population of this country didn't originate here, they were shipped across, willy-nilly, willingly and unwillingly. And the records of the emigration societies have been microfilmed, as well as the shipping lists. If you've got a name, and an approximate date, you can go through the card index in the genealogical section of the library. They're arranged by year, in alphabetical order. That's how I found the Kirksleys came out to Australia steerage!"

Mel sat at the table, reading the notes, now and then making herself another cup of coffee. After a while she heard the purr of Marc's alarm, then his early-morning grouch-grumble sounds. He opened the bedroom door, and started for the bathroom, realizing in midstep that something was out of the ordinary. One foot in the air, his eyes bleary, hair-on-end, he gaped at Mel.

"What *are* you doing?"

"Just reading," Mel said, shoving the book back in her bag. "Now I'll go to sleep."

But in the bed, still warm from Marc, Mel found herself restless. She stretched out, willing the ceiling to lighten with the dawn and wondering how many hours would pass before the libraries and archives opened. Trying to force herself to sleep, she coiled up fetally, her head under the pillow. While in this position Mel heard the bedroom door open—Marc saying a rare good-bye—but before she could extricate herself the door had closed and he was gone.

She could have run after him, and caught him in the hallway, but instead merely settled herself in the bed, experiencing something new and surprising: relief.

It started out small, Mel's report to Sorrel, with the only other person in attendance the watchful Nola, but before she had finished, Rube and the rest of Roxana, women she had only vaguely glimpsed in passing, or in the tearoom, and even the painters, had all crowded into the office—sitting on the windowsill, crouched on the floor, even propping up the doorframe. So much for open-plan offices, Mel had thought. Her words, heard over the partitions, had attracted a monstrous regiment.

Sorrel certainly hadn't expected much, that was certain. Her greeting was in typical sardonic style:

"Ha! Melvina Marie again. Any more on Merry Christmas?"

"Merry Christmas?" Mel repeated, puzzled.

"Ms. Mary Yule, the novelist."

Mel only shrugged, too full of her day and a half's work in the library to rise to this maggoty bait.

"Actually, there is."

Sorrel raised one eyebrow slightly. At this point Nola intervened.

"Think you should lend an ear, Sor."

"Do I really have the time?" Sorrel asked rhetorically.

"Kaye would, mate, if she was here. She'd say, Come on Mel, come on Nola, stop standing in the doorway like the Mormons, sit yerselves down."

And at that she barged into the office, Mel following, placing one foot in front of the other as if wary of mines in the carpet. Mel took the chair facing Sorrel, Nola another, piled high with manuscripts, on which she perched, parrotlike in her red and green plumage.

Sorrel glared at Nola for a moment, then said, "Oh, very well! But this has to be good."

"It is," Nola said, nodding her head emphatically.

"Then I suggest young Melvina Marie tell me in her own words."

Mel opened her mouth, froze for a second under the pressure of those two intense gazes, and began: "Yuill's an unusual name. . . ."

"Oh, cripes!" Sorrel said, standing up for a moment, then flopping down in her chair again with a despairing wave of her arms. "Not your projection again!"

"Bear with her," Nola cut in quickly. " 'Cos there was a Mrs. Yuill in Tolletown."

"Is that true?"

"It's in the *Chronicle*," Mel said. "On the same page as the twenty-eighth installment of *The Scarlet Rider*."

Sorrel retrieved the folio from the top of the filing cabinet and maneuvered it onto her desk.

"Personals column," Mel said. "Three from the bottom. After the ad for the Bellman."

"I am strongly reminded," Sorrel said, as she flicked through the pages, "of *The Hunting of the Snark*. The Baker, the Bellman, and the other alliteratives, off in search of the mysterious Snark. Are you Mel, going to produce a Boojum for Roxana? Ah, here it is."

She blinked, slowly and deliberately.

"It's spelt Yuil, not Yuill."

"Misprint," Mel replied. "Or maybe because the name was right at the edge of the column, the compositor got lazy."

"Typesettin' wasn't exactly up to Roxana standards," Nola said.

Sorrel hooded her eyes. "Do go on."

"Well, next I thought I'd check the frequency of the name Yuill, just in case there were any descendants."

"Through the male line," Sorrel said.

"It turns out to be an uncommon name. There's two in the phone book, mother and son, living in the same suburb. When I rang I got a thick Scottish burr on the other end of the line. Migrants from Glasgow, arrived twenty years ago. So I went through the microfilmed phone books, and before that the post-office directories—"

Giving herself an almighty headache in the process.

"—and found no Yuills, with one *l* or two. I gave up around 1900 and started searching from the other direction. Unless Melvina Yuill was a very early settler, or a transported convict, the odds are that she arrived in Australia in the gold-rush period, like most Anglo-Irish ancestors."

The Kirksleys, for one, and Dot and Nev's progenitor, for another.

"I started with the ship's records from 1850, and looked at the *Y*s. There were lots of Youngs and Yarrows—"

Adalbert, Albert, Angus, Arthur, etc., down to Zachary.

"But the name Yuill was absent, until I got to 1853. There I found a Yuill, Jeremiah, aged twenty-five, profession engineer, sailing from London. The following year, Yuill, Mrs., aged twenty-one, also arrived, on a ship whose cargo is listed as smoked salmon and whisky. An interesting diet, if they'd got shipwrecked."

Rube, who'd brought in a fax and remained to listen, smacked her lips.

"Twenty-one in 1854," Sorrel said, frowning. "That would mean thirty-two in 1865. A good first-novel age. Not that I necessarily believe a word of your narrative, of course."

"Well, wait till I get to the end. I didn't stop with the 1850s Yuills, but checked records of emigration almost to the moment *The Scarlet Rider* was published. There are no other arrivals with that name."

"Have you got a Christian name for Mrs. Jeremiah? Surely they'd have listed it on the passenger manifesto." The speaker was a ginger-haired woman, who had been pointed out to Mel as the cover artist for the Roxana Reul books.

"No," Mel admitted. "But what I do have is another name: Atalanta."

"Atlanta? That's where Kaye was last month."

"Cloth-ears!" Sorrel said sharply. "Atalanta. A character from Greek mythology, who ran so fast no man could catch her."

Mel nodded, fully aware that though she had a trail, a strong scent of the elusive Melvina Yuill, she had many hours of research ahead before her quarry could be sighted, let alone captured for Roxana.

" 'Gems which you women wear/are as Atlanta's balls, cast in men's views,' " Sorrel said reflectively. "John Sexist Donne, twisting things around, as usual. It was Atalanta's suitor who cast gold balls ahead of her, to make her slow down."

"BOLLOCKS," Rube said cheerfully, and the roomful giggled.

"Don't interrupt. Mel hasn't finished yet." For the first time, Spinach actually smiled.

"*Atalanta* was the name of a ship," Mel said. "A barque owned by a shipping firm with a classical bent. They also owned the *Mercury*, the *Pegasus*, and the *Bucephalus*. Those ships regularly traveled between England and Australia. But the *Atalanta* came only once, in 1854. On its return voyage it foundered off Kerguelen's land, in the Indian Ocean. Everyone survived, but they had to live off what the *Argus* newspaper described—see this photocopy here—as a 'peculiarly coarse and unappetising local vegetable' before they were rescued. On the voyage out, they at least could have had whisky and salmon."

"The voyage that carried Mrs. Yuill?" Sorrel said.

"Yes. Now turn to March 21, 1865, of the *Tolletown Chronicle*, page three. Start reading in column two, beside the headline SHOCKING ROBBERY ON OPEN ROAD."

Sorrel did, her precise English tones conveying all of her listeners, crammed into this small office, over one hundred years into the past, to a goldfield at night, after a hard day's mining:

The bucket was duly passed round, with its heavy golden load, and all the drinkers felt its weight, or even stroked the nugget as one might stroke a kitten, for the gold was indeed about the size of a young cat. If some of those present in the tent that night had covetous thoughts, they did not show them, instead being loud in their congratulations of the fortunate digger. Many a man on the diggings has loudly declaimed his luck, only to be later found beaten and robbed, sometimes even thrown down a mine shaft; and the diggers have thus become wary and secretive about their findings. This miner was a young greenhorn, and lucky for him it was that Aynsley, myself and Ned Metcalf were drinking with the company in the restaurant, ready to take the gold into our safe-keeping, until the escort should arrive on the following morning. Had we not been there, violence might have been done to the poor braggart; but I doubted greatly whether it would have occurred in this particular establishment, which I could see was ruled with a distaff of iron.

"I do believe that I have never felt such excitement in my life," the lucky digger said, quaffing his drink. *"Not even on the playing fields of my old school!"*

The woman behind the bar had been impassive all the while the bucket was being passed around her tent, but now she put down the glass she had been polishing, and leant her elbows on the rough counter, both hands supporting her face.

"Not having attended, thanks to my petticoats, the academies that manufacture fine young gentlemen for the Empire, nor having had any luck seeking gold myself, I cannot understand what you mean. Yet something about you reminds me of the day I stood leaning against the rail of the good ship Atalanta, *the wind tugging at my cloak, and heard the watch cry 'Land-ho!,' for at last we were in sight of Auriferous Australia, after so many wearisome months at sea."*

Sorrel's voice ceased, and all around the office rose a buzz of excited comment. Mel slumped back in her chair, triumphant but sick at heart. After her morning's work with the shipping records, she had gone to her room in Edie's house, and speed-read through the rest of *The Scarlet Rider*, looking for corroborating evidence. Thus she had found the *Atalanta*, and also a scene that she had not read, unless, possibly, subliminally while she had been flipping through the newspaper looking at the personals. Yet it had appeared in her dream, the dream from which she had awoken crying "Land-ho!"

Mel glanced at Sorrel and Nola, who were at that moment heads together, their tension forgotten, trying to work out when, timewise, Kaye Tollet was in the States, so they could phone her with the news. No, she thought, I can't tell you about dreaming a scene from *The Scarlet Rider*—it's too bizarre.

Instead, she leaned forward and let Rube shake her hand, up and down, so roughly she half expected to be dismembered. The force shook her hair forward into her eyes, so that she saw the office through a haze of bronze-red.

Red, she thought. Red Meg. She was the character talking about the *Atalanta*. Just how much did Melvina Yuill draw that character from her own experience? What did they have in common besides the name of an emigrant ship? She let go of Rube's hand, her mind leaping off and away, in pursuit of the elusive Atalanta.

TEN

Dislocations

As Mel approached the flat, key in hand, the *thock* of something hitting the inside of the front door was clearly audible. Thus she entered warily, the door momentarily resistant as it snagged on a paperback book, spread fanwise on the floor. Mel picked it up, and spied, scattered around the room, other books, similarly disheveled. Mayzee sat in her chair, bookless, her face like an ax.

By the window Mel could see Marc, arms folded, staring out at the view of brick wall and of streetscape.

"The Ma-monster rang."

That was Mayzee's name for Marc's mother.

"She's invited *you two* to dinnerkins tonight."

"Oh," Mel said. Marc's mother had visited the flat once, to deliver the fridge, at the start of the Happy Orphans' Club. She and Mayzee had mutually loathed each other on first sight.

Marc cleared his throat, and said, without turning, "She said she hadn't seen me all this year, and didn't want to wait until the next Christmas!"

"Umn. Perhaps you could have put her off. Said you were on shift tonight, or something."

"She'd only check up on me! She has friends at the hospital."

"Cowardy-custard," Mayzee said, softly but venomously.

"Well," Mel said, playing conciliator, "look on the bright side. Free gourmet dinner."

"For a price," Marc said sourly.

"And you won't have to do it again until Christmas."

They were both silent, and Mel moved around the room, cheerfully retrieving the tossed books. Roxana had cracked a bottle of champagne, in her honor, and a meal out would finish the day nicely. Mel could cope with the Ma- and Pa-monsters; in fact they had always seemed kindly disposed toward her.

The thought of family ties made her stand up suddenly, and, books still clutched in hand, head for the communal phone. Edie had made Mel promise to ring, once the interview with Sorrel was over, so she could hear how it had all gone. But what with all the excitement and champagne, Mel had quite forgotten.

The phone in the old house rang, ten, fifteen times, and Mel was just about to put it down when Edie lifted the receiver.

"That you, Mel? Sorry I took so long to answer, but I had settled down with *The Scarlet Rider*."

Mel had left it in the spare room, sitting on top of the desk, along with the rest of the Roxana paraphernalia, in her home away from home.

"You shouldn't have," Mel said, not too seriously. Sorrel, she knew now, was a pussycat.

"It's good, isn't it! The young policeman who wrote it, he had a sharp eye for the details of life."

"Hey!" Mel said. "Didn't I tell you my whole tortuous hypothesis about Mrs. Yuill and the *Atalanta?*"

"I hadn't read the book then. Now I wonder how a woman could know so much about the traps, as they called 'em. There weren't any female police in those days."

"Point took," Mel said. "But how do you explain the acrostic?"

"Oh, that's easy. Victorian men adored writing acrostics to their sweethearts. The writer was in love with Melvina Yuill. Maybe that's why the ship is there, too."

"I don't agree with you on that. Neither do Roxana."

Something occurred to Mel. Roxana seemed to have only women employees, and their list, as far as she could tell from the catalog she had perused in a tea break, was also exclusively female. If *The Scarlet Rider* wasn't by a woman, would they publish it? And if not, who would?

"Think I'm right," Edie said.

Mel glanced up to baleful gazes from both Marc and Mayzee. Better get off the phone, she thought.

"Well, I can't argue now. Bye!"

Mel put down the phone hastily.

"What was that wee confab about?" Mayzee asked suspiciously.

"Work," Mel said.

"The prunefaces?" Marc said, in the tones of disgust Mayzee usually reserved for the word. Within Mel something frayed, and snapped off short.

"No, it happened to be my aunt."

"Seedy Edie? Or Alice in Fairyland?" Mayzee drawled.

"Isn't it curious," Mel said, "the way you dish out nasty nicknames? It's so predictable. Anything you can't control, or maybe you see as a threat, gets the old verbal sorcery."

Mel had the unusual pleasure, mixed with fear, of seeing Mayzee rendered speechless. Marc glanced from one to the other, nonplussed, but still verbal.

"Mel-baby, that's not nice. Mayzee had a bad day with the doctors."

Mel was instantly if not totally contrite. But instead of apologizing to May, she was silent, merely walking over to place the pile of books in May's lap. The yellow brow wrinkled. She's cogitating over what was said, Mel thought, and there'll be consequences, later on. But just now Mel didn't really care.

"Tell me all about it, pets!" Mayzee said.

It was after one but she was still sitting in her chair. Mel was feeling bloated from the wine and three exquisite courses, and all she wanted to do was sleep. Instead she removed her coat, then sat down with Marc on the makeshift couch made from the mattress of his childhood bed, in the usual Happy Orphan ritual.

"Well," Marc said. "The flower arrangement course has obviously reached the advanced stage. The centerpiece was red roses and beech leaves."

"She had spent rather a lot of time over it, Marc," Mel said wearily.

"Beside it, a Tollet Chardonnay. Mel sang out how appropriate it was, as she was working for a firm run by a Tollet. Ma then had rhapsodies for approximately two minutes. Cue for Pa to chip in with a list of all the wonderful Tollet vintages he had consumed over the years. That occupied the time until the first course arrived."

"Smoked salmon?" Mayzee said.

"Correct!" Marc replied. "On thin circles of rye bread."

May closed her eyes a fraction, then opened them again. "I have a simply dreadful suspicion. Are you sure, Marc, that the

St. Cyr family didn't garner their moolah just in the last generation? Because they seem so totally noove."

"Maybe they've been lying to me all these years," Marc said, delighted.

"Then how do you explain the family pictures?" Mel asked.

"Acquired from antique dealers."

"They do look very like Marc's parents."

"Faked!" Mayzee said.

Mel was finding all of this rather tiresome. "Marc, you're forgetting something. Don't you recall the first time I went to your parents' home, your mother wanted to know if I was one of the Kirksleys of Appleby? She took me into the library to see the framed map, showing the St. Cyr property, and, fifty miles away, the station my ancestral Kirksleys owned before they went broke."

"I know, I know," Marc said. "Instant eligibility in the monsters' eyes. They approve of you! I should have presented May as my girlfriend!"

"Marc-pet, if only you had! Think of what May's missed over the years, the St. Cyr pretensions at first hand. The sheer fun of sneering at it all . . ."

"You manage quite well, secondhand," Mel said dryly.

Mayzee ignored her. "Marc, carry on. May wants every vicarious detail . . ."

Mel shrugged, got up, and went to bed. Even with the door closed she could still hear Marc and Mayzee in the living room, her metallic laugh, his deeper, but glee-filled at her sallies. Sometimes they can be so childish, she thought, shrugging off her clothes. Then she wondered at this perception. Maybe I've just sat through too many postmortems on the St. Cyrs, Mel thought as she climbed into bed. Then the wine cast a blanket over her, and she slept.

"Hallo, lass," Sammy said. Mel walked toward him, following his halting steps to the old car, which was parked under a tree at the far

*side of the country crossroad. That game leg's not getting any better,
she thought. She had never asked him how it got that way, and the
aunts had different stories, Alice claiming an accident, breaking his
leg and the school's high-jump record at the same time, Edie hinting
of sudden exits via drainpipes.*

*Should interrogate him about it, she thought, now I've got the
chance, but then she forgot, for he had opened the passenger door for
her, his habit when driving with a woman, and was beckoning impatiently.*

*She got in, and he arranged a tartan rug over her knees, a star-
tling divergence from routine, until she noticed the car was now a small
open carriage, drawn by a shaggy gray pony. Sammy closed the door,
tipped his top hat, and clambered awkwardly onto the driver's box.
He smoothed down his coachman's capes, dandy as ever, then cracked
his whip. The pony started down the road.*

"Where are we going?"

"To see a friend of mine."

*"Oh, Dad, still chasing skirt, even in the afterlife? Is it crinolined?
Mini? Pannier, like in the eighteenth century? I mean, there's eras
of women to choose from."*

He chuckled.

*"No lass, it's not like that. This one's a fine lady, for sure, but she's
not my sort. You'll see."*

*They were nearing a town, and as the cart passed between the first
rows of buildings, Mel saw they were giant dollhouses, their old-
fashioned façades crudely painted, with strips of lace, the strands as
thick as ropes, at the windows. She stared around, then back at
Sammy, intending a question—but he had gone, and so had the gray
pony. The carriage was rolling itself down the toy street, as if pushed
by some long-dead child. It stopped outside a wooden building, labeled
lopsidedly* COURTHOUSE. *The door of the carriage opened.*

*"Here?" Mel said, but nobody answered. She pushed aside the rug
and stepped out. The windows of the courthouse were tinted cellophane,
and she put her nose close to them, trying to see inside. Within were*

a collection of wooden dolls, toy policemen, witnesses, lawyers, even a judge in a cotton wool wig. They moved staccato-fashion, spoke in high-pitched voices, something between a mouse-squeak and the grate of knives on china.

"The accused will now stand!"

A figure seated in the center of the courtroom obeyed, but with fluid, human movements, not the jerkiness of the dolls. From the silhouette, of bonnet, full-skirted dress, and shawl, Mel could see it was a woman. She stood still as the judge squeaked at her.

"We find you guilty."

"Guilty! Guilty!" cried the other dolls, and the figure bowed her head, swaying on her feet as if about to fall.

Then there was light, and Marc's face, so close that Mel could see creases from the bed linen pressed into one cheek. He was grimacing.

"Bitch! You did it again! Sitting up and yelling 'Guilty!' as if you were in some courtroom drama."

"I was," Mel said, her head still full of the dream.

"I can't be woken up all the time in the middle of the night! Not with my hospital shifts."

"Try earplugs," Mel said.

"I'll try a gag on you first! Mel, this can't go on. Next thing you'll be sleepwalking. Go and see a doctor, first thing tomorrow."

"I can't, not with my job." The Melvina-chase was in full cry, and Mel didn't want to spend any time away from it. "Hey, why don't you diagnose me, and save me a trip to the GP? Doctor St. Cyr, aren't you?"

Mel had meant that to be funny and mollifying, but had miscalculated badly. Marc frowned.

"Get out!" he said. "Doss down in the living room and let me sleep in peace!"

Shocked and offended, Mel got up and stalked out, longing to slam the door, but knowing this would rouse Mayzee, buzzing with questions like a cloud of bees. In the dark living room she started to shiver, for it was icy cold, and Mel was barefoot, clad only in a threadbare nightshirt. She switched on the light, and saw, discarded on the couch, her duffel coat. Thankfully she snuggled into it.

Mel's shoulder bag with the notebook and her pens was in the bedroom, but she found a flyleaf from one of the tossed paperbacks on the floor. In the kitchen drawer was more luck—a stub of pencil. Using these poor materials she transcribed the dream from memory to paper, afterward folding the flyleaf to stamp size and putting it in her pocket. Shivering again, she turned off the light and lay down on the couch. It was narrow and too short for an adult but she drew her legs up and under the wool of the coat, and, amazingly, slept.

"Pet! Wakey wakey!"

Mel rolled over on the couch and tumbled onto the floor. There were only a few inches to fall, but still the impact woke her with a thump. She gazed upward, from a pair of velvet slippers, their purple nap and bead trim almost all worn off, to a torn satin dressing gown, once bright red, and above that, to Mayzee's sallow face and tousled shock of hair. How she has faded, diminished even, Mel thought, before focusing on what May was saying.

"May wants to know why you've gone sleepykins out here."

Behind May, she saw their wall clock. Eight A.M. Marc hadn't even woken Mel up when he left for the hospital, so that she could climb back into a warm bed. Bastard, Mel thought, then suddenly registered that Mayzee had hunkered down, and was shaking her by the shoulders.

"Pet! Pet! Answer when you're spoken to."

"No," Mel said, wrestling herself free, with such force that May fell spread-eagled across the carpet. "If you're so clever, work it out for yourself."

May stared, openmouthed, as Mel made good her escape. She shut the bedroom door, again resisting the temptation for a good, hard slam, then leaned against it, eyeing the small, squalid room. How like a prison it was.

Prison. Mel put her hand into her coat pocket and fingered the square of paper. The woman in her dream had been found guilty and was being sent to jail. Just as Red Meg, as Inspector Justperson had suspected, had a guilty secret in her past, one that had put her on the wrong side of the law, and ultimately of her lover, young Aynsley Dacre.

Red Meg. The woman in the bonnet and shawl. Melvina Mary. Were they one and the same?

ELEVEN

The Police Archives

*. ... a parcel of big ugly fat-necked wombat headed
big bellied magpie legged narrow hipped splay-.
footed sons of Irish Bailiffs or English landlords
which is better known as officers of Justice or Victorian police.*

—Ned Kelly, *The Jerilderie Letter*

On the other side of the door it was dead quiet
for several minutes, before Mayzee got up off the
floor with a groan and slip-slopped toward Mel. Only
plywood plus air separated them, and Mel folded her arms, still
combative. As if May could sense that, she hesitated. Then Mel
heard her move away, toward her own room, a cave of old
clothes, books, and medicine bottles, with barely room for the
bed. When that door closed, Mel dressed silently, seized her
bag, and was out of the flat without further confrontation.

It was back to Appleby again, not the ancestral station Mel
had never visited, but its suburban namesake. This morning the
terrace looked gloomy under the cape of the early-morning mist,
which also lopped off the tops of the tall city skyscrapers. Mel
knocked once, twice, but there was no answer, so she fished out
the key on its length of string. Inside, the house smelled of metal

polish and old newspapers. There was a note lying on the hall carpet, which read, "Mel, if you turn up I'm spending the day with Alice."

In Fairyland, Mel mentally added. She went into the kitchen, to find that the chandelier was no longer spread across the table, and made a cup of coffee, which she took upstairs to the study and *The Scarlet Rider*. The novel wasn't on the desktop where she'd left it! Alarmed, she quickly searched the top floor, first Alice's old room, with its massive mahogany furniture, inherited from Gran Kirksley: a four-poster bed; chest; a dressing table, its myriad drawers weighted down with heavy brass handles; and a wardrobe, whose twin long mirrors reflected a disheveled Mel. She tidied herself before the liver-spotted glass, wondering as she did so how many Kirksley ancestors had echoed her gestures in front of this mirror image.

Next door was the best room—the largest and sunniest in the house—where Sammy had slept during his infrequent visits. Now it was filled with Edie's presence, crammed with mementos everywhere the eye could see, mostly of her nursing overseas, from New Guinea masks to woven hangings to zoos of small animals, carved weirdly in wood. A true Kirksley squirrel, Mel thought. On the window seat, among a nest of ikat cushions, was the folder containing *The Scarlet Rider*. She reclaimed the text and took it back to *her* place in Appleby, the study.

What to do now? Pages and pages of densely printed Victorian text stared at her accusingly, daring her to dive deep into them and emerge with pearls of Melvina information. Instead, Mel looked out the window, at the bare branches of fruit trees stabbing the low gray sky, watched a cock sparrow first douse himself in the guttering of the old shed, have a good shake, then flutter away. She put her head down again, but, like the sparrow, found herself dipping in and out of the text, reading a paragraph here, a sentence there. It all seemed opaque, generalized; there was nothing she could seize upon for possible autobiographical import.

Maybe there's no more pearls to find, Mel thought. Maybe underneath all these words is rusty guttering, not seabed and oyster shell. The notion made her almost as glum as the day outside. Let's be methodical about this, she thought. Are there any more ships' names in the text, like the pearl *Atalanta?*

Mel speed-read through the novel, pen and paper at hand. After a few pages she began noting names, not of ships, but of people. Red Meg. Firefly the Bushranger. Colorado Jim, Hatter Mike, gold miners. Biddy the Irish washerwoman. Arabella, Miles the narrator's sweetheart, whom Sorrel had accurately characterized as saccharine, although practically all the males in the novel apparently considered her the apex of womanhood. Emma, a disconcerting goldfields urchin. Ned Metcalf, the lazy policeman. Inspector James Renfrew Justperson, the martinet. Constable Aynsley Dacre, Red Meg's lover.

Mel looked at her list of names, and slowly sorted them into categories. Goldfields types got nicknames, she noted: Colorado Jim, Scarface Tom. That was based on fact—people tended not to use their real names on the rough-and-tumble rushes. The women had little more than Christian names: Biddy, little Emma, Arabella. Miles also had only a Christian name, but being the narrator made him anomalous, she supposed. Mel put him to one side, mentally, and considered his fellow policemen. Then it struck her. Ned, Justperson, Aynsley, and the other mounted police were the only characters introduced with proper names, in full. . . .

Mel looked at her list again, then raced down the stairs like an avalanche. In the front hall she bent over the phone on its little marquetry table, and pulled out from underneath it the

White Pages directories. They landed fatly, heavily on the floor, bringing with them another book, bound in brown leather, which fell open beside her feet. Mel picked it up, glanced at the contents, then replaced it underneath the phone. An old ledger, containing an inventory of the contents of the "library" in Edie's precise hand, had no interest for her just then. What she was after was the police.

"Umn, hallo. No, I'm not reporting anything, I just wanted to know if you had an archive."

Mel was put on hold and forced to listen to what sounded like the theme from a TV detective show. Finally, a deep voice answered:

"Police Archives here."

Mel introduced herself, and her business, then almost immediately got the giggles, for he told her he was Constable Mick Hatter. How like Mike the Hatter, she thought, then acutely recalled the description of that miner from *The Scarlet Rider: a diminutive fellow, humpbacked and splay-footed, blessed in addition with such a wide mouth that he overwhelmingly gave the impression of a human toad.*

"Did I say something funny?" inquired this toad's near-namesake, his initial friendliness gone.

"No," she said hastily. "Just dust in my throat, from the victorian novel I'm researching."

Oh shit, here she was not thirty seconds into the conversation and already lying to a policeman. "It's got traps in it," she added.

From bad to worse. Mel knew that term wasn't at all complimentary.

"You mean, nineteenth-century colonial police?" he replied, his tone admirably calm despite the maniac on the other end of the line.

"Er, yes."

"Any illustrations of them? We collect photos of the *traps*."

"Unfortunately, no."

He gave a sigh.

"But can you tell me if you have a complete list of the colonial police on goldfields duty?"

Now it sounded as if he was choking. "Listen, have you any idea just how many men were employed in the force at the time? We had constables in every little rush and townlet."

Mel knew that, from the novel.

"And as for the sort of list you're after, by year, in alphabetical order . . . it doesn't exist. If you gave me a locality, maybe."

"I can't. The novel's set on an imaginary digging."

"Then no can help."

"Wait," Mel said, suddenly desperate. "There's some police named in the text. I don't know if they're fictional or not. Can I read them out to you? Please, don't hang up."

"Oh, all right!"

"Ned, I mean, Edward Metcalf."

"Doesn't ring a bell."

"Aynsley Dacre. Thomas Surtees. William Blanc."

"Ditto, ditto, ditto."

"James Renfrew Justperson."

"What?"

"James Renfrew Justperson."

Was Mel hearing things, or had his voice changed, from tones of weary boredom to acute interest?

"And who was this James Renfrew Justperson?"

"Police inspector and stickler for the rulebook. He turns up unexpectedly at the rush camps and dishes out fines if anything's less than shipshape."

"Then," he said, "I think you'd better come in here and look at the file on James Renkin Jesperson, goldfields inspector and the terror of his subordinates."

* * *

Mick proved to look nothing like a toad, not like his namesake Mike the Hatter, being a big man, with a beefy, cheerful, clean-shaven face offset by wary, hooded eyes. He met her in the front lobby of the gleaming, high-security edifice that housed these modern-day traps, and escorted her through an obstacle course of passages punctuated by doors, most of which Mick had to unlock. They finally dodged through a narrow courtyard filled with official-looking cars, before coming to the archive, a little brick building the color of a ginger cat, sealed with a heavy steel door, which Mick unlocked with the last of his keys. Inside was compacter shelving, heavy and gray, with the only free space Mick's office, which was furnished with little beyond a varnished, much-scratched pine desk and a glass case containing a dummy in full police uniform.

Mel inspected the dummy, a 1950s model with a chipped plaster face apparently modeled on Dick Tracy. Yet it was dressed incongruously like a cavalry officer: high shiny boots, skintight leggings, a blue jacket slashed across by a broad diagonal belt, and atop its head a glazed leather cap like a tin pot, held in place by a strap underneath the chin.

"Standard mounted-police uniform," Mick said, seating himself heavily at the desk.

"From what date?"

"Middle of last century."

"Then that's what Aynsley, and Ned, and Justperson wore. It's dashing . . . except for the silly cap."

Words Mel had dismissed as extraneous detail from *The Scarlet Rider* came suddenly to mind.

"Wasn't the cap usually covered?"

Mick eyed her. "They wore white cloth covers over the leather. I haven't got a surviving example, but it's illustrated clearly."

He got up and began moving the shelves on their rails, Mel watching in mild alarm lest he be crushed in the course of duty. Finally he returned unscathed, carrying an engraving sheathed in clear plastic.

"See here."

Mel held it, noticing first the two magnificent gleaming horses, their long manes and tails rippling in the wind. Their riders were similarly hirsute, with muttonchop whiskers and mustaches.

"I can't see any cover," Mel said.

"Not the sergeant, the constable at the back, on the black horse."

Mel looked again, and saw the tin pot covered with white, almost like a pith helmet.

"So that's a cap-cover. They were pests to wash, and the trick was to put them on wet, then leave them to dry. If you starched them beforehand, as Biddy the Irish washerwoman does in the novel, then they wouldn't fit at all."

"Then," Mick said, "your writer knew about the colonial police firsthand. I thought as much, when you mentioned Inspector Jesperson."

"Famous, was he?"

He paused. "No."

"But you knew his name, straight off, even though it was slightly disguised."

Mick reached out his hand for the engraving before answering.

"Let's say he's unusual. See, the senior officers of the colonial force, they were on the take. Jesperson wasn't. He didn't get a kick out of diddling the system, or from creature comforts, full stop. His thrill was making other peoples' lives a misery."

"Including a policeman's wife called Melvina Mary Yuill?"

"Run that past me again."

"Well, her novel was published anonymously in 1865 and it doesn't give Justperson/Jesperson the nicest press. . . . Maybe he fined her husband or something."

"That can be checked," Mick said. "Anyone fined by Jesperson got it entered into their permanent record sheet. I'll just have to look for a Yuill—can you spell it, please, on this pad—under his jurisdiction. But Jesperson was at several gold-mining areas, so this could take time."

"Can I help?"

He looked around the cramped space helplessly. "No. This is a one-man job. You just go home. I'll call you. Write your address down. And while you're at it, those other police names you mentioned."

Mel hesitated. If she wrote down the flat's phone number, what would Mayzee think if she answered the phone and found gruff Mick on the other end of the line? Already she could hear the barrage of questions—ones she didn't particularly feel like answering. So she wrote down Edie's number and the Appleby address instead. Mel would just wait by the phone, in her aunt's house, until Mick had finished his fossicking.

Mick's call came late that afternoon, as Mel stood in Edie's kitchen, watching the kettle for her umpteenth cup of coffee take its own sweet time to boil. At the sound of the phone Mel ran to answer it eagerly.

"Mick! Any news?"

"Some." He sounded weary, and Mel thought of those interminable filing cabinets, filled with records. "Bad stuff first. There's no policeman called Yuill. I went right through the records."

"Oh." From where she was sitting she could hear the bubbling of the unwatched pot, and see clouds of steam drift out of the kitchen and into the hallway.

"But the good stuff is that I found most of your other fellas. First was Edward Metcalf. In 1857 Jesperson fined him five shillings for losing part of his accoutrements."

"Could that refer to a lost button?"

"Yep, that'd be worth five bob, in Jesperson's book. He was upcountry then, in charge of an area that was basically empty scrub, and incredibly rich rushes. Best of the lot they called Aurealis. It's a blank spot on the map now, nothing but pasture. But in the 1850s, you could dig it like a potato patch and turn up nuggets big as spuds."

"It was nuggety," Mel said, "the goldfield in the novel."

"Metcalf was constable in charge at Aurealis. He only lasted a year—died in 1858 from drinking Blow His Skull Off. That was a tipple made of spirits of wine, turkey opium, rum, *cocculus indicus*—a dried berry which was normally used for stunning fish—and cayenne pepper."

"Lethal," Mel said, wondering at the inventiveness—or desperation—behind such a cocktail.

"Surtees and Blanc were in the force longer, till the mid-sixties. Didn't do anything exciting. From 1857 to 1858 they were stationed at Crimea, which was a rush about half a day's ride from Aurealis."

"In the novel it's Peg-leg Gully," Mel said absently. Her mind had divided into two parts—one half wondering how soon the kettle would boil dry and the other greedily considering the implications of the nexus at Aurealis. As if from a great distance she heard herself thanking Mick, and ending the conversation. Then she raced to the kettle. It was almost invisible behind the clouds of steam in the kitchen, but when she lifted it from the heat, she suddenly realized that Mick hadn't mentioned Aynsley Dacre. Did that mean Aynsley wasn't at Aurealis?

Mel ran back to the phone, but Mick had left for the day.

Maybe I've misread something, she thought. Better check the novel again. She headed upstairs, thinking vaguely, guiltily that she should really ring Mayzee and apologize for this morning's fracas. But the lure of Melvina Mary Yuill was stronger.

TWELVE

A Woman of Mystery

It was late afternoon before Inspector Justperson at last completed his business; and Ned and I farewelled him, standing stiffly to attention as the straight-backed figure negotiated his horse and buggy down the twists and turns of what passed for a main thoroughfare at Cornish Flat, finally disappearing from sight behind the tents. No doubt Ned was busy with his own thoughts, of relief at having survived another lightning inspection, which had left him five shillings short. I know that in my mind the image of the elusive detective's card, and what I could do to earn it, burned like a brass buckle in the bright Austral sun.

My arm grew sore, and my eyes twisted in their sockets, trying to stare at Ned; but still he stood like a soldier on parade. Were we to stay in this position until the miners came back from their labours and had a good laugh at us constables seemingly cast in wax?

"For heaven's sake, Ned!" I said through clenched teeth. "The Inspector's gone."

"Are you certain he's not turned his horse around and to take a second look at us?"

"Of course I'm sure, man! There's not room to swing a cat in that road, let alone turn horse and buggy!"

"Hooray!"

Statue Ned let out a whoop, and bending down, performed half a dozen somersaults up and down the knoll. I could not help laughing at his capers, although when I turned briefly away from Ned, to wipe a tear of mirth from my eye, I suddenly became aware that the road up from Cornish Flat, along which Justperson must pass, afforded an excellent view of the police camp. What the Inspector might think of his constable playing the acrobat did not bear contemplation; but, before I could warn Ned, he ceased his antics, and cocking his head at the hill, with the road winding up it like a length of sash ribbon, began brushing the fragments of grass and white dust from his jacket.

"Busy yourself, Miles," he said, "for that was an eyeglass I spied in our Inspector's saddlebag, and I have no doubt he will use the nearest vantage point to spy on us."

My gaze followed his, and I saw, not Justperson, but a tall and noble horse, just coming over the crest of the hill. Even at this distance I could judge the fine gait, the proud toss of the head that denotes a horse of spirit, one that I would not have trusted a woman to manage; but this rider was female. I could distinguish little of her beyond the long dark skirts of her riding dress, and the broad sunbonnet upon her head, but she seemed very much at home in the saddle.

I turned to Ned.

"Oh, a glorious sight," I said. "What I would not give for a race through the Australian bush, on that fine bit of horseflesh."

"The mare is called Vino," he said. "And many have desired

just that, even offered gold nuggets for the privilege; but she is not for sale."

Horse and rider had joined the road now, and I could clearly perceive the form of a small kanga-roo, swinging limply from the saddle-bow; and the pistol at the woman's waist.

"Ah, bless her," Ned intoned. "Just when I'd sworn I'd never eat another slice of that everlasting mutton! It's a treat in store, Miles, when kanga-roo tail soup is on the menu at The Golden Banner."

"The Golden Banner!" Half involuntarily I turned, to gaze down the hill at the tent which Justperson had pointed out to me as a vixen's lair.

"Tell me, Ned, who is that Amazon?"

"They call her Red Meg," he said, then suddenly laughed. "Oh Miles, look!"

"Ill met by sunlight, fair Titania," I thought, for coming into view up the hill was the horse and buggy. I do not know if the woman saw it, or not; but she suddenly spurred her horse, so that the mare flew like the wind towards Justperson.

"The devil!" Ned said. "He'll have her on a charge of furious riding, for sure."

Closer and closer drew the two horses, but just as it seemed that collision was imminent, the woman drew her mount up short, so that it reared in the centre of the road, blocking Justperson's path. For a moment the two faced each other, and we could distinguish the reins go slack in Justperson's hand, as he sat, still stiff-backed, but his mouth open in surprise; then Vino dropped to all fours again, and gracefully pirouetted round the buggy and down the hill.

"Well done," Ned said, clapping his hands. "Faith, it's small wonder Meg's the toast of Cornish Flat!"

"Indeed!" said I. Since coming to Australia I had observed how the daughters of squatters, indeed the women of any country household that could afford to keep horses, would, upon the slightest excuse, drop their needlework and saddle their mounts, backing them as well as any man in the district, and gallop head-long through the bush. Some of these fair maids acted as stock-riders on their fathers' stations, and could "give" the stockwhip with a vigour that, despite my policeman's uniform, quite sent a chill into my heart, on the occasions I encountered such a nymph in charge of a mob of cattle on the open road. In an older country, such behaviour would not have been countenanced in girls of their position, but despite its unwomanliness, I could not help admiring it. Then, as now, for though I thought the woman rash, to provoke Justperson in that manner, there was something in the spirit of horse and rider that made me mentally doff my cap to them.

Above us, Justperson furiously lashed his buggy up the hill; while the rider continued downward, crossing the log bridge over the creek with a sound like thunder, before she was lost to sight behind the clustering tents.

"Well!" Ned said. "It was worth the loss of my five shillings, to witness that little scene."

Here I bethought herself of the detective's card, and putting aside the image of that horsemanship, with regret, for whatever station in life a man may occupy, or however much a scoundrel he may be, I perceive some spark of worth in him if he handles a horse well, I determined to query Ned about Red Meg. How-ever, at this juncture, we were halloed from farther down the hill, by none other than the Irish colleen who had given me di-rections earlier. She clutched her baby on one hip, holding in her free hand a stout length of rope attached to a sturdy spiked collar such as a mastiff would wear, but which draggled on the ground, completely bereft of its canine occupant.

So we listened to the sad tale of Biddy's Towzer, and solemnly promised to search for the missing dog, until the washerwoman ceased her plaints and departed, leaving us con-stables to our own pursuits. Thus it was that we were lying on the grass of the police camp knoll, idly smoking, when I at last took the opportunity to raise the subject of Red Meg with Ned.

"I don't know her full name," Ned said, nonchalantly, "but that's common on the goldfields. You might have a sawbones and a barrister sharing the same tent, but to each other, and the world at large, they would be but 'Bill' and 'Tom.' "

It was the answer I expected, but one that I still had to ask. The melting pot of the goldfields is such that fine young gentlemen, with shaved faces and perfumed hair, soon disappear into the general mass of beards, wide-awake hats and Crimean shirts, living the rough life of a miner. All, despite their station in life, look much the same; and despite what the physiognomists would have us all believe, I myself could only tell the gentleman when he spoke.

"Does this Meg have a husband? I wonder how he feels at her riding about the countryside in that manner."

"She? Never! There's a woman as masterful and independent as any man, ay, and proud, too! I tell you, Miles, she could have had a hundred husbands over, men are so hungry for female company on these rushes, and not just common miners, but men of position back in England. There's something that draws you to her, in spite of her unwomanly ways. Look at her closely, and you'll see what I mean."

"I think not; from what you say she is about as far from my ideal of womanhood as she can well be. Me spooney on an Elinor Rumming, a tavern-keeper? Never!"

Ned laughed. "I could bet your next month's pay that you'll eat your words, with a nice humble pie crust, but I hate an easy wager. Once was enough, with young Aynsley. Sure he scoffed just like you, my fine young buck, but one visit to The Golden Banner, and he came back swearing that he had seen the finest woman as ever set foot on this earth."

Ned added, half to himself, "Who would have thought a

young face, with down on it instead of hair, would win favour where so many have earned uncivil words? She must have a softness in her heart for the boys!"

"What was that, Ned?"

"Nothing but what you'll witness later on, when Aynsley gets back from Peg-leg. But there she is! Hush now!"

While we had been talking, the goldfield had come alive, with the diggers downing tools for the day, heading for their tents, or the restaurants, or the creek, to wash themselves and change out of their rough mining attire in preparation for the evening's rowdiness. Amidst this movement, when even the flags, on their sapling poles, frisked in the wind, one more figure should not have caught our attention; but nonetheless our eyes were drawn to a woman emerging from The Golden Banner. She stood, gazing confidently towards the red, setting sun.

"What is she doing?" I said to Ned.

"Setting the time. Nearly every man on the rush takes his lead from Meg's shooting-iron. Watch."

Half of the round crimson had dipped beyond the hills; and as the other half disappeared, Meg raised her hand, which held a small revolver, into the air. Crack! it went, crack crack! the latter shots echoed by hundreds of firearms that had but waited for the woman's signal.

For those of my readers who have not been on the goldfields, I must explain that it was the custom for diggers to discharge their firearms at nightfall, for the dual purpose of satisfying themselves that the guns were in proper order, and to warn those miscreants amongst them that short shrift would be dealt to night prowlers after lawfully gotten gold. The gun discharged, the woman walked back to her tent, stately as a queen, and disappeared into its white canvas.

I turned to Ned, intending to question him again, but he was staring hillwards again, at another rider on the road, on whom even at this distance I could distinguish the blue of a police jacket, as he urged his tired mount into a trot down the slope to Cornish Flat.

"Hooray! It's Aynsley!" Ned said; and not too long afterwards we were joined by a dark handsome chap, tall, with a thin aquiline nose, eyes blue as a summer sky, and a fine head of curling black hair. Though he swayed on his police horse, with his face pale and weary, and his boots covered in dust, still he, at the sight of us, or perhaps at the sight of the tent with the golden banner, so close by, broke into one of the widest smiles I had ever seen.

"Ned! Oh, but it's good to be back at Cornish Flat!"

Ned introduced us, and as I reached upwards, to shake the thin white hand that only seconds before had been gloved and gripping the rein, I reflected that were I of the weaker sex, my heart would probably be susceptible to the charms of this young man. I could well imagine some daintily modest belle blushing at the sight of Aynsley Dacre; indeed I could think of one young lady (of my admittedly limited acquaintance) whom I would hesitate to introduce to him, lest I create for myself a rival. Yet could this youth have won the heart of that tall, stately figure below, so capable with a horse and a firing piece? It seemed impossible.

We saw to Aynsley, and his horse; and afterwards we three constables sat outside the police camp, hearing the news from Tom Surtees and his junior constable, Bill Blanc, at Peg-leg Gully, and watching the dusk settle over the goldfield. A pretty sight it was, seeing the tents transformed into a succession of giant lamps, as the light inside shone brightly through the cloth, casting the shadows of miners drinking or dancing or fighting on the canvas as on the sheet of a magic lantern. I could barely glimpse Aynsley beside me, except as a dark silhouette, yet I saw his gaze turned towards one particular "lanthorn."

"Shall we go to Meg's?" he said. Ned readily consented; with the proviso that we change from our uniforms first, for we stood the chance of having them taken off our backs permanently, should some fizzgig (that is, informer) report the sight of the blue and silver in a common shanty to Inspector Justperson. That done, we walked boldly down the knoll to The Golden Banner.

In the course of my duties, and otherwise, I had visited several "digger's haunts" on the goldfields, and The Golden Banner struck me as no different to any other, except in a higher degree of cleanliness. It was large, some thirty feet wide and long, with in its centre a long rough-hewn table, around which lolled the convivial drinkers. Soft blue wreaths of tobacco smoke made misty the light from the oil lamps, and rolled lazily upwards to the gables of the tent. At the back was the bar counter, a log erection, covered with zinc, with behind it a middle-aged couple, whom I later learnt shared Meg's tent and business, as a form of help and protection. Then a flap leading to the private quarters of The Golden Banner was pushed open, and the owner made her entry.

Red Meg was twenty-five at most, tall, with a slender, yet fully developed figure, outlined in a dress of simple black material. I looked, and looked again, but there was not a ring on her hand, nor even a brooch at her throat. This plainness of dress surprised me in its refined taste; for persons in this line of goldfields business were fond of extravagant show, loading themselves with ribbons, laces and nugget jewellery, easily acquired from the admiring diggers.

She moved amongst the bottles with more grace than a lady in her drawing room. In even the pouring of a glass there was a natural grace and suppleness that indicated she was far superior to her surroundings. What catastrophe has brought her to this pass? I wondered, staring at the handsome line of neck and head, which was crowned with a mass of splendid curling hair. Then, as we neared, she turned her gaze upon us. Such fine eyes!

I was glad indeed I had not wagered any money with Ned on this meeting.

"Well, if it isn't the traps of Cornish Flat!" she said. "Good evening, Constables Metcalf and Dacre!" As she spoke, she favoured Ned with a cool, ironic smile; whereas with Aynsley her reception had more of the demeanour of an elder sister. It did not fool me in the least, given Justperson's report, yet as she regarded me curiously I must confess I felt the blood mount into my face.

"Meg, this handsome young buck is a fellow trap, my mate Miles," Ned said. "And now, give us a whet, like a lady!"

She clearly knew what Ned's whet was, and after pouring him the shot of strong liquor the miners termed, all too accurately, a nobbler, pushed a bottle of claret towards me and Aynsley, placing two tumblers and a bowl of lump sugar beside it.

"Help yourself," she said softly. "I always give boys soft drinks. It's better for them."

Being described as a "boy" confused me mightily, so much so that I nearly dropped my purse as I drew it out to pay for what even I could see was good claret; but Aynsley, who had not taken his eyes from Red Meg once since she had entered the tent, waved it aside.

"I would never sell unlicensed liquor to a policeman," she said. "Such would be against the law, and foolhardy, for well he might use it in evidence against me. Nay, Ned, though we be friends, a woman such as I can never be too careful. Consider this hospitality my gift, as always."

I would have blushed again, like a schoolgirl, but just at that moment there was a commotion outside the tent: shouts, the din of metal beating against metal, even a pistol shot.

"By gar!" Ned said. "Soon as we turn our backs, Firefly the Bushranger gets up to his tricks again! Quick, Aynsley, run to the camp for our horses!"

Men sat rigid round the tent, uncertain whether to fight or

flee, but the figure that came bursting into the tent was only a digger, drunk with joy, holding a bucket in his hands. He shook it, and we heard the metallic noise again.

"Cornish Flat comes up trumps again!" he cried, and lowering the bucket to our gaze, revealed inside a huge nugget.

THIRTEEN

Bones and Red Ink

*I say this to you, you are empty shells. I am the
land. You will be doomed to the end of time by the
blood of my people.*

—Sam Watson, *Warana Festival Speech*

Mel looked up from fictional night into real
night, the blackness of Edie's garden outside the
study window. Before her was not the muted, eerie
geometry of tents lit from within by candles and oil lamps, but
modern house and streetlights—dazzle against dark. She put
down her pen and flexed her hand under the desk lamp, watching the shapes it cast on the pages of her notebook, a magic
lantern game.

Mel had been making a rough summary of the novel, in the
hope it might reveal something significant. Now she picked up
her pen again, and wrote:

"It's at this point that Meg mentions the *Atalanta*. While
she's talking, Miles, taking advantage of everyone in The
Golden Banner being preoccupied with the nugget, sneaks out
and finds his way into the tent where Meg sleeps. Under her bed
he discovers a box, containing personal possessions, among

them a sketchbook. Within it are several drawings of what he calls 'a distinctive and recognisable terrain,' signed by the initials 'M.L.D.' He hides the sketches under his coat and returns to the main tent, very pleased with this clue for Justperson."

Mel put down the pen again, and rubbed her eyes. There's no reason to drag in the *Atalanta*, she thought. It doesn't advance the plot, and Miles doesn't react as if it's a vital clue. But it isn't for him, though it is for *me*. It's almost as if the mystery operates on two levels, one in which Miles unravels the tangled web of Red Meg, the other in which I seek Melvina Yuill. But why would anybody write such a multilayered narrative, especially back in 1865, when the tools to decode the *Atalanta* reference, the shipping lists, weren't readily accessible? And why use the names of real police?

Mel drooped her head down on her hands, the lamp shining through her hair like sun on a closed eyelid. For a moment her mind was a blessed blank; then she was thinking hard, working at the problem again. There's so much unexplained! The novel doesn't really say what Red Meg looked like, nor why she got her nickname. Was she like me? She was tall, thin, and had curly hair, but of what color? Why was her mare called Vino? Did both horse and rider have red hair, as their names imply? Mrs. Yuill owned a chestnut mare in Tolletown, 1865. . . .

Mel wanted to stay at Appleby all night, just to think in peace, but below she could hear Edie's key in the lock, and knew she should go home and face Mayzee.

"It's a peace offering," Mel said, crouching in front of the swivel chair. For the first time since Mel had entered, Mayzee looked up from her book, taking hold of the plastic carrier bag.

"About bloody time. What is it?"

"Guess."

May looked inside. "Ah. Plonk."

Mel had tried for a Tolletown wine, but the local pub had only a limited selection.

"Open it!"

Mel obliged, fetching corkscrew and glasses. She sipped at her wineglass, then took one mouthful, then another, desperate for the sugar fix, for what with one thing and another, she had skipped breakfast and also lunch that day.

May had delved into the bag again. "Ooh, there's more in here! Butcher's paper . . . that means steak?"

It was May's favorite food, one they very seldom ate, owing to the expense. Mel held her breath, willing May not to realize that these purchases must have been made with the loan, but her friend thawed completely. "OK, petal, the offering's accepted. But never, *ever*, take out your love-tiffs on May again. D'you hear?"

"I hear." Mel bent forward and kissed the sallow cheek. "I'll cook the way you like it. Rare, you vampire . . ."

"De-lish!" May closed her eyes in fake ecstasy, squeezing the parcel, then opened them again, wide. "Oh, it's hard! With big knobbly bones!"

Then and there May unpacked the butcher's parcel, to reveal a lapful of large square tapering bones.

"Mel, I *don't* like osso buco!"

"It's kangaroo tail," Mel said. "And I haven't the slightest idea how to cook it, even if I wanted to."

The expression of affronted disappointment on May's face had Mel very nearly laughing, it was bubbling under in her throat.

"Oh, how gross!"

The hilarity, as impossible to suppress as a boiling pot, burst out, and Mel doubled up, spluttering and giggling.

"Pet! Are you playing a meanie trick on May?"

It was Mayzee at her most fearsome, but all Mel could do was snicker.

"No, just giving you a taste of old Australia. What they ate on the goldfields, as a special treat. They'd have preferred steak, but this was the only change from mutton they could get."

"You're shitfaced," May said. "Or nutso. Or both."

It merely set Mel off again, and May, temporarily defeated, rose from her chair and stalked away. Her bedroom door slammed, but Mel, lying on the floor, shook with laughter, the tears trickling down the sides of her face. After a while she got up and unsteadily wandered into the kitchen, where she ravenously made a meal of oddments from the fridge. Funny, despite the food she still felt faint, so she drank an extra glass of wine, and went to bed.

Mel woke, several hours later, struck by an unnerving thought. She got up, padded down the corridor, and opened the door to Mayzee's room. The smell of medicines and old books wafted around her, as she approached Mayzee's narrow, single bed. She reached out, found a bony shoulder, and tapped it gently.

"May! May! Wake up, just for a moment!"

The figure in the bed moved, and Mel could feel breath on her outstretched hand.

"This had better be an abject apology, naughty pet."

"Apology? Then I did do it. I thought it was all a dream."

"Dream? Mel, I just don't know what's gotten into you lately."

May shrugged off Mel's hand, turned away and snuggled into the warm mass of her blankets. Her voice continued, muffled:

"Go away!"

Mel went, to the living room, where she turned on the light, to see the bag of bones sitting forlornly on May's chair. She picked it up, sniffed cautiously, even touched the chunks, feeling slightly ill as her fingertip pressed into raw meat and her fingernail grated against bone. She *liked* kangaroos. . . .

It didn't make any sense. She remembered going into the butcher's shop, the blue-aproned assistant bending over the counter toward her, his five-to-five face shadowed and tired. She had felt a sudden rush of giddiness then, as if the raw meat had reminded her of the meals missed that day. Next moment— it seemed—she was standing outside the shop, the assistant revolving the sign behind the door to read CLOSED, the end of a long day's butchering. Yet what had happened in between, the ordering of the kangaroo tail, was a complete blank. Could he have made a mistake, she wondered, given me the wrong parcel? No—because you had to ask for roo specially, they kept it at the back of the shop. It was as if she hadn't done it at all. An ooby, out of body experience? she wondered. And yet she had somehow known, when May unwrapped the bones, what was coming, and had savored the joke.

Shaking her head, she put the bones into the rubbish and returned to her bed. Around dawn, she was awakened again, by Marc, back from his shift. Mel muttered something muzzily, and he put his arms around her, then after a pause, reached downward determinedly. Is that your peace offering? Mel wondered. If so, it's not good enough. She rolled away, to the farthest edge of the bed, and, to be blindingly obvious, imitated a snore or two. Marc sighed, then settled into bed. Mel waited, breathing deeply, until he started snoring, the real thing, not a bad pretense. Then she got out of bed, dressed as quietly as she could, and fled the flat for somewhere—anywhere—more like a home.

Mel arrived at Appleby to have her aunt open the door looking like a grizzled schoolboy in her plaid, old-fashioned dressing gown. "I'm making breakfast," she said immediately. "Join me."

In the kitchen, a pat of butter melted into golden bubbles over the disc of the big iron frying pan as Edie got extra eggs, bacon, and bread from the fridge.

"You aren't picky about cholesterol, are you?"

"No." But aren't you an ex-nurse? Mel wondered, her mouth watering like a leaky pipe.

"Sammy liked eggs and bacon," Mel said finally, when Edie handed her the laden plate.

"Is that a hint?"

Mel didn't reply, just slashed the face of her egg yolk and watched the saffron liquid spread across the toast.

"Mel dear, he went out like a lamp. And poor Alice lived like an ascetic, only to have her mind go bung on her. And so she waits, dependent and deranged, for her healthy body to decay and release her."

Mel took the fork out of her mouth and looked at Edie inquiringly. It was not like her aunt to be morbid. Edie opened her mouth again, but Mel, not wanting more reflections on mortality over breakfast, cut her off:

"Have you got any maps of this state, old ones?"

Edie paused, thinking. "There was a print that used to hang at the top of the stairs. It must be somewhere."

She went to look for it, leaving Mel feeling vaguely guilty at all the unreciprocated hospitality, guilty enough to wash up. She had just finished when Edie returned with a collage from Alice's room, photographs of Sammy, Mel, Edie, even Gran Kirksley, arranged with no attempt at composition within a large frame of extravagantly carved and gilded wood.

"It was in this frame, as I recall."

She set the collage facedown on the table and brandished an ivory-handled paper knife.

"Edie!"—but Mel's protest was too late. Edie had expertly slashed the brown paper at the back of the frame, to reveal brown cardboard underneath. She lifted this out, revealing a picture sandwich: the collage, the cardboard, and between them, an old faded map.

Mel spread it across the table, peering at the place-names

like black centipedes on the yellowed paper.

"There's Tolletown."

She lifted the frame, and placed the glass over the map again. "I need something to make temporary marks," she muttered, half to herself. To her surprise Edie went out to the hallway and returned carrying a red marking pen.

"I got it for labeling. Use it—the red'll wash off."

Thus reassured, Mel made a red dot over Tolletown and wrote, underneath, "1865."

"That's where the novel was published, and where we know Red Meg, I mean, Mrs. Yuill, was living in 1865. Now, let's find Aurealis."

"Aurealis?"

Mel relayed Mick's information, and Edie nodded. "I've read about the nuggety rushes. Out beyond Bendigo way. Let's have a look."

They bent over the map, red and silver heads touching.

"Kingower," Mel said. "Dunolly."

Edie echoed her, with more names: "Carapoee. Yawong. Gre Gre Village."

"You're too far west," Mel said.

"Well, I can't see any Aurealis, unless it's in the spot where the paper's torn."

They gazed at the tear; then Mel lifted the glass and smoothed down the map. Letters at the two edges of the rip came into view: an *A* and an *s*.

"It would be about there," Edie said. "I've seen Aurealis marked on a map, in the museum. Underneath was a huge nugget, cast from the original—plaster of paris and gold paint."

"Was it the length of a man's forearm and the shape of Cornwall?"

"It was shaped like nothing at all."

"That's what the novel says."

Mel replaced the glass again and made a dot above Aurealis,

adding, "Jesperson. Ned Metcalf, Surtees, Blanc, 1857–8."
Then, traveling downward, she made another dot over the city,
and wrote, in the blank space that was the harbor, "December
1853, Jeremiah Yuill arrives. October 1854, Mrs. Yuill."

They stared at the expanse of glass, now chicken-poxed with
red.

"Can you connect up the dots and dates?" Edie said.

"No. There's too many gaps, in place and time."

Edie frowned.

"Gaps conceal things, Mel. Did I ever tell you about your
great-great-uncle Alfred? He left Appleby late last century, and
apparently vanished into thin air. All I could find of him was a
letter, preserved in his mother's prayer book. He had written
from a station in Queensland. Inconsequential stuff, mostly,
but he mentioned shooting blackbirds one sunny afternoon.
That's odd, I thought, the colonists were much too fond of the
introduced birds, their reminders of old England, to kill them.
But then I was talking to a friend in the Genealogical Society,
and she put me straight. Alfred Kirksley's blackbirds were
human."

Mel, shocked, dropped the pen; but Edie, quick as a bird,
caught it.

"And from that moment, Mel, I lost the desire to write the
Kirksley family history, after all my hard work."

She opened her hand. The ink tip had pressed into her palm,
giving her a stigma of brightest red.

FOURTEEN

Silver-Nitrate Truths

The phone rang like a scream in the silence of the kitchen and Edie started, as if returning from a long distance. Her movements precise, she capped the pen and set it neatly on the table before hurrying out to the hall. Mel sat, her mind uncomfortably filled by the red mark, a negative, flickering image persisting in her vision.

"It's for you," Edie called. "The police!"

Mel ran out of the kitchen, grabbing the telephone receiver from Edie's hand.

"Hi, Mick."

"I was gonna mail you photocopies of those personnel records. But now I think you'd better come and collect them yourself. There's something else you should see—a photo of Inspector Jesperson in his police uniform."

"I'm on my way," Mel said.

* * *

"Here's the old tyrant," Mick said. "And doesn't he look it!"

"Mmn." Mel sat down on an uncluttered corner of Mick's pine desk, trying to extract the maximum of information from the image in front of her, not a Victorian print, but a modern copy, yet perfectly preserving the detail, the soft grays and charcoal of the original silver-nitrate image.

He's got freckles, was her first thought. Absurd, that such an authoritarian man should be freckled like a schoolkid. Otherwise, Mel fully agreed with Mick. Jesperson stood like an upright poker, the uniform on the tall, lean body immaculate. His face was hard and gaunt, the flesh tightly stretched over the cheekbones and the wide beak of a nose. But then there was the incongruity of that boyish, freckled skin. Boyish also, those whiskers, fine and straggly, like fronds of maidenhair fern sprouting from his cheeks. This man, if he had lived to a snowy old age, could never have featured in family photographs as a hirsute patriarch. The narrow slit of a mouth, the lips pressed firmly together—that was more like the Justperson Mrs. Yuill had described so mercilessly. And those eyes . . .

" 'Like pale green glass marbles, in which a man might fancy his misdemeanours, real and otherwise, were reflected, coldly and with censure,' " Mel quoted.

"That your lady writer Yuill? Drew from the life, didn't she?"

Mel wrested her gaze away from Jesperson for a moment.

"Mick, where did you find this photograph?"

To her surprise he looked away, as if confronted by the long-dead inspector.

"I didn't. There's somebody else researching Jesperson."

This news has to be taken standing up, Mel thought, and slipped off the edge of the desk. Now she acutely recalled Sorrel warning her of a bald man with a waxed mustache. Has he been investigating Melvina Yuill all this time? Oh please, no. She's mine!

"That's why you recognized Justperson as Jesperson," Mel said. "Mick, why didn't you tell me this before?"

"I was sworn to secrecy. You researchers! You're as paranoid as the fellas in the drug squad. Nobody's gonna shoot you!"

"I suppose not," Mel muttered.

"Your face ate lemons for lunch," he said. "Here, sit yourself down and let me finish. Charlie sent me the photo in the mail this morning, so I rang his Sydney number. He said, sure, show this Mel Kirksley the photo."

"What . . ." Mel took a deep breath and started again. "What does this Charlie know about Melvina Yuill?"

Mick wagged a thick finger. "You haven't been listening. I said Charlie was researching Jesperson."

"So he doesn't know about Mrs. Yuill?" Mel asked. Hope stirred inside her, like a bud about to blossom.

"He's never mentioned the name, so I'd say not. He's interested in Jesperson for other reasons."

"What reasons?"

Mick sighed heavily. "I think you and Charlie had better have a little chat, when he makes his next flying visit. I'm not gonna get caught in the cross fire."

Mel tried another tack. "What did you tell him about me?"

Mick cast his gaze up to the roof of the archives. "Sweet Jesus! It's like the locals and the Feds fighting over who gets first crack at a fizzgig!"

"That term's used in *The Scarlet Rider*," she said. Then, refusing to be distracted: "Mick, if you think I'm paranoid, you ought to meet my bosses at Roxana Press. I *have* to give them more information. Otherwise they'll come and knock down your door."

Mel rather relished the thought of Sorrel vs. Mick, and

maybe it showed in her tone, for he relented.

"Okay. I gave Charlie Mowbray a rough outline of what you were doing, without names, dates, places, nothing! And all I can tell you is that he has a document written at the end of Jesperson's life."

"A memoir?"

Mick closed his mouth and set his lips tightly together, almost like Jesperson in the photo.

"I see. But Mick, please, can you tell me this? What does Charlie Mowbray look like?"

"Shortarse. Stocky. Clean-shaven. Hair like JFK. Wears stud earrings."

So he isn't the bald man with the mustache, Mel thought, relaxing and examining the photo again. Then something struck her.

"Er, Mick, how do we know this is Jesperson? Apart from him fitting the description in the novel."

"And in the police records. I checked. But that's the old misery's signature on the back."

Mel turned over the copy and found nothing; Mick grinned, and dangled the envelope in which the photo had arrived. She lucky dipped in it and found a sheet of photocopy. There, in copperplate script, were the words: "To Darcy Ainsworth, from James Renkin Jesperson, in memory of an afternoon at Sackcloth's Studios."

"Sackcloth?" Mel put the photocopy down.

"On the photograph," Mick said, pointing. At the bottom, in a corner of the black surround, was, in tiny lettering, "S. Sackcloth, Slaggyford."

"That's the nearest sizable town to Aurealis," Mel said, thinking of Edie's map. "About fifteen miles away. So Jesperson visited Sackcloth the photographer. But who is Darcy Ainsworth?"

Her attention had been so caught and held by Jesperson that

she had hardly paid any attention to the second policeman in the photograph, except to notice that, on the back of the chair where he sat, Jesperson had rested, proprietorially, a broad, freckled hand.

"He's not as well dressed. Does that mean he's an ordinary constable?"

Mick nodded, and Mel stared at the image again. The man was young, thin, but not gaunt like Jesperson, being slender, almost of a girlish build. There was no hair on his face, but visible under his police helmet were thick dark curls. His nose was aquiline, like Jesperson's, but delicate, as were the long, thin hands. They reminded Mel of something; hands like that held . . . what? Then words from *The Scarlet Rider* came back to her and she thought, They held reins. A beardless boy, with dark curling hair, reaching down from horseback to shake hands with Miles the narrator.

"That's Darcy Ainsworth!"

"Ah," Mick said. "The only one of your fellas I couldn't find. But I was looking for Aynsley Dacre, not Darcy Ainsworth."

"The name was disguised, like Jesperson/Justperson. I think that means he was important to the novelist, not like Ned, or Blanc or Surtees. They were incidental characters—but Aynsley is Red Meg's lover, and Justperson her enemy."

"Your novel was what—1860s? Jesperson was a superintendent then. If someone was having a dig at him in print, it'd make sense to disguise his name."

"But what about Aynsley?"

"There'll be a file on him." Mick disappeared behind the wall of compacters again and Mel clasped her knee, rigid with anticipation.

"Eureka! Ainsworth, Darcy, mounted constable, joined the force December 1856, aged nineteen, stationed Aurealis January 1857, Metcalf's junior constable. Resigned February 1858.

Born Devon, single, religion C of E. Height five-nine, hair dark, eyes blue . . ."

"Aynsley had eyes blue as a summer sky," Mel said softly, staring at the photo. Make no mistake about it, Aynsley/Darcy had been a dreamboat.

It was curious, but all the while Mel followed Mick through the police corridors, in search of a working photocopier, she kept glancing at the image of Darcy Ainsworth. They copied the photograph and what Mick called the defaulters' sheets of Ned Metcalf, Surtees, Blanc, and Ainsworth, plus the thick file on Jesperson, and at last Mick escorted her out into the street. Almost before he had stopped waving, Mel had the crested police envelope open, and was feasting on the sight of Darcy.

Stop it! she thought. Anyone would think you were fourteen, with the latest issue of *Smash Hits*. She closed the envelope firmly, and wandered down the busy street. It was a sunny day in early winter, the wind crisp but intermittent, so that it was almost pleasant to sit down on a park bench, under the muted yellow-gray-green of a wattle tree about to burst into triumphant bloom. Mel clutched the envelope, aware her fingers were running up and down the flap as if playing guitar.

Distract yourself, Mel thought. Across the street was a phone booth, and Mel ran to it, hoping fervently that nobody from the police building was observing her jaywalking. She rang Edie's number first, but there was no answer. Then she dialed Roxana.

"HI MEL!"

"Er, hi Rube. Can you put me through to Nola?"

It was some time before Nola answered, and then Mel could hardly hear her above what seemed to be some sort of confrontation or celebration in the Roxana offices. There were at least three voices talking loudly in the background; that and a nearby fire engine at her end caused her to thrust the receiver almost down her ear as she strained to catch what Nola was saying.

"Mel, where you been these last few days? I rang your flat, the number you wrote on your personnel form, but just got this rude woman. She said she didn't know where Pet was and almost didn't care."

Mayzee, Mel thought. Oh, shit.

"The way she talked, you sounded like a dog, or a budgie."

"I know," Mel said. "Look, Nola, forget my flatmate. I've been doing Roxana work. Guess what? I've got photos of Darcy and Jesperson."

"Who the hell are they?"

"Aynsley and Justperson, in real life. And that's not all . . ."

"Hang on," she said, and Mel could hear her repeating the information across the room. Distantly, Mel heard the dulcet tones of Sorrel, then a third woman's voice, faintly Americanized. It neared, getting louder; then Mel heard clunking noises as the receiver was passed over.

"Mel Kirksley? Howdy! This is Kaye Tollet."

FIFTEEN

Kaye

"Dinner with a famous writer," Mel said, to the palm fronds above her head. "What do you think of that, you sparrows?"

There was no change in the twittering cacophony, the normal roosting sounds of evening. Noisy indifference, Mel thought, and hefting the leather satchel she had borrowed from Edie to transport the novel-baby in some sort of style to this meeting, she trudged onward wearily. She wanted to meet Kaye Tollet, but at the same time would have given a lot to be roosting just now in some warm haven, far removed from the city center on a frosty night. She swapped the satchel from one frozen hand to the other, feeling anew the dead weight of *The Scarlet Rider*, her notebooks, Mick's material, and, rolled up neatly in plastic, the map from Appleby. She and Edie had mended the tear over Aurealis with sticky tape, but the paper was so fragile that Mel seriously doubted whether it would survive handling over the table. Could *Mel* survive the dinner? Every shopwindow she passed showed her face wan, with dark shadows under her eyes.

Nonetheless she persisted, and a block and a half later reached the rendezvous, the George Sand restaurant. Pressing her nose to the window like a waif she saw, already seated, Nola, Sorrel, looking more like Virginia Woolf than ever, and a third woman, head bent over the menu, so all Mel could see of her was a big black trilby hat. I should sneak away, Mel thought, go have a snooze. But no, they've seen me.

"Mel!" called Nola, and waved. As Mel entered, Ms. Trilby rose and came rushing toward her. Mel was just able to register a piercing gaze, pale skin, paler blond hair, lank and long, before she was wrapped in an embrace, satchel, duffel coat, and all, and almost lifted off the ground. She's tall, Mel thought, very tall, and bony—the hug was the most uncomfortable she had ever experienced. Then Kaye stood back a moment, her hands resting on Mel's shoulders. Unnerved though Mel was, she still noticed that Kaye had a nice smile.

"So here's our literary detective."

"Oh, don't say that," Mel muttered, coloring.

"Well, 'tis true. All the time I was among the heathen, those people who tell me I have a cute little accent, call our dear old wattle trees acacias and think South America means Arkinsaw, I got phone messages and faxes extolling your virtues. A paragon you were, a Miss Marple, a V. I. Warshawski, even perhaps a Roxana Reul! So come and satisfy my curiosity."

She released Mel, who went and sat at the one vacant place at the table, beside Nola, and across from Kaye and Sorrel. Mel untoggled her duffel, then was heartily embarrassed by the waitress, who wore what looked like a man's evening dress, taking the coat, Marc-stains and all, and hanging it on a peg behind the door, beside Nola's cardigan coat, Sorrel's classic English mackintosh, and a black cape that must be Kaye's. She *would* wear a cape, Mel thought. I bet it's got red silk lining.

Kaye's long beringed fingers were now toying with a cigarette. Sorrel proffered a lighter, small and silver, as deadly in appearance as Roxana Reul's gun; and while the exchange of fire took place, Nola turned her head toward Mel, and winked, from the eye invisible to the women on the other side of the table. The movements of all three coincided so precisely that they might have been choreographed by a director. Have we suddenly stepped into an arty movie? Mel wondered. This reality was too perfect to be real.

Nola poured a fourth glass of wine.

"A toast!" Kaye said. "To Rosie, the two Melvinas, and incidentally, to nepotism!"

"Nepotism?" Mel said, confused.

"From *nepôte*, nephew. I must coin a female equivalent. You see, once we knew what a treasure Roxana had in you, Nola confessed to being your good fairy stepmother."

"Almost-stepmother," corrected Nola.

"I had guessed as much," Sorrel said affably, "although the exact relationship did come as a surprise."

Mel looked at her sharply, suddenly aware of a sea-change. Sorrel and Nola were no longer tense in each other's company, for they smiled at each other and at Kaye, touched even, in the act of pouring wine or passing bread rolls, with perfect amity.

"Wake up, Mel!" Nola said, and obediently she reached across the table. All four women clinked glasses with the noise of a chandelier in a typhoon, then drank. The wine was a soft pink-yellow-red, a quintessence in color of the pastel tablecloth, the centerpiece posy in its cut-crystal vase, and the light of the wax tapers. What superb art direction, Mel thought, then asked, "Is this a Tolletown rosé?"

"Yes," Kaye said. "One particularly apposite." She turned the label toward Mel, revealing a name: MARY ROSA TOLLET.

"Lil's—a vintner's immortality, to name a special wine after a special person. The first time I tasted it was at the belated wake Lil, Nola, and I held, when I finally got around to revisiting Tolletown. After the second bottle, Nola and I drunkenly agreed to sort out Rosie's Place."

"She knows the rest," Sorrel said.

Kaye glanced at Mel. "Do you now?"

"Well, not all. I got two accounts of how *The Scarlet Rider* was found, one eyewitness from Nola, another from Sorrel, apparently not eyewitness . . ."

Mel was about to add, *and both simultaneously*, but Kaye interrupted:

"My fault, I'm afraid. As we three were going out the Roxana door, a minor crisis arose. Somebody had to deal with it, and I'd promised Lil, so I tossed a coin, to choose between my two lieutenants. Sorrel won, or lost, depending upon your point of view."

Virginia Woolf smiled, as if forgetting her grievance, at being left behind, Mel realized.

"I guessed at something like that. But I don't know what happened next. Who is the bald man with the mustache that nobody wants me to meet?"

"How like a spy novel it sounds." Kaye addressed Mel, but her gaze was fixed on the waitress, who was looming. "French onion soup."

"Escargots," Sorrel said. "Kaye, it was *extremely* like a spy novel. I insist you write it up."

"The mixed horse doover plate," Nola said. "Yeah, thanks a million, Kaye, for telling Geraldo what you thought of him—"

"Oh, can we have a carafe of water as well?"

"—then buggering off to Yankee-land."

The waitress noted down the orders imperturbably, not even the faint dark mustache on her lip twitching.

"And some more bread," Sorrel added. "Kaye, you deliberately left Nola and me to cope with unpleasant legal letters, threatening phone calls . . ."

"Well, of course I did," Kaye said. "Because you two are dependable. Mel, you've not ordered!"

"Roxana'll shout," Nola said. "Have the most expensive dishes on the menu. C'mon, you've earned it."

Mel gazed nervously at the waitress. "Er, prawns, and the duck à l'orange to follow. But I have to ask . . .?"

The waitress leaned forward expectantly.

"Is Geraldo the bald man with the mustache I was told to avoid like the bubonic plague?"

"For second course, coq au vin," Kaye said quickly to the waitress before answering Mel. "How perceptive of you, my Marple-ette. Of course he was."

Nola grinned widely. "Told ya Mel was a smart girl! Told ya! And pepper steak for me!"

"Blanquette de veau, please," Sorrel said.

Somehow amid the confusion the waitress took the orders.

"Aah," Kaye said, as the waitress departed. "I feel the storytelling urge coming on. Sorrel and Nola stopped at the opening of the magic trunk, didn't they? Well, several chapters later Geraldo appeared."

She blew a smoke ring, which floated over Sorrel's head like a halo. Mel sat back, eyeing the face under the trilby hat, and thought, no, the feeling of being directed, in a movie, has to do with the personal ambience of Kaye. She is living theater, she processes raw reality into artifice, the Roxana Reul stories; and thus even being in her presence is to feel like a character in the personal novel of Kaye Tollet, crime writer.

"Imagine, Mel, the wide verandah of the family home at the Tolletown vineyard, now Lil's, with a heap of cushions, a bottle of wine, and me, lounging and reading *The Scarlet Rider*. Every now and then I would pass a section I'd finished on to

Nola. It was very quiet, the only sound birdsong, and the occasional incredulous gasp. My ancestors were hopeless miners, Mel, but I know gold when I see it.

"Over dinner that night, with Lil and her daughter Varney, who is extraordinarily beautiful and intelligent, Nola and I audibly wondered how to find who the author was. Lil suggested her latest beau, who was doing a history of Tolletown. Geraldo was at a conference, but we could leave the paper and he could look at it when he returned. And at that Varney made a moue."

She paused to wave her cigarette over the ashtray, the cylinder of ash falling tidily off, *by itself*, as though timed to the second. It's the Kaye effect, Mel thought.

"Nola and I left Rosie's treasure at Tolletown, and drove down to the city again. Well, weeks went by, and not a peep from the winery. I rang up now and then, but the history man either was out, or couldn't be disturbed, or similar specious excuses. On the tenth try I got lucky. A whiny tenor voice answered the phone. After our brief and evasive exchange was over, I remarked casually, to the nearest person, who happened to be Rube . . ."

She took a sip of her wine.

"I said: 'He sounds like a cad from a 1920s thriller. Even the name is pat. Geraldo Abernathy.' "

"Rube went 'EEK!' at the top of her lungs, momentarily deafening me. When I got my hearing back, she confessed—well, the worst."

She blew another smoke ring.

"Rube told me that Geraldo had been thrown out of her uni for trying the fuck-or-fail gambit on the vice-chancellor's goddaughter. A lot fitted into place then, like a pornographic jigsaw. Varney's moue, for instance. Lil's a good parent, tough in business, makes killer wine; but she has attacks of romance. For six months, regular as clockwork, the sun shines out of the current object of desire, whether he be a Hare Krishna, a banjo player, or a hippie capitalist like Varney's dad, Lil's only husband, who was responsible for the child being christened Nirvana. Lil's had a thoroughly mixed assortment of men."

Mel sipped at Rosie's rosy wine. Lil sounded like a female version of Sammy.

"Thus Varney, for a ten-year-old, is an astute judge of the male sweetie. If the name Geraldo makes her wince, I thought, then I have entrusted Rosie's treasure to entirely the wrong person."

She paused and drank a mouthful of water, like an athlete preparing for a final effort.

"Here's where it gets all suspenseful. I had about eight hours before I was due to catch the plane for the U.S. tour. Nola! I yelled, you know the way to Tolletown, get me there ASAP, if not sooner! So off we scorched in the Roxana van, me praying to the patron saint of crime fiction—St. Agatha of Mayhem Parva—for no speed cameras, nor punctures. When we reached the outskirts of Tolletown, I made Nola take the back road to the vineyard, for an inconspicuous arrival. Halfway along we met Varney, on ponyback. Suddenly the narrative switched genre, to Girl's Own Adventure. Nola, I said, keep the motor running! With hardly a word spoken, Varney led me, following in her hoofsteps, to Geraldo's lair."

Her eyes narrowed at the memory.

"He'd taken over Rosie's cottage, converting it to as close an approximation of an academic study as could be faked in the wilds of Tolletown. There were shelves of books, Great-grandpa Tollet's walnut desk, and an expensive computer, with screen save drawing pretty origami patterns all over its face.

"Geraldo was up at the main house and had left the door unlocked. I stationed Varney and pony underneath the roses, as lookout, before I went inside. First, the computer. I scuttled the mouse around on its little pad, and retrieved the document that Geraldo had been writing. It was a letter regarding *The Scarlet*

Rider, which Geraldo claimed to have discovered. LIAR, I typed. This extraordinary novel, brilliantly prefiguring Conan Doyle, blah blah, the work of some unknown master . . . OR MS, I typed. The letter was directed to a multinational publisher with despicable politics, whom Geraldo seemed to think would be ideal to publish *The Scarlet Rider*, edited and with an introduction by G. Abernathy. I typed: NOT ON YOUR NELLY!

"The Scarlet Rider sat on the desk, pleading to be rescued from this appalling fate. I grabbed it and fled out the door and into the vineyard, running between a row of twilit vines, Varney galloping and giggling beside me in the parallel row, to the waiting van. When Geraldo returned, he found the bird had spread out its pages and flown away.

"Of course, while we were zooming down the freeways, Geraldo rang the phone off the wall to Roxana, long-distance. He phoned again, just as I was collecting my suitcases from Sorrel's office. 'You deal with him,' Sorrel said, for she had already been earbashed beyond the call of duty. The first thing he said was 'Thief!' 'Not at all,' sez I, ' 'twas my keepsake from Rosie, like Lil promised.' 'I don't think that will stand up in court,' he said.

"Nola was making hurry-up gestures from the doorway. I made an intelligent, considered suggestion re his sexuality—"

"Involving manglewurzels," Sorrel said happily.

"—and sped to the waiting seven-forty-seven."

"Leaving Geraldo in the poo," Nola said.

"And paddleless," Kaye added. "No other *Tolletown Chronicles* survive from the 1860s."

"Roxana holds the unique text of this hot literary property," Sorrel said.

No wonder you didn't want me to copy it, Mel thought, almost feeling sympathetic in retrospect. A black-sleeved arm, serving from the right, deposited a plate of sizzling prawns in front of her. The sympathy dissolved immediately into rabid hunger.

"But now," Nola said, "he's flying the white flag."

"Not surrender, but truce," Kaye said. "We got a fax proposing a bury-the-hatchet lunch."

"But why?"

Kaye had a mouthful of wine, so Sorrel answered. "We wondered that, too, although we have suspicions. Geraldo, when Nola and I were still talking to him, kept arguing that Roxana couldn't possibly publish *The Scarlet Rider*, because it was written by a man. Indubitably, he actually said. True, Boy's Own Stories aren't in our charter. Kaye's guess is that he thinks he's got proof of authorship."

"But I've got proof that it was by Melvina Yuill!"

Nola patted her hand. "Yes, but you don't tell him that."

"Me? Have lunch with this, this . . ."

Mel dropped the heavy silver fork, with prawn still attached, onto her plate with a mighty clang. The waitress winced, but nobly refrained from serving a plate of piping hot soup into Kaye's lap. It wouldn't happen, Mel thought. The Kaye effect would stop any pie in face, because slapstick isn't in her personal novel.

"You don't have to do much," Kaye said. "Just act the young naive researcher, and let him talk about his discovery."

"But how can you be sure he'll tell me?"

"Young and attractive women bring out the braggart in him. Ask Rube."

SIXTEEN

Geraldo

And after that, it was Mel's turn at narrative, to tell Kaye all about Melvina Mary Yuill; not as well, Mel knew, but then Mel hadn't the practice of writing all those Roxana Reul novels. By the time Mel had finished, which was around the time of the dessert menu, she was drooping, utterly exhausted. She could dimly remember being helped into the Roxana van at the end of the evening, Nola in the driver's seat, while Sorrel and Kaye sat in the back, chatting. Her eyes closed, and images, precursors of dreams to come, flitted across the screen of the eyelids.

Somehow Mel ascended the stairs to the flat, but after that she must have been sleepwalking. When she awoke, in dawn light, beside the hummock of Marc, she found she was lying on top of the coverlet, still fully clothed, in her coat and boots. She let out a moan, at this new evidence of her increasing eccentricity, and at that Marc opened one eye. Please, Mel thought, don't let him wake up. Mayzee will have told him all about the roo, and he'll think I'll have gone completely bats. His eye rolled, surveying her, but he must have assumed the sight was a dream, for he turned, snuggled into the pillow, and after a moment started snoring.

Moving very slowly and softly, Mel got off the bed, and went to the bathroom, where she inspected herself in the mirror. Young and attractive—that was how Mel was meant to look for Geraldo, at the lunch, scheduled for one o'clock today. Instead she felt one hundred years old and looked elf-ridden. Vanity, thy name is woman, she thought, as she filled the basin with water. She bent down to wash her face, then suddenly reared up, cheeks dripping.

A memory had come to mind, somehow connected with the ride home, but blurred by dream, as if Mel had passed into REM sleep in the van, or else repeated the trip subconsciously during the night. Mel stared into the smeared, filthy mirror, trying to remember. Somehow, she had a distinct impression that Sammy had been driving the van, instead of Nola.

She tried vainly to pin it down. There had been a drunken discussion of what she should wear for the meeting with Geraldo, and at that—did she drift into sleep at this point?—a voice next to her, from the driver's seat, had piped up with Sammy's favorite adage on female vanity. Laughter had sounded in the back of the van then, silvery, almost musical, quite unlike any of the three Roxanas. Someone had leaned forward and spoke into her ear: "Buy a pretty dress for Geraldo!" The accent had been English, but in Mel's memory it differed from Sorrel's sit-com tones.

Mel didn't take much notice of the command until several hours later, when, idly glancing from the window of the tram that was lugging her and a load of office workers into the city, she saw *it*. At the next tram stop, Mel leapt off and ran back to the little shopping center. In front of the Opportunity Shop was a phone booth, and without taking her gaze from the dress in the window, Mel dialed Roxana.

Nola sounded seedy. "Oh gawd, Mel. I'd say, wear black leather and biker boots, but then I'm hungover. Sorrel! Mel wants to know what she should wear to the lunch."

Sorrel said, in the background, "Something feminine and demure."

It sounded nothing like the English voice she had heard, not at all. Roxana didn't tell me to buy a dress, Mel thought; but somebody else did. Either way, it was sound advice.

Minutes later she was staring at an image of herself, perhaps not demure, but certainly very feminine. The dress was fifties era, of sage-green wool, thick and soft, the full skirt draping almost to her ankles. The sleeves were three-quarter length, with a frill of lace at the wide cuff, matching the collar. The bodice was cut to give the impression, quite erroneous in her case, of voluptuousness. Mel adjusted the sash again, and regarded the changing-room mirror with joyous disbelief. The garment could have been made for her.

It was only later, as Mel passed the windows of the Victoria and Albert Hotel, that she noticed something else about the frock. She had worn it out of the Op Shop, carrying her old sweater and skirt crammed into a recycled bag. Now she stared at her reflection against the antique background. Yes, in the dress, Mel looked quite fifties, almost as retro as Sorrel in her thirties garb. But at the same time, another era was evoked—with a few more inches of skirt, the garment could have been Victorian.

Geraldo's reaction to the dress was to look her up and down, lingeringly. Mel stood like a model, smiling slightly as she made a tick in a mental notebook: from her briefing with Rube, less than an hour ago, she knew his reaction was typical. One short glance was all Mel had given Geraldo—this figure, waiting impatiently outside the bistro, was even from a block away unquestionably her luncheon date. He was taller than her, tending toward the fleshy, with his most noticeable features the expanse of shiny bald head, partly natural, partly shaved, Mel decided, and the waxed mustache, which verged on the handlebar.

"Have you been to the Fox and Hounds before?" he asked, pulling back the chair for her. Chivalry, Mel thought, as she sat. A prelude to horseplay? The bistro had definitely an equestrian theme: there were prints of hunting scenes on the walls and the matching place mats. But the suits around her were not hunting pink, but pinstripe and gray, worn by men who maybe rode exercise bikes, but never to hounds. Yet they talked at the top of their voices, quaffed quantities of beer, and devoured large hunks of meat, as though breaking from a strenuous ride across the countryside.

"Sorry, I was miles away. No. I don't go to restaurants much."

"I'm an honored customer here," he said. "Though not so often, since I met the lovely Lillian, and acquired the lifestyle of a country squire."

The leather elbow patch on his tweed jacket squeaked alarmingly at this point, as if agreeing with him.

"But this remains my favorite city eatery. And do you know who agrees with me?"

Reverently he dropped the name of a minor novelist, and Mel made another tick against her Geraldo checklist.

"You look blank, my dear. Never heard the name before? I suppose you only read *women's* literature."

"Actually, no." It occurred to Mel that for the last few years her reading, textbooks apart, had consisted of Paperback Exchange hand-ons, whatever Mayzee pronounced suitable. Would *The Scarlet Rider* pass the May test? She rather thought not.

Geraldo continued, oblivious of her brown study. "We're dear old friends. Even shared the favors of a lovely lady."

And why should you wish me to know that? Mel wondered.

"Which he put into his novel, but I've magnanimously forgiven him now."

Mel smiled sweetly, recalling Rube's indignation: "HE ACTUALLY RECOMMENDED THE TUTORIAL READ THE BOOK!"

"And did you?" Mel had asked.

"NAH, DROPPED OUT OF FIRST-YEAR HISTORY INSTEAD."

Her lack of response must have disconcerted Geraldo, for he turned his attention to the wine list, his skull rising above the equestrian scene on its back like a pink sunset.

"Pinot noir? Not Tollet, alas."

What with the plonk and Rosie's rosé, Mel seemed to have imbibed a bit too much lately. "No, just water."

"The path to an extremely virtuous and boring old age," Geraldo said, frowning. "Well, allow me at least to advise you on your meal. Steak is the house speciality and I particularly recommend the T-bones. No objection? Good. Garçon!"

Having ordered, he cast his gaze, like a pair of grabby hands, upon her.

"Now, while we wait for the meal, perhaps you can tell me a bit about yourself, starting with qualifications."

It was like a card game, for her humble B.A. (Hons) was quickly trumped by his Ph.D. Since all he had wanted to establish was her inexperience, he continued solitaire, with a monologue about himself. Mel nodded from time to time, not really listening to the history of Geraldo, starting with his Scottish and Paraguayan ancestors, Utopian socialists and the subject of their scion's first book; nor his childhood, school, and brilliant university years, although she did note a sharp unexplained blip between Geraldo the academic and Geraldo the freelance historian.

"So, in my series of winery histories, I turned to the Tolletown winery, and ultimately, to the lovely Lillian. In fact, I had researched much of the district history before the advent of *The Scarlet Rider*. And thus I had the cutting edge on Roxana."

Two enormous steaming hunks of meat were placed in front of them, surrounded by potatoes in foil and minimal green vegetables. The servings were so generous that the broad china plates were almost invisible beneath them. Could I ask for a doggie bag, she wondered, in the Fox and Hounds? I'll never stomach all this man-food.

Geraldo sniffed appreciatively, added pepper and horseradish copiously to his meal, then suddenly shot a name at her:

"Augusta Turk."

"Schoolteacher," Mel replied, recalling the Tolletown directory.

"I see you are not just a pretty baby. But do you know what happened to her?"

Mel shook her head.

"Aha! She caught the eye of young Frederick Tollet, heir to the vineyard, married, and produced ten sons. And Mary Rosa Tollet."

"In the trunk were keepsakes of Rosie's mother," Mel said, remembering Nola's description of the tobacco-brown dress.

"Correct. I wondered why Mrs. Frederick Tollet kept a magazine serial. She would have hardly any time for reading, being in an almost perpetual state of fecundity throughout her married life. Between pregnancy and lactation, she probably never had another period."

Mel watched him slice into his steak. It was rare, as he had ordered, and hemorrhaged slightly, a counterpoint or contradiction to his words.

He put a sizable chunk into his mouth, chewed once or twice, then said, without swallowing, "*The Scarlet Rider* obviously had special significance for the woman."

"Maybe she liked a good book," Mel said, unwrapping one of the gargantuan potatoes. It put her in mind of a Christo installation.

"No. Rrromance!"—with another leer.

He really is a sex maniac, Mel decided.

"Tolletown last century was hardly a hub of literary activity. There were few likely candidates for the authorship of *The Scarlet Rider*. I investigated the local police first, as the passages regarding the mounted force hinted at some disgruntled plod. However, when I examined the police records for Tolletown, I found men barely competent in the English language."

Wonder if he went to the archives, Mel thought. Must ask Mick. Did they get on? Doubt it, somehow.

"Police eliminated, there were two obvious candidates. Horace Polk-Smith, editor of the *Tolletown Chronicle*, a man fiftyish, with a large family, but just possibly the answer to a wishful maiden's prayer. Miss Turk was a plain little thing, just like her daughter. And without a farthing to her name."

He swallowed, and hacked at his steak again.

"Another candidate was much more attractive: Charles Alonso Ellis, the head teacher. A man with a face like a Hellenic statue, athletic, golden-haired, and in 1865, unmarried."

Mel nibbled at a sliver of potato. The sight of Geraldo's bloody steak had quite put her off her T-bone.

"He left Tolletown in 1870, as I discovered, in the wake of a religious crisis precipitated by a traveling hellfire-and-brimstone preacher. I was able to trace his subsequent history, which was spent in China, as a missionary. In the 1890s he authored a volume of moral tales for children, an extremely rare book, not even in the British Library. Nonetheless I was able to obtain a microfilm copy, from where I have no intention of telling you. Its evidence of Ellis's literary aspirations is conclusive. Miss Turk either was told or guessed the authorship of *The Scarlet Rider*. Naturally she treasured the work of her first love."

Or did she treasure the work of a friend? Mel wondered. Tolletown was a small place and Augusta quite probably knew Melvina, by sight at least, if not more—they were two bookish women in Hicksville. As if summoned by that notion, mischief, like a small mouse, stirred within her.

"Maybe Augusta wrote it herself."

"My dear young lady! On the evidence of the family letters Mrs. Frederick Tollet was nothing more than a Victorian hausfrau."

"She might not have been, when she was single."

"Really?"

"Well, she must have had something going for her, to be penniless and yet catch a Tollet," Mel said. "With the family so fond of marriage as a form of investment brokerage."

It was an invention, as suppositional as Geraldo's romantic tale of Augusta and Alonso, but it caused him to go quite red in the face.

"Where did you hear that?"

"A little bird," Mel said, thinking: You fortune hunter! You utter gigolo!

It was clearly a topic he did not wish to pursue. "If Roxana's line is that Mrs. Frederick Tollet wrote *The Scarlet Rider*, then you are seriously in error."

"Maybe. But unless you can prove that Alonso could have written *The Scarlet Rider*, Roxana will publish the novel as a woman's text."

"No female wrote that book. I can prove it beyond doubt. And when I do—"

"If?"

"Don't interrupt, girl! *When* the novel is positively attributed to Ellis, then it will be of no use to Roxana and can be returned to me."

"Perhaps," Mel said. The sight of Gerald bristling over his steak bone was so dire that she glanced away, only to have her gaze arrested by a hunting print, bloodthirsty even for the Fox and Hounds. That poor little fox, Mel thought, it's like *The Scarlet Rider*, the text being literally torn between two hounds, Geraldo sinking his teeth into one end, and me hanging on grimly at the other. So much for my fantasy of being Mel the huntress, hot on the trail of the mysterious Melvina. At the end of every hunt is a kill . . . and I'm no killer.

The thought depressed Mel, all the sudden confidence of her spar with Geraldo evaporating. Vaguely she wondered from whence it had come. A whopper red herring like Augusta Turk, authoress, was not normally the sort of thing Mel could produce under pressure. She stood up, crumpling her serviette in her fist.

"Going? But you've hardly touched your lunch. However, I never come between a woman and her diet—not that you really need to."

Mel concentrated on counting out Roxana money to cover her half of the bill, not wanting to hear another word from him, but being obliged to, all the same.

"This was a most delightful lunch. Not only because dialogue was resumed between myself and Roxana, but also because I had the pleasure of meeting you. Miss Kirksley was not what I expected from cousin Kaye, not at all."

He drained his red wine.

"Before I met the lovely Lillian, I had several girlfriends among the gay sorority. Occasional girlfriends, but very charming. They would ring up now and then, if they felt like a touch of heterosexuality, and of course I would oblige."

"Er . . . Yes . . . Good-bye!"

Mel left the Fox and Hounds at a dignified pace, but with the distinct feeling of yelps and hot doggy breath behind her. Only later, as she collected herself in the closest haven, the ornate ladies' lavatory by the Town Hall, did it occur to her that though Geraldo's final message was perfectly clear, why he had couched it in such terms was quite obscure.

Mel had taken a lot of trouble with her appearance that day, not quite twinset and pearls for that swine, but close. So what about her had made Geraldo assume Mel belonged to the sorority? Because I work for Roxana? she wondered, and her eyes went wide, as she recollected the absence of men in the publishing house, the teasing glances, little touches, between the three at the restaurant last night, the tension she could now identify as sexual between Nola and Sorrel. Not only feminists, but . . .

Well! she thought, then started to giggle. What would Sammy have thought of it!

SEVENTEEN

Life Like a Sensational Novel

"You look like a visitor from another century," Edie said.

"You noticed?" Mel asked, as Edie shut the Appleby door behind her. "I didn't at first."

"It's a lovely dress, the color almost matching . . ." Edie put her head on one side, surveying Mel critically. "Yes, it does match!" she added, half to herself. "Mel, close your eyes! I've got something to show you."

Mel obeyed, feeling very silly. Edie's footsteps retreated, going into the library, then returned, bringing with them a strong smell of mothballs. "Now we need a long mirror." She took Mel's hand. "No, you can't open your eyes yet! Trust me."

"Until you break both our necks," Mel said, but let Edie lead her upstairs. She felt polished board under her feet, then worn rug, and guessed that they had come to Alice's old room, with its heavy furniture and antique mirror.

"Stop here!" Edie said, and Mel did. She heard a creak as the mahogany chest was opened; then a swathe of something light and soft was thrown over her shoulder. Edie's patent-leather boots squeaked slightly as she stood on tiptoe, lowering something down onto Mel's head. Through her hair Mel felt a slight weight, and smelled the indefinable musty fragrance of age, overlaid with moth-killer. Edie's cold fingers scrabbled under her chin, tying a strip of silky cloth.

"Now, crouch a little!"

"This is ridiculous!" Mel said, but did as she was told.

"Now you can open your eyes!"

Mel did, and saw facing her, a Victorian lady, in a long green dress, with draped over her shoulders a white silk shawl embroidered with flowers, her great-great-grandmother's, and on her head a bonnet of silk and lace, decorated with little sprays of velvet leaves, with a dull-green bow tying it under the chin. The dress Mel had worn all day, the shawl she had seen on her first visit here, and the bonnet was presumably something Edie had discovered during her house cleaning; but together the effect was too much, alien, as if a redheaded stranger stared back at her. She moaned, and fell toward the reflection.

"This isn't smelling salts," Mel heard Edie say, as if from a great distance away, "but 'twill have to do."

Something wafted increasingly sickly and strong under Mel's nose. When she opened her eyes, Edie was clutching a stick of burning incense like an Indian fakir. She gave a tremulous grin, and stuck the incense into an empty flower vase on Alice's mantelpiece.

"Mel, you fainted, just like a lady in a Victorian melodrama, with her stays too tight. In fact, you wouldn't come to until I applied a Victorian remedy!"

Mel realized she sat propped against the side of the great mahogany bed, a pillow behind her head. Over her shoulder was draped not the white silk shawl, but a bathroom towel, spotted with red. Cautiously she touched her nose, which felt sore, then her forehead. She winced, and withdrew her hand, to find it smeared with blood.

"I thought you'd have shattered the mirror, you hit it such a whack! Instead you bruised your forehead—"

Mel felt it, a lump like a halved egg above her brow.

"—and made your nose bleed."

"Victorian ladies," Mel said, "generally had someone to catch them when they fell."

"Sorry about that, but I'm not as spry on my feet as I once was."

Mel wiped her hand on the towel. "Did I bleed all over . . . the antiques?"

"No. The bonnet was only loosely tied, and it slipped down your back when you fell."

Mel turned her head slightly, and saw the confection of lace, velvet, and green ribbon sitting beside her on the bed. Beside it was the shawl, pristine as far as she could see.

"Stay there. You might be concussed. I'll bring you a brandy."

She left, and Mel gazed into the glass, now ornamented vertically with a streak of blood. The woman in the reflection was curd-pale, except for the livid bruise, but without the hat or shawl not overly Victorian. Why had she fainted? It had been a long day; and the latter half of it, after reporting on Geraldo via phone to Roxana, had been spent at the old library, running up and down the wrought-iron spiral stairs of the stacks in search of Charles Alonso Ellis's literary corpus. Her native guide had been the friendly androgyne, and they had braved the dust of the 200s, venturing into the unmapped, uncataloged jungle of nineteenth-century miscellaneous missionary-society publications. However, Alonso had proved elusive, and they had not even been rewarded with a sighting of the library ghost, rumored to haunt the theosophy shelves. . . .

Ghost, Mel thought. When I looked into the mirror, it was like seeing a ghost: my quarry, Melvina Yuill, as I interpret her through her character, Red Meg, who seems to look like Myrie Kirksley and me. I felt like a huntress early in my search, but Geraldo reversed the chase, in the Fox and Hounds, making me prey, the creature hunted. He lost me, but there's someone else in pursuit, who's put an *a* in the "hunted," making me feel *haunted*. . . .

This disturbing reverie was thankfully interrupted by Edie, entering with brandy in a glass balloon. I scared her, Mel realized. She's trembling.

"Did you eat today?" Edie asked as she seated herself on Gran Kirksley's hard little beaded occasional chair, eyeing Mel worriedly. Mel nodded through the ball of glass, then, as proof, launched into the story of the horror lunch with Geraldo. Slowly Edie relaxed, even laughing at Geraldo's "sorority" line.

"Was Sammy ever like that? I know he was lecherous, but did he brag about it? In the same breath as making his pass?"

"No. My brother had tact. And charm. Not a lot else, but it got him by."

"Geraldo didn't have any. And he didn't know it! If only there'd been a mirror in front of him, so he could see how charmless he was."

Her gaze flitted to the wardrobe glass, then away. It still spooked her. Then Mel met Edie's eye. The older woman gave her a haggard smile.

"Mel, in my professional opinion, I don't think you're concussed, but you do look shaken."

She glanced at her watch.

"It's after eight. I think you should stay here until you look less of a wax effigy, or for the night, whichever comes first."

Very carefully, Mel stood up, avoiding all possible eye contact with the mirror.

"All right. But in the study, not in this room."

A high wind blew up that night, and in the dark outside the study window Mel could see tree boughs shaking in a dervish dance, leaves tossing like tresses in the gale. The house creaked, and needle-sharp drafts edged through the gaps around doors and window panes.

Mel slept for a while, then awoke, lying in the dark and listening to the wind. When she was tired of that, but not tired enough for sleep, she ventured downstairs to the library, returning with the family album. She sat in bed, the eiderdown wrapped around her shoulders, and flipped through the heavy, photo-laden pages. Here were images of her in christening robes; Sammy, with an unidentified lady clinging to one hand and plump toddler Mel to the other; Edie and Alice youthful and pretty in matching dresses; Gran Kirksley, dressed like Sorrel; and farther back, top hats, long skirts, stays—the nineteenth-century contingent of ancestors.

All along, the fact had been staring her in the face, but it had taken the image in the mirror to make her realize, belatedly, that the similarities in names and physical appearance between her and Red Meg/Melvina Yuill went beyond simple coincidence, to perhaps . . . atavism. Everybody's been researching their ancestors, Mel thought: Edie, Nev and Dot, even Geraldo. It's a compulsion, a disorder of the will. The cousins said something interesting about that—what was it? Something about feeling the "oldies" almost bodily pushing them into the library. Is that what's happening to me?

Maybe, Mel thought, I know things because of information encoded in my genetic matter. The solution to Melvina Yuill could be hidden in my DNA, my personal double helix, like those stairs in the library stacks. If the DNA can transmit eye shape, pigmentation, family traits, then maybe it can transmit memory as well. All my hunches and successful guesses could be the memories of my ancestor Melvina.

Mel closed the album on her Kirksley ancestors, thinking: It can't be on Sammy's side. Edie would know if any Yuill had married into the family. Myrie's a better bet—she gave me her looks, that were Red Meg's also. But I know very little about her: a country girl from the south of West Australia, Sammy said, working in a hotel when they met, no relatives worth speaking of . . .

No, Mel thought, start at the other end. Look for records of Yuills in the nineteenth century, starting the year Melvina arrived in Australia. She came by herself, unaccompanied by off-spring—but she might have had a child or children later. If so, the record will be in the Births Index.

When the library opened that morning, Mel was waiting outside the great door wearing a beret borrowed from Edie, pulled low over her bruised forehead, "in case people think you a battered wife," as her aunt had said. One of the first people inside the great door, she found the building eerily quiet, almost dreamlike in its desolation. Genealogy was temporarily free of its senior citizens, in fact of everyone except the staff. Without having to wait, for once, she selected from the fiche carousel a fan of birth records, covering the *Y*s. They encompassed the years 1854, when Melvina arrived, to the 1880s, the biological limit of her fertility. Only 1855 was missing, probably misfiled—but Mel was too eager to pause long enough for a sustained search of the gills.

At the reader, Mel moved the microfilm in its glass sandwich, and names sped across the screen, alas none of them Yuill.

That was 1854. She pulled out the fiche, and inserted another, then another. The pile of discarded fiches beside her mounted, all proving Yuill-less. She withdrew the last of them and sank back on the chair.

Then immediately sensed a presence standing behind her, as if poised to strike.

EIGHTEEN

Gold

Mel twisted in the chair, afraid of seeing what was behind her, and yet making the attempt, all the same; and beheld first a white dustcoat, over tweed, then an Eton crop, decorated with cobwebs. It's only the Androgyne, Mel thought, but her heart hammered and she felt close to fainting again. The librarian spoke, and with a great effort she concentrated on the words:

"I investigated, as a last resort, the collection bequeathed by Dean Orlando Burnett, five thousand divinity volumes of such stupendous dullness that they were stored in the roof, in the hope that they would molder away before funds became available to catalog them."

Mel slowly became aware that the dusty hands were presenting her with a paperbound, very dirty book, pamphlet-sized. Taking it, she read the title, *Sabbath Tales for Little Friends*, and underneath, the words "by C. A. Ellis."

* * *

"And thus," Mel read into the phone, "Barnabus and Nicodemus, formerly Wei-Ping and Wei-Fang, forsook their heathen ways and took their first steps upon the golden path of Christian righteousness."

There was a strangled gulp from the other end of the line, Roxana's end, and also signs of restiveness from the lengthening queue behind her at the library phone.

Kaye's voice said, "When you started reading I switched the office phone to conference mode. You've got a mini-audience here, including Rube, who made the vomiting noises. Well, thank you for that insight into Charles Alonso Ellis."

"The next story's called 'A Mongolian Daniel,'" Mel said temptingly.

"Spare us. Well, that convincingly proves that Geraldo's ascription of *The Scarlet Rider* to Ellis is wishful thinking—what lousy dialogue, not to mention the flat-as-a-board characterization and bleeding obvious subplot . . ."

"That's one of Geraldo's claimants down," Sorrel said, from the background.

A hand tapped her on the shoulder. "Will you be much longer?"

"Don't hassle me," Mel hissed, "or I'll read 'A Mongolian Daniel,' *very slowly!*"

"Leaving Horace Polk-Smith," Kaye mused. "Unlikely, I should think. Did you read his editorials in the *Tolletown Chronicle?* Typically Victorian. Would never use one simple word when two or three flowery ones could be fitted in. Calls a spade an agricultural implement."

Now it was Mel's turn to make strangled noises. At the mention of the newspaper, she had glanced down at her feet, to find the expected bulk of *The Scarlet Rider* missing.

"Excuse me," Mel said to Kaye, "other people want to make their calls."

"Thank gawd," said a voice from the queue.

She slammed the phone down and went running through the reference center, pausing only to drop *Sabbath Thoughts* in front of the Androgyne, who was in position at the walnut desk, monarch of all he/she surveyed. The satchel containing *The Scarlet Rider* was too large to be allowed in the library: she must surely have stowed it in the locker room. The problem was that she had no memory of carrying the novel under the Shakespeare pediment that morning, nor of when she had last seen it. She felt in her sage-green pocket and found one of Edie's handkerchiefs, but no locker key.

Shaking her head, Mel wandered out to the portico, which was deserted, except for the usual clutch of diehard smokers found outside a public building. There were two statues at either end of the space, Victoria and, inevitably, Albert. Mel walked between them, like an intermediary in a tiff—surely the royal couple must have had them—trying to remember.

She marched up to Victoria, thinking of *The Scarlet Rider*, in its folder, heavy as a baby under her arm. There was a pigeon perched on the Britannic crown. About face, and back to Albert. When had she last felt that weight? Not with Geraldo, and with that Mel gave a mental sigh of relief that she had not left the book with the enemy, in the Fox and Hounds, and quickened her pace.

On the day of the lunch Mel had been carrying something, but what? She thought of herself reflected in the windows of these royals' namesake hotel, and saw the plastic bag from the Op Shop, with her old clothes in it. Hallo, Consorting Prince Albert. About turn again. Try recalling the previous day, Mel thought, and mentally gave a yelp, for she saw herself walking to the restaurant, the satchel just about wrenching her hands off.

She remembered Kaye at the dinner table, the pages of photo-copy piled beside her. After that the fate of the novel was un-clear. Victoria again.

Mel stopped dead and stared upward into the blind stone eyes of the matronly queen. Where did I leave *The Scarlet Rider?* she thought, then realized, from the stares of the smokers, that she had actually spoken the words aloud. Suddenly decisive, Mel strode back into the library, across the black-and-white marble, then across the carpet of the reference center, finally to the bare boards of the corridor housing the library phone booth. The queue had dispersed slightly, but she still had to wait impatiently for about ten minutes to use the phone again. Mel rang Edie first, but she was out. She sighed, clenched her teeth a moment, then dialed the flat.

"Hi. May?"

"Pet," Mayzee said, the syllable long and drawn out, like a snarl. "Where you been?"

Now Mel thought of it, last night Edie *had* suggested she ring home, "to let your flatmates know you're all right."

"Flatmates? You met Marc and May at the funeral."

"Ah, the ones holding your hands. I remember. It was hard to tell which, or perhaps both of them, you loved."

"Marc's my boyfriend, but Mayzee's my best friend," Mel said firmly.

In fact, Mel had suddenly realized, they were her only friends. Edie had raised her silver eyebrows and let the matter drop. In fact she must have dropped it down a deep well, for Mel had completely forgotten her flatmates.

"Pet! Pet! Don't you go sulky on me, May wants to know where you were!"

There was only one way to respond and that was with the truth. "I had an accident."

"Walked into a door?' May's tone was arch.

"No, actually a mirror. I've got a lump like an egg on my forehead."

May was silent a moment, digesting the information. When she spoke again, she sounded slightly mollified. "Oh, poor petal."

"Apologies about not ringing, but I was feeling pretty horrible."

"You might have made an effort. We were worried! Marc doesn't need that sort of hassle, and neither does May."

"Sorry, sorry, sorry!" Mel said, suddenly sick of this line of conversation. "May, could you do me a favor?" And, before she had time to query or prevaricate, Mel blurted out, "Go and look under the double bed in our room."

"What?"

"Please, please. It's important!"

May gave a pity-poor-me sigh and put down the phone. Mel waited, holding her breath.

"Underneath your bed is dust, several dirty socks, and a bag."

"Of old leather?"

"Uh-huh," May said reluctantly.

"Full of paper?"

"As a matter of fact it was."

"Then that's all right," Mel said, the adrenaline-fueled anxiety within her dying down. But she had left a gap in the conversation and finding it, Mayzee pounced.

"Mel, stop putting May off. Where were you?"

"I've got to go," Mel lied. "Other people want to use the phone."

Mel could hear May screeching as she lowered the receiver: "Pet! Pet! What's happening to you? You're not yourself—"

Click, and May's voice was stilled.

No, Mel thought, turning toward the genealogy section

again. I'm not myself, in fact I'm practically Melvina Yuill. Where Mel had left the book was proof of it: in the novel, Miles had found Red Meg's sketchbook, her most precious and dangerous possession, because it concealed the key to her past, underneath her bed. Mel and Marc's double bed was nothing like Red Meg's, "built around gum saplings, once growing in virgin bush, yet even after they had been trimmed as part of the furniture of a dirt-floored tent, still hopefully pushing out round green leaves"—yet still Mel had stowed *The Scarlet Rider* beneath it.

Her feet led her, voluntarily or not, to the carousel. She stretched out one hand, caressing the gills, and their fiche inserts; so much information, childbirth, marriage, suffering, contained on slips of plastic, smaller than an envelope. Mel selected without consciously looking, then headed for the fiche machines. Dot was in the distance, behind a pile of street directories; Mel waved at her. The strip of plastic slipped in the glass tray, so, the light went on, so. A list of names appeared on the screen, a sequence of *Y*s.

At first Mel could not believe the visual evidence, and withdrew the fiche, checking that it was indeed the missing 1855 Birth Index card, Watson to Zander, that had come to her hand as if summoned. Ouija fiche, she thought. She slipped it back into its glass envelope and then glanced at the screen again. Babies Yakonov, Yates, Yowell, moved past her gaze. Last in the sequence of *Y*s was . . . Yuill.

A baby, unnamed but female, had been born to Jeremiah and Melvina Mary Yuill, 2 September 1855, at Sailor's Gully. That name rang a faint, distant bell, and as if a door in her mind had been opened in response, she saw her smaller self, with Sammy, and his ladylove of the time. The old car was stopped at a country crossroad, and they were peering up at a sign. "Home is the sailor, home from the sea," said the ladyfriend, who had a poetical bent. "And the hangman home from the hill, I suppose,"

Sammy had replied. The sign had pointed in one direction to Sailor's Gully and in the other to Hangman's Hill.

They had been driving to, to . . . Spur Rock, once a huge alluvial goldfield, now a picturesque tourist trap, complete with working mines and people in polyester copies of Victorian costume. Sailor's Gully had been maybe ten miles out of the main rush, a satellite settlement in the 1850s, now verging on suburb. It was also midway, on the map, between this city, where Melvina Yuill had disembarked, and Aurealis.

Mel said, loudly and inelegantly, "Gotcha!"

At that, Dot looked up from her pile of directories, grinned, and came over.

"Hi. I've got a birth record for my Yuills, but I don't understand the system. What do these numbers at the beginning of a record mean?"

Dot took Mel's hand, in congratulation, and said, "Only an abstract of the record is indexed, dear. You go to the Births, Deaths and Marriages Registry, a block away, quote that number at them, and get the full record. And find out, if you are lucky, that your great-grandfather died of an overdose of cough mixture. I'm not making that up, it's all there in the old family tree."

Half an hour later, Mel sat on the wide step outside the registry, reading the photoprint in her hands. She had paid double, for quick service, and thus had used up not only Mayzee's advance, but the remainder of the money Roxana had given her for lunch with Geraldo. Almost-but-not-quite broke, she stared at the record. Baby Yuill had not been baptized or named, and the birth had been registered by one James Arthur Smith, miner. His relationship to mother Melvina was not stated.

Where were the parents? Mel wondered. Surely they would have registered their own child? The odd sense of passivity, loss of control, that Mel had felt when she had discovered the lost 1855 fiche returned again. Let your feet do the walking, Mel thought. Standing, she moved forward like a sleepwalker, slowly and then with increasing urgency heading back toward the library. Of course! Mel thought. Spur Rock was a larger settlement than Tolletown, big enough for a daily newspaper, covering not only the main rush, but the whole district. Reproductions of the early issues were sold in the shops, for the *Spur Rock Sentinel* had been preserved, complete, continuing even today in an unbroken run since the 1850s. Depend on it—if the Yuills of Sailor's Gully had been newsworthy at all, they would be mentioned.

But seated at the microfilm reader in the newspaper section, she felt less hopeful: the *Spur Rock Sentinel*'s definition of "news" was wide. Visiting clerics of whatever denomination got column inches, as did parliamentary news, chiefly, Mel noticed, British. It was a different, more leisurely age: the latest information from the Crimean War, brought by fast sailing vessels, was several months out of date, by CNN and satellite standards.

Yet it fascinated her, and she was soon, as she had been doing with the *Tolletown Chronicle*, reading every word, again impressed with the social history thus chronicled and how accurately *The Scarlet Rider* depicted life on the rushes. Little details resonated: a miner, found robbed of his gold; others, luckier, on drunken sprees; and goldfields children running wild, stealing dogs.

Then, as she scanned the Poet's Corner, Mel felt a sudden adrenaline thrill. Her heart beating hard as a quartz crusher, she stared at the verses, first puzzled, then disbelieving as the visceral reaction connected with her conscious mind. She had found gold, a pure nugget, one very familiar to her:

> *My eyes behold a beauteous world*
> *My ear hears naught but merry glee . . .*

The poem was signed M.M.Y., Sailor's Gully.

NINETEEN

The Death Index

In her excitement Mel ran from the library to Roxana, arriving too winded to speak. Frustrated by this inability to communicate, she waved the photocopies of the poem and baby Yuill's birth certificate at Rube wildly. The receptionist stared at her wide-eyed, then put both fingers in her mouth and whistled, summoning the entire office. It was only when Nola produced the first-aid kit that Mel put hand to brow and realized that Edie's beret had slipped half-off. Yesterday's bruise had been exposed, still violet enough to look new.

"No, no," Mel managed to gasp, although by now the heavy cavalry, Sorrel and Kaye, had arrived. Kaye bent down and tilted Mel's head upward with a slim finger under the chin.

"Who did this to you? Geraldo?"

Mel considered saying yes, and thus having the whole Roxana posse storming off in the company van, armed with softball bats. Then she decided honesty was the best policy.

"A mirror did." Or rather, her reflection in it. "We collided."

At this point Mel's brandishing of the photocopies before her employers' eyes had some effect, for Nola focused on one document, and went beady-eyed.

"Lookee, lookee! Mel's clutching proof of the original Melvina, Ms. Yuill, doin' a spot of sprogging."

And Kaye kissed Mel full on the mouth. Is this a come-on? Mel wondered uncomfortably as they disengaged. No, she's demonstrative, I know that already. And besides, she's already got Nola. Or Sorrel. Or both of them.

Again, she wondered what Sammy would have thought.

Much later, Mel emerged from Roxana, still feeling somewhat otherworldly. She had tried to explain to various Roxanas her feeling of being swept along, like a toy duck in a storm-filled gutter, the sense of losing all conscious volition, that had intermittently recurred all day. She had thought that she was getting through to Nola, but at the end of her somewhat confused speech Nola had merely said:

"Delayed shock, mate, from that knock on the head. I'm surprised you're still standing, let alone functioning."

After that, Nola and Kaye had given her strict instructions to take the afternoon off.

"You've earned it," Kaye had said. "And this."

Mel stopped at the foot of the Roxana stairs and inspected, disbelievingly, the envelope in her hand. Nola had finally added up her untidy time sheets, and there had been a cash bonus from Kaye, for being a good investigative reporter. She was clutching over five hundred dollars. For lack of anything else to do with it, she put the envelope into her sage-green pocket and ventured out into the alley.

It was one of those rare days when mood and weather coincided precisely, Mel's dreamy sense of achievement matched by a sunny, almost balmy winter afternoon, not a cloud in the sky, and even the biting winds absent. She wafted down the street, her feet, it seemed, hardly touching the ground. Pedestrians, police horses, traffic, all passed by ethereally.

Then she was suddenly arrested by a shopwindow, a jewelry display. Trays of tiny, exquisite rings caught her gaze, stones glinting from beds of velvet, pearls in long lustrous strings, gold intricately cast, twisted, beaten into leaf shapes, rosettes, even coy little animals with semiprecious eyes.

Words from *The Scarlet Rider* echoed, almost as if spoken, inside her mind:

"I will wear no gold," said Red Meg, "for it is so easily got on these diggings, that were I to mount a nugget on a pin, and wear it as a brooch, it would mean nought, save that I had flattered some miner. Were I to accept even one gift, I could not reject two or three, and soon I would be so laden down with gold that I would not be able to conduct my business for the sheer weight of it. Who would fardels bear, indeed! Yet, gold wrought in beautiful forms is a weakness of mine, and in the old country I could not pass a jeweller's window without dawdling."

Aynsley had put down his glass, and now he spoke to the woman, softly, but with an intensity.

"Is there no golden gift that you would accept?"

She glanced down at her hands before answering.

"Ay, there is one gold thing I would wear gladly, plain though it would be."

What *Mel* wanted was not a plain gold band. Although she had been living with Marc for years, she had never really yearned for the bride-price of engagement and wedding rings, nor indeed for any jewelry in particular. Yet as she stared in the window, she found herself mourning Gran Kirksley's jewels, which had been sold to pay private-school fees—for Sammy, but not the two girls. She had never seen the ornate tiny art-

works that had adorned the Kirksley ancestresses—and Red
Meg/Melvina Yuill too?

Suddenly she was hooked, as if the barb for insertion into a
pierced ear struck, even through the security glass, into her
flesh. Never before had Mel possessed the least desire for a pair
of Victorian earrings. These, though, were exquisite—dangling
teardrops decorated with intricate designs in gold wire, center-
ing on two tiny flowers, their centers seed pearls, the petals
made from flakes of turquoise. The glittering bait drew her inside the shop.

Mel asked to see the earrings, held the chill gold in her
hands and felt it warm from the contact, even removed the
copper-hoop keepers Marc had bought her years ago at a hippie market, and inserted, in their place, these miniature mas-
terpieces. They hung heavy from her lobes; as she moved her
head the gold kissed her neck. Mel knew she had to own them,
though they cost nearly all of her pay.

That was the high point of the afternoon; from then on it could
only be downhill, with Mel's mood darkening as she headed
back to the flat. After all that time away, she felt like an alien,
and looked it too, for previously the mirror by the barber's shop
had reflected a gawky, ill-dressed girl, with a downtrodden expression on her face. Now it showed an elegant stranger.

Trudging up to the flat, Mel felt increasing trepidation,
which was confirmed by the view, as she unlocked the door and
entered, of Mayzee's grim yellow face. Her friend had a heap
of papers, and a calculator, in her lap. She looked up unsmilingly, focusing on Mel's getup.

"Where did you dig that up from?"

"Op Shop. Where else?"

"You look like an antique."

"You think so?" and Mel pirouetted, as if the remark had been complimentary.

"Marc'll hate it," May said flatly. "You'll see."

Mel stopped in midswirl. Marc doesn't have to agree with you all the time, she thought, he's got a mind of his own. Or has he? a little nagging voice said.

"Since you've deigned to come home, petal, you can spill your guts and tell May where you were last night."

"At my aunt's. The woman you call Seedy Edie."

Mayzee looked distressed.

"Mel, aren't we the Happy Orphans' Club, sufficient unto ourselves?"

Mel came and kneeled down by the chair, the long folds of her skirt spreading across the carpet like a green wave.

"Oh May, we are." Lie, she thought, lie convincingly. "But I had a knock on the head, I could hardly think straight."

She pushed back the beret, revealing the bruise. But Mayzee was staring down at the papers in her lap again.

"Rent's due. Also, gas, telephone, and electricity bills. You owe me moolah. Cough up, pet."

"Oh, that's easily done, I just got paid. . . ."

Then Mel froze, feeling the weight of the gold. Just at that moment, Mayzee looked up, suddenly seeing, not only the bruise, but the antique earrings.

"Where did you—"

"Dig those up from? That's what you were going to say, wasn't it? They're Victorian. I bought them this afternoon, with my Roxana money. And that's why I can't pay you, just now."

May struck Mel with the flat of her hand, full in the face. Moving quickly, automatically, Mel scrambled to her feet and out of May's bony reach, hands to her face, ready to ward off another slap. Tears had started to her eyes, and when she withdrew her hands, she found one palm red: May had set her nose bleeding again.

"You bitch!" Mel said nasally, trying to stem the trickle from staining her dress.

"You asked for it, for being rude, and pushing, and playing meanie tricks on May . . ."

She continued, but Mel ignored the list of grievances. Her forehead ached appallingly: the blow had landed on the bruise, whether intentionally or not, she didn't know. Without turning her back, she walked crabwise to her room, seeking the bedside box of tissues. Clutching a big wad of the soft paper to her nose, she reached under the bed, and withdrew the precious satchel containing *The Scarlet Rider*. From now on, she thought, mentally addressing the novel, you go and live at Edie's, where you'll be safe!

As she straightened, clutching her bundle, there was a screech from the living room: "Pet, Pet! Don't you dare leave! May's still talking to you!"

With as much dignity as Mel could muster, she returned to Mayzee, not at her bidding, but because the living room was the only exit from the flat.

"Yes, May, but I'm not talking to *you*."

And she left, clumping down the concrete stairs, to the shrill accompaniment of May, who had followed her out to the landing:

"Have you forgotten that stress is a big no-no? You'll be the death of May, you will. . . ."

Outside in the street, a tram was lumbering up to the stop; Mel ran for it, and soon was seated in the comforting warmth, thankful for this quick getaway, in the physical sense. Mentally, though, Mayzee's parting shot was still very much with her. "The death of me" was a line Mel hadn't heard for some time; it meant, she realized now, that May wasn't getting her way, so was using her medical condition as the ultimate argument.

"The death of me," Mel repeated to herself, then felt a sudden chill. The phrase was used in *The Scarlet Rider*. She bent down for the satchel, and hoisted it into her lap, aware she was getting curious glances from the other passengers. With one hand she held the tissue to her face; with the other she hastily pulled her beret over the bruise again, before searching frantically through the pages of photocopy.

Was this it?

It was a letter from my sweet Arabella, back in England, each line beloved to me, even when detailing the smallest headache or listlessness of her dear Mamma, whose mysterious illness, baffling to the most eminent specialists, seemed ever to recur at the slightest deviation from maternal rule. I have often observed how effectively dominion is exercised from the sickbed, with the Damocles Sword of imminent death a sure means of ensuring the most abject devotion, and in this case it stood in the way of my darling's passage to Australia. Unchristian though it may be, I had often hoped that the invalid's fears might for once be well-founded, so that I might receive a black-bordered letter from Arabella, announcing her imminent departure for these shores, and ultimately, my welcoming arms.

Melvina, if speaking through the persona of Miles, certainly disliked manipulative invalids. Mel wondered what she'd make of May. Then she put the comparison between living and fictional character out of mind, as she continued her search. Was this the passage?

"There are queer stories about the woman," said Ned. "She was married, for she calls herself a widow, but any allusion to her husband makes her eyes blaze and her fingers clench."

"What are the stories?" I asked, my mental notebook ready for any information I could pass to Justperson.

"Idle tattle, mostly, though young Emma tells a tale of picking wildflowers in the bush one fine day and stumbling across Meg weeping bitterly over a curl of baby's hair."

No, further on, near the end of the novel.

We rode silently through the bush for some time, my poor police "screw" scarcely keeping pace with the mare Vino, as I waited for Meg, who I now knew to be the wife of Firefly the Bushranger, alias Arthur Dalvean, to continue her confession. At last rain began to fall from the lowering sky, and as if that was a signal to her she spoke again, her voice scarcely louder than the sound of the drops striking the hard, auriferous earth.

"I could not stay with such a man; and he freely admitted he was tired of married life. Thus we made a pact, over the cradle of our sleeping babe, that he would make no claim on me again, and I would tell no one living about the robbery of the gold escort. Arthur knew I would keep my word, for how could I hang the father of my little child?

"We parted, but three months after my husband left my life, the baby died, and I was all alone. I thought that would be the death of me too, and so it was, in part, for when I arose from my bed of grief I was no longer Margaret Dalvean, the sweet innocent helpmeet, but that hard businesswoman, Red Meg, resolved never to feel for anyone again. Ah woe is me, that ever I laid eyes upon Aynsley, for he broke my resolution, and has broken my heart as well!"

Mel put the novel away, thinking very hard. Red Meg had a baby; so did Melvina Yuill. Did the parallels between writer and heroine go further, with the death of the child autobiographical? That scene has the grim ring of truth about it. She wrapped her arms around the satchel protectively, so agitated that it was a miracle her nose ever stopped bleeding. When she looked up, she saw she had reached the city center, all its golden afternoon glory gone as sunset neared. The tram stopped in front of the library and she disembarked, unable to stop her search for the truth.

Please no, Mel thought, as she thrust *The Scarlet Rider* into a library locker. I don't want Melvina Yuill to lose her baby! The desire was largely selfish, she knew: without this child there could be no genetic link between her and Melvina, for no other baby Yuill was listed in the fiche index.

But when Mel scanned the death records, on microfiche color-coded not with the Victorian mourning shades of purple and black, but shrieking yellow, there was no doubt about it. The Yuill baby had died, at Spur Rock, less than a month after her birth. Mel jotted down the index number, aware that the registry had closed, and thus she would have to wait till tomorrow for the full biographical record.

Outside, in the portico, she leaned her head against Victoria's stone skirt and cried.

Revulsion

After that, Mel didn't want to talk to Roxana, to confess that Sorrel had been right, all along: she had been projecting herself into the shadowy void of a lost author, seeing her as a mirror image, even imagining Melvina as an ancestress. Mel didn't seek solace with Edie either, for aunt was almost as involved in the search as was niece. That left only one alternative where the subject of Melvina Yuill would not be raised, and so she went back to the flat, to face the Marc-and-Mayzee music.

When Mel unlocked the door, both flatmates were seated in front of the television, with a tin of sardines and a biscuit packet on the floor between them; it was obviously Mayzee's turn to cater. They turned, initially hostile, but the sight of her woebegone face was disarming.

Marc leapt up, solicitous, and when Mel unhooked the duffel, took it from her, even lifted the beret from her head. At the sight of the bruise he drew his breath in sharply.

"May, you never said Mel-baby's bruise was concussion-size. No wonder she was acting strange."

He put his arm around Mel, walking her across the room.

"Even before the bruise she was acting nutso," Mayzee said sharply. She rose, and as she neared, it was all Mel could do not to flinch away. One of May's thin fingers touched Mel's cheek, and a tinge of pity sounded in her voice.

"Poor petsy's sorry enough now. But really, Marc! Spending all her moolah on earrings!"

"Never mind that now," he said. "I'll put her to bed."

All this time, they had been talking as if Mel were merely an object, a doll in a game between two children. She could have spoken, contradicted them, but she felt utterly drained, without the energy to open her mouth. Marc led her into the bedroom, helped her undress, even brought a cup of herbal tea. As Mel sipped it, he reached forward, to take the earrings from her lobes.

"No," she said, speaking for the first time. "Leave them. I'll do it."

He looked slightly hurt.

Mel said, "Thanks Marc, but all I really want to do is sleep."

"Okay, okay. I won't disturb you."

He kept his word, for when he went to bed, he did not wake her; that came later, about four in the morning. Mel had been dreaming again, confusedly, of Sammy at the Sailor's Gully/Hangman's Hill junction, which was followed by the sudden impression of staring out at a sunny landscape through a barred window. But then the dream was lost, for she jerked wide awake, to find that Marc had rolled over, almost on top of her.

She clenched her fists rather than strike them into that sleeping face. These dreams, with their introductions, always featuring Sammy, as if he was her personal gatekeeper into the world beyond, were worth their weight in golden nuggets to the Melvina research. But the temptation to violence grew stronger as she lay beside Marc and finally she slipped out to the living room, where she stretched out on the couch, with her coat for bedding again.

Sleep Mel craved, to continue the dream, but all she could do was think, mostly about Mayzee. It was like picking at a raw spot of resentment, so instead she pondered the dream, as if recalling each hazy detail would restore the message in full. But it didn't work—all she had was Sammy, and the image of staring through bars.

Maybe she did prison visiting, Mel thought wishfully. Yet that's not right, for the viewpoint looked out, at light, rather than into the darkness of a cell. At the same time she recalled the earlier dream, the dolls in the courthouse shouting *Guilty, guilty!* at a woman in a bonnet and shawl. Put together with the vision of the barred window, that meant something, she decided.

Mel rolled over and closed her eyes. Look in the *Spur Rock Sentinel*, she decided. First thing tomorrow.

What Mel found, as she scrolled the newspaper's issues for late 1855 across the screen, was an inquest. The beginning of the report was missing, for the paper had been damaged at this point, but what followed was all too clear:

Eliza Smith deposed—I am the wife of James Smith, living at Sailor's Gully. The accused I have known about three months, since I came to this diggings. Her husband and mine were mates in a claim together, but bad luck on the goldfields had made Jerry Yuill a drunkard. He would be bad-tempered in his cups, quarrelling with anyone who crossed his path at such times. My husband remonstrated with him, vowed that he would find some other mate, but Jerry knocked him down. While his wife silently wept, and I attended to the poor un-

conscious body of my man, Jerry took what little gold we had, and fled. Nobody on the rush has seen him since.

When it became clear that Jerry would not return, his sad deserted wife took sick. I was her nurse, for she had nobody else to help her, and Doctor Curlewis delivered her of a baby daughter. She recovered her health, but her wits were astray. Sometimes she would deny the baby was hers, other times that it was merely a wax doll. The little thing was so still and wan, sometimes it looked waxen even to my eyes. Though she was not unkind to the infant, she was careless of it. Once I came out of the tent and found the tiny creature lying on the bare earth, with a dog sniffing at its wraps. I snatched the baby away in time, before any mischief was done. The accused was away wandering in the bush at the time. It did no good to upbraid her, she was like a little child.

Mel wondered at the court reporter, and the accuracy of his transcription. Would Eliza Smith, who seemed plain-speaking and down-to-earth, have referred to the woman she had nursed as "the accused"? Were questions put to her, and then omitted from the printed account, as her somewhat staccato speech indicated?

My husband would not take another mate, after Jerry Yuill, so to keep the claim I had to tuck up my petticoats and work like a man. I could not give all my attention to the accused as well, so I asked for help from the few women who were our neighbours. They were busy cradling gold or cradling babies, or so they said, but I believe they feared contagion from a poor woman wandering in her wits. I took to bringing the accused to the claim with us, but soon as my back was turned she would wander off.

Yesterday, the 21 inst. . . .

Mel's suspicions were confirmed. Eliza Smith would not have used such legalistic language.

Yesterday, the 21 inst., about half past one, a boy came to the claim and said he had seen the accused carrying the baby into the bush. A storm was brewing, and covered all in dirt as I was, I went round to the miners. I said: "You will stop your grubbing for gold and help me, for the love of Christ. She has taken the child into the wilderness, the poor mad thing, and it will be on your conscience if you do not come and search for her." They were ashamed, and downed their tools just as the storm broke. We searched until about four, through the wind and the rain, and at last Sam Orenshaw called out that he had found the lady. The accused was sheltering in the lee of a quartz outcrop, clutching a bunch of wildflowers. I ran up to her, crying: "What have you done with dolly?" She replied: "I would not leave a wax doll in the sun to melt, so I put her down in the shade, with a flower in her little cap, but I cannot remember where."

Sam Orenshaw deposed next, but added little to this fearful account. The next witness was a Cornish miner, speaking through an interpreter:

I am John Tregowan. I do not know the accused, but have seen her carrying her baby around the diggings. On the 21st inst., a countryman of mine came to the claim, and said: "Come join a search party, for the madwoman has taken her baby into the bush and will surely murder it." Around twilight, I was ready to give up when through the shadows I thought I saw a white duck amongst the native grass. It was the child, soaked through and ice cold to the touch. When I picked it up it moved feebly, so I knew that it was still alive.

Dr. Curlewis was the last witness:

I am Simeon Curlewis, doctor of medicine from Glasgow University. I attended the accused's confinement, delivering her of a perfectly formed, though premature girl. It is not uncommon for the pains of childbirth to affect a female's wits adversely. In some cases the presence of the little one brings them to their senses, in others not. Therefore, my action was to give the accused a few weeks' grace before committing her. She did not show hostility towards the child on the several occasions I examined her, indeed her delusion inclined her to cherish the "doll."

On the 21st inst., I was busy with a case of fever, and could not

join the search. I had just returned to my tent when a crowd of min-
ers burst in on me, carrying the child wrapped in a Crimean shirt. I
did what I could, but life was extinct before morning. An infant with
a stout constitution might have survived the wetting, but the Yuill babe
was sickly. There is no evidence the child was maltreated, death was
as a result of being exposed to foul weather.

Another tear in the paper.

During the course of this evidence, the accused sat still, as perfectly
composed as if in church, but wearing a bonnet fantastically orna-
mented with wildflowers and ribbons.

At that detail, tears suddenly blurred Mel's view. Wiping her
eyes, she removed the microfilm, and took it to the copier.
When the sheets of paper crept from the machine, Mel lifted
them out, reading as she did, and for the first time got to the
end of the inquest. The verdict was death due to willful neglect,
and the accused—"Melvina Yuill"—was committed to the Spur
Rock Asylum.

Mel spent the rest of that morning in the medical section of the
library, tracing the sad history of postpartum psychosis, not
named as such by the Victorians, though they knew enough of
the condition to distinguish a baby's death in such circumstances from the all-too-common infanticides. One could be a
hanging offense; the other, as she had seen, meant relegation
to the madhouse. A nineteenth-century asylum was hardly an
environment in which a woman would spontaneously recover
from postnatal mental illness; yet the *Index Medicus* testified
that such cases occurred. How else could Mrs. Yuill have been
free, in Tolletown, by 1865?

Mel sat in the library tearooms, eyeing the photocopies and
notes. All she felt was revulsion. I didn't want to know this, she
thought. The novelist she had admired, identified with closely;
but not a mother who exposed her own baby.

If Mel felt this way, what had Darcy Ainsworth thought, a man from a society that created impossible, unbridgeable dichotomies between good and bad women? The fictional Aynsley's reaction was plain enough:

Even after changing horses at Peg-leg Gully, to the great amazement of Surtees and Blanc, and probably their resentment as well, for they could not gainsay Inspector Justperson, we were quite unable to gain ground on the eloping pair. It was several hours before we clattered into the prosperous mining town of K - , well known in the district for having a parson who took his fee without questioning the couples he married. Justperson stopped just once, to ask of a passing miner the whereabouts of the church, and hearing it was close by, spurred his horse furiously onwards.

"Make haste, Constable!" he shouted over his shoulder to me. "For I fear we may be too late to prevent this travesty of a marriage."

Ahead was the little timber church, and tied to the sliprail outside Vino, and Aynsley's bay horse, easily distinguishable by its police brand. We added our own nags to this equine congregation, then, not even pausing to brush the dust of our travels from our uniforms, went into the church.

Justperson reached the heavy wooden door first, and flung it open, to reveal, at the other end of the church, standing before the altar, a parson in his robes, and before him, our miscreant couple. Seated to one side were two men, by their garb tradespeople of this town: the witnesses.

"I require and charge ye both, as ye will answer at the dreadful day of judgement, when the secrets of all hearts shall be disclosed, that if either of ye know of any impediment why ye may not be lawfully joined together in matrimony, ye do now confess it," droned the parson. He was plainly not expecting a response; yet he got one.

"Stop!" shouted Justperson, and taking off his dusty white gloves, he strode down the aisle towards Aynsley. I followed in his footsteps. The parson looked nervous at this interruption, the witnesses concerned, Aynsley angry, and as for the bride, I could tell nothing of her

feelings, for she wore a white satin wedding bonnet, the veil decorously concealing her face.

Aynsley opened his mouth to speak, but Justperson gave him no chance, immediately declaiming the story of the detection: of how I had discovered Meg's sketches of a now extinct goldfield; my travels there; the search, from rush to rush, for the individuals who knew Margaret Dalvean's history; and finally, the slow accumulation of evidence before Justperson, leading to our precipitate arrival at Cornish Flat, only to find the lovebirds had flown.

"Thus, Aynsley," concluded Justperson, "the woman who has bewitched you into marriage, which we thankfully arrived just in time to prevent, is not only a common tavern-keeper, but a known associate of a bushranger, one with the blood of several mounted constables on his conscience! She was his wife, Aynsley, and indeed may still be, for though Arthur Dalvean, alias Firefly, was sorely wounded at the hold-up at Whispering Flat, no one saw him dead. We have not only saved you from a degraded union, but from possible bigamy as well!"

During this speech, the witnesses had quietly excused themselves from the church, and though the parson remained, his agitated mien indicated that he very much wished that he, too, were absent. The woman had sunk down, as if her legs could no longer support her, onto one of the rough-hewn benches that served as pews; she sat, her head and shoulders drooping. Aynsley had stayed standing, but the blood had gradually drained from his face, until he was as ashen as a corpse.

Justperson ceased, and watched Aynsley eagerly, but no answer was forthcoming. Instead, the young constable tossed down his police cap, and turning away from the woman, spake these words:

"I thank you, Inspector, for your detection, and thank you not!"

He marched down the aisle to the open door, stood for a moment silhouetted, then shut the heavy door behind him. Justperson turned red as a cassowary, and went running after Aynsley, completely forgetting his dignity. The door closed a second time, and there was silence inside the church, save for a faint rustling, of cloth against cloth. I turned and saw the woman, in the act of untying the satin ribbons

under her chin to remove her wedding bonnet. Her face, when re-
vealed, had such an expression of dejection upon it, that I could not but
pity her. She set the bonnet neatly beside her on the bench, and stood.

"Parson, a gift for some poor girl of the parish, hard pressed to
buy wedding finery."

She faced me, her eyes dark and imploring.

"Miles, I see from your face that you alone have not judged and
condemned me as a wicked woman, without allowing me a word in
my defence. Perhaps, then, you will grant me the favour of escorting
me back to Cornish Flat. I have The Golden Banner to attend to, for
nothing else is left me now."

TWENTY-ONE

A Rival Researcher

Mel sat at the Appleby kitchen table with Edie, watching her aunt read through the pages of photocopy. Whatever Edie thought of this strange twist of events, Melvina Yuill the murderess, even though temporarily insane, it didn't show on her face. Edie would have made a perfect straight woman, Mel thought irritably, and without further ado, dived into conversation.

"Well, what do you make of it?"

"It's so terribly sad. Postpartum psychosis always is." Edie blinked and Mel realized that she, too, had been brought close to tears, though not outright bawling, by this antique tragedy.

"It doesn't fit with the image in *The Scarlet Rider*," Mel said after a moment.

"You thought she'd be tough. Maybe that came later."

There was a long pause; then Edie said briskly, "Well, it's

wonderful material, and you should be happy to have discovered it."

"I'm not. In fact I'm angry. With Melvina."

"Did you expect her to be perfect?"

"Like a Dickensian heroine? No. But I felt . . . that she was like me. It went beyond us having the same Christian name. I was drawing her in my own image. And then I found that she was different, disgustingly different. I—I can't identify with a baby-killer!"

Thump. That was her fist striking the table. Mel lifted her hand, stared at it in surprise, then stowed it for safekeeping in her armpit.

"Mel," Edie said. "Mel dear. You're holding something back and it's making you more and more upset. I think you should speak it."

Now Mel was hugging herself, head bowed. "I disinherited myself, that's what. Remember I asked who named me? I got it into my head 'Melvina' was from Myrie's side of the family, that I might have been descended from Ms. Yuill. It did seem too much of a coincidence."

Edie sighed. "Mel, if only you'd asked a bit more . . . You see, I don't think Myrie knew much about her family names. She grew up in an orphanage, Alice said. I wish Alice's memory hadn't disintegrated, because she could tell you so much more than I could! Being overseas at the time I only knew Myrie secondhand, through Alice's letters: how happy Myrie was to be having a baby; how she had found a name both she and Sammy liked in an old book of poetry; how Mother would have been rolling in her grave."

Mel raised one eyebrow, then regretted it—it was the brow beneath the bruise.

"Mother spent her whole life grooming Sammy for a good marriage to restore the family fortunes. He reacted by developing a taste for women quite unmarriageable, from Mother's viewpoint—not debutantes, nor moneyed, nor even middle-class. Even after Mother had gone aloft, Sammy kept picking women for their shock value."

Mel thought of Nola, with her blunt, earthy speech, and then of the photos of prim Gran Kirksley in the family album. The contrast made her lips twitch, then stretch into a smile. Edie smiled also, but with a tinge of sadness. She seemed to be about to add something, but then the phone rang. Mel wandered out to the hall and lifted the receiver.

"Hallo."

"Are you Mel Kirksley?"

"That's me."

"I'm Charlie Mowbray."

Mel said, "Rival research."

"Come on," said the drawling male voice at the other end of the line. "I let Mick show you the photo of Ol' Rectitude, didn't I?"

"Is that what you call Jesperson?" Mel laughed. "It fits."

"I'm glad we agree on that," he said. "Perhaps we can agree on something else. Drinks?"

Mel had thought he was going to suggest another lunch, with what dire potential she could only guess. Relief that he hadn't caused her to actually accept.

"Good," he said. "This afternoon, two o'clock, at the Old Colonial Club. Take down these directions, because it's hidden away."

After Mel had the instructions, Charlie rang off, and she returned to the kitchen. Edie looked up quizzically.

"That was more to do with Melvina Yuill." Her voice caught at the back of her throat, and with an effort she controlled it. "I don't identify with her anymore. In fact I almost hate Melvina the child-killer. But I can't seem to get away from her."

"Do you really want to?"

"I suppose not."

Images of a Melvina-less life came to mind: no Roxana, Kaye, and Nola, for starters. And if Mel hadn't contacted Edie at the beginning of this research, there would have been no visits to Appleby either. Her life would have comprised: the flat; Mayzee, her heaps of paperback books; sardines and dry biscuits; Marc, her lover Marc . . .

It just wasn't enough anymore. Like it or not, Mel couldn't disengage from Melvina Mary.

Stocky. Shortarse. Stud earrings. Hair like JFK. So Mick had described Charlie Mowbray, but as he uncurled himself from the studded leather armchair Mel noticed other details. He moved like a cat, with a grace that seemed partly natural, partly studied. There was study, also, if not calculation, in his dressing, for he had offset an elegant European double-breasted suit with a lurid green tie decorated with geishas. A clash like that had to be premeditated.

His hand was cool and dry. "Welcome," he said. "Welcome to the Old Colonial Club. Do sit down."

Mel did, observing that all around them, well-heeled, mainly middle-aged men and women were drinking and chatting, in an ambience of old gentility.

"What is this place?" Mel murmured.

"Haven to the secret masters of this state, the people whose ancestors gobbled up the best land and resources before the gold-rush riffraff got here."

He gave a flicker of a smile.

"The service is good here, as is the food. But I really come here for the ceiling."

His chin pointed upward, and Mel saw, painted above their heads, orientalia in riotous colors, minarets and marketplaces, men in turbans, veiled women, sheepish-looking camels, genii, oil lamps, forty clay jars, all observed in a painstaking style halfway between high Victoriana and the Pre-Raphaelites.

"It's the Arabian nights," Mel breathed. "So beautiful."

Charlie drooped his eyelids slightly and Mel realized some further response was expected. She glanced upward again and this time noticed that the eyes of the women visible above their colored veils all had the same expression, lascivious and demonic. Once that jarring feature was noted, other images obtruded: the grin on Ali Baba's face as he poured hot oil over a potted thief; a cat, toying with a wounded mouse; and, central to the composition, the Old Man of the Sea, teeth bared, turban blowing wildly, half strangling Sinbad.

"And sinister," Mel added. "Especially the women."

Charlie gave a slight nod.

"Jubilee Goodman was the artist. I've written a book about him. A fascinating subject—most nineteenth-century males had odd ideas about women, but Goodman . . .! Consider his mother, immortalized in this ceiling."

That was a challenge. Mel glanced upward again, but all the images of women were young and lissome, not matronly at all. Then she noticed the painted eyes of the Old Man of the Sea, seeing them also full of sensual evil. Suddenly her perception of the figure changed, as she realized its true gender: what had seemed to be a turban, unwinding in the sea wind, was in fact ragged white hair, above unmistakable wrinkled dugs.

"The Old Woman of the Sea," Mel said.

Charlie nodded again. "Goodman's *Arabian Nights* is a minor classic, both as Victorian kitsch, and for its subtext of weird eroticism."

"It *is* classic," Mel said, aware now that Charlie was setting, if not traps, then a series of tests for her. Let's try the direct approach, she thought, and see what happens. "But I get the feeling you are not being simply conversational. Does Goodman relate to our mutual research interest, Ol' Rectitude?"

He looked at her over steepled hands.

"They had something in common?" she asked.

His gaze went up again, not in exasperation, but inviting her to inspect the ceiling again. Mel noticed this time the lovingly observed depictions of the half-naked, brown young men, and had the answer.

"Jesperson was a misogynist, like Goodman. And my research shows he could get rather overattached to pretty young policemen. Are you suggesting . . . ?"

Playing Charlie's game now, Mel looked at him quizzically.

"Almost textbook repressed homosexual. Freud would have adored him—as a case study, of course."

"If you say so."

Charlie must possess, Mel thought, a document which reveals far more of Jesperson than Melvina's poisonous, but probably fully deserved, portrait. And he won't produce it unless I prove myself. We are bargaining here, with information. He made the first move, with the photograph. Now I should respond and see what he does in return.

As an immaculate waiter took their orders for drinks, Mel told of Roxana, the newspaper serial, and, finally, the revealed Melvina Mary Yuill. It was a long narrative—the drinks arrived, scotch and soda for Charlie, white wine for Mel, and were almost finished by the time she finished. They ordered refills for Charlie's side of the story.

"I congratulate you," he said, "on your sleuthing. How fascinating to find an author whose life is an open book. My tale is less in the detective genre, more of a character study, the hero not talented, like Ms. Yuill or Jubilee Goodman, nor even particularly interesting. But Pluckrose had a hobby that makes social historians thank God for his existence. Even the atheists."

"Pluckrose?"

"Henry Pluckrose, 1840 to 1905, Anglican clergyman."

"Like Dean Orlando Burnett?" Mel said, thinking of the dusty theological books stored in the library roof. She was not entirely surprised that Charlie knew the name.

"No, a smaller fry, although both were collectors. Pluckrose was born in India, where cholera wiped out his entire family, only little Henry surviving. He was packed off to relatives in Australia, attended school and university, took holy orders. I think his adult life was happy. His career path, mostly spent working as a chaplain in places where he came into contact with the moribund, prisons or sanatoria for the tubercular rich (which was where he met Jubilee), precisely coincided with his interests. Even as a student he made rubbings of funerary inscriptions and amassed mourning jewelry in quantities excessive even for an age as pathologically morbid as the Victorian."

"Was he good-looking?" Mel asked.

Charlie again drooped an eyelid.

"The only photos of Henry are from middle age, when he was portly and balding. But his bone structure was good."

"Yes," Mel said. "Otherwise Ol' Rectitude would never have been friendly with him. And Pluckrose collected something of Jesperson's, didn't he?"

A slight nod. "He collected lives. It was a method he developed in his ministry, a means of psychologically preparing his subjects for 'the great translation,' as he put it. He asked them for their histories, written by themselves if they were literate and still able to hold a pen, or taking dictation otherwise. These biographies he had bound, in booklets, hundreds of lives lining his study. He had the idea of writing a monumental religious tome, documenting how 'the individual soul struggles towards God,' as he says in one of his marginalia. But he never quite got round to it, being a collector rather than a creator."

He paused, and finished drinking the whisky from its cut-crystal glass.

"I think of Henry as a conduit, something through which water, whether clean or polluted, flowed, he directing it into the reservoir of the written word, without attempting to purify it first. He had too much respect for 'souls in proximity to their dread Maker,' as he called them, to interfere with these personal histories. Thus he collected the bloody confessions of scaffold-bound bushrangers, and the immaculate records of tubercular virgins, with complete editorial impartiality. In his biographies you hear a myriad of voices, not the slightly disguised tones of an Anglican clergyman. The first ever voice was Jesperson's."

"When did they meet?" Mel asked.

"On Pluckrose's twenty-fifth birthday. He was a curate then, in a country town near the South Australian border, and one day he paused in the street to watch the district superintendent of police gallop by. The next moment he was picking Jesperson out of the dust. It was a breezy day, and the wind had flipped the frilly bonnet from the head of a small child, and blown it into the path of the police horse, who shied violently. Jesperson never walked again."

"Spinal injuries?"

Again the slight nod. "The superintendent took a year to die, watched over devotedly by Curate Pluckrose. I think they were happy, Pluckrose because he adored dying people, Jesperson, despite his pain, because he had an attractive young man so friendly with him. Jesperson was so warped that his complete inability to respond sexually to Pluckrose suited him just fine. He actually addresses Pluckrose as 'purest and dearest of men.' It was accurate: Pluckrose was a total innocent. I doubt he re-alized the subtext of Jesperson's life—the search for the perfect young man—at all."

"So it's a catalog of crushes, what Jesperson writes?"

"In the purplest of prose. It gives me the giggles."

"Where is it?" Mel said, obviously too eagerly, for he gave her a long, cool, admonitory look.

"Ah, therein lies a tale. The middle-aged Pluckrose attended the sickbed of a young but wealthy widow, and, as was his habit, had a splendid platonic relationship with her, bringing flowers and reading aloud from his favorite book of sentimental prayers. The widow enjoyed herself so much she recovered, and much to Henry's surprise, he found himself still attracted to her, even though she was healthy and hell-bent on matrimony. She plucked his rose, inevitably. After they married he collected no more biographies, his squirreling urge apparently satisfied by sex. He must have been a nice husband, for after his death Mrs. Pluckrose cherished the roomful of booklets. She lived to a great age and in her will bequeathed the collection, and her own carefully invested fortune, to the National Library. It was only when the booklets were being belatedly cataloged that it was realized what a gold mine they were. Eyewitness accounts of Aboriginal massacres. Bushrangers in their own colorful words. Even the confessions of an octogenarian former 'colonial woman'—that's Tasmanian slang for a gay male convict. Pluckrose missed the point of that one, too. Such a sweet idiot of a recording angel."

"You've given enough information," Mel said cautiously, "for me to locate the Jesperson memoirs. Does that mean I should respond in kind?"

"Not really. Jesperson is incidental to my study; indeed the only interest he had for me was that Pluckrose classified him and Jubilee together, recognizing the mother-complex, if nothing else. I can wait until Roxana publishes *The Scarlet Rider*. By the way, do you like my tie?"

Puzzled, Mel bent forward, as he flipped the green geishas forward, showing the reverse, so that she could see, for the first time, just what the figures were doing. If the ceiling was implicitly pornographic, then the tie was explicit. Mel laughed.

"And that's something I'd show to very few people, particularly in the Old Colonial Club," Charlie said, flicking the tie back into place. "You're all right."

He drew, from beside the chair, a manila envelope.

"Here's Jesperson's confession, the parts relevant to your study. Best wishes for the edition."

He stood up, straightening his suit.

"I must fly, literally, back to Sydney. No, don't gulp down your drink—you can stay as long as you like, any guest of mine is okay with the management. Oh, before I forget. You mentioned Geraldo Abernathy, and his plans for a rival edition. I didn't want to interrupt your flow then, but I was a student with Geraldo, before I specialized in art history. A word of advice. If he asks you to lunch at the Fox and Hounds, decline. Otherwise next day he'll be telling the lads in the front bar how you rate sexually."

"Thanks," Mel said. "I really wanted to know that."

TWENTY-TWO

Jesperson's Story

The photocopied handwriting before Mel was spidery and shaky, but still recognizably that of the man who had proudly inscribed the photograph to Darcy Ainsworth:

Debarred as I am from most of the inviting though alas imaginary sources of happiness, it is a vast consolation to reflect that the true panacea for all earthly ills lies within my grasp, viz, contemplation of the life to come, to which my thoughts have been so kindly and strongly directed in recent months. I may go further and add that the position in which I am placed, my isolation from the turmoil and fierce struggle of existence, is singularly favourable for a reflection upon the events of my life, as has been urged upon me by my beloved friend, the purest and dearest of men.

Mel groaned inwardly. She had thought the ponderous utterances of Inspector Justperson were artistic license on Melvina Yuill's part; but the reality was even worse. Her eyelids began to droop after the first page, and she had initially the greatest difficulty not to nod off. And yet slowly the testament gripped her, with what she slowly realized was a growing pity for that poor cankered soul, James Renkin Jesperson.

However roughly the world may use a man, most can remember a time in their lives when they lived in the perfection of happiness, when each night closed with the recollection of innocent pleasures, when the progress of each day was cheered by the experience of unlooked-for joys, and when the awakening to another dawn was a pure physical delight, unmarred by those anxieties for the fortune of the hour which are the burden of the poor, the ambitious and the intriguing. Little by little, by contact with the world, the trustfulness inherent in youth becomes effaced, but most men can look back on a golden time, when interposed between the young soul and worldly debauchery was the devotion of a pure woman, caring not for fashion, nor fame, only to be a good mother to her little lambs.

Alas, my first initiation into the business of living was under different auspices. My father died before I was born, and thus I came into the world the only child of a rich woman, who maintained a mask of piety and decorum when married, but once the prescribed period of mourning had passed, lived but for the gratification of social and literary ambition. She fancied herself a second Sappho, forsooth!

Was his mother a lesbian? Mel wondered, perplexed. No, in context it means something different. His mother was literary . . . just like Melvina Yuill.

None among her crowd of flattering admirers would speak truthfully to her on this or any other matter, and thus I believe a miserable collection of her verse, showing nothing but how little the muse had smiled upon her, by "A Lady," and published at her expense, did in fact grace the fashionable bookstalls, if only for the lavishness of its binding, for none ever read it.

She lived in Paris, or London, patronising the dandies, artists, and scribblers who form, in both cities, the world of pretentious idleness, and thus I was thrown, when still a boy, into witty and wicked circles, where virtue was conspicuous only in its absence. ~~My mother~~ My parent never cared to inquire how I spent the extravagant allowance, which her indifference rather than any inherent generosity permitted me to squander. Thus I was suffered at sixteen to ape the vices of sixty.

You can guess the result of such a training, and dear friend, I will not sully your eyes with a full account of my sinfulness. Suffice it to say that I discovered, at twenty years of age, that the primrose path I had trodden so gaily led to the insane asylum or the debtor's prison, that a beautiful young woman's love was an item for sale, that friendship was assured only by the expenditure of large sums of money: in short, the totally barren and godless nature of my existence.

This discovery, which surely saved me from a rapid destruction, was made through an event as sudden as it was astonishing—my parent, who had seemed in rude health, died suddenly at a fashionable watering hole. Of the fortune my father had bequeathed to her, to hold in care until my majority, almost nothing was left: it had all been frittered away on earthly vanities.

The sale of furniture, paintings, plate and other chattels brought enough to pay the funeral expenses, leaving me heir to several hundred pounds. My relatives, who had previously showed not the least interest in my fortunes, stared, shook their heads, and insulted me with pity. Conversely my friends of the fast life were not "at home" when I called, or else "cut" me in the street when I passed, for these cynical drones worshipped nothing but Mammon. Desirous now only of avoiding those who had known me in prosperity, I claimed the remnants of my patrimony and vanished to the Antipodes.

During my days of vice and wealth I had read avidly in the newspapers of the goldfields discovered in the Austral El Dorado, never thinking that the reports of fortunes so rapidly and effortlessly made might come to seem peculiarly apposite to me. For did not these deceitful travellers' tales speak of golden nuggets to be found on the streets of Melbourne or Sydney? So, vain and foolish youth that I was, in my imagination I began to regard my fortune as already recovered *on the diggings, and indulged in gilded dreams of castle-building during the greater part of my voyage into exile.*

Upon my arrival in Australia, matters began to assume a somewhat more practical, business-like appearance. Together with a small group of my shipboard companions, all ardent young adventurers such as I (though, as I was soon to discover, small as my means were, they were vastly superior to those of my "friends," as they had taken care to ascertain before attaching themselves like limpets to my ~~person~~ pursestrings), I outfitted myself & Co for the goldfields at the exorbitent rates then common in the colony.

Mel turned the page, to find the next photocopy blank, with a neat note in green: "Leaf missing here, but I doubt anything relevant to your research has been lost. Cheers, C."

The bitter draught of experience had now taught me, as it would teach many others, that the diggings were to be regarded as a kind of lottery, which offered on the one hand many prizes, indeed, and some of them of great magnitude; but that on the other hand the bounty of fool's gold vastly preponderated. The scales having fallen from my eyes, I quitted Heartbreak Gully, knowing that I could get no recompense for the depredations of my false friends; in fact I left with their jeers pealing loudly in my ears. At that point, the nadir of my young fortunes, I bethought myself of the colonial police, for should I don the blue and silver uniform I would be in a position to exercise ~~vengeance~~ justice on the persons who had cheated me, should our paths ever cross again. Thus I took my wounded pride to the great city, applied at the office of the Chief Commissioner, and soon was accepted and enrolled as a member of the mounted cadet force.

The police force was then very ineffective; murders, stabbings and other outrages were of frequent occurrence in the city, and throughout the country round prowling ruffians, often escaped convicts, were ever ready to waylay and murder the wandering digger for the sake of his aureate load. Any real ability to deal with the prevalent disorder was conspicuous, and received its just reward; twelve months after my arrival in the colony I had gone from a humble cadet to the com-

mand of a goodly company of twenty, all strongly built fellows of some six feet in height in their stockings,

Mel, suddenly apprehending the mental image of a Mountie in suspender belt and fishnets, suppressed a giggle.

a glorious sight to the eye as they clattered down the streets on their police horses, each armed with a brace of pistols and a cavalry sabre.

When, my beloved friend in God, you ask me to consider the good I have done in this mundane life, I think of the young men who have passed through my care, whose lives I attempted to guide into the path of righteousness. What changes time wrought with them! Some rose to eminence in their respective areas of duty, receiving the admiration of the crowd. Others sank into obscurity and nothingness, although no less happy than the more aspiring—and not a few degraded and debased by vice blighted their own fortunes, crushed the fondest hopes and wrung the anxious bosoms of their families. The grave in all probability has closed over many, as it will shortly close over me, paralyzing the throb of many a bosom beating yearningly.

I recall Alaric Blain, Superintendent of Detectives, when he was but a dewy youth, with the softest head of golden curls I ever did see, and a mouth so bright as to seem carmined. Walter Burrows, now the finest steeplechaser in the colony, would in the barracks strip to the waist, displaying a torso that would not have disgraced Greek statuary, and challenge all comers to wrestle. I never took a fall with him, as I must needs maintain my officer's dignity, but I watched his display of manly skill often like a delicate child forbidden rough play. *Zavitowsky, a Polack, was ambushed by bushrangers, and horribly mangled by a bullet in the face, left to die—I strung the blackguards high for wantonly destroying his beauty, for he was a Raphael incarnate.*

A catalog of crushes indeed! thought Mel, and skipped a couple of pages, looking for a familiar name.

And now, you ask as I prepare to stand before the glorious throne of my Maker, is there aught that troubles me, a matter that must be settled before my spirit is at rest? You asked me last Sabbath-day, and at that time I was silent, reviewing the annals of my earthly existence.

I believed myself always on the road to righteousness, I would not stint myself from my proper duty, nor stint others; thus I know that I gained the respect of my commanding officers, my peers in the force, and the men who served me, if not their friendship. I was the scourge of the old Vandemonians and villains I encountered; they hated me, for I was a hard man. And yet there was an instance where a little softness of touch, such as I might have learned from a sister, had I been graced with one, full of kindness, calmness, and thought, might have not lost me the one person who not only respected, but truly liked me.

One day a young man came to me with a letter, from Home—the writer was a distant cousin of mine, now living in reduced circumstances, for he had been obliged to send his only son (the bearer of the letter) to the colonies to seek his fortune. I perceived in this youth, Darcy Ainsworth, a pure soul, clad in a perfection of form that seemed to belong to the angels. The daguerreotype I had taken of the pair of us in our police uniforms refreshes my memory, for though I presented it to Darcy, when he left the service of the police he did not take that image with him. It shows a sweetly handsome boy, his nose aristocratically aquiline, the nostrils as fine as a thoroughbred's, eyes as blue as forget-me-nots (ah, how those flowers have ever since reminded me of him!), the dark hair resting wavily on a forehead as guileless as a child's, the hands dainty and marble-white. His whole mien expressed a true nobility of spirit, but, and here was a sign of coming danger, predominant in his physiognomy was candour and innocence, chinks through which the wicked world may so easily strike down a man.

For his sake, and his father's, a man of decent repute, I did all in my power for Darcy, obtaining him employment in the goldfields Mounted Police, and seeing that he was posted to areas without peril, either mortal, from the ranging highwaymen of the bush, or moral, from the company of officers I knew were venal, or less than honest. He was grateful for my efforts; and I took joy in his gratitude. Alas! I had other duties, and while I was far from Darcy, administering my district, my vigilance elsewhere, that innocent youth fell under the power of a Sorceress.

I have always, when in exercise of my police duties, found that women with flame-coloured hair are the wickedest; and indeed that proved to be the case in this instance, for my Darcy fell head over heels in love with a vixen, her profession being that of a common goldfields tavern-keeper. Oh, he swore she was a lady, brought low but not falling by widowhood in a country far from Home, where she had no friends or relatives who could save her the ignominy of working, and certainly she could ape a lady's manners quite convincingly, in the eyes of everyone save me. Observing some slight furtiveness in her, such as I had found a sure badge of guilt, I began to make enquiries as to her past, for I had no doubt as to some concealed infamy. Rather than enlist my colleagues in the detective force, or any of my fellows or subordinates, for I did not trust them with this valuable charge, I resorted to fizzgigs, disreputable men on the goldfields who would do my bidding, for fear of the charges I could well have brought against them.

So much for Miles's complicated tangle of detection and deduction! Mel thought. The truth, for once, was simpler than the fiction, though more sordid.

One fizz, a bellman, of whom I knew enough to hang him, eventually brought me gold, and such a prize! The Scarlet Sorceress had committed child-murder, though escaping the three-legged gallows mare by feigning dementia. Moreover, her husband, a common thief, probably still walked this vale of tears, though nobody had seen him alive for some years. Armed with this information, I made haste to Darcy's station, for months had passed in the search, and though I had delayed the marriage by keeping Darcy's request to wed unsigned, and unapproved, he was young, and like most youths, impetuous.

Alas, I was too late, for Darcy, disobeying the police regulations for the first and only time, had yielded to impatience, or to the importunings of the Sorceress, she perhaps being suspicious of my delaying tactics, and had found a curate turned gold-miner to unite them. I came to the wedding feast like the Mariner in the modern poem, uninvited, and with dire revelations. The tavern-tent was decked with boughs of flowering wattle, baked meats were on the table, liquor flowed, and an assembly mingling promiscuously the district members of the Mounted Police with the disreputable customers of the Sorceress were applauding as the bridal pair danced to the squeal of a gipsy fiddle. Truly a fine conjunction for the son of an English gentleman! I walked up to the couple, as if requesting the next waltz, bodily interposed myself between them, and declaimed my discovery to the company, as was my beholden duty to do.

And as I spoke, I saw the face of the bride go ashen, though her lips (no doubt painted, giving the lie to her protestations of being a lady) and hair remained bright; the contrast made her seem an example of that fearful German spectre, the Vampyre. At the same time, I saw a fire kindle within Darcy's eyes, a rage not against the woman who had deceived him, but as I slowly realized, against me! In exposing his bride as false before his fellow officers and the goldfields rabble, I had humiliated him utterly, gaining no friends by my action and indeed losing the only one that I had (until thou, brother in Christ).

He resigned from the force forthwith, and I, sick at heart, could not but let him go without a word beyond the regulation formalities, nor would I punish him for his presumption in marrying without permission, for his pride had suffered too much. A fizzgig of mine tracked him to Adelaide; but from that metropolis he went I know not where.

His false bride remained on the goldfield several days, to my fury receiving many gestures of sympathy from the rough miners, and even those who were gentlemen—then she too vanished (though not, as I ascertained, in the same direction as Darcy). Perhaps she feared that I would charge her with bigamy; though in the absence of any sign of her husband, alive or dead, the charge would have been difficult to prove. Justice had been done already, although as a consequence all, including my superior officers, who should have known better, thought me vindictive. Their disapprobation in time grew too much to bear, and I eventually betook myself to South Australia, and the service of their colonial police force, with some idea of seeking Darcy— but dear friend, I found you instead!

Ah, but what could I have done otherwise? Should I have held my *peace and let the false marriage stand, bigamous though it may have been? Such would have broken the heart of Darcy's poor father, and would not have been my duty. And yet . . . and yet the Sorceress might have made a virtuous wife and mother, for as you have so often said to me, does not the Lord permit even the most hardened of criminals the chance of repentance, and in doing so, forgives us all? It is his heavenly wisdom which men must bow to, not take it upon themselves to anticipate the divine judgement.*

My thoughts also linger upon the case of Mad Jack the Bushranger

Here Mel turned over, to find another blank page, with the now familiar green writing: "That's all about Darcy, folks! I'll spare you the rest, which is 90 percent religious mania. C."

She sat thinking for a moment, running the new information through her mind. Then, responding to Jesperson's tale at the physical level, she rolled her eyeballs up to heaven, or rather the section of the painted ceiling immediately above her head. For a moment Mel gazed at the Old Woman of the Sea, then blinked, staring, with cold fingers of adrenaline playing scales up and down her spine.

Just for a second it had seemed the monkey on Sinbad's back, the mother-wraith, white-haired, wrinkled and half-naked, had winked one bright demonic eye at her.

TWENTY-THREE

The Divine Mirror

Time blurred between that painted wink and Mel coming to a halt, out in the street, several blocks away. Her ribs heaved painfully as she gasped for breath, unable to run any farther. What an exhibition I made of myself, she thought, dashing out of the club like that. They'll never let me in again—and with that she felt a joyous relief at thus escaping the gaze of the Old Woman of the Sea. But the image, even in memory, had force: it pricked her mood like a bubble, leaving her somber again. What was she so scared of? A painting couldn't wink, not in a sane world.

She saw nearby a drinking fountain, and as she bent toward the nozzle she startled a sparrow perched on the rim. The fan of its wings flickered sunlight and shadow on her face. Something like that, she thought, an interruption of the light, an optical illusion, happened inside the Old Colonial Club, and made me running scared. It wasn't the happiest of explanations, but she clutched it to her, as she turned away from the fountain, thinking despondently that it was time for her to return to her— now so difficult—home.

Yet despite Mel's fears, she got a respite that night, for the Day-Glo DO NOT DISTURB sign, signaling one of Mayzee's migraines— "My horror-movie headaches," she called them—was on the door of the spare bedroom. Knowing from that not to make the slightest of sounds, Mel moused around the flat. The only loud noise came as she was showering, with the slam of the front door. Marc, she thought, tensing against the flow of the water. It seemed a long time since she had been glad to see him.

When she emerged, in dressing gown and towel turban, he was sprawled in front of the television.

"Um, is that low enough? I mean, May . . ."

"If it disturbs her, I'll sort it out, okay?"

All this time he hadn't turned. He's cross with me, she thought. Well, small wonder—I'm cross with Mel myself. Nervous as a thoroughbred I've been lately: fainting, shying . . .

That silent back was getting to her. She knelt down and walked on her kneebones, stopping at the touch of his jacket. No response. Cautiously she slipped one hand under his elbow, and down, stroking his chest through the layers of clothing. If you can't sort things out in bed, then you'll never sort them out at all, she thought. Sammy, Book 1, Chapter 4.

Marc cleared his throat. "It's been a long day."

Gently she withdrew her hand. "You been at the hospital?"

A nod. Wish I could keep track of his shifts, she thought vaguely. Then I'd know what to expect. She sighed, and at that he turned and gave her a quick peck of a kiss.

"Not tonight, Mel-Josephine. But soon, okay?"

"Okay," she said, but he was immersed in the television again. Just to keep him company, or to have company herself, she sat on the couch for a while, toweling her hair dry. But he was watching what she eventually recognized as a Stephen King movie, defanged and deblooded for a TV audience, but still eerie. Unbidden, the wraith eyes came back to her. Get thee behind me, Satan, she thought sternly. Or Satana. It didn't work, and with another sigh, silent this time, she picked up the nearest paperback and retired to the bedroom.

When, some hours later, Marc came to bed, she was still reading, unexpectedly engrossed in the book, a pulp detective novel but impossible to put down, trash though it was. Marc undressed and flopped into bed, with a mumbled "Lights out, Mel."

She obediently shut the book and reached under the crinoline of the lamp for the light switch. In the sudden dark, she lay staring up at the dimly glimpsed ceiling, her eyes like peeled onions. Marc stirred beside her, settled, but did not immediately slip into the breathing rhythms of sleep. Not so tired tonight, she thought. But still not Mr. Willing, Ready, and Able.

She reached out for the book again, and, without turning on the light, slid out of bed. Marc made no response, even when she shut the door of the bedroom behind her. She turned on the living-room light and settled on the couch, wrapping her coat around her yet again. My bed away from bed, she thought. In the electric glare she felt better, like a child with a nightlamp, safe in the knowledge of a visible room, with no shadows to hide ghoulies and ghosties. Nothing can sneak up on me, she thought, no hags of the sea with flowing air and evil eyes, for instance. Yet her gaze fluttered away from the book, to the window, and the door again, particularly when she got to the bit where the serial killer's victims were exhumed.

I exhumed Melvina Mary, she thought. And what I've found about her is a skeleton in the cupboard indeed: desertion, madness, exposing her own baby, a very public jilting. She wanted like any author to be known, for her work to be admired, to reach a bigger audience than the *Tolletown Chronicle*. But at the price of having her sensational and sordid secrets open to all?

An angry ghost could give Mel more than bad dreams. And so she kept on reading, with the light on, until top eyelid inexorably met the lower and consciousness deserted her. If she dreamt, it was forgettable, not the intense Melvina visions. Now and then she roused slightly, gazing at the world through a slit of eye barred with lashes. In these moments, everything seemed as remote as television: Marc bending over Mel, then firmly switching the light off, leaving steel-gray dawn; May eyeing Mel anxiously; the two flatmates in whispered, worried conclave; then separating, Marc to work, Mayzee back to bed again.

Mel eventually roused properly in midmorning, with a head full of emotional cobwebs but thankfully alone. Ghost or not, the search called her. She could not willingly abandon it, yet she had no clear idea what trails of inquiry she could next follow in pursuit of her elusive quarry. For something to do, she rang Appleby, but there was no reply. Frustrated, she kicked the nearest object, her bag, which as if in response suddenly disgorged the notebook of handy hints from Edie. She knelt, reading the almost illegible transcription of her aunt's rapid speech:

"NB if your subject ever got in trouble with the law there's courthouse records that's how I got your grandfather's breach of promise suit and also the reports from each police station they're in the Public Records Depository, out in the suburbs . . ."

Of course, thought Mel. How could I have forgotten the Depository? She knew why soon after, as, map in hand, she surveyed the maze of public transport routes leading out to the depository. They barely connected—it would take hours to get out there. Learn patience, she thought. The miners rode, on horseback or in oxcarts, or simply walked from rush to rush, over dirt roads, taking a week to traverse what a car would cover in a few hours.

Nonetheless, as she alighted from her third suburban bus outside the door of the Depository, some two hours later, she was hot, sticky, and in a foul temper. The weather had that day chosen to be unseasonably warm. Perspiration was trickling down her neck and absently she stripped off her heavy black woolen sweater, tying the sleeves shawl-fashion over her grandfather shirt, then twisted her back hair into a knot, high on her nape. She gazed with real envy at the neat lines of cars parked in the concrete waste of the Depository car park. Oh, to get from A to B at speed, safe in your cocoon of metal and glass. While she waited for the second bus, she had copped a hail of obscenities from a carful of youths. "Grow up, baby boys!" she had yelled back, but her voice had been drowned in the traffic.

Inside, the Depository alternated the institutional with the antique, the archive furnishings offset by shabby historical artifacts: a desk, with plaque proclaiming what important document had been signed there; framed nineteenth-century architectural diagrams; a large mirror, its gilt frame fantastically decorated with clouds and fat putti; and a wag-on-the-wall clock. She glanced at it, realizing she had only a few hours before the Depository closed. Well, here goes, she thought, and strode toward the reference desk. Surely she couldn't have come all this way for nothing?

Retrieving files from the Depository archives was a slow and complex process of forms, registers, and delivery timetables, intensely frustrating even to Mel, who had learned from the library Androgyne that the hounds of information sometimes ran long, roundabout trails in search of their quarry. At least he enjoyed the false starts, the red herrings, she thought. Her first request was for the register of county cases, which did not include Aurealis, so next she tried for the police records.

When the box came out, she eagerly untied the dirty cotton tapes around it, as if expecting a present. What she found inside was blue, fading stationery, crumbling in the corners, stained with age and neglect. Rusty pins were stuck through the corners; the staples and paper clips of the Victorian era, she realized. She lifted one document, then another, reading at first eagerly, then with increasing disappointment: the records were extremely incomplete. Occasionally the familiar names appeared—Jesperson's signature on dispatches, Blanc investigating a suicide, Metcalf appearing as a witness in an interminable dispute about a bale of hay. But there was no Ainsworth, nor, more importantly, Red Melvina Yuill.

She looked up, longing for some Dot or Nev equivalent she could exchange notes with, but the Depository researchers sat apparently glued to their desks, heads down. As she had been, she grudgingly admitted, while searching for the traces of a century-old love story in the dusty police records. Still restless, she got up and wandered toward the mirror, for a better look at its over-the-top decoration. Close to, she stopped, transfixed, at the sight of a woman wearing a black shawl over a high-collared blouse, her hair drawn back tightly—as if the mirror had metamorphosed into an antique portrait. She was reflected here, she knew, but the sight seemed alien. As she stood, she saw, in the mirror, movement over her shoulder, and glanced at it without turning to see—

A young man. Eyes as blue as the summer sky. Slender, almost girlish. Beardless, pale, and with an aquiline nose. Dark hair . . .

Behind her stood Darcy Ainsworth, to the life.

TWENTY-FOUR

Daniel

For a moment the world reeled around her and she swayed on her feet, struggling to keep from fainting. From nowhere a thin white hand came, steadying her.

"You've gone wan," a male voice said. "I startled you. Sorry!"

"Who are you?" she muttered.

For a moment her brown eyes met a clear blue gaze in the mirror. The reflected lips moved as he spoke:

"I'm Daniel Darcy Ainsworth."

She registered for the first time that the hand had not the chill of a ghost.

"Get me out of here before I have hysterics," she finally said, and his hand turned her away from the seductive, frightening mirror. Each step seemed to consume vast resources of energy, and when he eventually led her into a bleak little space, the Depository tearoom, she flopped down in the nearest chair. He brought her a polystyrene cup, filled with murky liquid from the coffee dispenser.

As Mel drank, she gave Daniel an over-the-rim scrutiny. On second glance the resemblance to Darcy was not so startling—his hair straggled untidily to his shoulders and he wore a discreet wire ring in one ear. Most un-Victorian, she thought. Ditto for his jeans, runners, and denim jacket. She noticed more divergences from the daguerrotype—his hair was straight, instead of coiling, for instance. Yet Daniel was still recognizably . . .

"You're a descendant of Darcy Ainsworth," she said.

A quick nod. "Great-grandfather. And you must be Mel Kirksley, who knows a good deal about my ancestor's early life."

"How . . . ?" she breathed.

"A little bird named Charlie Mowbray said I might find you here. He gave me an ID. Look for a tall apricot-colored girl, he said, who doesn't dress Victorian, apart from her turquoise earrings, but has an indefinable faraway look, somehow suggestive of the era, in her face."

Mel considered that description for a moment, as the room filled with the sterile tones of an announcement that the Depository would be closing shortly.

"I think we shall have to continue this conversation elsewhere," she said.

"There's still half an hour of research time."

"Do you want to stay?" she asked.

"Not especially. And you?"

"Not after the divine mirror."

To her surprise he responded with a few words of what sounded like French, so heavily dialectal as to be incomprehensible.

"What *did* you say?"

"Nothing much. I thought you were making an allusion, that's all."

"I merely meant that with all those putti, and gold and clouds, it was like a window into heaven."

"In which you thought you saw my great-grandfather, assuming he went to heaven, that is?"

She laughed, ending with a cough of embarrassment. "You're quick. Yes, I did. Charlie told you I'd seen the photo, right?"

"I've got a copy of it in my car."

The announcement of closure repeated, more insistently.

"We'd better go," Daniel said. "If you're up to it."

"Oh yes." She stood. "But just one thing . . . what did you think I was alluding to?"

"In the Haitian mythology," he said, "the divine mirror is the afterlife, the reflection of this earthly world. I thought myself of it, when I was gazing into the space between those gilded clouds."

Their eyes met, for the first time since the reflection in the mirror.

A return journey seems always to pass more quickly than the voyage out, when novelty prolongs the trip. Such was the case now with Mel, who found herself spared another session of public transport, for in the Depository car park was a small, dusty car, with West Australian number plates: Daniel's.

"You're a sandgroper!" she said. As the words left her mouth she suddenly recalled where she had heard the term before: Sammy had once thus described Myrie, who had also come from the other side of the continent.

"Yep, fourth-generation Westralian," he replied as they got in. The car was well-traveled and lived-in, with maps, bags, books, tape cassettes, and other oddments strewn over floors and seats, even a bulging folder on the front passenger seat she was obliged to displace to the footwell in order to sit down. So far so messily normal. But on the glove box was painted a design in white, like a cross, its arms ornamented with curlicues, as if made of iron lace.

"A vévé," he said, following her gaze, despite apparently being intent on the logjam of homeward-bound researchers at the car-park gates. "It's a symbol of an African god, whose worshipers traveled in the slave ships to the New World. His name is Legba and he is guardian of doorways, with power against thieves."

Mel laughed. "That's much more imaginative than a wheel lock."

"After I painted the symbol, it occurred to me: Legba has jurisdiction over crossing points, paths and roadways. God of the street. So what better name to call a car, for when you're in a mood to own the road?"

Suiting action to words, he accelerated down the road from the Depository, heading toward the freeway.

"There's Mazda cars . . ."

"I never heard of the Zoroastrians declaring a *fatwa*, or claiming copyright on Ahura-Mazda. Anyway, Legba is a better name for a car. He has many titles: Maître Carrefour, that means master of crossroads, his sacred place; Papa . . ."

Mel was suddenly oblivious of this comparative theology, for the folder at her feet flapped open as Legba sped onto the freeway, revealing a photocopy of the antique image she knew so well, Darcy and Jesperson. She picked it up, staring at that youth, so like, and yet also unlike, Legba's driver. Fourth-generation sandgroper, she thought, recalling Daniel's words. So that means Darcy went to West Australia, she mused, and then realized, from Daniel's quick nod, that she had spoken aloud.

"I never would have thought to look so far afield for him."

"Possibly neither did Jesperson and the Sorceress."

"Her name was Melvina Mary Yuill," Mel said, feeling a

shivery thrill of anticipation, as if she and Daniel were about to exchange kisses rather than information. He gave her a quick sideways glance, as if sensing her excitement.

"We have a history and a herstory to tell each other," he said. "Who goes first?"

"Shall we toss for it?" she suggested.

He reached down into the space between the seats, pushing cassettes aside, his hand emerging like a diver's on Greek Easter, clutching a coin. It wasn't from any country she recognized, and she glanced at him inquiringly.

"Haitian. An old coin—that's Papa Doc Duvalier."

"What an ugly head," she replied, eyeing the dictator with distaste.

"You prefer tails?"

"No, I'll stick with Papa Doc."

Without apparently taking his gaze from the freeway, he flipped the coin, then caught it. His clenched fist opened like a flower, at the center of his palm Duvalier.

"I start, then," he said ruefully. "But where to begin? With a painting of an elderly bearded man, that hung above the mantelpiece in my grandparents' home? He didn't look anything special, but they called him the Parliamentarian. I noticed once, that I'd inherited his eyes and nose—"

He rubbed it self-consciously.

"—but didn't take much note of it, until I got to university and took a unit of Westralian history. My tutor was Charlie Mowbray—first thing he asked was whether I was related to Darcy Ainsworth. I found out the Parliamentarian had been quite important: he had a hand in all sorts of interesting legislation, his fingers in every political pie. You should investigate him further, Charlie said, a suggestion I left on the back burner. In the meantime I finished my unit and eventually my degree. Not knowing quite what to do next, I took a couple of years off and worked for foreign aid, thinking that from the experience

I might get the materials for a doctorate, something postcolonialist. I got sent to Haiti . . ."

He paused, his eyes distant and shadowed.

"By the time I came home I had decided it was wrong to study other cultures as if they were interesting exotica, that you couldn't understand others without first knowing yourself. Back to roots, I guess. At around the same time the last of the grandparents died and left me the family papers. There was enough material for a political biography of Darcy Ainsworth, Ph.D. material, and maybe publishable."

Mel watched the fast-approaching city skyscrapers, thinking, There's not enough time to tell both our stories during this trip, we'll have to stop somewhere. She turned her head, assessing Daniel: not pretty, not a dreamboat like Darcy, but still . . . intriguing.

"I was able to piece together much of Darcy's life, from his speeches, and family letters, and by writing to my distant Ainsworth relatives, back in England. Yet there was a crucial gap in the record. He told an interviewer that he 'hazarded his fortune' in Australia because his family lost their West Indian estates in a famous bank crash. From that I could date his departure from England quite accurately. His arrival in West Australia was similarly documented—when he wanted to appeal to parochial sentiments he would quote the exact date. Trouble was, it was three years after he left England. What happened in between setting out on the voyage, which should only have taken a few months, and his stepping off the coastal steamer in Albany was a complete mystery. Where was he in the meantime?

"I was planning a systematic search of the emigration records, in every Australian colony and maybe even New Zealand, but then I went to a conference and ran into Charlie again. He stared at the sight of me, just like you did. Now I hadn't seen him for a few years, I'd been living rough in the Caribbean—but I didn't think I'd changed that much. He knows something, I thought, his eyes have gone all hooded. You've met Charlie, so you'll know what I mean: he plays with information as if he's in a card game."

Does he ever! thought Mel.

"He led the conversation, a little too casually, around to my ancestor, and when I told him about my thesis, he laughed in his pussycat way. Our interests coincide, he said. Apparently he'd been trying to locate me ever since he'd read Jesperson's memoir. But what really made him grin was the synchronicity: only yesterday he'd been going through a box of uncataloged photographs in the Pluckrose collection and he'd found my twin! The Parliamentarian as a young man, when the family had no snaps of him before middle age. And in police uniform too."

"You'd no inkling he'd been in the police force?"

"Not in the slightest. The moment the conference ended, I came down here in search of archival material, as fast as Legba and the traffic laws would allow."

"Find much?" Mel asked.

"A ship's passengers list, an advert he placed in the *Argus* when he arrived, for return of stolen property, a personnel record from Mick the police archivist . . . and now you."

"Charlie said nothing to me at the Old Colonial Club about an Ainsworth descendant," she mumbled.

"Oh, he likes his little surprises. Did it to me too—nary a word until he'd checked you out. Then he gave me the glad news, also your phone number. Nobody answered the times I rang, but this didn't worry me. I felt sure I'd bump into you at some research site sometime. As Charlie said, the whole business was clearly in the lap of the gods. Which gods I don't know . . ."

"Legba?"

"I've never heard of a god or patron saint of historical research. I just feel that something is looking down benignly on all our hard work."

"Are you serious?" she asked, unable to gauge his tone.

"Half and half."

She left it at that, as they shot across an overpass and down into the city center.

Daniel said, a little hesitantly, "I could either drop you off at a tram stop, or at your front door."

"No," she said, rather too forcibly. "Not home. The flat's in no state for visitors."

She meant not untidiness, but the emotional mess existing between the Happy Orphans ever since, it seemed, Melvina had become almost an obsession for namesake Mel. With the thought, she felt a grim hopelessness fall upon her, like the shadow of a skyscraper. A flash of bright gold roused her and she lifted her head, looking around curiously. They had stopped at an intersection, hemmed in with pre-rush-hour traffic, trucks, cars, and taxis. Legba inched forward slightly and sunset rays streamed upon them, reflected from a mirrored façade. For a moment it seemed as if they were surrounded by gold, the gilt of the antique looking glass. The divine mirror was here, now, heaven experienced in the middle of a traffic jam, with car exhaust instead of clouds. Only the putti were missing.

She wondered whether to share her fancy with Daniel, but before she could voice the thought, the traffic lights changed. Legba moved ahead, out of the reflected sunlight, and into darkness again.

TWENTY-FIVE

Out in the Cold

By the time she got back to the Happy Orphans' Club, it was evening and icy, once the warmth of the sun had gone. Mel entered warily, relaxing once she found the flat was free of problematic company. Dropping her bag on the floor, she thought briefly but intensely of Daniel, then grabbed the phone off its hook. Edie would be rapt at this latest installment in Mel's personal detective serial.

The bell rang in distant Appleby but then she put the receiver down hurriedly as the door, left ajar, admitted Marc, sudden as a thunderclap. He saw her hand on the receiver, and said "Aha!" sharply. She gazed at him, puzzled as to why he stood rocking slightly on his heels like a pugilist, his face full of furious triumph.

After a moment he said, "So . . .," but with such absurd emphasis she was immediately irritated.

"Marc, you're talking like a soap opera. 'Aha!' 'So!' . . . So what?"

"So I know why you've been acting so strangely, like you've turned into another person."

She started, thinking of the reflection in the mirror, and he smiled, not nicely.

"It's because of another person . . ."

How can he know about Melvina Yuill? she thought, perplexed. I've not told him anything about the research.

At her lack of response he suddenly shouted, "The tall dark stranger! I saw you, drinking coffee and laughing together."

"Oh, that," she said, light dawning.

Daniel had driven her to the trendily boho part of town, in search of a coffee shop he said Charlie had recommended, but it had proved elusive. Instead, they had bought takeaway coffee from an upmarket milk bar and taken their cups to a nearby park. There, on a lawn strewn with the bright coins of dying leaves, Mel had told her detective story of Melvina, the flip side of Jesperson's biased tale, between sips of coffee. Silly Marc! She laughed now, thinking of what the scene must have looked like, then stopped dead, for Marc had gone red in the face.

"Have I said anything funny?" he demanded.

"No, not from your point of view. But from mine . . ."

Marc cut her off short.

"Points of view! Whichever way you look at it, there's no mistaking the way you two eyed each other."

She paused, thinking, Yes, I am attracted to Daniel. And he to me? Then she said, a little lamely, "Daniel's just a relative of my research."

"How interesting! I never knew 'research' was a synonym for 'hanky-panky.' "

She was stung. "What if I talk to a man—"

"Young, handsome!"

"—since you insist, yes! Does that give you the right to make a scene?"

"I would suggest it does, after all these years."

"All these years!" she repeated, thinking of everything that phrase encompassed: sardines, the moldy walls of the flat, constant study and poverty, the sense of being worthless . . .

"All these years of what? From where I sit it looks like years of nothing much!"

The purpose, the new joy in life, had not come from Marc and Mayzee, but from a seed planted years earlier by Sammy: Nola.

Marc said, very slowly and deliberately, "Well, if that's your attitude . . ."

His fingers stroked the white cloth of his intern's coat, which had hung over his arm while they argued. She was riveted by the motion, suddenly thinking very hard.

"So you watched us, without coming near. Did you follow me home after I waved good-bye to Daniel? Waved good-bye, not kissed good-bye, you must have noticed. You surely did follow, on the next tram, to get back so quickly, within a few minutes of me. But what were you doing in that part of town? We don't know anyone living there, and it's not nearly posh enough for your parents. You're dressed as if you've just done a shift, but the hospital is on the other side of the city center, nowhere near the park."

He started to speak, but she carried on regardless.

"How could you have seen us? We were in the center of the park, out of sight of the street, with only trees around us. Either you were peeping from behind one of their trunks, which is *creepy*, or else you were spying from above, from one of the overlooking buildings, I'm not sure what they are, flats or offices . . ."

As she paused he began to swear at her, at first softly, then with increasing venom and volume, no sense to the words, just inarticulate outpourings of rage. She cringed, hands over head, and at that he strode past her and into the bedroom, where she heard the cupboard door slam against the wall, the banging of open drawers. She chanced a peek and saw, lying on the double bed, Marc's Gucci suitcase, with socks, T-shirts, and underpants flying through the air and landing in it, as neatly as if aimed at a basketball hoop. She turned away from the sight, quite stunned. They had hardly been loving lately, but this . . . ?

He finally emerged, lips set hard, packed and closed suitcase in hand.

"Where are you going?" she murmured.

"I imagine that would be of no interest to you," he said coldly.

She tried to protest, to say, Yes, it would, but her tongue lay fat and still in her mouth. Could I voice that, she wondered, with enough conviction to be believed?

As he reached for the door handle she finally managed to speak:

"Will you be back?"

He opened the door before replying.

"For the rest of my things, sometime." He had barely opened his mouth to retort, and the words hissed out, as if from a steam press. Then she heard the slam, and his footsteps walking away, down the concrete steps, first loud as jackboots, then fainter and fainter.

In the new, sudden silence, she thought of Melvina Yuill's break with Darcy, the fictionalized desertion at the altar, the real interrupted wedding feast. Her ending with Marc was not as dramatic, but nonetheless she knew it was equally as final.

She sat on the couch a long time, the dusk shading into darkness, feeling incapable of any coherent action. In the end soft steps sounded outside, the key grated in the lock, and May stood silhouetted in the doorway, the light from the stairwell making her hair momentarily as vivid as a dandelion. She entered, switching on the light with one decisive slap of her hand. Mel blinked, knuckling her eyes, but still registered that May had purple shadows under her eyes: the sign of a bad day's dialysis.

Mayzee said nothing, as if forbearing to comment on any more of Mel's eccentricities. When at last the absence of greeting had made the atmosphere unbearably reproachful and tense, Mel said, "Hi, May."

It sounded banal; and worse, with this breaking of the silence, May had gained a small tactical point. She immediately went on the offensive.

"It's freeze-your-tits-off cold in here! Why couldn't you be a considerate pet and put the heating on?"

Mel put her hands to her cheeks, for the first time realizing they were icy.

"I was thinking."

"Obviously not of May!"

Maybe that's my problem, Mel thought, that I've been thinking too much of other people, trying to please them, and it's left me no space to be myself . . . until Nola and Melvina Yuill gave me a way out.

"May, I can't anticipate you all the time," she said, in what she hoped was a reasonable voice.

"You might at least make an effort. Remember Marc and May wiping the tears off you all night, when your scallywag of a dad died? Or all that moolah I lent you out of my starveling pension?"

"Gratitude is not a bottomless pit," Mel said.

The reaction was shocking: May came up close to her, so that all Mel could see was her white face, flared nostrils and mouth, drawn thin. Mel held that intense stare, noticing, almost clinically, that May had a lump of dried, yellowy mucus lodged in the corner of one eye.

"Don't you think, pet, that you owe May and Marc, for putting up with you all these years?"

Jesus, Mel thought, it's not been a one-way transaction! Then, emboldened, she voiced it. May blinked, backed away a step or two. She stood on one spindly leg, then the other, her face turning from aggression to pathos. For a second Mel believed it and felt guilty, then realized the calculation as May spoke:

"Mel, when May's been so sick . . ."

"I know that," Mel said wearily. "I also know there's a thin line between being in a pitiful state and trading on it, which you've crossed a number of times."

May looked momentarily dumbfounded. Then she sat down in her chair, resting her head in her hands.

"Oh Mel, we were so cozy in the Happy Orphans' Club."

"People change," Mel said. "Or grow beyond things."

"No," May said. "You don't change. Stay my sweet pet Mel."

"I can't!"

"You're making May and Marc all miz. What's got into you?"

"Melvina Yuill," Mel said.

"What? Oh Mel, you're nutso. May's gonna sit here and talk horse sense into you. Don't you see what you're doing? You're breaking up our Happy Orphans' Club. May won't be your best girlfriend anymore and Marc won't be your boyfriend, either!"

It had to be said, at last.

"Marc's gone already."

"What?"

"Take a look in the bedroom."

May got up and investigated.

"When did this happen?" she demanded.

"About half an hour ago. We had a row. He thought he saw me with another man, but he got it all wrong. I don't have another lover."

"No," May said, coldly. "I don't see how two men could put up with you."

"Anyway, he didn't give me a chance to explain, just stormed out."

As she spoke, she thought, That's not quite right. I could have patted Marc down, if I'd tried. But in a sense I'm past trying to hold on to him. Yet she knew that was not the whole truth, not at all, for there was an area that remained mysterious: Marc's loss of temper. He had not gone out of control over Daniel, only when she had asked what he was doing in that part of town, how he could have spied on them in the park.

"Hup, pet!"

She suddenly noticed that May held the front door gaping wide.

"On your feet! You're gonna find Marc, say very very sorry to him, and bring him home. We can't afford the Happy Orphan Clubrooms on my pension and your irregular income, especially if you keep splurging it."

Mel looked at May, astonished.

"But I don't know where he is."

"Then go and find out!"

"May, don't be silly. You complained about being cold earlier, and you'll freeze if you keep that door open."

She got up, intending to reason with May, but the other woman stood firm, her hand on the knob. Mel grasped May's wrist, meaning to break her grip gently, but found the muscles were bunched hard.

"Don't you touch Mayzee!"

May jabbed at Mel's midriff with her free hand, hard. Next moment they writhed in struggle, silently, girl wrestlers, with not a bikini nor any mud in sight. She's strong, for an invalid, realized Mel, as May shook one wrist out of her grip. Or desperate. May's hand snaked upward, and Mel thought, *She's aiming for the bruise again,* fading though it is. She struck at the hand, like a cat boxing a moth, deflecting it sideways into her hair. May caught hold of a strand of curl, then released it, instead grasping gold, jerking hard. . . .

A moment of intense pain. Mel screamed, clutching at her ear. The pendant was warm and sticky against her palm, and feeling acute nausea at the thought of it falling free from the torn lobe, she fell to her knees across the threshold. May's booted foot approached, and she dodged the anticipated kick, rolling onto the concrete of the landing. Nothing happened—except that the door behind Mel slammed. She heard it lock, then the rattling as the latch and security chain were secured.

"May . . ." she breathed, too stunned for anything louder than a whisper.

She looked up at the spyhole, seeing it dark, blocked by the eye of Mayzee.

"Don't get your panties in a twist. It's only a scratch."

"May, you ripped the earring out!"

"No I didn't. I just gave it a wee pull, and how you reacted! Feel if you don't believe me!"

Mel felt, finding a thin loop of flesh between lobe, hook, and empty air. Wincing as the hook grated against raw meat, she withdrew it. Even bloodstained, the pendant was beautiful. She wiped it clean on her handkerchief, then stowed the golden prize safely in her jeans pocket. A trickle of blood ran down her neck, unstaunched.

"You'll have to do what you're told now," the voice behind the door said. "May's not gonna let you in, without Marc."

Her key, Mel recalled all too clearly, was in her bag, inside the flat.

"May, I'm wounded."

Silence. Try another tack, she thought.

"I've hardly any money on me." She felt in her other pocket with her free hand, finding her coin purse. She opened it, displaying for the benefit of the spyhole her all-day ticket and some small change.

"It's cold. I've no coat."

"You've a nice warm sweater on."

"MAY!" She closed her eyes and shouted, a primal, rebel yell. The response was a high-pitched giggle. Mel clenched her fists, resisting the urge to pound at the door until it—or more realistically her fists—broke. The moment past, she switched to the voice of cold reason.

"May, stop being childish."

Silence.

"At least give me my bag," Mel pleaded. Then she realized that May couldn't, for it would mean opening the door, with the possibility of Mel forcing her way back in.

"Na." The muffled voice was gloating now.

"Is that final?"

More silence.

"May, you're out of your mind!" Mel said, seeing that fact, cold and clear, for the first time. She stalked away, faintly hearing the response, like an echo from a faraway playground, the atonal chant of child superiority, chilling in this context: "Na-na-na-na-na!"

No, she would not play May's game, nor turn and shout at her that she had given up on not only the argument, but her "best friend," forever.

TWENTY-SIX

Cradled in Velvet

She had no idea what to do next, but outside in the street she found one of the infrequent late-night trams. Her resolve crystallizing at the sight, she clambered up the steps, into the light and warmth. Get away—that urge was dominant. To Edie's, she thought, for coffee, disinfectant, and sympathy.

She sat down, feeling the pressure of stares on her face; when she looked around the few other passengers glanced away guiltily. Turning, she surveyed her reflection in the night-opaqued window: a Mel pallid as a corpse, even her lips drained of blood, clutching a handkerchief to her ear like a Van Gogh self-portrait. Do my eyes look mad? she thought, staring at herself. They're wide, with too much white showing, but not crazed like Mayzee's.

Sammy never met her, she thought, with the wisdom of hindsight. He was away on holidays when I moved into college, and then into the flat. When he came back he was preoccupied with Nola, and somehow there was no time for a meeting with Marc and May. She recalled now that the excuses and missed appointments had all been on the Happy Orphans' side, recognizing the symptoms, now she could identify them, of Marc's phobia of families, May's possessiveness. Didn't Sammy always say that thin and nervy is bad in a horse and in a woman? S. Kirksley aphorism no. 9, or 1009. He'd have recognized May right away as something to avoid, but would I have believed him? No.

The tram trundled through the night as she sat quietly, numbed by events. When her fingers felt the blood on her ear clot, becoming jam-sticky, she removed the handkerchief, now more gore than cotton. She closed her eyes at the sight, shutting out the world, the visual aspects of it at least, temporarily. When she opened them again, she found that the tram was nearing Edie's stop, and that she was almost the sole remaining passenger.

She alighted, dimly aware of someone else also leaving, from the back exit. Walking down the street to Appleby, she heard night sounds: distant barking dogs; a cat's yowl; a ticking sound that might be a meter, or a bat; and behind her, footsteps. The streetlamps seemed very far apart, and she sped up, almost running through the darkness between each pool of light, even in her shocked, post-Mayzee state feeling unnerved.

Appleby was black. She halted, incredulous, then glanced at the lighted numerals on her watch. Eleven o'clock. What could an old lady be doing out at this hour? Maybe Edie had decided on an early night. She opened the gate, like a sober, daytime visitor, resisting the impulse to vault it and run toward the house. She rapped with the knocker and stood, huddled against the door, rehearsing words: I'm sorry I woke you, I'm sorry I woke you, look at me, look at my torn ear, help me! Edie sleeps like a petrified log, she concluded, after about ten heartbeats of silence, and rapped again.

When the fourth rap had been unanswered, she stepped back, staring up at the house disbelievingly. Well, if Edie wasn't in, she had to find somebody who was. The terrace on the right was also dark, but on the left light shone through cedar blinds. Feeling really spooked now, she ran up the neighbor's path, pressing the doorbell hard.

After a long wait, she saw movement behind the etched ruby glass. An outside light came on, illuminating her in a cone of bright yellow. The door opened, releasing the sounds of soft, saccharine rock and the smell of perfume. A woman stood there, apparently naked and oiled, until Mel realized she merely wore a flesh-colored Lycra bodysuit over a figure dieted to the scraggy stage. Her face was square and vacuous, with a layer of red lipstick over cord-thin lips.

"I'm looking for Edie."

"Never heard of her."

"From next door. She's my aunt."

The woman shrugged. "Look, I only just moved here, and I work late Monday to Friday, weekends I ski, or party. I don't have the time to be neighborly."

"Look," Mel said, "it's very important that I find her."

Behind her came a faint noise, the sound of something scraping on pavement, and Mel glanced nervously over her shoulder, realizing too late that she had thus given the neighbor an eyeful of her torn ear. When she looked back, Ms. Lycra had retreated a step, looking frightened. Mel self-consciously put one hand to her lobe, felt the crust of dried blood, and felt sick all over again. She swayed on her feet, toward the woman, who drew back farther, pulling the door almost to, so that only a slit of her showed.

"I need help," Mel said.

The woman fidgeted.

"How do I know you're who you say you are," she finally said, her voice hard. "I don't know this Edie. Are you homeless?"

Involuntarily Mel responded with the truth: "Yes."

The one wide, vacant eye visible blinked, then a door slammed in Mel's face for the second time that night. Mel leaned her forehead against it for a moment, as the cone of light vanished, leaving her in darkness again. She slouched out to the pavement, eyeing the house on the right. Were there new neighbors there too? She guessed that anyone who might recognize her from the days of little Mel, staying with Alice, would be long gone.

Because she had nothing else to do she continued down the street, suddenly aware that the footsteps were back again. She stopped, as if struck by a thought, and the echo also halted; she moved on, hearing the steps slowly gaining on her. Ms. Lycra would never come to the door if she heard a scream from outside, she thought, she'd just hide under the bed. For a residential street, the houses she was passing were eerily dark, seemingly deserted. Lose him, she thought, remembering the maze of back alleys behind the houses that she had explored when staying here as a child, had even blazed, drew maps of, a hidden country of her own. She walked on, thinking very hard of those drawings made in colored pencil and crayon. An alley between two houses was coming up, and as she considered it, she heard from behind her a murmur. She could not tell whether the words were comprehensible, or whether her imagination supplied them, but the message was clear:

"Girlie, don't wanna hurt you, only wanna kill you!"

She darted sideways, running full pelt. Even before she had gone very far into the lane she realized that the hidden country had changed, with new garage doors in the brick on either side of her. But the steps behind her were speeding too, now, and she had no choice but to press on. A junction loomed, one arm she recalled going up behind Edie's row of houses, to eventually meet with the cross street, and she took it, her heart on overdrive, from both fear and exertion.

Even the streetlights barely penetrated here; she wanted to slow, to try and gauge where she was, but not with those feet behind her. Turning a corner, she skidded on rubbish, ending up on hands and knees in front of a brick wall. From somewhere near a dog barked deafeningly. But as she stared at the brickwork, she saw, half obliterated, a design in white, semiluminous paint, the M for Mel, and suddenly recalled what this blaze signified—the wall of bricks was old, and pitted, with just enough holds for a child to climb over the top and onto the shed roof of Appleby.

Mel had no time to wonder if the holds would take an adult or not; in desperation she simply scrambled up, scratching her hands, breaking nails, managing to roll over onto the roof just as the footsteps rounded the corner. She fell into a clammy damp softness she recognized as a layer of dead leaves, blocking the shed's guttering and incidentally providing a quiet landing.

Now she lay still, trying to suppress her panting. The dog had gone into frenzy at the smell of another intruder and she could hear it leaping up and down, the scrape-crash of paws and body against the wooden fence. A back door slammed, and a man shouted at the dog. The footsteps had stopped—as the dog owner came down his garden, grumbling at "Rambo," she heard them retreat, and sidle back down the lane.

Nonetheless, even after the dog had been quietened and silence filled the night again, she remained motionless, listening intently. Who was he? she thought. Somebody creepy, after a scare, or after much worse? Did he really say he wanted to kill me, leave me a bloodied corpse like Red Meg, with some modern-day Miles—Mick, maybe?—to read the riddle of my death? I looked vulnerable on the tram, with my torn, bloody ear, a waif and stray with nowhere to go home to, easy prey. . . .

The damp of the leaves was soaking through the wool of her sweater, an icy wetness. She found herself listening to a faint tapping sound, bone against bone, then realized it was her teeth chattering. Slowly she sat up, edging across the roof to the branches of the old quince tree, smaller than in memory, but still reaching upward, coaxing her to descend.

She saw the dark house before her, stars reflected in the black windows. Break in? She stood in a flower bed, pressing her hands against one window. Tired though she was, the idea of violating Appleby was taboo. She sighed, and wandered back to the shed, thinking to shelter in it until the lights came on in the house again, signaling Edie's return from a wild night on the town.

Almost immediately she blundered into softness, dry not damp this time, and redolent of must and mothballs. She felt, her fingers reading the shape of the Saratoga trunk, sitting dustily in a corner of the shed as long as she could remember, but now open and muffled by its contents, spilling free—the acres of Gran Kirksley's old velvet curtains, torn and faded, but most importantly *warm*. She wrapped herself in them as if in a cocoon, huddling at first, then as she became less chilled stretching out a little, her feet against the trunk and her head toward the door, watching and waiting.

Before long she knew that the warmth and her extreme tiredness—physical, mental, emotional—would not let her stay awake. She slumped, head drooping, eyelids descending inexorably. An image returned, from the deep past, of Sammy solemnly following her down the alleys, paintpot in hand. What had occasioned that? Oh yes, she had climbed over the wrong fence, and ended up tearful, treed by a Pekingese. Sammy had, for once, been on hand to soothe the irate neighbor, and when he found out what had happened he had simply said, "You need a sign."

And so he had hobbled down the bluestones with her, and painted, on Alice's brick wall, the *M* for Mel, child-height.

"See," he said, "that M means, climb here, not into yards with yappy little dogs."

That memory was suddenly so strong, she could almost hear his voice. Yeah, Sammy, she thought, I did climb, thanks to you. She snuggled more deeply into the velvet, having, before consciousness finally left her, a sense of pure safety, as if the shed was a cradle around her, the curtains blankets, and she a child with someone watching benevolently over her.

TWENTY-SEVEN

Bad News Travels in Company

Waking came slowly, through a confusion of sensory impressions. Noisy birds, Mel thought, then wondered how she could hear the dawn roosting, for there were no trees near the flat. Against her cheek was something that felt like silky, musty fur, and she opened her eyes a slit to see she was enveloped in dark green. Marc! She sat up, only to have the events of yesterday crash down on her like a castle made of blocks. Marc was gone, May she never wanted to see again . . . and where was Edie?

She struggled free of the velvet and out into the garden, every muscle in her, it seemed, complaining bitterly. It was not long after dawn, she guessed from the light, and when she pressed her nose against the kitchen window she saw from the wall clock that it was seven o'clock. She glanced up, at the window of Edie's room, and saw the blind open, as it had been last night. She stood still, listening—but there was no sound from inside, beyond the tick of the clock. Edie had not come home at all.

On top of everything else, she thought, do I need to worry about someone so self-reliant? Nonetheless, she felt bothered. More pressing, though, was the need for food, water, TLC, and reluctantly she bent down and picked up a loose white rock from the edging of the flower bed. I'll pay Edie for the glazing, she decided, if I ever have money again. As she lifted the stone, a faint gleam beneath it caught her attention. She knelt, and saw, pressed into the ground, a circle of metal. Dropping the stone, she pulled at it, the earth disgorging a slightly rusty, but perfectly usable key. She eyed it, thinking very hard.

Suddenly she was at Sammy's funeral again, bending toward Edie under the arc of an umbrella, hearing her aunt say, with a toss of her head at Alice and her flowers, "She's got it into her head lately that she'll be locked out of Appleby, and she keeps hiding the house keys, under flowerpots, the dustbin, I've been up and down to the locksmith, getting spares made, and then she hides those too!"

The key fitted the back door, and inside the kitchen Mel found on the table a cup of black coffee, icy cold. Old people fall, she suddenly thought, they break bones easily and lie there, waiting for somebody to find and help them. Forgetting her hunger, filth, and exhaustion, she scurried through the house, checking each room.

Relieved, but not relieved, at the absence of an anguished form on any of the floors, she returned to the kitchen. To wash her hands in hot soapy water, in the sink, seemed an absolute luxury, and after that she made coffee, in the largest mug, and a breakfast consisting of a heaped plate of the nearest things to hand: cheese, pickled onions, fruitcake, a woody but sweet apple, raisins, leftover corned beef, dates, and a half bottle of faded hundreds and thousands, eaten with spittle on fingers. Thus stoked up, she attended to the outer Mel, cleaning and dressing her ear while the bath filled.

She wallowed in it, as content, under the circumstances, as the previous day's catalog of disaster would let her be. For a long time she simply luxuriated in earthly pleasures, mind a blank, without worrying thoughts, until at last she was roused by the increasing tepidness of the water, and from the street the sounds of a vehicle parking in front of the house. Wrapping a towel around her, she ran to the one upstairs front window, Alice's, but found her view blocked by untrimmed ivy. All she could glimpse through its interstices was a mass of bright pink.

Determined to be prepared whether she had a visitor or not, Mel returned to the bathroom and dressed in yesterday's clothes, as she did, assuming with their dirt almost a look of fear/care. Coming downstairs she inspected herself in the hall mirror, and saw a Mel wan and wild-eyed, a veritable feral kid. Then she opened the door, to see Dot from the library locking a pink van, at the same time talking to Ms. Lycra, clad this morning in running shorts, Reeboks, leopard print T-shirt, and matching headband. Their gaze drew her, and she ran down the path.

"That's the niece I've been looking for," Dot said. Then, to Mel: "Dear, why didn't you say you were a Kirksley? I thought you were a Yuill, and me knowing Edie so well from the family history course we did . . ."

It struck Mel that she had never told Edie about meeting the cousins—she had meant to, but somehow, with all the Melvina information, it had never been communicated.

"Something's happened to Edie," she said flatly.

"And something's happened to you too, by the look of it!

Dear, I'm so sorry to tell you this, but Edie's in hospital. She fell down in the milk bar. Heart, it was."

Mel reached out for something to steady herself, found her fingers grasping a shrub, and transferred them to something more substantial—the gatepost.

"How did you . . . ?"

"She asked for me, though we hadn't seen each other in months. She asked for you first, but the hospital couldn't reach you. Then they got on to me, and I thought I'd go round to Appleby just in case you were there."

Ms. Lycra was looking at Mel accusingly. "How could I have known you really were a niece? I'm all alone, I can't let strangers into my house!"

"Dear," Dot said, quietly yet firmly, "don't make it even worse for yourself. Mel, can we go in and talk?"

Once the front door of Appleby was shut behind them, Dot said, "Know that type. Having an affair with the bathroom scales and the exercise bike, she is, too wrapped up in her body shape to think of anybody else. Well, you've made her feel guilty, for an hour at least."

"How's Edie?"

"Not good."

"My father died of a heart attack."

"She hasn't, not of this one, but she may have another, she's that agitated about you. The hospital didn't tell her, but they told *me* that when they rang your home—"

Oh shit, Mel thought. The May-monster.

"—the girl at the other end said she didn't know where you were and didn't care."

"I got thrown out of my flat last night."

Dot's mouth opened in a soundless O. "My dear, evils don't come singly, do they? But why were you knocking next door? Edie gave you a key, she said so."

"I left it at the flat. But I climbed over the back fence and found the spare."

To tell Dot about the creep, the chase through the back alleys would have been too much; Mel knew she would have started to weep uncontrollably. The human animal cannot bear too much commiseration.

"Thank goodness you did," Dot said absently, "even if you made a mess of your clothes. Where can I get you a change? Anything of mine would just fall off you, and you might not like pink."

"Never mind about that. Let's hop in your van and go see Edie."

Mel had broken her arm once as a child, falling off a parallel bar at school. When she thought back on this event, the memory seemed fractured, incomplete: one moment she stood triumphantly atop the bar, next she lay on the earth below. What happened in between had vanished.

Fractured, too, were the impressions of this bad time, when it seemed nothing could get much worse . . . and yet it did. Foremost, she didn't know why, a dog was lying in the gutter, licking an open sore on its side. When did she notice that? Was it after she saw a flower stall as they went through an intersection, and shouted at Dot to stop? She couldn't remember leaping out, only returning at a gallop, her arms full of snapdragons.

Another disconnected fragment, like a piece from a jigsaw puzzle, showed Dot's little house, its pastel and pink prettiness decorated with photos from the genealogical research, and unexpectedly, Koorie activist posters. Dot looked up at Mel, saying, with quiet authority, "Dear, you're in no state to go back to Appleby alone. Have some tea, sit down for a bit."

Now Mel was waiting in a corridor, watching a woman wandering around in a hospital gown, strings half untied, naked back and bum for all the world to see. "She's half out of her mind," somebody said. Mel thought, How much more does it take to go crazy? How much more before I break?

Plaid shirts, a heap of them, on Dot's spare bed. "My son's," Dot said. "Best I can do for you, while we wash your clothes. Here, I've bought you matching leggings, like all the young girls wear. You can get away with them, not like me, I never had decent pins."

"Nonsense," Nev said loyally.

The dog licked hair, circling the wound. She stared, fascinated and repulsed.

Tucked up in the narrow bed, wearing a T-shirt also belonging to Dot's absent son, she heard the cousins' voices from the next room, Dot's bedroom. The digital clock said 2 A.M. That and the tone of the voices suddenly clicked information into place like a numeral: Cousin-lovers. Is it incestuous? she wondered. Surely not at second and third remove.

The dog ran its long pink tongue over the sore, tasting lymph fluid and blood. Spittle heals, Mel recalled. Imagine the pain, though, as that hard raspy surface meets raw, living meat. But the dog tolerates it, maybe even relishes it in a masochistic way, even if it does not know that by cleaning the wound a healthy scab forms and healing ultimately takes place. She circled the sore spots in her memory, accessing scenes at Dot's house, the hospital corridor again, before running a mental tongue over her own raw pain, hurting yet cleansing herself. Now Mel's past-self entered Intensive Care, and approached the bed, with its helpless, pathetic form. She winced mentally, but pressed on.

Edie was corpse-pale, limp as a pillow put through the wash, half the stuffing knocked out of her. She opened one eye, then another, and at the sight of Mel, animated slightly. A white hand, puppetlike, the string a tube, bottle at one end, at the other a needle, feeding into a pale blue vein, moved, clasping Mel's own healthy apricot mitt. The grasp was feeble, but warm. Mel could have held it forever.

Whispered words, not many at first, but later, much more, spilled through the colorless lips.

"So much to tell you . . . so little time."

TWENTY-EIGHT

Words

Mel said—at this visit or another? it hardly mattered—"You knew you were ill."

"They always say health professionals can't diagnose themselves, but *I* knew the old ticker was winding down. And I thought, Just as well. In this family, the heart goes or the mind goes when we get old. . . . Believe me, I know the Kirksley deaths for generations. I'd rather a heart attack than end up like Alice."

Something came back to Mel, from a long distance away.

"I knocked over a book on the hall table. I only glanced at it, not meaning to pry, but it had a list of everything in the library."

"Not only the library . . ."

"You were making an inventory of Appleby?"

A wobbly smile. "You look at that inventory. Hospital storeroom standard, it is."

"And all the cleaning and tidying up, too . . . ?"

The smile grew wider. "Putting the earthly chattels in order, so that nobody could think me a sluttish housewife. Spring-cleaning for the Great Reaper."

Later: "Mel, I had a dream. I was wearing a nightgown I owned years ago, turquoise silk with pearly buttons, but three had come off, and were lying on this bed. What do you think that might mean?"

"I'm not sure. I dreamt of Melvina Yuill, and the dreams told me a lot about her. But what can you learn from a pearl button?"

"Three buttons, it was. Bad things come in trios. I've had two heart attacks, Mel, one in poor Aphrodite's milk bar, another before Dot brought you in here. Don't think the mortal coil could cope with another. Somehow I doubt I'll be having many more dreams."

A long pause.

"Oh Mel, don't you cry."

Then, shockingly, Edie went to sleep, leaving Mel still hungry for words.

Another day, another mood. This time Edie was agitated, breathing heavily, tossing her head, as if running the emotional equivalent of a race.

"What's up?"

Besides pulse and breathing rate, that was.

"I can't stop worrying about Alice. I know she's well looked after, and I suppose she won't even notice my not visiting anymore. But Mel, it's so sad. She's forgotten her name. She can only remember if you say, 'Sammy, Edie, and who?' Then she grins like a kid and says, 'Allie!'"

"Does she remember me?"

"Hard to say."

"I'll go and see her."

"Good girl. Thought you'd rise to the occasion."

"You manipulative old puss!" Mel said.

Edie gave her rare, feeble smile, then a moment later was reflective. "Mind, don't take her to my funeral. Not after the last time."

"No."

"Not that I'd be there to see, if she ran amok. . . . You see, I don't believe in life after the good sleep, Mel. No sitting on clouds for me. Dot, dear, I know you think your ancestors nudge you here and there in your research—"

Dot, sitting quietly by the bed, smiled serenely.

"—but I'm not going to be an interfering old ghost."

Mel suddenly realized that these two had discussed the subject previously.

"Not unless I was unquiet, with unfinished business."

Mel started, suddenly recalling Melvina Yuill. Is that why I sense her presence? she wondered. Because she has an ax to grind? Then she put her obsession forcibly out of mind, for Edie was speaking again:

"I've done everything I had to do, Mel. There's no need of an afterlife for me."

Her tone carried utter conviction.

After one visit, when Mel exited with the silent Dot and Nev, she heard Edie remark, in the general direction of nobody:

"All these people here! They won't let me go."

"There's something I've been meaning to tell you. Something important. These damn drugs! I can't remember."

Edie fell into silence for a while, seeming not even to notice the pressure of Mel's hand. When she finally opened her mouth again, near the end of visiting time, she was perhaps delirious, for her words made little sense:

"Just as well you came back, Mel. Those poor dogs and cats! You'll have to make it up to them somehow, take in a kitten, maybe."

"I will."

"Promise?"

"I promise."

She kissed Mel's hand, and the touch of the lips was tepid, as dry as fallen leaves, about to be whisked away in the wind.

The next visit, Edie was asleep, and they left her undisturbed, though inwardly Mel was frustrated: How many more conversations could she exchange with her aunt?

This time, the voice was so faint Mel had to bend over the colorless lips in order to hear.

"That you, girl? See, I've been holding on, trying to remember, and I think I've got it now."

She struggled for breath, then continued.

"Allie knew, but I doubt the information's still accessible in her poor old brain. Mel, she's lost so much! Well . . ."

Suddenly she addressed Dot, and Mel had to repeat the words, for Edie's voice would not carry far.

"Dorothy, you remember—"

"You remember."

"—telling me about your adopted son, about the poor little children taken away from their parents, for being light instead of dark brown."

"Telling Edie about the Aboriginal half-caste children,

brought up in care," repeated Mel, suddenly understanding the Koorie posters on Dot's walls.

Edie's voice raised slightly, enough for Mel to retreat and let her aunt speak for herself.

"I went back to Allie, and said I'd never heard of such a dreadful thing before. She said she had, when she edited those little booklets the Anglican Aboriginal missions put out. Then she giggled. She was just starting to lose her grip then. 'Sammy said I was never to tell,' she said. 'Tell what?' 'Myrie was shy,' she said, 'like me, but now and then she let things out. Like growing up in an orphanage, with her parents alive.'

"Now, that didn't make sense to me when she said it, but Myrie wasn't the sort of person to be interrogated, even I could see that. It was something I'd have to store away in the old curiosity shop. A few days later I was cleaning out an old trunk, looking for the Kirksley christening gown. Myrie watched me over her belly as I sorted out the family rubbish and suddenly burst into tears. I got up, cuddled her, and after a while she started to talk. She said she was crying because she didn't have rels, although once, when she'd been working in a hotel in outback WA, she thought she saw someone who looked like her brother being refused a drink. Unlike her, he couldn't pass . . . Then she bit her lip. I noticed, as if for the first time, that Myrie was light brown, light brown apricot peach. It shocked me. Sammy might have liked tweaking Ma's spectral nose, but marrying a girl with a touch of the tar . . .

"Still, Myrie was carrying his babe, and that was what counted, although he was cross with both of us, when he heard the black cat had been let out of the bag. Sammy was ashamed of his own wife! I had to promise not to tell anyone. Yet, 'Ede'—and this is what Allie said to me—'does it matter with my own sister? You and I are getting on, and we'll die without the little girl ever knowing. That was what Sammy wanted.' "

Edie paused and drew a deep breath.

"Mel, I no longer care anymore about Sammy's wishes. You ought to know, and be proud of your ancestry, on both sides."

Mel sat, unable to absorb the information, dimly aware that Nev had thumped her on the back, and that Dot was dabbing her eyes with a lace handkerchief, delicate as frosted spiderweb. What would Melvina Yuill make of this? she wondered. Victorians were notoriously racist. But then she put the thought firmly out of mind—Edie, at this moment, was much more important.

"Congratulations, Mel, you're a real Australian," her aunt finished.

Almost her last words, Mel thought. Did she say anything much of consequence after that? If she did, I can't remember. The next time we came to see her it was too late. Edie lay on her bed, waxy and still, all personality gone from her face. The number-three pearl button had been and gone.

Suddenly, Edie wasn't there anymore. That was how Mel later expressed it to Dot. All that was left of the woman were reflections in the Kirksley photo albums, first as an infant, her expression happy and intelligent as a Buddha; then the small girl, supporting the new baby Sammy, Allie on one side, Edie on the other, the sisters identically dressed, with big bows in their hair; several years later, Edie dressed up as a mini Charlie Chaplin for a fancy-dress party, with Sammy as The Kid; then teenage, astonishingly pretty, on the arm of an American soldier.

After that shot the images of Edie smiling were fewer, and tended to show her standing in front of hospital buildings in stiff linen apron and headdress like a folded table napkin. What happened to that soldier? Mel wondered. Was he the love of her life? How little I know about her.

And how little it took, too, for a vital personality, shaped by life into an attractive mix of idiosyncrasies, to be suddenly . . .

gone, with the world rolling on as if nothing had happened. Phrases came back to Mel, from an otherwise boring first-year English class: an Anglo-Saxon noble, comparing life to a sparrow, flitting through a dining hall, in one end and out the other, with nobody in the hall knowing where it had come from or where it was going to. Only the passage through the room, the beating of tiny wings, was perceptible. You may not have been a high-flyer, Edie, Mel thought, but your flight had grace.

She closed her mental album. It was time to go to the funeral.

TWENTY-NINE

Two Funerals

"Shouldn't we be making a move now?" That was Nev again, nervously punctilious.

Dot answered, in amused exasperation, "Well, if you want to be an early bird, dear. Yoohoo, MEL!"

"I'm on my way," Mel called. Quickly she checked her reflection in Dot's mirror and adjusted her earrings again. Today was the first day that she had been able to wear both, with the right earlobe, the one that May had ripped, no longer swollen and sore. Until it had healed, she had combed her hair over the wound, so that nobody could remark on it.

Yet otherwise she had hardly thought of that eventful day, nor of anything much beyond the bed and its occupant. Edie's leavetaking had dominated her existence, and there had been no time to think of what she might do next, where she would live . . . but she put that out of mind. The leavetaking was not finalized yet; they still had to attend the last act, the *carnevale*, farewell to flesh and blood.

"Let's go," she said to the waiting cousins. They trooped out to the van, a somber little company, with even Dot toning down her usual pink, her dress almost more cobalt than fuchsia, with matching hat.

Their destination was a necropolis in the outer suburbs—Edie's choice. Her aunt's forethought had extended to putting money aside for the ceremony, even making a deposit with the funeral directors several months back. "She opted for cheap and efficient," Dot had commented. "How like a nurse!" The wastes of brick veneer land didn't seem like Edie at all, but it was difficult to define what would have been preferable. A Viking ship burial, perhaps?

"Gate three!" Nev lifted his head from the map book, directing Dot. They drove into the necropolis, a curious area of grassy parkland, with surgically trimmed rosebushes so tidy as to seem artificial, interposed with low brick walls, adorned with square brass plaques. "Chapel Three parking that way." He gestured. The pink van negotiated the roadways, finally coming to a stop, among the more soberly colored vehicles in the parking lot, like a flamingo in the company of crows.

Their destination was a brick building whose shape suggested, but only slightly, a church. As they neared, Mel was struck by the number of people waiting outside, mostly middle-aged women with a no-nonsense air to them. "Old nursing buddies," Dot said from underneath her hat. "Sticks out a mile."

"But so many of them!" Mel said.

"She had quite a career," Dot said.

"People do read the obit notices," Nev said. "Only way to keep up with your friends when you get to a certain age."

By one side was a group of three elderly men, vaguely familiar to Mel, although she could not place them until she noticed they all had long noses, reminiscent of ski runs. Cousins, she recalled, but Donaldson, not Kirskley. She rubbed her own shorter snub, thankful for this genetic legacy from Myrie. The trio all wore tweed, in harmonious shades of charcoal gray, just as, she recalled, they had the last time she had seen them. These cousins might have been a prop, stage furniture from the burial scenes of Mel's experience.

The thought took her from the thin sunlight to gray weather, rain drizzling down on a grim little stone church, the umbrellas of those arriving shiny with wet, leaving tracks of damp behind them, like snails. As the mourners had been almost exclusively women, the umbrellas had been frilled, or paisley, or flower-patterned, contrasting oddly with the black dresses and glum faces underneath. In that milieu, the trio of Donaldsons had been conspicuous by their masculinity, and their plain brollies.

"Gawdalmighty, who are those ads for Harris tweed?" Mayzee said, twisting around in the pew.

"Edward, Sarjent, and Timothy Donaldson, gent's outfitters and Dad's cousins," Mel said, also gazing around. At the sight of her face the Donaldsons had nodded gravely, sympathetically, but, since they did it in unison, also comically. May went pink in the face, and spluttered. "Stop it!" Mel whispered frantically, then in a moment caught the infection of laughter, and had to cover her mouth with a handkerchief. She felt a pang of conscience—the Donaldsons were very proper, and mind-numbingly stuffy, but they had at various times in her childhood presented her with toffee apples.

Marc came down the aisle, slipping into the pew beside them. "What have we here?" he said to May, and got the reply "The entire contents of Sammy Kirksley's little black book, also Tweedledum, Tweedledee, and Tweedleyourthumbs, whom Mel says are rels. Any more of your bizarre family in evidence?"

"My aunts," Mel said, enjoying despite herself May's sallies.

"Where?"

Mel tried to gesture unobtrusively with her head and the Happy Orphans' Club craned sideways. Alice and Edie sat in the pew on the other side of the aisle, in matching black, linked by the clasp of their gloved hands, their Kirksley noses very noticeable in profile. Mel surveyed Edie with real curiosity; it was the first time she had seen this aunt in years, as throughout Mel's childhood Edie had been nursing at various South Seas hospitals, with only flying visits home to Appleby. Her look of calm was in contrast to Alice, who continually fidgeted, eyes moving back and forth wildly.

"Names!" May had said, a grin at the corners of her mouth.

"Well, the one nearest us is Edie—"

"Did you say Seedy?" Mayzee said, eyes wide.

Mel felt quite sure she had spoken clearly, but repeated: "Edie."

"Edie. Seedy Edie!"

"Oh, well done!" Marc said.

"And the other is Alice."

May's eyes narrowed. "She looks in Wonderland. Alice in Wonderland it is."

Mel was distracted from these unpleasantries by the sight of a woman in full-length silver mink, bizarrely overdressed for a funeral. She greeted Edie, and Mel guessed at her being one of Sammy's private school flames, all of whom, to Gran Kirksley's fury, had subsequently married their old money to more of the same, consolidating existing wealth and status, rather than raising Sammy to the dizzy heights of the upper middle class. As Edie replied, Alice took advantage of the diversion, slipping her hand free, then nipping out of the pew like a wayward child.

"Oh, no!" Mel goggled as Alice wandered up the aisle. She made a circuit of the coffin, looking bemused, then reached out and started picking flowers from the wreaths. One she stuck in her hatband, and another went into her buttonhole, before a charcoal-colored blur came up the aisle, decorously but rapidly, Sarjent or Edward or Timothy Donaldson to the rescue.

"Wow!" cried Mayzee. "I wouldn't have missed this for the world."

Chapel Number Three was half filled already, with more of the nurses, and, judging from the nods in Dot and Nev's direction, a fair selection of the genealogical researchers. Mel looked at the backs of the heads in the pews before her, searching for some familiar sign, to indicate that someone was here whom she knew, apart from the Donaldsons. Tears chafed her eyes; it was asking a bit much for May or Marc to have come, but still . . .

Spread along one entire pew was a bewildering selection of heads, not with white or rinsed blue hair, but the colors of youth: brown, bobbed, or shoulder-length; blond, lank, and long under a black hat; and fluorescent-dyed dreadlocks. As their little cortege passed up the aisle, Mel saw the faces behind the hair—Sorrel, Nola, Kaye, and Rube. Roxana Press had come to the funeral.

Mel stopped, momentarily finding herself without words.

"But how . . . ?" she mumbled.

Nola, who sat nearest, on the aisle, reached out and took her hand. "Kaye reads the obits column."

"Hatches, matches, and dispatches are a great source of inspiration. Plus it's one way of keeping up with the various branches of Tollets," Kaye said. "And when I found the name Kirksley there, we knew why you'd suddenly disappeared from the planet Roxana."

"We thought Geraldo might have kidnapped you." That was Nola.

"That bitch at your flat was no help," Sorrel said, scowling.

Mel boggled at the thought of Sorrel vs. May, but said, "Oh, I'm so glad you came."

"Just as long as you're back on Monday," Sorrel added.

"We've got a conference for you to go to," Kaye said.

"Hey, don't overload her!" That was Nola again. "Can't you see Mel's only got one thing on her mind at the moment?"

Indeed, while they had been speaking, Mel's eyes had overflowed with tears.

"GO AND SIT DOWN," Rube boomed.

"We'll give you the gossip later," Nola said, and gave Mel a little push, kindly but firm. Mel took one step forward, somehow registering, blurry though her sight was, that the couple in the pew opposite were the St. Cyrs, Marc's parents.

"What are you doing here?" she blurted, her voice barely in control.

"Why shouldn't we show our respect?" Marc's father said, a little defensively. "We are your in-laws, de facto or not."

But not anymore, Mel thought. How to tell them? As she momentarily pondered, the Ma-monster hissed, "We thought Marc might be here, he . . ."

"Ssh!" Nev said firmly, looming beside Mel and taking hold of her elbow. "Come and sit down. The show's about to start."

And indeed Nev rather than Dot had been right about the time: if they had dawdled any longer they would have been late for the funeral. Mel let Nev guide her to the foremost pew, as the funeral celebrant, a bland man in a dark suit, neared the podium with the air of being about to read the night's TV news. She sat, for the first time noticing the pale pine coffin, which struck her as absurdly small. Had Edie really been so tiny? How little it looked, to encompass sixty-seven eventful years.

* * *

"Man that is born of woman hath but a short time to live, and that is full of misery," intoned the minister at Sammy's funeral.

"What sexist lingo!" May said audibly. Anything to create mischief, thought Mel, who knew that sexism in language bothered Mayzee not at all. Behind them came several indrawn breaths, then a cracked little voice retorted, "How lovely to hear the funeral rite from the Book of Common Prayer as it ought to be, not translated into modern slanguage!"

In response to the minister's voice an emotional tap had started to drip within these already overwrought women: the lady in mink wiped her eyes with a silk handkerchief; two identical stick-thin women, whom Mel vaguely realized must be the Penhaligon sisters, Merle and Gladdy, notorious in the family annals for Sammy's two-timing twin with twin, were sniveling; and a Filipina-looking woman, quite young, whom Mel could not place, was sobbing unrestrainedly. Didn't he go to Manila for his last but one holiday? she wondered, before the emotional charge caught up with her too. She sat still, shrouded in grief yet unable to cry, with the melancholic, archaic phrases from the service resounding in her head.

"He cometh up—"

How appropriate for Sammy, Mel thought, as May, beside her, emitted a soft snicker.

"And is cut down like a flower, he flieth . . ."

Away like he did all his life, why should now be different? she thought. If any woman got a little too close to him, off he was on the road, in his car, being a lone wolf, a love-you-and-leave-you man. There were exceptions—Myrie, Nola, the women shackled to him by blood—but even they never really got to know Sammy. What might Nola have made of him? Clearly those two were birds of a feather, for the almost-stepmother had run away too.

Self-pity brought tears to her eyes; and she snuggled her face into the angle of Marc's neck. There was no fatherly shoulder for her now—Marc and Mayzee would have to be her family. As if in response, two sets of arms encircled her; she succumbed to them, and to sorrow. After that the rest of the service was a blur.

The celebrant declaimed, "We have all gathered here today to say our good-byes to Edith Adah Kirksley . . ."

Mel listened, leaning back, her hands folded. How sensible of Edie, to keep organized religion out of her funeral service! This was a farewell it would have been impossible for Mayzee to disrupt, for here was not convention, followed blindly, no matter how beautiful the words might have been, but a spontaneous, unstudied series of tributes. The celebrant summed up the life, Mel realizing now that Edie had, as Nev had said, quite a career in nursing, in Australia to begin with, then Borneo, New Guinea, Polynesia. Afterward followed a succession of the nurses, sharing their memories with affection and pride; Ted Donaldson, with a sentimental retrospection that made Mel suddenly aware he must have been quite sweet on his cousin as a teenager; and finally Dot, recalling Edie's work as treasurer for the Genealogical Society, which sounded every bit as efficient as her nursing.

And then, suddenly, it was all over, the coffin trundling away behind a curtain, the action reminding Mel irreverently of an airport baggage carousel in reverse. The living contents of Chapel Three spilled out into the sunlight, thoughtful, and blinking a little. Suddenly Mel was the center of attention, people swooping down on her from all sides. The Donaldsons, in succession, shook hands with her, remarking, as if allocated, one pleasantry each:

"A very fitting service, if I may say so, even if not Christian." (Tim.)

"Good send-off for the old girl, I thought." (That was Sarjent.)

"Hear she left the funeral chappies strict instructions about having her ashes scattered around a rosebush. What a woman! Thought of everything." (Edward.)

One of the nurses, overhearing, said, "And it had to be a Lorraine Lee! Any significance to that?"

"Who knows?" Mel said, thinking that there probably was a reason for the request, but one Edie had kept to herself.

Marc's parents neared, and Mel was acutely aware that her smile was becoming forced.

"Can we possibly talk about Marc?" the Ma-monster said ominously.

Dot interposed herself: "Of course not. Mel's got a wake to go to."

As Dot spoke, Mel was distracted by the Roxanas.

"Good-bye Mel," Kaye cried merrily. "I hope you don't mind, but I did need a funeral service for the next chapter of my novel. This will do very nicely."

"Vampire," Nola said amiably; then, to Mel: "See you on Monday, right?"

"You've got work to do," Sorrel added.

The St. Cyrs had vanished. Mel bent under the fuchsias of Dot's hat and whispered, "Thanks, but what a dreadful whopper! There's no official wake . . ."

"I know, dear, but it got rid of them, didn't it?"

"Who were they?" asked Nev.

"My ex-in-laws. It's just that they don't know it yet."

"Ah," he said. Before he could comment further, about ten nurses in succession came up and shook Mel's hand, then an elderly couple, who introduced themselves as former neighbors of Edie and Alice's at Appleby. After that, there was a lull.

"You know," Dot said, "I dips me lid to Edie. Like that old

dear said, she really did think of everything. Fancy arranging the disposal of her own ashes!"

"Oh, it has to do with what happened at my father's funeral. You see . . ."

Two more nurses neared, arm in arm. "We're off to the pub to drink Edie's astral health. Do join us."

"I'll be in on that," Nev said. "I'm parched! Dot, care to whet the old whistle?"

The fuchsias nodded.

"And Mel?"

They were all looking at her, she knew, but all she could do was stare at the figure approaching over the lawns.

"No, no thank you, you're very sweet, but I'll stop a while here. . . ."

"But how will you get back?" Nev said.

"Don't worry, I've got transport," and breaking free, she stepped forward to greet Daniel.

THIRTY

In the Garden of Baron Samedi

Mel felt like hugging Daniel, but instead all she said was "Hey, you too read the obituary columns!"

"Now and then. It wasn't how I was expecting to find you, though."

"I was incommunicado."

"I'm sorry."

Almost without thinking they had started to walk away from the little group remaining around Chapel Three, into the Park of the Dead, with its velvet grass and manicured roses.

"Was Edith a nice aunt?" he said.

"Yes."

"I've got nice aunts too. Mad, but nice."

Mel paused in front of one bush crowned with pink roses.

"D'you know if that's a Lorraine Lee? It may sound silly, but I don't know what they look like."

"The ones my parents grow are less of a nail-varnish shade. Why'd you ask?"

"Because my aunt wanted her ashes fertilizing that brand of rose. I think somebody must have once called her Lorraine."

An American serviceman, perhaps?

"Are you going to scatter the ashes?"

"No, as I keep explaining. She said ashes and tears just made gray mud, and the undertaker should do it."

"What forethought," he said, bemused, and at his expression Mel suddenly felt glorious peals of laughter leaping up and down in her throat, like children nearing the end of a school day. Feeling no longer under control, she sat down on the lawn, and released them.

"No, no . . ." Daniel was kneeling beside her. "I'm not hysterical, it's just I'm remembering how at the last family funeral I went to, it was my father and, and . . ."

She laughed again.

"I wasn't exactly paying attention to the disposal of the ashes, what with every woman Dad had dated in the last forty-five years fluttering around and trying to weep on me. In fact I forgot clean about his mortal remains for a fortnight. When I phoned the funeral directors they said that the ashes had been collected already, by Miss Vera Kirksley. There's no such person. They gave me a description—plump, gray-haired, middle-aged—but that could have fitted about twenty of Dad's ex-girlfriends. One of the old floozies had actually gone and snaffled Dad's ashes! She's probably got him on her mantelpiece still, among the silk flowers and china poodles."

"That's macabre."

"I tell you, it happened. That's why my aunt left instructions. Though it would have been nice if somebody had wanted to steal her ashes . . ."

She sat up, suddenly serious.

"You've had a bad time," he said.

"You can tell?"

"It shows." She fingered her left ear for a moment, then released it. Should she tell him now, of the string of disasters since they had parted in another park? No, wait.

"I had my own disaster. Nearly didn't get here."

She raised her eyebrows.

"Legba broke down on the other side of the necropolis. You try getting your car fixed in a cemetery! Luckily these police came by and summoned up a tow truck via mobile phone. Then I went walking through the park from Chapel Two, looking for you."

She stood up, trying to see if anybody was left at Chapel Three, but all the little ant figures had vanished. "But how . . . but how will we get out of here?"

"With Mick. Constable Mick Hatter, of the archives. He's here today, at the same funeral as those police I met. In fact, he's a friend of theirs. He won't be free for an hour or so, as the Chapel Two funeral is running a bit late, but we can join him then for a lift home."

She shook her head, incredulous. "It's too much of a coincidence, having Mick here too! Like it was written in the stars or something."

"Or Legba and Samedi teamed up."

Legba and what? she thought. It sounded like Saturday, in French. But he continued before she could query the word: "You haven't heard the deputy police commissioner had a stroke? His funeral is today, but the necropolis is so big, you'd hardly know there's thousands of police here all paying their respects."

"No, I tell you I've been living in a complete media blackout all week."

They walked on silently, across a blazing white gravel path. Without anything being said, they paused here, Daniel toying with the gravel, Mel, arms folded, staring at the lines of roses.

After a while she turned, and saw he had found a loose stick, amazing in this pristine setting, and was scratching a design among the tiny sharp stones.

"An asterisk," she said.

"Asterisk in one cultural context, a *point d'arrestation* in another. Stopping point. We are halted here."

He drew again.

"That's from your car," she said.

"The vévé of Legba. It's a path, so I can draw it here, although the cemetery is Samedi's territory."

His stick delineated a third symbol.

"The vévé of Baron Samedi. Brother god of Legba. Legba controls roadways and gates, including the portal between this world, and the divine mirror, the next. Samedi is Lord of Graveyards, another meeting point. It was an unholy conjunction between the two, maybe, that got you, me, and Mick here on the same day."

The design finished, he stared at it a moment, then obliterated all three sketches in gravel with his feet.

"Are you a pagan?" Mel asked nervously.

"No, sorta agnostic. It's just . . . from experience . . . I have respect for a couple of religions. Nothing monotheistic, though—the universe isn't that simple, I think. Like the man said, there are more things in heaven and earth . . ."

A chill little breeze had sprung up, scattering red rose petals like drops of blood all over the white gravel of the path. Mel wrapped her arms around herself, shivering, and for the first time, it seemed in eons, suddenly thought of Melvina: of the dreams, iconic transmitters of information; of the strange guesses she had made, as if someone anticipated her every research move; and above all, the eerie sense of being watched, when nobody was in sight.

"This may sound like a bizarre thing to say in the middle of a cemetery, but do you believe in ghosts?"

He looked up at her. "I don't disbelieve in anything."

"Do you believe the dead walk through people's dreams?"

He looked concerned. "You've been dreaming about your aunt?"

"No, about Sammy, my dad . . . and someone else."

"A dream can mean different things in different contexts . . . cultural for instance."

Now he stood, brushing his hair out of his eyes, his face wary, as if judging what next to say.

"Hell, when I was in Haiti I dreamt about Legba and Samedi."

"What did that dream mean, in that particular cultural context?"

He hesitated. "It could mean they were saying, 'Come hither.'"

Suddenly he shivered, as she had earlier, but more violently.

"Mel, do you mind if we continue this conversation later, and elsewhere? It's giving me the creeps, here, in Samedi's garden."

"You feel it's maybe tempting fate a bit?"

He shook his head, and in an undertone he added the following, apparently to himself, but still audible to Mel:

"No, tempting some very capricious guys."

Mick, when they met him, was red around the eyes, and Mel was momentarily shocked that this tough man had been crying. Vaguely she wondered if Jesperson had ever wept; and if he had, would it have been good for him? Nonetheless, Mick seemed pleased to see them, even to chat inconsequentially while he drove from the necropolis, realm of Samedi, to the emergency garage where Legba's namesake languished. There, they found that Daniel's car needed another hour's work. Mick said to Mel,

"You don't want to be hanging around an old garage, do ya? Lift home?"

"Go," Daniel said. "It's been a long day. But before you do, tell me where to find you again."

She sat, a passive passenger in the back of the unmarked police car, thinking that, with Mick in uniform, it could look to casual observers as if she were a villain, being driven away for questioning. "It's been an evil day," Mick said, without looking around. "The Big Fella, and then your aunty . . ."

"She had a pretty good innings," Mel said. "No, today wasn't so evil for me, compared to the last week."

She leaned forward, hands against the back of the front seat, addressing the back of Mick's neck with the tale of her troubles, so carefully kept to herself. He listened, commenting now and then:

"You go and report that guy in the alley. Creeps are ten a penny . . . but you never know, as the lads in the sex-offense squad say."

Later he spoke again:

"Pity you didn't make a statement before your ear healed, it would have been evidence. You had other things on your plate, right? But Miss Mazy May coulda been charged with malicious wounding and a few other things."

"I don't care, except that she's got almost all my possessions, shut in the flat. I need my purse back, also my bankbook, so I can stop sponging off Dot and Nev . . ."

"No worries," Mick said. "We just make a detour on the way home."

Back at the old, familiar street, Mick parked his car in front of the block of flats, and made to get out.

"No, wait here. This has to be done on my own, or I'll feel like a total coward for the rest of my life."

He nodded, then glanced up at the flats. "Sure she's in?"

Mel eyed the fourth window on the second floor, the living room, providing the Happy Orphans' Club's only street view.

"Sunday isn't a dialysis day, the Paperback Exchange is closed . . . nowhere else she could be."

"Orright. But if she takes a squiz I'll be standing by the car, having a smoke and looking scary."

Had Mel been away only a week? It felt like years, and the block of flats looked smaller, as if last encountered by the child-Mel, its bricks more dingy, the concrete steps filthier. I have grown, Mel thought, trudging up the stairs, not outwardly, but beyond the limits of last week's self, who ran away from trouble, rather than confronting it. She touched her earrings briefly, then knocked at the door, feeling detachment, not trepidation. A bad event anticipated is always less hurtful than one that creeps up unawares and hits you over the head.

From inside the flat she heard slippered footsteps.

"Knock, knock, who's there?" May said.

How odd her voice sounded! Had Mel never noticed before how glutinous it was?

"Mel. If you go to the window, May, and look down, you'll see my escort. I didn't bring him up here, but he'll come, if you don't let me in to collect my belongings."

A long pause; then chains and bolts began to click back, until the door swung open, revealing May, and the flat in a state of unusual squalor. A pile of crumpled junk-food packets surrounded May's chair, and on the table were several empty wine bottles, and a single, dirty glass: nothing had been cleaned up since Mel the maid, however slovenly, had left. The smell, too, of old books, cheap food, mold! I'm well out of here, Mel thought.

First thing she did was walk past May and secure her bag, which was still lying on the floor. She checked its contents, and found nothing missing, then went into the bedroom, to find it as Marc had left it, with the wardrobe gaping, open, empty drawers, oddments Marc had discarded when packing strewn all over the unmade bed. She reached up, to the top of the wardrobe, and retrieved her old battered suitcase, borrowed from Sammy but never returned.

Myrie's photo was the first thing that went into it, wrapped up in the folds of her sage-green dress. Other clothes followed, with the exception of the duffel coat, too shabby and full of old, bad memories to be taken with her. The bedroom emptied, she moved from room to room of the flat, excepting only Mayzee's, taking only what was incontrovertibly hers, for she wanted no part in anything jointly owned; that might lead to further wrangling, further contact with this past.

Finally, suitcase filled, she stood in the living room, staring at the back of May's chair. She circled it, and it started to turn, away from her, until, suddenly angry, she reached out and arrested the motion. The mass of egg-chick hair did not move; May kept staring into the depths of her latest paperback.

"You read, you read all the time, but do you ever take a look at the obituary notices?"

"God no." It still sounded glutinous. Mel waited, for the follow-up, but when it didn't come, she merely shrugged, calm again. May's silences meant nothing to her now.

"Well, no matter. Do you know where Marc is?"

A shake of that fluffy head.

"I saw his parents. We didn't have time to talk, but they seem worried about him."

May finally looked up; Mel met her gaze unblinkingly.

"You didn't find Marc."

"I had other, more important things to do. Like avoid being raped and murdered, which nearly happened the night you threw me out on the street."

"Spare me the Mel-o-drama," May said in tones of cool disbelief.

I hate you, thought Mel, but controlled herself. "Well, I'm

not playing Little Orphan Annie with this suitcase, I'm leaving for real."

"What about the moolah you owe me?"

Mel paused, pondering this impediment to a clean break with the flat and its inhabitants.

"The deposit we paid on the flat—one month's rent in advance. I came up with one-third of it, didn't I? My aunt Alice gave it to me. Keep it."

She reached into her bag, found the key ring by touch, and, not taking her eyes away from Mayzee, removed her copy of the flat's key. She flipped it at May, and with a faint thud it landed on the open book.

"You went and smashed up our lovely Happy Orphans' Club," May said, softly and venomously.

"Not me. Another Mel." Ms. Yuill, in fact.

May started to speak, but Mel reached forward and touched her on the lips gently, closing that mouth and its protests.

"It's over. Ssh. Not another word."

She moved back, releasing May and also the chair, which spun away from her, expressing unspoken rage. At the door, she said:

"Good-bye, May."

No answer. Had she wanted or expected any? She went out the door, burdened by the suitcase, but ready to skip down the stairs. Halfway down, she grinned wryly, suddenly recalling a passage from *The Scarlet Rider*:

"Stop!" cried Red Meg. Aynsley and I had been about to intervene, to separate the brawling miners, and hard work we expected of it too, for they were big, burly men; but the dulcet tones of the woman halted the fight immediately. Fists still upraised, California Joe and Scarface Tom turned to look at her, mouths open in amazement, as if they had been transformed into bronze statuary.

"Did I not say to either of you, no fighting in The Golden Banner? I hereby ban you from my establishment."

Scarface Tom started to protest, but she came closer to the combatants, still carrying the ivory fan, Aynsley's gift to her, which only a moment before she had been twirling like an innocent girl of sixteen at her first ball. Now she furled the pretty, fragile fairing, delicate as a butterfly, and tapped the tip of it against those rough lips, looking straight at the man as she did so, her gaze that of an Imperatrice.

"Ssh. Not another word."

THIRTY-ONE

The Shadow-Self

Back at the little pink house, Dot answered the door with the telephone receiver to her ear, at the end of the extension tether, for all the world like a child's toy pulled by a string. Seeing that the fat woman seemed agitated, Mel walked past and let her continue the conversation. It consisted, at this end, of "Yes, dear," "All right," and "I see."

She dropped her suitcase down at the end of the hallway, under an immense Yothu Yindi poster, and went into the kitchen. On the benchtop were a pot, a knife, and the ingredients for stew. To make herself useful Mel began to prepare the meat and vegetables, cutting them into tidy chunks. Paring down my life, she thought, that's what I've been doing. Slice! There goes Mayzee, into the bin. Slice again! The flat. All finished and gone, letting me concentrate on the important things. She held a peeled carrot in her hand, admiring the streamlined shape. Melvina, for one. Roxana. Daniel?

Standing there, carrot in hand, she began to laugh again, with the same fierce joy she had felt on leaving the flat, until her sides ached and tears trickled from her eyes. In the sudden silence after Dot put down the phone, the sound filled the house. Next moment the fat woman's footsteps thundered toward her.

"Oh," Dot said, assessing the scene. "Get a rude carrot, did you? What my son calls cocklecarrots?"

Mel wiped her eyes, shaking her head.

"Oh. Well, that was him on the phone."

Dot popped a chunk of celery into her mouth, as if to chew out a mental turmoil.

"Long-distance, reverse charges, as usual. I love every penny of it, especially when it's to say he's coming to visit. With some family, of course. His real family."

She sighed.

"Twenty years back, how were me and my husband to know? We thought we'd do the proper thing, adopt an original Australian, a little orphan from the bush. It seemed so right, too, when we saw this beautiful café-au-lait baby, with the biggest googly brown eyes you ever did see. We fell in love on the spot. Nobody told us his mother hadn't consented to give him up, nor that she was only fifteen. So we took him home, to this suburb, with nothing but white faces for miles around, and did we find out all about prejudice. . . ."

Mel thought suddenly and acutely of Myrie's brother, her uncle, who couldn't pass for white.

"By the time Keef was fourteen, he was in trouble with the law. With any other middle-class kid, the police would have laid off, knowing his dad had died only the previous year, and I wasn't coping too well. But all they could see was the black blood. Then one day I looked out the front door to see the kid in the arms of a woman crying fit to bust. She was darker, but apart from that they were dead spits. It was Keef's ma, come looking for her firstborn. He went from being an only, lonely kid, to one of six brothers and sisters, with an extended family in the hundreds."

She was calmer now, reflective.

"It was the saving of him. He's still in trouble with the law, but it's all in a good cause, the Koorie cause."

She reached out and opened a drawer in the kitchen table to reveal a photo, which she handed to Mel. It showed Dot in her usual pink, clutching a placard trailing streamers of yellow and red and black, the Koorie colors.

"My first-ever demo. The Old Ancestors, as Nev calls 'em, were sweet Christian dissenters, pro all the good causes from breastfeeding to antislavery. So Keef and I belong to a proud tradition."

Mel handled the photo carefully, then returned it to Dot.

"But now I'm in a pickle, dear. He's showing up tomorrow morning, early, along with he's not sure how many yet, all coming to stay in this little shoebox. I never could say him nay, but what about you? Keef'd say the more the merrier, but I don't think you could cope with crowds right now."

"I'd like to see him," Mel said. "I never met a black person before."

"In good time, dear. When you're ready for it."

Mel stuck out her lower lip.

"You're just trying to get rid of me."

"Oh I don't doubt you'd have a good old chat with Keef and Company, but I'd rather you did it when you're in a less volatile state."

"Volatile!"

"It's more than just grief. You're all over the place, emotionally. I think you need to be quiet, by yourself, to sort out what sort of person you want to be."

"What do you mean?"

"Nev said to me, 'I can't put it into words properly, but half the time that's not the same girl we met in the library. And yet half the time it is.' I don't want to use pop-psych terms like personality crisis, but that's what it looks like to me."

Mel sat still, her scalp prickling. Is Melvina that obvious? she wondered, and with that thought felt a great yearning, to pare down her life even further, to do as Dot suggested, leaving the pink house to concentrate on the search for the woman behind *The Scarlet Rider* again. And if I find Melvina? she thought. Locate a little bush grave, like the one in the last scene of the novel, and have a plaque put on it, to coincide with Roxana launching the book? Will her business with me be finished, and her presence vanish like a pricked balloon? Taking this newfound strength, this courage and confidence, with only the old timid Mel remaining? I don't want that!

"I'm going to Appleby," she said.

"But . . ."

"You were the one who said I should be alone."

"I did, but I was also thinking: who owns that house?"

Mel put down her paring knife. "Just now, I couldn't give a damn."

"No, dear, but you ring up the lawyer, or whoever's your aunty Alice's trustee, and find out what the situation is."

Mel picked up a peeled carrot. "Dot, you mean well, but it's"—here she snapped the carrot in two—"too much for me to think about at the moment."

She bit into it viciously.

Dot helped herself to another carrot. "Good for us, aren't they?" she said, and soon the pair were crunching in unison.

"Here I am!" Mel said to Appleby. It seemed appropriate—the house had, after a week of being shut up, the air of reproachful neglect. She put her suitcase down and moved from room to room, switching on lights and lowering blinds as if to ward off prying eyes, outside in the night. It was like retracing her steps in the dawn search, over a week ago, for Edie; but now she knew that the crumpled body she had been anticipating had vanished into ash, rose-food.

Nothing to worry about—but as she moved around the house, now a box of light, little reminders of Edie began to gnaw at her, like spirit mice. On the stairs, the dirty old housecleaning shoes. A feather duster stuck in an empty flower vase. In the best bedroom, the cumulative effect of the souvenirs finally was too much; she slumped across the neat coverlet and cried hopelessly into Edie's old dressing gown.

The emotional storm over, she brought her suitcase upstairs and to the little room of her own in Appleby, where she unpacked distractedly, for outside the wind blew, swishing through the trees and rattling twigs against the windows, like rapping fingers. What if that creep's out there again? she thought. Watching out for me. Can I bear to be alone, here? Should I call Daniel, ask him and Legba to drop around, stay with me? No, hold your horses, girl, you hardly know the man. . . .

Memory came to her aid: Hadn't she survived a night, out in the shed, sleeping soundly after a series of waking nightmares? Take courage, she thought. What would Red Meg, or more importantly, Melvina Yuill, do?

She stared at the electric light switch, then decisively, switched it off. Next she yanked the window curtain back, and opened the room to the night wind. At first the darkness seemed total; then she adjusted to it, becoming owl-eyed, able to see by the gleam of neighboring streetlights, and the seven-eighths-full globe of moon. Emboldened, she circled the house, opening and darkening each room.

Finally she stood on the landing, amid a shadow theater of charcoal dark and silvery moonlight, animated by the currents of air that swept through the house, ruffling papers, billowing curtains, jangling chandelier pendants and the shell wind chime in Edie's bedroom. The whole house was full of busy movement and soft noise, as if children scattered through it played hide-and-seek in the dark. Yet one point of stillness caught her attention: moonlight shining through the skylight, onto a framed sampler hanging on the wall beside her. She read it aloud:

"Yea, though I walk through the valley of the shadow of death, I will fear no evil, for thou art with me; thy rod and thy staff comfort me."

She was without fear, completely at peace, and alone? No. The sense she had before, in the shed, of someone watching over her, as she slept in her cocoon of green velvet, had returned, but stronger, its intensity almost a presence. She pirouetted, dancing with shadows, certain that just out of her sight, something eluded her gaze. It was a game, which she played until she suddenly stopped, near-giddy from the twirling.

"Welcome, Melvina," she said.

THIRTY-TWO

The Last of Marc

There were too long intervals of silence when each doubtless chewed the cud of sweet and bitter fancy.

—Susan Meade, shipboard diary

It was absurd and infuriating, but the next moment the intimacy shattered, with the phone ringing loud and unwelcome as a cock crow. Mel jumped, filly-like, landing on the edge of the narrow stairs, where she teetered, then fell forward into the dark pit of the hall. Her arms flailed, catching a banister, which checked her momentum briefly, before her grip broke and she rolled, bumping all the way down the steps to the hall carpet. Her shoulder struck something, which toppled with a crash, and from the following total silence she deduced that she had knocked over the phone table.

Mel lay on her back for a long moment, moonlight patterning her prone form. The wind had lulled, as if associated with the sense of the other, the shadow-self keeping her company, who had been chased away by the intruding noise, perhaps irrevocably. Now she was completely alone.

"Halloo?" a tiny voice said.

She saw by turning her head slightly the receiver lying close to her, at the end of its spiral cord. The call was still, miraculously, connected. She sat upright, muscles protesting bitterly, and grabbed the receiver.

"I hope you realize you nearly broke my bloody neck!" she snarled.

There was a pause, and then the person on the other end of the phone began to cry helplessly. A woman's tears, Mel realized. Whoever she was, she kept trying to talk through the sobs, but was unintelligible. Oh cripes, Mel thought, suddenly contrite. Probably some old crony of Edie's, who's only just found out what happened.

There was a scuffle at the end of the line, then a man's voice, familiar:

"I told Margie she shouldn't try to ring you at your aunty's house, the night after the funeral, but would she listen?"

Margie, Mel thought. Marguerite. Of course, the Ma-monster. "Hallo, Mr. St. Cyr," she said coolly.

"And hello to you too, Mel." His voice was tense—from the background noise, the Ma-monster was crying on his shoulder. "There, there, Margie, settle down. It's not as if the boy's been killed. . . ."

"You found Marc," Mel said, even more coldly.

"Found? He just reappeared, after causing all this botheration."

Mel gripped the receiver hard. "Look, as I was trying to say at the funeral, I'm not in an in-law relationship, de facto or not, with you anymore. Marc and I—"

"He told us, and we're very sorry about it, too. That's not all that's ended, either. He's walked out of his internship."

Mel became suddenly thoughtful, the calm reflectiveness experienced at the end of a jigsaw puzzle, when the bigger picture, seen only in fragments, is complete, visible in its entirety.

Of course, she thought, there was much more to that fight than Marc suddenly getting sick of me. . . .

"Well?" she said.

"We thought you might talk with him."

Mel wanted to say, No offense meant, but I really couldn't give a damn. She reached out, mentally, in the dark, for Melvina, but there was no response. Despite herself, she was curious to hear what Marc had to say for himself.

"If he wants to talk to me, I suppose I can listen, but there's no going back, understand? We ended, Marc and I."

She stood up and flicked on the hall light, picking up one-handed the table and assorted bits of Kirksley rubbish from the floor, while Mr. St. Cyr nattered on. Nearly everything she touched was a memento mori of Edie, and that meant she paid very little attention to what he said. "Well, what do you say to that?" he said finally.

"Yes," she replied abstractedly.

"Then that's settled. Afternoon tea with Marc at our place, three-thirty tomorrow," he said, sounding a little surprised. Mel put the phone down, then seconds later gave a heartfelt scream, as she realized just what she had agreed to. It exhausted whatever resources she had left at the end of this long day, and suddenly desperate for rest, she closed up the house and went upstairs. After a cursory check of her body for broken bones (nil) and bruises (several, but none too bad) she climbed into bed. The thing she saw before switching off the light was *The Scarlet Rider*, sitting safely on the desk. Despite that, her sleep was utterly dreamless.

Coming back to Roxana the next morning, she felt as if she had been a long time away—everything looked different. She said as much to Nola over coffee.

"No, it's you been bitin' the apple of life and seeing things new, just like old Adam and Eve in the garden of Eden."

Mel looked at her sharply. "That was something Sammy used to say. Generally when he was feeling sadder but wiser."

"Yeah, and I used it on Kaye. She liked it so much she put it into the mouth of one of her characters."

"What sort of character?"

"Sweet older guy. Ex of one of Roxana Reul's lovers."

"How . . . autobiographical," Mel said. Nola looked mildy rueful.

"You twigged at last. Wondered when you would."

Mel eyed one of the framed book covers, Roxana Reul against a tropical-beach sunset. "You met Kaye when you ran away to Bali, didn't you?"

"And Sorrel."

"I thought as much. There's electricity between the three of you."

"And sparks, if there's only two. Just works that way. We need a third, for . . ."

"Equilibrium?"

"I guess so."

Mel shook her head. "If Sammy could see you now . . ."

"Mel, don't you underestimate your dad. He had a lot of tolerance, for all sorts of things. Wherever he is, or whatever, if you believe in reincarnation like the Balinese do, he'd be glad I'm happy."

During their long and thoughtful silence, Sorrel entered with a gray bag, which she dumped in Mel's lap. Mel looked up, astonished at the weight.

"What's this?"

"From Kaye, who's sorry she can't speak to you now, but she's locked herself in her office until Chapter Seven is done. It's a portable laptop computer, in carrycase."

"For me?"

"To write about Mevina Yuill," Sorrel said, handing Mel a

glossy pamphlet. Mel unfolded it, and read, "*The Self and the Other: Writing Lives* . . . Conference on Biography/Autobiography . . . distinguished international guest . . ."

"The list of speakers is on the other side," Sorrel said, lip-smacking anticipation in her voice. Mel read on suspiciously, before stopping with a mental screech of brakes.

"It lists Mel Kirksley as speaking on 'The Mystery Behind *The Scarlet Rider*'! How COULD you?"

"Very easily," Sorrel said. "Once we heard Geraldo was presenting a paper at the conference on Charles Alonso Ellis, mystery writer."

Nola grinned. "We did things you don't want to know about to get on the program."

"Cajoled, appealed to feminist solidarity, and bribed with advance proofs of the next Roxana Reul," Sorrel said. "We had the luck that one speaker refuses to be in the same room as Geraldo, let alone the same conference, so we took her spot, which happily precedes his. Now all you have to do is write your paper. Use the computer—we'll show you how to use it."

The full impact of the flyer belatedly struck Mel, and she gulped like a fish several times. "Why? Why me?" she finally managed.

"We've heard you present your findings," Sorrel said. "You're an impressive speaker, when you forget about being diffident."

"But a conference . . . with important guests!"

Sorrel sighed theatrically. "Of course, Kaye could always write it for you, and present it, if you're going to be a nervous nelly. But the poor thing's got a deadline. . . ."

Mel looked down at the flyer again, registering for the first time the date. "So have I—the conference is less than two weeks away. All right, all right, I'll do it . . . but you're a bunch of—"

She stopped short, unable to think of an appropriate word.

"Publishers!" Nola said, laughing, as Sorrel swept triumphantly out. Annoyed, yet finding the situation funny herself, Mel joined in. When she sobered, it was to be suddenly aware of the computer in her lap, a square plastic pet. She looked down at it.

"Well, I suppose I'd better get started then. But I'll need some money, either borrowed, or an advance on my pay."

Nola said, "Ask, and you shall receive." Then, lowering her voice, she leaned close to Mel. "Talking about receivin', didn't your aunty leave you anything?"

"I really don't know," Mel said, genuinely surprised.

"Find out, then. She liked you, didn't she?"

"Not at first, after all those years away. Later, I think we loved each other."

After an impromptu computer lesson with Nola, Mel left Roxana, the computer hanging heavily from her shoulder like an electronic Old Man of the Sea—or Woman, she thought, recalling Jubilee Goodman's painting. She went first to the Victoria and Albert tearooms, but felt too self-conscious to set up the device and tap away in the midst of all that antique elegance. Then she thought of the library, and even found a quiet spot; but the little gray screen bothered her, so much so that she could do little more than stare at it perplexedly. Eventually she gave up. Even without the off-putting new technology, Marc was too much on her mind. What could she possibly say to him?

Initially, though, she merely said "Hi!" The ride to the moneyed part of town where the St. Cyrs lived had exhausted her into conventional banality. Marc nodded curtly and closed the front door.

"You being butler, then?" she said, reviving a little.

"Thank God, they've never been that pretentious!" he said loudly.

"I take it your parents are not in earshot," she replied.

"They're being discreet—watching vids in the master bedroom," he said. "But they've left us a tea party."

Mel turned slightly, and saw the mahogany tea trolley in the living room, carefully positioned between two overstuffed chintz chairs.

"It looks too cozy for words," she said.

"At least we agree on something," Marc said, and flung open the French doors into the formal garden. Next moment he was wheeling the trolley through and across the paved courtyard, coming to a stop at a brick wall decked with Mr. St. Cyr's pride and joy, espaliered roses, heavy and scarlet with blooms. Mel closed the doors and followed. Though the wind was chilly, the walled garden created a shelter, warmed by winter sun. Marc had pulled one of the heavy garden seats over to the wall, and she did likewise, leaning back and soaking up the warmth of sundried brick. For some minutes they just sat side by side, looking down the terraces of the garden to the river view below.

Marc poured tea for Mel without a word, for he did not need to ask about milk or sugar. Mel took the proffered cup, but declined a slice of cake. I'm not going to speak first, she thought. That's up to Marc. But the silence continued, and finally she snapped.

"Marc, I can't believe you want to talk to me."

"We didn't exactly part on friendly terms . . ." he mused, without regret. She looked at him hard. He sat relaxed, a slight smile playing across a face that expressed primarily *contentment*. That's new, she thought. When did I last see Marc looking like that?

"Your parents seem to think I can influence you."

He looked even more amused. "Funny about that. You couldn't care less, could you?"

She nodded, not at all reluctantly.

"I guess I felt the need to . . . explain myself. Satisfy your curiosity. You can't deny that."

"Marc, I've guessed a lot already. When your parents rang me, suddenly a lot of jigsaw pieces fell into place. The row, for one. You must have left the internship already by then."

He nodded, a short up-down bob of the head.

"How else could you, when supposed to be at work, spy on me and Daniel instead?"

She finished angrily, but his response was mild.

"I wasn't an intentional spy. It just happened that I looked out of the window and there you were."

"What window, where?"

"In the block of flats overlooking the park. That's where I'd been going for the previous three weeks, keeping shifts, but not at work."

"Doing what?"

"Watching fish, mostly. Shibunken."

Mel looked sideways, at the ornamental fishpond, to see underneath the lilypads a flash of red, like an animate autumn leaf. She never had understood what the St. Cyrs saw in overpriced goldfish.

Marc laughed, with a nasty edge.

"It was all due to Ma's fish. Otherwise I'd never have got friendly with Noboyuke. He's Japanese, a proctologist, and nobody talks to him much, 'cos of the job, I guess. He had a fancy fish magazine, in Japanese, in the hospital canteen, and I started talking to him about it. He doesn't make friends easily, just like me . . . which is why I joined the Happy Orphans' Club."

Yes, thought Mel, we three were spirits made kindred by loneliness . . . but I'm not like that anymore.

"Anyway, he had to go back to Japan for a couple of months, some complicated family crisis, and he asked me to care for the fish in his flat. It's a nice place, decorated Japanese style, high-tech with a dash of Zen, very relaxing, very peaceful. I thought of taking you there, and doing naughty things on his pure white rug. Then I thought, No, I'll keep it to myself."

Just as, thought Mel, I was unable to share Melvina with the Happy Orphans' Club, though I doubt now whether that was entirely my volition.

"But it wasn't easy, caring for the fish, being the perfect trainee doctor, *and* dashing back to the Happy Orphans' Club. For one thing, Nobby had chosen his flat for the view rather than proximity to the hospital. The three sites formed a triangle, the sides about equally distant from each other. One day I got to the flat with about five minutes to feed the fish, who were about ravenous enough to take bites out of each other, before heading off to another session of sick, cross, ugly people, and yells from the registrar. I think something gave way, deep inside. I looked up from the fish, and saw the five minutes had stretched into two hours. And there was nowhere else I wanted to be, just then."

"So you never went back to the hospital?"

"No. I didn't want to tell lies, or crawl and say, I'm sorry for playing hooky, take me back and I'll be a good little doctor for ever afterward, amen."

"I thought you liked medicine," she said, after a moment.

"I was mistaken."

"All those years of training . . ." she said, wide-eyed.

"Stop it! You're sounding like the Ma-monster."

"I only meant that you must have seen this coming."

He broke off a rose and tore it apart.

"Only in the sense of a generalized unhappiness, that got worse and worse."

"Marc, I had no idea . . ."

"May spotted it," he said.

She was silent again, digesting this new information. "Well, what happened next?"

"Not a lot. I kept shift hours, but at the flat. It had become my home away from home, the place where I could sit and not worry how I was going to tell everyone what I'd done. Then one day I looked out of the window and there you were. It made me see red, Mel intruding on my special place. Then I noticed the man with you. I felt like a traffic light—red and green-eyed."

Anger *and* jealousy, thought Mel. Also, injured male pride, just like Darcy Ainsworth, with the only response to run away, though not as far as West Australia.

"So I followed you back to the flat. When I got back to the fish that night, with my suitcase, I felt better. Relieved, almost, because now I knew why you were being such a different person, from the old fancy-free Mel I had loved."

Past tense, Mel thought.

"And knowing that, I could forgive, and walk away from you."

Now Mel was scattering petals too, venting her annoyance to the innocent rose. "Marc, do you know what happened between me and May, while you were feeling sorry for yourself and staring at fish?"

He looked aggrieved at being checked in his flow of self-justification. "She told me."

"May told you? When did you see her?"

"Yesterday. When I finally felt like leaving Noboyuke's flat, she was the person I went and talked to."

"She reproached you, I suppose."

"Not at all. She said I should have done it long ago. Turns out she'd spotted that my shifts were out of sync, with me spending more and more time with the fish. She's very perceptive—it's like telepathy."

"But wasn't she cross at you disappearing for a week?"

"I wrote her a postcard, telling her not to worry, I'd be back soon."

Mel felt hot, as if her blood really were, in the words of the old cliché, boiling.

"To her, but not to your parents, who were so worried they actually went to my aunt's funeral in case you were there!"

"I'm sorry about that," he said after a pause. She looked at him, realizing that that small point was all he would apologize for, and that it contained some relish for him, in that his impeccably mannered parents had committed a social gaffe. She was suddenly tired, rather than angry with his perversity, although the urge remained to wipe the barely suppressed smugness off his face.

"So what are you going to do now?"

"Think. Take it easy. Not do what anyone wants me to anymore."

Except maybe May, thought Mel, who approved of your leaving the internship. With that thought, another piece of puzzle came to hand, ready to be slotted in. She stood.

"Well, Marc, it's your life, and it's nothing to do with me anymore. No, don't see me out, I know the way." This was said over her shoulder, as she crossed the courtyard. "Just one question . . ."

"Yes," he said, a little nervously.

"Has May been to Noboyuke's flat?"

"Last night," he said. Was that a faint blush in his cheeks? Whatever, the piece was now slotted into the jigsaw, Mel's suspicion confirmed. Maybe her face gave her away, because he said, pathetically, "I thought, because you looked like me, you'd be like me."

"Are you trying to say," she said, as she wrenched the French doors open, "you loved what you perceived as a reflection of yourself? Marc, don't be so feeble! *Nobody* is like anybody else."

Except maybe me and Melvina?

The glass doors slammed shut behind her, and as she headed out, Mr. St. Cyr appeared, hands raised in supplication.

"No," she said, in passing. "I can't make your son grow up. He's got to do that himself!"

Another door slammed, and she strode down the pathway, feeling free enough to turn a cartwheel in this decorous, old-money street. A thought occurred to her as she straightened, fallen red maple leaves stuck like stigmata to each palm.

Off with the old love. And on with the new?

THIRTY-THREE

Séance with Claret

Daniel phoned that evening, as Mel was contemplating the first page of her conference paper, rough draft she knew, but still intensely satisfying to her. Recognizing his voice, she stroked the receiver, grinning dopily, she saw from her reflection in the dark study window.

"How's the conference paper going?"

She was incredulous. "You know about *The Self and the Other*?"

"I saw your name on the flyer."

She laughed. "Well, I've been writing for the last couple of hours."

"Feel like a break? I could bring around some takeaway."

He moves fast, she thought, feeling again the anticipatory surge of adrenaline she had experienced as they drove down the freeway in Legba.

"What a lovely idea," she said, trying not to sound too eager, but failing ecstatically.

She put down the phone, then went charging up the stairs like the Light Brigade. Entering Alice's room, she stared boldly at the mirror, defying the glass to show her anything but a Mel Kirksley. Nothing happened, and she smiled triumphantly at her reflection, realizing it held no fears for her now; she had accepted, indeed welcomed, Melvina's intrusion into her life. Nonetheless, she felt anxiety—at not looking ideal enough for Daniel. The dress was her best, the sage-green wool perfectly offset by her turquoise earrings, but something still seemed missing. What had happened to those embroidered shawls?

Then she turned, recalling the creak of the mahogany chest's lid, as she had stood, eyes closed, waiting for Edie's surprise. The box had always been a repository for Kirksley treasures. She opened it to find the two silk shawls uppermost, wrapped in tissue paper. Pulling out the white silk, she draped it across her shoulders. Better . . . but her reflection still didn't look right. She looked at the chest again, realizing the matching bonnet must also be hidden in its depths, but in the end shut the lid, determined not to tempt fate.

She neared the mirror, staring critically at her face and hair. Makeup? No—most un-Victorian, for only whores painted their faces. Was that information in *The Scarlet Rider*? she wondered. If not, how did I know it? She ran her fingers through her wild halo of hair, eyeing it with loathing. Usually she liked the unkempt look, but now to her it seemed she had a bird's nest on her head, of copper wire.

In the bathroom, Mel found a comb, and carved a center parting in her hair. She smoothed it down on either side of her head, using water from the tap, for lack of any . . . any . . . What is the word? she thought, annoyed at the amnesia, and from somewhere came a term she had never used before: *pomade*. Don't I mean hair spray or gel? she puzzled, then put the thought out of mind, as she separated her hair in regular, thick strands, then began coiling them around her fingers.

She had just finished when the expected knock came at the front door, and pausing only to rearrange the shawl she ran down to meet Daniel. At the sight of her he nearly dropped their dinner.

"Do you like it?" she asked.

"I almost didn't recognize you," he said testily. "Not in a fancy dress and shawl, nor with those ringlets."

Mel fingered the long loops of curls, her smile, already tremulous, dying altogether at his following words:

"I got a shock to find Elizabeth Barrett Browning waiting for me. I always thought she looked like a poodle."

"That's unkind!"

"Sorry, but I never was a great fan of Victorian fashion. Now are you going to let me in, or do I take my chicken vindaloo elsewhere?"

She was almost cross enough with Daniel to slam the door in his face, but grudgingly let him pass. In the kitchen they opened the containers of food, eating hungrily, but with a certain restraint between them. She was still annoyed that he had not appreciated her effort; he for his part kept glancing at her, an unnerved, wary look on his face. It was almost a relief when she went to make coffee, then found . . .

"There's no milk!"

"Shall I take Legba and get some?" Daniel asked.

"No, I'll go myself. You stay here."

A walk, Mel decided, would clear the air somewhat. She had no idea where the nearest milk bar was, but headed out nonetheless. It was still early in the night, and the street was dotted with people: a few late commuters; children on skateboards; and dogwalkers. Creep time would be later, when the law-abiding were shut in their houseboxes, and only the night creatures roamed at large.

The wind had freshened—she felt it flap her heavy skirt like a sail, cold fingers of breeze teasing the oh so carefully arranged ringlets out of her hair. She felt no regret—while disbelieving she had resembled a poodle, she preferred not to shop as if on her way to a costume ball. On the other side of the tram stop, light shone from a corner store, and she entered to find a centipede of people being served by a young and cheerful woman, her eyes rimmed with red, from fatigue, and black, from Kohl. Mel waited impatiently with her milk, but the queue was chatty, small talk delaying the speed of service.

So this is Aphrodite's milk bar, she realized as the woman behind the counter gave an eyewitness account of Edie's heart attack. It was almost too much to bear, but as Mel hesitated, contemplating flight, the last customer left. She wondered whether to say, "That was my aunty you were talking about." Then she met Aphrodite's tired gaze, and decided that even with her new, Melvina-inspired assertiveness, there were times when making a scene was not appropriate.

Back at the house, though Legba was still parked outside, Daniel was missing. Has he run away? she thought, then noticed light spilling down the stairs from the open door of the study. Daniel had invaded her personal space at Appleby; he sat at the desk, *The Scarlet Rider* open before him. Even the short while she had been away, he had got through a fair chunk of the novel.

"Couldn't resist temptation," he said, without turning around. "I had to know what Melvina Yuill said about the young Parliamentarian."

"Roxana'll crucify you!" she said.

He tore his attention reluctantly away from the book, facing her with complete unrepentance.

"But they're not going to find out . . . unless you tell them, of course."

"How do I know you're not another Geraldo?" she said, aggrieved.

"Because I'm still here, reading, not speeding away with the text, fast as Legba can go."

Their gazes met, blue staring into tawny brown staring into blue. "I believe you," she said finally. "But you shouldn't have done it."

"I know, but I couldn't put it down. Even now, I can't wait to find out what's going to happen."

"I can save you the trouble by telling you. Where did you stop?"

"I speed-read to where Red Meg has just taken off her wedding bonnet."

"Well, after the debacle at the church, Miles escorts Mel— I mean Meg—back through the bush to Cornish Flat. They talk, with him pumping her for information about her missing husband, Arthur Dalvean/Firefly the Bushranger, she just trying to get things off her chest. Then, as they near the rush, she tells him to fall back, they would set tongues wagging if they arrived together, a respectable mounted constable in company with a notorious woman. He protests, but she spurs the mare Vino ahead. His last sight of her is a silhouette at the crest of the hill, the light of the sunset tinting horse and woman. 'As if she were indeed a scarlet rider,' he says to himself."

"Go on," Daniel said.

She sighed. "It's an ominous image, for next day she's dead. Yes, I know it's unfair, but not by the literary conventions of the 1860s. Kaye says I must read about a baker's dozen of early crime novels, *Lady Audley's Secret*, *East Lynne*, to understand that Melvina's subversion could only go so far. Victorian morality meant women had to be angelically good, especially in literature, and that bad girls had to suffer sticky ends. Meg must be punished, literally killed off."

"How?"

"Shot with her own little pistol: an apparent suicide, but Miles recognizes that it's murder. He solves the case."

"Oh. Whodunnit?"

"Scarface Tom, who's really Firefly, unrecognizably disfigured since the holdup at Whispering Flat. He's lying low, but keeping a watchful, jealous eye on Meg. When he hears about Aynsley he sneers at her, and something in her retort makes him think she's realized his identity. So he lures her into the bush before she can inform her 'pretty policeman.'"

"Nice guy."

"Resourceful Meg, though, even in her death agony seizes a loose button from her killer's shirt, concealing it in her sleeve for Miles to find. He traces it, and arrests Firefly."

"Justice is done?"

"Correct. Dalvean/Firefly is hanged, Miles gets his detective's card and his mimsy sweetheart. The last scene of the book has Miles and Arabella laying flowers on Meg's quiet bush grave. *We lingered for a while, watching birds going about their business in the ti-tree, in our ears their soft calls and the breath of the wind amongst the native grass, before leaving that quiet spot, where such a turbulent soul had found perfect peace.*"

His eyes went wide as he turned to the last page of photocopy. "You have the final sentence word perfect."

"Oh, I've read it a few times."

"Too perfect," he added. She pretended not to hear and he put the novel aside, following her downstairs. In the hall he suddenly clapped his hand to his brow: "How could I forget?"

And he dashed out into the night, returning with a bottle.

"Tollet claret," she said, pleased. She uncorked it in the kitchen then, playing the wine buff, poured a little into her glass and sniffed at it delicately. Next moment she clutched at the table for support. Strong, she thought, her head reeling. Daniel stared at her, so collecting herself she filled their glasses.

"What are you doing?" His voice appeared to be coming

from a long distance away, and she became aware she held a jar in her hand, the lid half unscrewed.

"Oh. Sugar lumps. For the coffee."

"You haven't made it."

"Ah." She chuckled, the sound seeming to continue a for a long time. "I will. . . ."

Very deliberately, he filled the kettle at the sink, and set it on the stove.

"Now put that jar down."

As he took it from her the lid shot off, clanking and rolling under the table. He bent to retrieve it, then shot up like a jack-in-the-box.

"You did something, then!"

"Me? Never!" Helplessly she started to giggle. He grabbed her by the shoulders, shaking her as gently as one would a wayward kitten, but shaking her nonetheless.

"I saw your hand move!"

"Don't be daft! Do you think I don't know what my own hand is doing?"

Mel broke free, and seizing her wineglass she opened the garden door. A gust of night air blew into the house, drawing her outside, as surely as if a dance partner had put his arm around her, leading her into the waltz. Although she walked on grass, and the only thing that had struck up was the wind, she sashayed across the lawn, finishing with a wobbly curtsy. Daniel appeared in the doorway, and she raised her glass:

"A toast, to old Australia!"

She drank, then next moment hiccuped with laughter, red droplets spraying all over her chin.

"Oh, it's revolting—like mulled lollywater!"

Daniel slipped delicately, then spat into the flower bed.

"Claret and lump sugar is certainly foul. I wonder about my ancestor's taste buds, if he drank the concoction."

He set the glass down, and walked to where she crouched, still shaking with mirth. He pulled her to her feet.

"You should say, Can I have the next dance, not boldly grab," she said happily, then yelped as he lifted her off the ground.

"Hey, put me down! What is this!"

"An old Haitian remedy," he replied, crossing the threshold of the house as burdened as a bridegroom. He set her down on the kitchen table, her feet dangling, and set about making coffee. Sitting there, kicking at air, she slowly sobered, but her head only seemed to fully clear with the first strong, hot mouthfuls.

"I put sugar in the claret, didn't I?" she said.

"Making 'soft drink,' just as Meg did for Miles and Aynsley."

She closed her eyes, the better to recollect.

" 'S funny. I remember pouring the wine, even holding the jar in my hand. But not dropping the cubes into the claret."

"I don't think," he said carefully, "that you did it."

"Then who did?"

"You know who it was."

"Yes," she whispered. "Can I get down now?"

He nodded, and she slid down, the soles of her shoes meeting hard tile with a jarring shock. Daniel relaxed, as if he had half expected something else to happen.

"Good," he said. "Now, if we could take our coffee into a place with comfortable chairs . . . because we have some explaining to do, filling in the gaps in our respective stories."

She lit a fire of pinecones in the library, and they sat watching each other in that red light, Mel on the rocking chair, Daniel on the couch. She longed to sit beside him, but his body language warned against it—for whatever reason, he was keeping his distance.

"When you told me about the Melvina search, in the park, it seemed you must have phenomenal intuition—all those hunches, turning up gold. Now I think you were being prompted."

"Dreams," she said, and told them, one by one. To her astonishment he questioned her most about Sammy:

"And your father appears at the start of the dreams? And always at a crossroad?"

"That's what I said. What else do you want to know? That he was the original boudoir bandicoot, and that he had a gammy leg?"

"Legba is an old man, walking with a stick. And a great one for girls."

She poked at the fire irritably.

"Are you suggesting that when I dream of my father, he's actually a Haitian god? Daniel, that's silly!"

"No sillier than you playacting Red Mel Yuill. Legba is the gatekeeper to the world of *les invisibles*, and when the spirits manifest in Haitian ritual, he appears first. Same as when I dreamt of Legba and Samedi in Port-au-Prince. They both appeared to me as houngans—that's voodoo priests—of my acquaintance."

"You really got into it," she said sardonically.

"Be thankful I did. Because of Haiti, I can recognize what is the matter with you."

"The matter of Melvina," she said, unsurprised at his quick nod. She told him more, of the gradual estrangement from Marc and May, the buying of kangaroo tail instead of eye fillet. . . .

"It happened before, then," Daniel said grimly.

"My going dizzy, then enacting a scene from the book?"

"It's more than that," he said.

"You may be right. I don't understand why the meat substitution trick happened, although it certainly got May hopping mad."

"My guess is that Melvina couldn't stand her . . . or Marc. From what you said, it sounded you were quite content to live in their peculiar little world, until the Melvina research."

"My ghost is a jealous ghost," Mel said.

"So I thought. And you started seeing them through her eyes . . ."

Perceiving Marc as immature and weak, and May as insanely domineering?

"It *was* like seeing from another point of view," she said. "A clarification . . . and an obscuring, as well. I never noticed Marc's shifts were out of whack, nor that my aunt was dying in front of me."

She stretched her hands out to the blaze, suddenly chilled by the idea of a haunting, which they could so calmly, rationally discuss. And yet it made perfect sense.

"But that means I must have been seeing you through Melvina's gaze, which would have been approving, given your resemblance to, and descent from, Darcy."

He didn't reply for a moment, then said, "I thought you might say that."

"So I fed you sugared claret."

"You were *saoulé*."

"What?"

"It's a Haitian word, meaning tipsy."

"I was pissed on the smell of alcohol?"

"No, you were in a state of near-possession."

She stood up. "Daniel, if you are seriously suggesting I was on the point of *being* Melvina . . . then I think I do really need a drink. I'll get the remaining claret."

"No tricks with the sugar?"

"No tricks." The moment of almost-but-not-quite losing control had passed.

They sat for a while in silence after she returned with the wine, drinking and watching the firescape in the grate, a topography from Mercury, or the sun. Finally he spoke:

"If what I say is to have any sense, I must tell you about Haiti. I didn't know much about voodoo when I went there—only zombies, pins in dollies, all that populist crap. When I got there I saw the bigger picture, how religion holds the island together. It's a dirt-poor place, but rich in spiritual culture. Where else could you go to a church social that was also the best disco you'd ever been to, and watch people commune with their gods? It's intensely experiential—the spirits enter into their worshipers, possess them."

Mel stared into the fire, gradually becoming drowsy from the warmth and wine to the point of near sleep, waking REM, for as Daniel spoke it seemed images appeared on the red in front of her. First appeared a picture from a travelog: acres of shacks made of cardboard cartons, strips of tin, any old rubbish, the scale of a cubbyhouse, but housing whole families. Then came a moving image, an urchin bent over, pushing down a garbage-strewn alley a toy horse on wheels, with riding on its back a red-coated soldier, with helmet and curly mustache. The child and the horse were black, but the soldier's face and hands had been painted ghost-white. Another still: inside a hall, decorated with balloons, flags, crepe bunting, chalk vévés drawn on the floor.

He kept talking, not looking at her.

"I had a sort of girlfriend by then, called Angélique. She was a trainee mambo, that's priestess, and she'd take me along to ceremonies. The first possession trance I saw happen was a young man named Ishmael, shy, quiet-spoken, gentle. One minute he was dancing, the next . . . his personality had gone on holiday. This Ishmael walked like a lame old man, but leered and accepted homage—a walking stick decorated with carvings and ribbons—like a party boss. When he spoke, his voice was husky and he foamed at the mouth like a bronco. It was Legba, riding on the back of Ishmael, being a divine horseman. That's how they see the relation of spirit and medium, in terms of rider and horse."

She blinked, thinking of the child dragging the toy through the alleys of Port-au-Prince, then by association, of the policeman and their steeds in *The Scarlet Rider*, and finally of Red Meg, that fearless horsewoman.

"The third or so time I went partying with the spirits, *something* happened. I felt drunk, my mind a very great distance from my body."

She nodded, recognizing the symptoms.

"Next thing, Mait' Jacques, head houngan there and a massive guy—the Samedi of my dream—picked me up bodily and carried me away from the music and dancing."

"Why the lifting off the ground?" she asked.

"That's how the spirits enter, feet first, striking upward like a bolt of lightning."

She shivered, reaching out to the flame again.

"When I felt more normal, Angélique explained that I'd been on the edge of the trance state. For a white boy with a black god, not even an initiate, that's a transgression."

"So what happened after that?" Mel asked.

"I came home. Angélique and Mait' Jacques said that if I stayed much longer, I would become a horse—*un cheval blanc*, Mait' Jacques said, as if that amused him. Of course, coming home on the plane, I rationalized that I'd merely been very suggestible. I do hypnotize easily."

She drained her glass. "Me too."

"My materialist interpretation of possession is that the worshipers identify with their deities so much that when they trance, they become the godhead, in their own belief. But hedging my bets, I painted the Legba sign in my car, even had it made up by a silversmith."

He drew out from under his shirt a fine chain, with the Legba symbol dependent upon it, like a distorted cross.

"I thought I would invoke him as protection, to prevent my psyche being stolen, however briefly, away. I set Legba to guard my personal gateway."

He lifted the chain over his head, slipped forward onto his knees on the hearth rug, and put the charm into Mel's hands.

"I think you need this more than I do."

She felt the silver in her hands, warm from his body.

"Melvina's not a voodoo god."

"She's a spirit. Same powers, if you believe in her sufficiently."

"My aunt Edie said she was unquiet," Mel mused. "Does that mean evil?"

"Some cultists I knew talked about soul-eaters. The spirit devours your personality: you die inside and walk around an empty husk, the spirit always with you. A state of permanent possession, if you like."

Mel leaned forward, reaching out to Daniel, returning the cross.

"Look, I'm sorry, but it's just too alien for me. I never heard of anything like this before. Darcy's family had a West Indian connection, and that's maybe why you were affected by voodoo. Me, I'm from Kirksley in Yorkshire, with—as I recently discovered—some Southwest Australian Aboriginal in me."

"That makes you a Nyoongah," he said.

"Nyoongah," she said, rolling the word around her mouth, trying it for sound. "Do *they* believe in spirit possession?"

"It's foreign to this continent. Nearest is Indonesia. But I can tell you one thing Aboriginals do believe—to name, to think on the dead, makes them unquiet. I suggest you do as a Nyoongah would do and put Melvina out of your mind completely. Because she's likely to destroy you otherwise."

THIRTY-FOUR

Resigned Unto the Heavenly Will

"No," Mel said. "I don't believe that. And I can't let Melvina go."

"At least don't give that conference paper," Daniel said. She realized he was pleading.

"That's all very well for you to say. Roxana would fry me alive, for starters."

"I do get the impression those ladies are formidable," he said wearily.

"Besides, there's Geraldo . . ." She stopped, gagged by a yawn. "The record has to be set straight, otherwise Charles Alonso Ellis will be credited as the author of *The Scarlet Rider*."

"True," he said. "But you could always write the paper and give it to Kaye to read on the day, saying you're sick."

"Daniel, you're a researcher, and you suggest I give up an opportunity to flaunt my research skills?"

"Touché," he said.

"Besides, I *have* to give it, as . . . as propitiation, I think. If Melvina is unquiet, wherever she may lie, then if I prove she was the author of *The Scarlet Rider*, I'll lay her."

Tired though she was, the word set off a chain of associations in her mind. Lay a ghost, she thought. It sounds sexual, like the horse/rider analogy of the trance cults. Lay Melvina . . . and Daniel?

She spoke, rather than ruminate upon that thought: "I know I'm biased, but I don't get a sense of evil from the Melvina presence. Jesperson called her a sorceress, but I can't believe she would be a soul-eating ghost."

No response. She glanced at Daniel, and saw his head droop; he was nearly falling asleep where he sat. She reached out to shake him awake and her hands lingered on his shoulders. He opened his eyes.

"You love Melvina, not me," he said.

Startled, she disengaged.

"When first we met, you seemed otherwordly, preoccupied. You would smile to yourself the way people do, when they think of that special person. It drove me crazy, as I didn't know who you loved. Now I know it's a ghost, a jealous one, you said."

She rubbed her eyes. "Daniel, I swear, I had no sense of Melvina as a third party, when I've been with you."

"Two's company, three's crowded."

"You find Melvina off-putting?" she asked belligerently.

"She desired Darcy. Was that relationship ever consummated? I don't know, but the thought of it, and of you looking at me with Melvina's eyes . . . is quite inhibiting. Otherwise, I'd happily snuggle up to you."

She looked at him, thinking, There's only one way to resolve this, Sammy would say. Cautiously she reached out, took his hand.

"Let's go upstairs."

He stroked her fingers, then abruptly released her. "Not with Melvina around."

"At least come to my conference paper," she said. "See me propitiate the ghost."

"Or . . ." but he did not finish the sentence. Become her, she mentally finished.

"You will be there? Promise?"

"I don't know about that. I've got to go back to Perth ASAP, to get more travel funding from my department."

"Can't you do that from here?"

He shook his head.

"But you'll come back?"

"If they fund me."

He yawned and she said, "Stay here. You're in no fit state to hit the road."

"Oh, Papa Legba will look after me."

On the doorstep he hesitated, then gave her a swift, soft kiss on the lips.

"Take great care, Mel."

And then he was gone.

Mel brought the eiderdown from the study and huddled on the couch awhile, thinking of Daniel and staring into the dying pine embers. She slipped into sleep imperceptibly, waking finally to the dawn racket of sparrows roosting in the ivy on the front of the house. Watch out, noisy birds! she thought. Didn't Edie say I should get a cat? The oddness of that remark, especially in its deathbed context, suddenly struck Mel. How could I? she thought. Landlords don't allow pets and how would I take it from flat to flat? Cats aren't portable, not like dogs. She tried to remember Edie's exact words, and after a moment retrieved them. Edie had made her promise to make it up to the cats and dogs, had suggested she take in a kitten. . . . It still didn't make any sense.

Shaking her head, she got up, undressing, showering, and dressing again, regretting that her sojourn in Appleby, this pleasant place, might be brief. Better call the solicitor, she thought, and find out what's in the will. But I can't remember the name of the family's firm! The problem niggled in her mind as she sat at the kitchen table, breakfasting on reheated leftover vindaloo. Address book, she finally thought. Where did Edie keep it?

In Edie's bedroom she soon found what she sought in a plain black leather handbag, hanging behind the door, and read through it. The book yielded a bewildering array of names, some she remembered from the funeral, and one useful piece of information: under the name Alice was the address of the nursing home where her only surviving relative now lived. Must go and see her, Mel thought. I promised Edie. How manipulative the dying are, as is their right. She tied me up with obligations in her last few days, first Alice, then that damn pussycat. . . .

She closed the little book. Perhaps the name of the lawyer would be hidden with the Kirksley treasures in the mahogany chest. But when she threw the lid open, lifting out the contents one by one, careful despite her urgency, she began to feel black disappointment: all in here was antique, records from the bush Appleby, rather than the town house. Then her gaze was arrested by a flash of silver, protruding from it a folded paper, covered in Edie's writing.

She pulled it out, finding the silver a picture frame. When she pulled the paper loose, an image was revealed of bygone Kirksleys, girl and boy on great horse in a garden, from a hundred years ago. Of more interest to Mel just then was the writing on the paper:

Mel, I may not have a chance to tell you who these people are, and you won't know otherwise, as I never wrote the family history. The little boy on the horse is Jonathan Kirksley, the girl his sister Adah. She was a wild bush maid, forever galloping around the countryside on her beloved chestnut mare. I always loved the look of her, wondered what she might have become. It's so sad—they both died in the same week in 1882, Adah in a fall from her beautiful horse, Jonathan from eating green apples, the family said, although it sounded more like appendicitis to me. They lie buried side by side in the little bush graveyard at Appleby.

Mel thought: Edie wrote that for me to find. And that means . . .

She put down the photo and galloped downstairs, taking the steps two, three at a time. More words from the dying had come back to her: You look at that inventory, Edie had said. Mel had last seen it on the hall table, and she searched under, around, and finally *in* the thick phone books, but no inventory could be seen. Where might Edie have put it? Or, more importantly, what was she doing last thing, before the fatal trip to the milk bar?

In her memory another box opened, the Saratoga trunk in the shed, spilling old green curtain. Moving with speed now, as intent on this search as she had been with Melvina, she ran out to the garden, into sunlight pale as a primrose. The dark mouth of the shed doorway gaped at her, and she entered, scanning the small space: boxes, oddments for gardening arrayed on rickety wooden shelves, the yards of green cloth, but no leather-bound book.

Think! Mel said to herself. Edie was busy here, going through the boxes of Kirksley treasures, and wouldn't have had a free hand. Where might she have put the inventory, while she worked? Mel knelt in front of the trunk, her knees on a hummock of rumpled velvet. There, just below her eye level, was a shelf, and on it, the familiar brown scuffed leather, bookmarked by a ballpoint pen.

She opened it, and saw lines of neat writing, the itemized chattels of Appleby. Flipping through it was like a guided tour of the house, with page after page listing the contents of every room. Impatient, she turned to the page marked by the pen, finding entries for the shed, which stopped in midpage, for the inventory was incomplete. After that came no further writing, only the foxing of time. She stopped turning the creamy, antique pages, and shook the book, holding it upside down, but nothing fell out. She righted it, ruffling the pages from cover to cover, and this time noticed, at the end, more writing, highlighted by a frame of red ink.

> *Mel dear!*
> *Bartelby our family solicitor is off on hols, and his son always did give me the irrits, so I've made an appointment for when the old man gets back. Just in case something happens, I thought I'd better put things in writing.*
>
> *Love, Edie*

On the opposite page was more writing, which Mel, her eyes filling, could only read in snatches: *I, Edith Adah Kirksley . . . hereby revoke earlier will . . . beneficiary the Cat & Dog Home . . . the contents of this book . . . my share of the house Appleby . . . to my niece Melvina Marie Kirksley.*

Underneath were two signatures of witnesses, Nick and Aphrodite Stougiannos. The name rang a bell, and she recalled A&N Stougiannos, Proprietors, painted on the door of the milk bar. If only I'd made that scene, so Aphrodite knew who I was, she thought. She hugged the book to her, mentally adding: No, better to find out this way. Edie gave me a clue, the sly old thing, and I followed it through, just as I did with Melvina.

THIRTY-FIVE

Conferenceville

In the days that followed, Mel almost appreciated Daniel's absence, for her time was fully occupied. More of her conference paper slowly appeared on the gray computer screen, and she also made excursions: to Bartleby's, Mel clutching the ledger tightly to her like a shield; to the nursing home, making the first of her promised visits to the sweetly vague shell of Alice; to Roxana; several times to the library; and even to the depository.

She had it, finally, her paper completed, details checked as much as possible, the whole a logical, coherent argument to the best of her ability. Now Mel stood staring out at a sea of faces, a lecture theater full of *The Self and the Other* attendees. Nola and Sorrel had inspected her limited wardrobe the night before, selecting the Philippine silk blouse and most respectable skirt, to be worn with a beautifully cut jacket—on loan from Kaye.

"She insisted," Nola had said. "Just as well, 'cos nobody else in the office would have fitted ya. She even suggested we buy you a deerstalker, as the crownin' touch!"

Sorrel had added, "But we talked her out of it. You can't look Victorian in any way."

Mel had replied, "As if I'm identifying with the subject?" But I do, she had thought. Then, unable to resist a dig at Sorrel: "As you identify with Virginia Woolf?"

"Only with her dress sense!" was the retort.

"Sorrel's right," Nola said. "You'll give the wrong impression."

"OK, but at least let me keep my earrings."

Having won that concession, at least, she lightly touched the gold for luck, as the conference MC for this session finished his announcements, leaving the microphone free.

"I want to start this paper, like a murder mystery, with a body of text, published anonymously, with no apparent clue as to whodunnit."

The little knot of Roxanas smiled encouragingly in the front row—Sorrel, Kaye, and Nola, the latter a self-appointed minder, bringing Mel orange juice prior to the session, plucking copper hairs off the borrowed jacket. Concentrate, Mel thought. Somewhere toward the back of the audience, she knew, was a bald head, a waxed mustache, but she preferred not to seek Geraldo out, for the message, her propitiation, was too important to allow any distraction.

Click!

"The image on the slide projector is of the first page of *The Scarlet Rider*, as published in the *Tolletown Chronicle*."

Click!

"This slide shows a detail from that page, the poem which begins the novel, anonymous, like *The Scarlet Rider* itself."

Despite her resolve, her gaze wandered among the audience. She avoided the temptation to glance sideways, as if seeking approval from Dr. Ana B. Milne, the keynote speaker, formidable

in a Chanel suit and stiletto heels of almost fetishistic height.
She sat to one side of the stage, beside the MC, for her speech
came immediately after Mel's.

"A tad unfortunate," Kaye had said. "You being the warm-
up act for the lion of this biography circus. But on the other
hand you have the benefit of Ana's considerable audience. She
used to be Andrew Milne, conventional biographer of the art
canon. But then Milne lopped off the 'drew' and other ap-
pendages, becoming Ana, resurrecter of forgotten women
artists, the weirder and woolier the better."

"Sort of what I'm doing," Mel had cut in.

"Yes! If she likes you, we'll know we've won, proved Melvina wrote *The Scarlet Rider*."

"If," Mel had replied.

Indeed, the Roxanas were all gazing worriedly to the left, as
if reading Dr. Milne's expression. With a great effort, Mel ignored them and continued; nothing was more important than
to communicate her message.

"It now had to be established, since there *was* a woman
named Y-U-I-L or Y-U-I-L-L in the Tolletown area in 1865,
if she was a Melvina Mary, as suggested in the acrostic. This involved checking through the available colonial records. . . ."

She glanced up and nearly waved, for she suddenly had
noticed Charlie Mowbray seated toward the back. Nonetheless
she pressed on, finishing her paragraph before raising her eyes
again.

"In this search for a detective novelist, the quest imitated art,
with clues dropped in the text, dark suspicions sown in the
mind of the reader. One such suspicion was whether the act of
self-referentiality, the hiding of the author's name in the poem
at the start of the text, might indicate more auctorial in-jokes
hidden in the novel itself. Take the names of the police, for instance . . ."

A face in the audience smiled at this—Mick from the Police

Archives, in plain clothes, squeezed into one of the narrow lecture seats. She looked again, at a flash of bright pink, and saw Dot, with Nev in attendance. Beside them sat a bulky, dark, very handsome man, obviously Keef. On the aisle sat the librarian, as androgynous as ever. And, slipping unobtrusively through the door at the back of the theater, Daniel. Had all her friends, her real friends, not the Happy Orphans' Club, rallied around her at this testing time? For a moment the computer typescript in front of her blurred, and she paused, very close to tears. Yet she carried on, gaze on text, until there was no more to read, for she had finished her story, the mystery resolved, the woman behind it revealed.

Applause, and she stood back from the lectern, gulping a glass of water, as the MC briefly commandeered the microphone. Now and only now did she do a head-by-head inspection of the audience, for Geraldo . . . but he was nowhere to be seen.

"We have time for a few questions before the next speaker," the MC said.

A girl in the second row, with an ethereal, Pre-Raphaelite look to her and much silver jewelry, raised a jangling, bangled hand.

"When did Melvina Mary Yuill die?"

In the Roxana enclave, Nola rolled her eyeballs upward, as if to say: The question we didn't want!

Mel took the microphone again.

"That, to be perfectly honest, remains a mystery. I have been through death records of Yuills for the whole of the nineteenth century and into the twentieth. There is no sign of Melvina Mary, even if she'd lived into her hundreds."

"Maybe she's a vampire, still alive," somebody said sotto voce. Mel thought it sounded like Charlie, but he looked innocent as the audience giggled.

The girl continued regardless: "I wondered why she hadn't written anything more."

An interesting point, thought Mel. Why is *The Scarlet Rider* a singleton text? Does this mean I have to go through all the dusty colonial newspapers, searching for Melvina's further works, even if anonymous?

She said, "That remains to be seen, at this point of research."

The girl smiled. "I await the next installment, with interest"—and was graciously silent.

Nev raised his hand. "I was wondering, as Jesperson was still alive when *The Scarlet Rider* was published, could he have read it? What might have been his reaction?"

She blessed kind Nev for this question, so easy to answer.

"Seeing as the novel sent him up unmercifully, I imagine his reaction would have been choleric."

More laughter.

"But *The Scarlet Rider* was published in an obscure, regional newspaper and at the time Jesperson was hundreds of miles away, on the South Australian border, slowly dying. I rather doubt he saw it."

Pluckrose would have been censoring his reading, she decided, saturating Jesperson with religious tracts. As if her thoughts had been communicated aloud, she saw Charlie nod.

But now Daniel had caught the eye of the MC.

"Does your answer also apply to my great-grandfather, Darcy Ainsworth, who was in West Australia at the time, starting out in a political career?"

All around the theater, people craned to look at Daniel.

"I also doubt he could have seen it, being further afield even than Jesperson. But, I'd like to ask you, as a legitimate descendant of Darcy's—"

"Oh, yes," Daniel said and the audience twittered.

"—when did he marry your great-grandmother? He wedded Melvina first, and although Jesperson torpedoed the wedding feast, with stories of dead babies and husbands possibly still alive, though miscreant, that union had legal validity. I haven't found any record of a divorce, and they were difficult to get at the time, and expensive. Did Darcy commit bigamy subsequently, having only a 'poor man's divorce,' that is, via desertion?"

Daniel grinned, enjoying this cut and thrust.

"Darcy didn't marry until he was in his fifties. To the teenage daughter of his chief political ally."

Cradle snatcher, thought Mel, then tossed another question to Daniel: "Does the delay imply he waited for news of his first, notorious, wife's death?"

Daniel shrugged. "When Darcy eventually married, he was a prominent man, featured in newspapers, and not only in West Australia. He may have thought, since his first wife hadn't arrived on the doorstep, demanding restoration of conjugal rights, she was well and truly dead. Certainly he never said a word to my great-grandmother, in their twenty years of happy marriage, not even on his deathbed."

"Thank you," she said.

The MC was checking her watch. "One more question . . . ah, Dr. Milne!"

Mel froze, seeing that the keynote speaker had come up onto the stage, conference paper in hand.

"I just have to ask you—"

The voice was husky and deep, like the growl of a hunting cat.

"Why do you think Melvina Yuill wrote this novel?"

Oh, thought Mel, and almost grabbed at the lectern for support. The most difficult question of all.

"Well, inasmuch as one can get inside the mind of a writer from a hundred years ago . . ."

Sorrel was staring fiercely at her, as if saying: A lot depends on your answer!

"I would guess—revenge, a desire to set the record straight, if anyone was reading who might guess at the true story behind

The Scarlet Rider, the simple desire to make life art, to expurgate private demons by writing them out, the graphomanic desire to get into print . . ."

Ana B. Milne spread her hands wide, a who-knows? gesture.

"All or any of the above. Whatever her reasons, she did it, otherwise I wouldn't be standing here talking about a love triangle from a hundred and fifty years ago."

"She created a mystery story for us, her life coded within her fiction," Ana B. Milne said. *"Cherchez la femme*, and you found her, Ms. Kirksley. My compliments to the sleuth."

Ordeal, or act of exorcism, over, all Mel felt like was a stiff drink, but she was obliged to sit beside the MC while Ana B. Milne delivered her address. It was an anticlimax, for her, but also oddly soothing, just to be quiet and listen. Moreover, Ana was a pleasure to hear, communicating her enthusiasm professionally and effectively: despite Mel's never having heard of the subject, one Frances Broadford Greene, an American artist and spiritualist.

She noticed notetaking in the audience, though none as incessant as that of the Pre-Raphaelite girl, the clank of her bangles a constant accompaniment to Ana's growling delivery. How irritating, she thought, seeing Ana purse her lips slightly, then realized the motion had more to do with content than crowd noise. The bulk of the paper was about Greene's painting, which from the slides was strange stuff, portraits of spirit guides, done in a style that eerily predated surrealism, yet each time Ana spoke of spiritualism, it was with perceptible reluctance. The bangles might jingle furiously at the mention of ectoplasm and ouija boards, but Ana's voice would grow cold, and her lips momentarily pucker.

Disapproves, Mel thought. As I would have, before Melvina. Now I know that there are more things on heaven and earth than can be explained in any materialist philosophy. But the mechanism, the calling into being of the biographical subject, so that it is felt almost as a presence, eludes me. Is it a psychic necromancy, identifying so much with the person researched that you somehow will them into a shadow-existence? I don't know.

The hard candy of this thought occupied her, completely obliterating for Mel the latter part of Ana's paper, and also the following queries, a show of hands, so many that a number of questioners, including the Pre-Raphaelite, were never answered. Finally the MC called a halt, and the conference attendees trooped out for refreshments in the foyer. Once outside, Mel was grabbed by Kaye, who waltzed her across the room. It was crowded, but given the Kaye effect, they completely failed to bump into anyone, far less capsize the groaning table of books beside which they finally came to a full stop.

"Kaye's pleased with you," Sorrel said unnecessarily, as she caught up with the waltzers.

"Indeed, Miss Mel Marple! We can now go ahead with a reprint of *The Scarlet Rider*, edited and with an introduction by Melvina Marie Kirksley."

"Lookee!" Nola said, and unrolled a flyer, with indeed those words on it, in fancy lettering, and the announcement "Forthcoming from Roxana Press."

"When did you print that up?" Mel demanded.

"Oh, it was just somethin' we had ready."

"Optimists!" Mel said.

"Why not? It was abundantly clear that the Force was with you," Kaye said cheerfully.

The Force? thought Mel. Of what? Melvina Yuill, that forceful personality?

"But Kaye, I've never edited anything in my life."

"We'll help," Sorrel said.

"But first," Kaye said, "Mel deserves champagne."

"Here? A conference isn't a pub."

"It is when a book is launched into the ocean of the marketplace, to swim or sink."

Mel turned, at the display of volumes behind her, and saw with a start, the image, familiar but small-scale, of the Old Woman of the Sea strangling her Sinbad-son, the image repeated over and over, from cover to cover. Remembering her panic, but determined to face it, she stared into that malevolent gaze, and this time had no illusion of a wink. Now she could see beyond the image, to a familiar name on the cover.

"My baby book," Charlie said, from behind the arc of a champagne glass. She noticed that he wore his geisha tie.

"Congratulations!"

"Same to you. I enjoyed that paper, having deliberately positioned myself where I could watch its effect on Geraldo. You routed him completely."

"I didn't even notice he was there."

"Oh, he left after the infanticide. Must be squeamish."

Someone pressed a cold, full glass into her hand; she took it, turning, and saw it was Daniel. Charlie smiled, excused himself, and wafted off into the crowd.

"I thought you weren't coming!"

"And miss a chance to talk about the Parliamentarian? I almost set a land-speed record!"

But their colloquy was interrupted almost as soon as it started by another biographer, wanting to ask Daniel about Darcy Ainsworth's relationship to *his* subject, a radical politician of the 1890s. Laughing a little into her glass, Mel left them to it. Mick appeared, with congratulations, followed by the librarian, then Dot, Nev, and Keef. Mel was in such a happy daze she could barely concentrate on what they said, although one exchange fixed itself indelibly in her mind:

"Now that's over with," Dot said, "you can go and find out all about Myrie and your Nyoongah heritage."

"Too right!" Keef said.

Then Mel was alone, aimless, wandering through the crowd. Total strangers would smile at her, and she felt stunned—at having achieved something substantial with her life, perhaps? As she stood, still center in the whirling conference, she became acutely aware of ambient conversation, as if tuning to a common mental wavelength:

"—Dream about him? Of course I dream about him—"

"—oh, I never have. It's the wife that has the dreams. She says she wishes I'd pick nicer subjects, she'd sleep easier at night—"

"Victoria Glendinning told the audience that she had the urge to wear huge rings when she was doing Edith Sitwell, and when she was doing Vita Sackville-West, she had the urge to—and she paused dramatically here—throw logs on the fire and take large dogs for walks."

Mel sipped at her champagne and moved on, listening intently.

"—it's a very special relationship I have with my subject. We're good mates—"

"—I can always tell when an informant is lying, I don't know why, it's a sixth sense—"

"—just sometimes, when I happen to write something critical of the old bugger, I have this odd feeling of someone looking over my shoulder disapprovingly."

Daniel, released at last, appeared at her shoulder.

"I'm surrounded by horses," she said. "Kindred spirits."

He looked for a moment alarmed.

"People like me, not quite their usual self, because they are intensely involved with another person, their object of research."

"How true," Charlie said, reappearing with a refill of champagne. "Professional biographers tend to go quite barmy, but differently, with each biography. Thespians too—one actress I knew played Ophelia, and then couldn't get rid of the character until she went for a swim one day, and effectively drowned the milksop of Elsinore."

"I thought it was just me," Mel breathed.

"Richard Holmes wrote that biography's central tenet is empathy, something that can be quite eerie when writing the lives of that silenced majority, the dead. In my opinion, biographers belong to two camps, the spiritualist and the materialistic. You, Melvina-Mel, are otherworldly, but friend Ana is a perfect example of the rationalist biographer. Which is why it is rich seeing her coping with Fanny Greene's ectoplasm and automatic writing. But pray, where is the lady?"

"Being buttonholed," Daniel said.

"Then I shall release her, so that she can launch my book. But before I go"—and now he bent toward Mel—"a little suggestion. Have you read Symons's *The Quest for Corvo*? A wonderful book, the story of a biographical hunt. Seek it out, because I think you could do likewise, most successfully, with your search for Melvina."

A sudden image came to Mel's mind, her desk in Appleby, with open on it the computer's gray screen. No, she thought with absolute certainty, that's not right. An old ledger book, writing longhand, the Melvina way, is the only appropriate way, for her story . . . and mine.

"Don't tell Kaye Tollet that idea," she said, "or she'll make me do it."

"Then of course I must tell her. But first, the rescue of Ana."

He strode away, the crowd parting for him, as if he possessed biblical, rather than merely auctorial, authority.

Daniel said, "There's a copy of the Symons on the bookshop table. I saw it earlier."

"Oh well, I'd better do what Charlie said, and buy it."

Daniel nodded, and they eddied through the crowd, passing, as they did, the returning Charlie, with a flustered Ana on his arm.

"At the Connecticut colloquium a man all in black *kissed* my hand and gave me an ouija message from Fanny, and now this lunatic! Pages and pages of notes, and she said it was automatic writing, done by Fanny's spirit while I talked ..."

"Hazards of the biography trade," Mel said to Daniel.

"Obviously."

Later, as they inspected the display of books, he said, as if this was a question that he had been chewing on, "I must belong to the materialist end of the biography spectrum. I don't get a ghostly feeling from the Parliamentarian."

"You wouldn't necessarily," a voice said, and, looking up, Mel saw the Pre-Raphaelite girl, staring at them fixedly over a hardback biography of Madame Blavatsky. "He's part of your genetic inheritance, and thus is manifest within you."

Under the bangled arm, Mel suddenly noticed, was a pad covered with indecipherable scrawl. Automatic writing ...

"You asked me about Melvina's death date," she recalled. "As if you knew I desperately wanted to know it."

The girl bent closer, her gaze a pale, insane blue.

"You could so easily find out. Why don't you come to my séances? All your questions would be answered."

Mel felt Daniel squeeze her arm, prompting.

"No," she said.

THIRTY-SIX

A Trip Upcountry

What does it matter if you eat my soul?
If you do we will go about together.
—Nigerian Bori cult song to Ladi
Mayo (Ladi the Sorceress)

The rest of that day and night continued as a party, with the launch of Charlie's book shading into the conference dinner. Yet far more important to Mel than being a social butterfly was talking with Daniel again.

"I nearly didn't come back from West Australia. You see, I worried you would fail to exorcise the ghost. But in the end I decided that even in a worst-case scenario I ought to be present."

She drew a deep breath. "You think the propitiation worked?"

"Well, you're still here, and you don't *seem* otherworldly."

"Good," she said. "Now, are you coming to the dinner? Roxana booked a table!"

"Would I be allowed?"

"Allowed? What is this? Are you scared of feminists?"

Like Marc, she remembered, and also May.

"They're not only feminists," he said.

She turned, glancing back across the foyer, at Kaye and Sorrel, who were getting on famously with Charlie Mowbray. Damn, she thought, as Charlie winked at her, he's gone and told them his idea for the Melvina biography. And now they'll badger me incessantly until I write it, when I don't even know if I have the ability to make the Melvina-narrative interesting to others.

"Somehow I don't think they're separatists."

"That's what Charlie said . . . about you."

"Did he now?"

"Quite the Cupid, he was."

She laughed. "Little matchmaker!"

Their gaze met again.

"He matched right," Daniel said.

Hatches, matches, and dispatches. Halfway through the conference dinner, a torrential thunderstorm struck, thunder crashing overhead, followed by the lights flickering, then blacking completely out. Kaye merely laughed and lit the centerpiece candle with her cigarette lighter, as all around them similar small bulbs of flame slowly appeared in the darkness, palely illuminating the diners.

"Candlelit dinner," Kaye said, "how romantic!" with a meaningful glance at Mel and Daniel, although it was Sorrel and Nola's hands she sought. They sat in companionable silence for a while; then a bobbing pocketlight approached the table. It swung upward to illuminate the face of Rube, her bright dreads dripping rain.

"MESSAGE FOR KAYE!"

She unzipped her leather jacket, extracting a postcard. Kaye bent over the candle, reading intently.

"Oh, what a useful little spy we have!" she said, and passed the postcard around the table. Mel took it, seeing on one side a pony, and on the reverse childish, rounded script, which read: "Geraldo's six months are over!!!! Hip hip hurray, V." The arms of the *V* ended in tiny hearts.

"*V* for Varney?" Mel asked.

"Yes, the sweetie."

The conference dinner was soon over, as without electricity coffee could hardly be served, nor after-dinner speeches made. Mel and Daniel quietly slipped away, driving Legba back to Appleby, the thunder and lightning having abated, leaving only torrential rain. They went upstairs to the study, where they sat under the eiderdown, drinking leftover launch champagne and listening to the drumming of the rain on the roof. Gradually they drew closer to each other, Daniel no longer affected by the presence of a third party, the voyeur Melvina.

Nothing happened, and yet everything happened. The meeting of their bodies was tentative, not quite satisfactory, as is only to be expected when two people are lovers for the first time; and yet had the promise of better things ahead. He's more sympathetic than Marc, Mel noted, but making comparisons is odious. She took hold of the Legba cross, still on its chain around Daniel's neck, and clenched it briefly, the shape of the vévé temporarily impressed in her palm.

Much later she said, "You laugh when you come."

"Sorry, involuntary."

"No, don't apologize. It's endearing."

Mel woke next morning, to find Daniel had made them breakfast, and strewn the bed with stiff, crackling paper.

"What's this?"

"Maps. From Legba," Daniel replied. She sat up, to see from the study window the garden bright with sun, its greenery shiny-clean and sparkling with raindrops.

"It's a glorious morning," he said, bending over a map. "Just right for a trip to the country."

"Today?" she said, rubbing her eyes.

"Why not? I always intended to go and see the Parliamentarian's old haunts—"

Not the right choice of word, she thought.

"—at Aurealis."

"And you want me to accompany you."

"Unless you had other plans than being my navigator."

"As if I would!" she said.

An hour later, they were on the road, Mel perusing the maps as they negotiated their way through the inner suburbs, heading for the upcountry freeway.

"We'll have to go through Spur Rock," she said, after a while.

"The gateway to the goldfields," he said, quoting the tourist brochure.

"More the gateway through which Melvina emerged a tainted woman, after Jerry Yuill's crime, her madness, and the death of the baby."

"True, but it made a novelist of her."

She was silent, ruminating on this notion.

He continued: "I'd quite like to be a bloody tourist and stop at the mining village. And why not go the whole roadhog and do Tolletown?"

Mel demurred: "That'd make a long day's driving—we might have to stop at a motel."

"That's no problem," he replied. "Not after last night."

Mel gave him a look, but he kept his gaze on the road.

"We could visit the Tollet winery," he said, changing the subject.

"See what Lil Tollet's new boyfriend looks like. And meet the invaluable Varney."

It took them two hours to reach Spur Rock, with stops for inferior coffee in service-station cafés. The day was balmy, unseasonal greenhouse summer humidity in nascent spring, with everywhere signs of last night's storm, as if the contents of a celestial bucket had been dumped on the land. Puddles lined the road, and the lowering, overhanging hilltop of the Spur was so freshly washed that thin cascades of rainwater were still running down its nooks and crannies. The mining village itself was closed for flood repairs.

"I don't grieve," Mel said as they stood in the mud outside the wooden gates. "Even as a child I thought it far too tidy, a Victorian toy town."

Like the toy village of her dream, in which she had ridden in the horseless carriage down to the courthouse, to see the dolls declare Melvina guilty?

"Now I can't see it as anything but false, having read *The Scarlet Rider* and also the inquest proceedings. I mean, when Melvina was here, the village consisted of tents, or at best slab huts, in a sea of brown earth, frantically being grubbed up in search of golden loot. Nothing National Trust, nor picturesque, no polyester crinolines . . ."

"That came later," Daniel said. "It's not false to the subsequent history of the town, when the quartz mining had meant there was some permanency, a chance to build."

"That may be, but it's not m . . . Melvina's history. Or herstory."

She had nearly said: my history. With any luck, Daniel hadn't noticed. He was staring at his maps again.

"Well, as we can't see the village, what about driving to Sailor's Gully?"

"And retrace the search for Baby Yuill? No thanks!"

"You still identify," he said.

"I think I always will."

On the way out of town she willed herself not to see it but

still couldn't avoid the sight of the mental hospital, a Spur Rock institution for over a hundred years, the building squat, of khaki brickwork. Once, the site had been a log enclosure, as her research had shown, housing the cases of delerium tremens, depression, postnatal pyschosis—all the minds cracked by life in Spur Rock and the surrounding goldfields.

"Such a shame," Daniel said, "as you commented in your paper, that the madhouse records were immolated in the great bushfire of 1870."

Mel sighed. "I'd have liked to know how and when she got out. We know she did . . ."

"Because she reappeared in Tolletown, sane, and in literary spitting form."

"Another mystery," she said.

At this point, Legba circled an outcrop of the Spur, and the madhouse was, thankfully, left behind them. They sped on, into a day that was beginning to be almost uncomfortably hot. Mel wound down her window, smelling warm eucalyptus, mixed with the scent of those early blossoms not stripped from the trees by last night's storm. Birds called; insects filled the air, buzzing and swooping, some splatting wetly against Legba's windscreen. When they stopped the car briefly, to let an enormous cow cross the road, Mel heard rustling, faint mouse peeps from the roadside tussocks; she looked up to see a crucifix against the sky, the form of a hovering, waiting hawk.

"Lunch break?" Daniel said, as they slowed, to pass yet again through a one-horse town. Mel looked at the sign, and whooped:

"Slaggyford! Nearest settlement to Aurealis. No, let's press on—we can't stop now."

As they drove down the main drag, with its inevitable row of memorial elms, she inspected the shops, hoping to glimpse a faded sign for S. Sackcloth, photographer. Instead, she saw rural depression, black windows, boarded-up businesses, a contrast to the rude health of the natural world. As they passed the little white weatherboard church, last building in the town, Daniel said, "Aurealis wasn't on any of the maps I bought, which means it might not even be signposted. We may have to estimate distance to find it."

Mel thought hard, remembering: "There's fifteen miles between Slaggyford and Aurealis."

"And Legba measures in kilometers! We'll just have to make a rough estimate from the odometer," he said, as the macadam gave way to dirt road. Legba slowed in a cloud of dust, and they drove for a while through a changing backdrop of scrubby pastureland varied with bush. The only sounds came from their passage: the purr of Legba's engine, and the crunch of rocks and twigs underwheel.

"To think," Mel said, "of all the oxcarts and horses coming up and down this road, from the teeming, prosperous goldfields."

"And now it's deserted," he said.

They continued on, Mel repeatedly glancing at the odometer, conversion calculations running through her head.

"I think," she finally said, "I think fifteen miles would be about here."

Legba stopped, in a river valley denuded for pasture. On both sides were bare hills, between them an expanse of lumpy grass, dotted with the occasional emaciated sheep. Mel got out of the car, waving aside bush flies.

"Well, it's a river flat," Daniel said, also getting out.

"Like *The Scarlet Rider*. With hills around." She shielded her eyes against the sun, which was unpleasantly hot on her hair. "I suppose this is it."

"You'd think they'd erect a plaque. 'On this spot in eighteen-whatever, was found a humongous nugget.' "

" 'Shaped like nothing in particular.' " She walked up to the barbed-wire fence, and looked around, trying to imagine this bleak space filled with tents, an aggregation of people lured across the globe by the gleam of gold. The vision eluded her. Melvina's text was testimony that Aurealis/Cornish Flat had once been vividly alive; but without it, or the few primitive photographs Mel had examined at the library, miners posed stiffly around nuggets, it would be hard to believe this wretched, overgrazed farmland had any significance at all. Once Aurealis had been golden, the backdrop to myriad tales of greed, woe, and love—now it was worked-out desolation.

"Let's go," Mel said. "Unless you want to take photos."

"There's nothing here to record," he said. "Except absence."

They left Aurealis behind them, Mel bending over the maps rather than sit and watch the drear vista. The car was now hot enough to make them both sweat, and she thought longingly of Tolletown, still some distance away, by her estimate. A glass of cool white wine . . .

"Late lunch at the wineries?" Daniel said, as if reading her mind.

"Sounds perfect. But I'm parched now."

The road shot into welcome shade, a patch of lush bush, trees stretching over the road, with birds flitting from branch to branch. Daniel slowed Legba, making the most of the eucalypt cool, as they rolled down an inclining bend toward a middle-sized river, brown and swollen by rain.

"There's a sign on that tree," Daniel said.

"What?"

"Red, yellow, and black. Koorie colors."

They stopped by the riverside, got out, and inspected the plaque. "Historic canoe tree," Daniel read.

Mel stared up at the huge white skeleton of the river gum, the wound clearly visible now, where an expanse of bark had been hacked out with flint axes, to make, as the sign said, a canoe. She reached out, stroked the wood, over a century dead, but still standing. Although she knew that it had been Keef's an-

cestors, possibly, who had been the canoe builders, not her Nyoongah forebears, the touch still thrilled her, as if an emotional
electric shock had been transmitted.

Without a word spoken, they returned to Legba and hit the
road again, which meandered parallel with the river, heading
gradually upstream. They came at last to a deeper and wider expanse of water, a swimming space, complete with picnic facili-
ties.

"Stop here for a break?" Daniel said.

She nodded, and he brought Legba to a halt in the mini car
park. They got out, walking down to the water through shivery
grass with large brown seed heads. Mel noticed the seed heads
rustled like rattlesnakes, the sound faintly echoing. She did an
odd little dance: two steps, look back over the shoulder, two
steps again.

"What are you up to?" Daniel asked irritably.

"It's the grass. See how it keeps vibrating even after I've
passed, as if someone walks behind me."

"No, I don't," Daniel said, stooping to drink at riverside.
Mel bent also, finding the river water very fresh and cold, although slightly silted. Mischief struck her, and scooping up a
cupped palm's-worth of water she dumped it over his head.

"Cut that out!" He lunged at her, but laughing, she dodged
out of reach, running along a small platform built over the water
for diving.

"Watch out," he said. "Those timbers are slippery."

Annoyed at his old-maidish tone, she stood on the end of
the pier, daring him by her proximity to the water.

"Don't fall in," he said. "That water's cold. And the current
looks quite inexorable."

She pretended to teeter, giggling maniacally.

"Anyone would think you'd been at the Tollet wineries already," he grumbled. Then his voice rose in a near scream:
"Mel, you're *saoulé!*"

Alarmed, she started and teetered for real this time, as a wave of dizziness struck her. For a moment she looked into brown, moving water, then hit it bodily. She felt cold, wetness, slimy leaves against her face—

—and stark terror. Suddenly it seemed she had never learned to swim, for she sank like a rock. She tried to kick, but her legs moved sluggishly, as if entangled. Am I caught in weed? she thought, but nothing restrained her, although for a second she thought she glimpsed black cloth, trailing lace and frills, swirling around her. Her feet struck the riverbed, and she tried to kick upward from it, but seemed to have minimal control over her body. All she could do was flail, sending up dense clouds of brown silt.

Now she couldn't see the hand in front of her face, and worse, the current was bowling her downstream. It flung her against a submerged rock, so painfully that, forgetting she was underwater, she opened her mouth wide to scream. Instead she swallowed water, and choked, the river sending icy tendrils down her nose. She was running out of air now, the silty brown in front of her eyes darkening, to deepest black . . .

THIRTY-SEVEN

Horse and Rider

Danbala ap monte I (Danbala is riding her)
—William Gibson, *Count Zero*

Mel stood on the river's surface, looking down at the still shape beneath her, almost invisible through the silt except for a submerged white hand, reaching upward. Three silver spheres were suspended in the water, buttons, she thought, like Edie's dream. No, the bubbles of my breath. The realization did not strike her with any fear; she felt detached, uninvolved with the drama in the water. So this is what an out-of-body experience is like, she thought calmly, and walked away.

She walked lighter than a water-skipper, her steps leaving no imprint on the river, nor did the surface beneath her feet feel any different as she stepped onto dry land, bushland. A dirt track led away through the gum trees, twisting and turning; she followed it, the track widening into a primitive road. Between the trees she could glimpse a shiny surface, rippling like foil in the wind, a huge liquid mirror. The road met with another, forming a crossroad, one arm leading into the mirror, the others into the bush. She neared the center of the cross, then halted, seeing an old-fashioned, strangely familiar car parked in her path. She tried to step around it, but—without apparently moving—it blocked her way again.

"Hallo, lass," a voice said, and, turning, she saw a small elderly man, handsome despite his age. He stood by the car door, leaning on a stick.

"Sammy?" she said.

"Not entirely."

"How nice," she said, "personalized Legba," and tried again to sidestep the car. Once more it blocked her way, and this time Sammy (or Samedi? she wondered) sighed, a heavy sound like silk rustling, totally alien to the father she remembered.

"Not so fast."

"But aren't I . . .?" She looked at the mirror, seeing momentarily through it the form of a barred gate, the Samedi sign, sculpted in metal.

"Not quite. You still have a chance."

She looked back at the river. "But what am I supposed to do?"

"Come walk with me." He offered his arm, the tweed not warm and rough to the touch, rather slippery, siliceous. They took the road parallel to the river, she adjusting her strides to his halting steps, as if they had last walked together only yesterday, not three years ago. She glanced behind them once, seeing trees rather than the wall of mirror, but otherwise having no sense of distance traversed.

"Here," said her companion. She looked around, to see a fence of rough, split rails, enclosing a hillock of grass, with a lump of quartz set like a pillow at one end.

"You know it?" he said.

"It's the grave of Red Meg, from the last scene of *The Scarlet Rider*."

Seated just outside the fence were two dolls, a cloth police-man with dashing painted mustachios, and a fine porcelain lady, golden curls neatly sculpted on her bonnet head. Across their laps rested a bouquet of bright pink roses.

"Miles and Arabella," Mel breathed. But Sammy allowed her no time to dawdle, instead hurried her along the path, as much as his game leg would permit. They neared the river again, walking across a clay flat, flood overspill land.

"That, back there, was what *she* wanted. A pretty little bush grave with attendant mourners. But this is what she got."

He released Mel, poking with his stick at the side of a small bank. She saw him unearth fibers from the clay, strands that after repeated prodding blew free in this still air, proving to be hairs, very long and white. Two depressions in the clay nearby she recognized now as empty eyeholes in a human skull. She watched, and the damp clay moved, coating the skull as if being molded by a forensic artist. Eyes, nose, lips were formed, at first red-brown as the clay, then becoming flesh-colored as a layer of skin spread over the head. A cluster of little white stones embedded in the clay linked together into first fingerbones, then a living hand, cuffed with lace. The bank heaved and a figure stood upright in front of them, as unnaturally and abruptly as a puppet levitated by string.

Mel stared—at a woman not particularly like her, with a narrow Celtic face, the features finely cut, the eyes vivid green, the skin pale as milk. She had been redheaded, like Mel, once, but now the wildly flowing white locks showed only traces of the original color. Yet this woman was not old, for the faint lines on her skin indicated she was at the most forty. She wore a black, heavy gown of thick cloth; a riding habit, for in one hand she clutched a whip.

"Scarlet!" she said to Mel.

Her voice was silvery, as English as Sorrel's, but with an accent perhaps Irish, or Scots. With that naming Sammy vanished, leaving horse and rider alone. The woman leaned forward, tapping Mel on the neck with the crop, a gentle, yet imperious touch. Mel crouched, feeling the cloth of the skirt rasp her naked skin, as the rider mounted, piggyback, horseback. She stood, feeling the woman's familiar weight, then walked forward, on all four feet, wind and rain disheveling her mane of hair. The river flowed before her, swollen high and running fast; the whip stung her flank and she started, leaping forward into the water.

For a few steps, she could feel the stones of the ford beneath her, then she swam, with difficulty, for though this chestnut mare had strength, the current of the water was even stronger. Yet she responded to the voice and crop, struck out vigorously, might even have reached the opposite bank—had not a heavy chunk of flotsam cannoned into them. The mare Scarlet heard a cry, felt a desperate clutch, as her rider lost hold, was washed off horseback . . .

Mel stood on the bank again, holding Sammy's hand, the pair of them watching in the water a frozen, struggling tableau of two women and a chestnut horse.

"I thought she was gone before," Mel said.

"You don't get rid of *Madam* so easily. She has to die again, be nothing, to go completely."

"Taking me with her!"

"She didn't mean to hurt you," Sammy said. "But when you hit the water it all came back to her."

"Because she drowned in a flooded creek," Mel said. "Victorian women weren't taught to swim, and furthermore she wore a heavy habit, with long skirts. I felt them, entangling me, pulling me down."

She shuddered, and the pressure of his hand grew firmer.

"It's very clear now why I couldn't find a death record. This region was only sparsely populated in the 1860s; and the body was never found. Without habeas corpus, the death couldn't be registered."

"Clever girl," he said.

Mel shivered. "She lost her horse but found *me* instead."

"And what are you going to do about it?"

"I don't know."

"Didn't I say you were clever?"

"Yes, but I need a helping hand!"

Like a pricked bubble, he vanished, leaving her alone on the bank, wind snaking through her hair, and turmoil in the center of the river, the three-way battle for life. As she stood helplessly, she felt a prompt at the back of her mind, and pulled at it, a scene from the novel resurrecting from memory, words translating into vision. A boat came down the river toward her, at first tiny in the distance, its passenger doll-like, like the toy Miles and Arabella at the grave, then slowly resolving into a canoe, paddled by a grown woman. Mel focused hard on this little vignette from Miles's search, the one appearance that her ancestors, the original people of Australia, made in *The Scarlet Rider*. It was ambiguous, as if drawn from life:

Down the river, in a primitive bark canoe, came a solitary female of the native tribes, whom I halloed, in hope she would be able to provide some indication of where the inhabitants of this once bustling goldfield had gone, but whether from lack of the English tongue, or justifiable fear, for I wore the uniform that had brought British law to so many, alas, of her people, she replied not.

Paddling toward her now was a woman in a possum-skin cloak, young and healthy, her face like Mel's, or Myrie's, but dark.

"Poor primitive race," that silvery voice said, and turning her head, Mel saw Melvina Yuill standing on the riverbank beside her. "Doomed to extinction."

With those words, the woman in the boat shriveled, becoming a decrepit crone, her jaw distended, brow shrunk to minuscule, her face subhuman as a gorilla's and pocked with sores.

Melvina spoke again, in tones of patronizing regret: "All we can do is smooth their dying pillow."

Mel screamed, "No!" She stared at the Koorie woman, by strength of will seeing through her own perceptions, not Melvina's. Slowly the face twisted into the shape of the dark Myrie again.

"That's my great-grandmother!" she said, with the certainty of dreams.

"Then you are an octoroon!" Melvina replied, gazing at Mel as if seeing her properly for the first time.

"Yes," Mel replied proudly. Without a moment's hesitation she dived into the water, and the maelstrom of rider and horses. As she joined with her own drowning body, pain and fear nearly overwhelmed her—but still she kicked upward with all of her remaining strength. She saw rushing toward her a silver mirror . . . divine? no, the water's surface. Her head broke through into air, and she thrashed, fighting to keep afloat. Though she had regained control over her limbs, the current bore her rapidly downstream, too forcefully to swim against. She was not out of the water yet, not at all.

A shape like a giant duck neared, keeping pace with her, steered by quick dabs of the paddle. Mel looked up, into dark eyes; then a hand reached down. Though it was cold, stiff, and hard, she grabbed at it, and at that moment the canoe swerved, banging heavily against her. She saw not stars from this blow on the head, but a brief vivid picture of the chestnut horse, stumbling onto dry land, shaking water from its mane.

And as the image vanished, she knew that she had crossed back from the dreamworld, that in-between place, to reality. Her body gasped for breath; she felt battered, waterlogged, ready to vomit . . . but alive. Water eddied fiercely against her, yet her progress down the river had been arrested, by something that felt like rough wood under her clutching hands. When she opened her eyes she saw dimly, through her wet lashes, a mass of white: the trunk of a huge, stark, dead tree, its branches nearly spanning the flood, its roots, still dripping wet earth, rearing up from the bank to the sunny sky.

Crashing sounded from the bush behind her and Daniel came running into view, barefoot, stripped to T-shirt and jeans. At the sight of Mel, he stopped, chest heaving.

"I thought . . . dive after you . . . current too swift . . . nothing to do but chase . . . see if I could catch you in shallows . . . somewhere . . . anywhere!"

She tried to pull herself out of the water, but failed, for she was as weak now as a half-drowned kitten. "Don't!" he said, and clambered over the roots, crawling down the tree toward her.

"Heard the noise . . . the tree falling . . . bit of history gone, of course . . . but oh what timing!"

She opened her mouth, tasting blood from a cut on her lip. "What do you mean?"

"Why, this is . . . was . . . the canoe tree."

She leaned her head against naked wood, blessedly thankful. Next moment his warm, living hands reached for her, pulling her out of the water and up onto the trunk. She vomited then, a mixture of brown water and blood; he held her shoulders, waiting patiently. Then very slowly, like a double inchworm, they edged their way back along the tree-bridge, crawling over the plaque and the great wound left by the cutting of bark, eventually reaching the riverbank.

And as Mel stepped onto solid earth, she felt the difference, half-drowned as she was: unencumbered, no longer ghost-ridden, she walked free.

Available by mail from

PEOPLE OF THE LIGHTNING • Kathleen O'Neal Gear and W. Michael Gear

The next novel in the First North American series by the bestselling authors Kathleen O'Neal Gear and W. Michael Gear.

SUMMER AT THE LAKE • Andrew M. Greeley

"[This] story of three friends who spend a memorable and life-altering summer at a lake near Chicago...is a riveting story of love, crime, and scandal laced with the Roman Catholic orientation that is Greeley's forté." —*The Chattanooga Times*

MAGNIFICENT SAVAGES • Fred Mustard Stewart

From China's opium trade to Garibaldi's Italy to the New York of Astor and Vanderbilt, comes this blockbuster, 19th century historical novel of the clipper ships and the men who made them.

DEEP AS THE MARROW • F. Paul Wilson

When the president decides to back the legalization of marijuana, organized crime decides that he must die and his best friend, his personal physician, must kill him.

A MAN'S GAME • Newton Thornburg

Another startling thriller from the author of *Cutter and Bone*, which *The New York Times* called "the best novel of its kind in ten years!"

SPOOKER • Dean Ing

It took the government a long time to figure out that someone was killing agents for their spookers—until that someone made one fatal mistake.

RELIQUARY • Lincoln Child and Douglas Preston

"The sequel to the popular *The Relic* hits all the right buttons for those looking for thrills and chills....Another page-turner that cries out for translation to the silver screen." —*The Orlando Sentinel*